RIPPED - The Price of Loyalty

Everhide Rockstar Romance Series – Book 1
by
Tania Joyce

EVERHIDE
ROCKSTAR ROMANCE

For the lovers of music.

Chapter 1

GEMMA

I stormed out of the Madison Square Garden's dressing room, slamming the door against the concrete wall with a bang. *Crap.* I hadn't meant to open it that hard. Late for soundcheck, my fluster had gotten the better of me. I had one more show to get through tonight, then tour was done. Nine months of traveling the world and singing to sell-out crowds would be over. *Finally.* But my head spun. A deep throb pulsed between my legs. Fire coursed through my veins. My heartbeat thudded in staccato after yet another wicked dream. All I'd wanted was a ten-minute power nap, not another hot mindfuck.

These dreams had to stop. Stop now.

I wasn't about to ruin my life over some stupid delusion.

Music was everything. Hunter Collins and Kyle McIntyre, my fellow Everhide bandmates, were my world. We'd worked too damn long and too damn hard to get to the top, I wouldn't fuck that up. Not for anything. Or anyone. Not ever.

"Gem, wait!" Hunter laughed, rushing out of the dressing room behind me. "I'm sorry I had to wake you." *No he wasn't.*

"Slow down. Wait for me." Kyle jogged after us with takeaway coffees in hand.

Sucking in a deep breath, I lifted my chin and strode along

the corridor like I was on stage in front of thousands of fans. *Just ignore the guys. They'll stop . . . eventually.*

"Gemm-maaa." Hunter's voice rumbled low, husky and deep. "You were moaning and muttering our names in your sleep. Sounded hot. Want to tell us what you were dreaming about?"

My breath hitched, but my stride didn't falter.

Shit. They'd heard.

They'd seen.

Fuck. Fuck. Fuck.

I stopped. Spun around. Kept my poker face in place. But two pairs of eyes beamed at me—Hunter's azure and Kyle's espresso. Both guys had smiles as wide as the Brooklyn Bridge. They exchanged a quick glance, then burst out laughing.

"Did you have a wet dream, Gem?" Hunter bobbed his head in a slow, rhythmic motion and gave me an *oh-you've-so-been-busted* grin. "About us?"

Heat shot up my neck. Knots twisted and tightened in my stomach.

"You wish," I sneered and snapped, refusing to give them an inch to play with. "As if I'd ever have a dream, wet or otherwise, about you two. That would be more like a nightmare."

But . . . I'd lied.

To myself. To them . . . my two best friends. But some things were better left unsaid. Especially things that would cause issues.

"Here." Kyle winked as he handed me a coffee. "This will help you feel better . . . and cool down. Latte, just the way you like it."

"Thank you. You're the best." I took a sip, savoring the dash of cinnamon topping. But I needed buckets of ice thrown over me to lower my body temperature, not a hot, delicious, belly-warming latte. It had been a fucking hot dream.

The mischievous glint in Hunter's eyes sparkled. "Gem, do you need to change your panties?"

"What?" I threw him my most evil glare. "No. Don't be ridiculous." I did, but he didn't need to know that. And going by my dream, I wanted him to do more than just take them off. *Ugh, don't go there.* The guys could tease me all they wanted. I wouldn't let them get to me. It was just another ludicrous, stupid, unwarranted, reoccurring dream. *Yep. Just a dream.*

"I could help change them." Hunter held out his hand, but I slapped it away.

Kyle elbowed Hunter in the arm. "Okay, dude. Enough."

So true. Shaking my head, I spun on my heels and marched along the corridor. But my whole body was still on fire. As I sipped my latte, I tried to erase the images flickering through my mind. *Naked bodies. Steamy kisses. Roaming hands. Shit.* It was impossible. With each step, my heart lurched hard against my ribs. Every breath sent a shudder through my entire system.

Fuck.

Who was I kidding?

I had a problem.

A huge, fucking problem.

I'd suppressed it, hidden it, denied it for months, but it grew stronger and stronger every day. It wasn't just in my dreams.

I was . . . without a doubt . . . in love with Hunter.

How did that happen? This shouldn't have happened. Since high school we'd been nothing more than best friends. He was a playboy. God's gift to women. He'd never had a girlfriend. I had no desire to be a name on his long list of conquests, or to clock up another failed relationship to rival my mother's long list.

After my shitty track record, I wanted no part in love. I remembered all too well what it was like to be hurt, betrayed, and let down. First, by my father, then my ex-boyfriend, and always, always, *always*, my mother.

People left you. Hurt you. Lied to you.

I'd survived, thanks to these guys. I trusted them with my life.

"Kyle, it's okay." I could handle being teased. They knew that. I waved over my shoulder as they followed. "Hunt's just being Hunt. He's trying to cause a stir when he knows he's wasting his time."

I was certainly over the craziness going on in my head. The first steamy dream I'd had about Hunter was funny. The next few, rattling. But after four months of them occurring every few days, enough was enough. Hunter was my friend. That was it. End of story.

Surely, after tonight's show, a vacation and some time apart this nonsense would disappear. With a new album to work on and a busy schedule ahead, I wouldn't gamble with the uncanny bond I shared with the guys. Our band had been our life since we were fourteen. Our fame had come at a huge cost. We'd survived in this industry because we had each other. I wouldn't fuck up what we had for anything. Not even my heart.

"Gem?" Hunter called out. "I could try harder."

"No, thanks. I'm good."

We already had enough problems. I didn't need this mess to create more.

I'd already pissed off our label, SureHaven, pushing and poking them for more creative control on our next album. I hated wasting our songwriting talent and was over SureHaven telling us what to sing. After one more record, we'd have the power to negotiate a new contract—one where our future albums comprised songs and music we'd written, not anybody else's.

That had been our dream since high school, not some stupid, steamy fantasy.

We'd been through so much together. The horrid teenage years—being bullied at school, teased, and ridiculed. Difficult home lives—the neglect, abuse, the fights, and broken households. The three of us loved music, and it had united us from the moment we'd met. We'd overcome the odds and had become a phenomenal success. No matter how strong my feelings for Hunter were, there was no way I'd tamper with my band's dynamic. We were a trio. Equal. Together, we were a stronger force than nature.

Taking a calming breath, I entered the backstage area. The place was alive with the crew prepping for tonight's show. Trusses and scaffolding towered overhead. Large video projection screens slid along metal tracks, ready for testing during soundcheck. Electric bass and loud drumbeats reverberated through the floor. Our backup band wouldn't be happy with us for being late.

I cruised past the rack of electric guitars where Amie, our band manager, stood talking to a crew member. She threw me an arctic glare and tapped an impatient finger against her watch. I returned a thin grin and made my way over to the table where our in-ear monitors lay next to the mics and transmitters.

I sucked in a deep breath, then let it out slowly.

One more show. In our hometown. At Madison Square Fucking Garden. Oh yeah.

Adrenaline surged through my veins. The caffeine kicked in. *About freaking time.*

I downed the last mouthful of latte, placed the cup on the table and grabbed my in-ear monitors. Kyle and Hunter jostled beside me like teenage fans vying for front-row positions at one of our concerts. *What are they—twelve? Not twenty-three?*

"You sure you're okay, Gem?" Kyle put his arm around my shoulders, giving me a comforting cuddle. He kissed the top of my head, then reached for his transmitter and stuffed it into the back pocket of his jeans. "You want me to kick Hunt in the ass? Just say the word."

Hmmm. He would if I asked him to.

"Go on, Kyle. I dare you." Hunter turned and wiggled his ass. Laughing, Kyle half-heartedly swung his leg toward Hunter's butt, but Hunter jumped out of the way in time. He shook his dark brown shoulder-length hair back and hung his in-ears around his neck. "Gem, you have to admit it was funny we caught you writhing around on the sofa." *Yeah, maybe a little. I'd laugh about it later.* "You want me to make those fantasies of yours a reality?"

My heart skipped a beat. Going by his reputation, he probably *could* make every hot dream come true, but it would be nothing more than sex. Hunter didn't do meaningful.

But damn. What if he did?

What if he felt the same way about me as I felt about him?

Nope. Don't go there.

"You?" I thumped the back of my hand against his chest, making sure my calm remained in place. My ex's betrayal may have been behind me and hooking up with random guys during the tour had lost its thrill, but Hunter was a no-go zone. I had to get him out of my head. "No thanks. I'd sooner take care of myself."

Hunter stepped back. He placed his hand over his heart and clutched at his shirt. "You hurt my feelings."

"Doubt it." I gave him a *you've-got-no-hope-in-hell* smile. I was one of the very few females who'd crossed his path who'd always said no to him. Now that had become one of my biggest challenges . . . I had to keep saying no.

Hunter bent down, meeting me face to face. Silver shards shimmered in his electric eyes. "Maybe we could get down and dirty together at the after-party tonight." His flirtatious wink and suggestive nudge against my arm sent heat rushing to my cheeks. If only he knew the effect he had on me.

Stupid heart. Stupid head.

"In *your* dreams." I covered his face with my hand and pushed him away. My plan was show, then party, then bed . . . by myself.

After putting on our ear-monitors and transmitters, Kyle pushed Hunter toward the stage. "Hurry up. Let's get soundcheck over and done with."

I bounded up the metal-grid stairs onto the elaborate stage and waved to our band at the back. The Garden's empty auditorium stretched out before me. The magnificent circular-paneled roof loomed overhead. Rows of chairs filled the floor. In a few hours, nineteen thousand screaming fans will be here to see us play. Even after thousands of live performances, my belly still somersaulted before each show, especially here in our hometown of New York.

Gone were the high school days of us jamming in Kyle's garage—me on electric, Kyle on bass, Hunter on keys—and playing small-time gigs in Montgomery, New Jersey. Now we were performers, singing to crowds of thousands with a backup band rather than playing our own instruments. Winning a Discovered-On-YouTube contest five years ago, and signing with SureHaven Records & Entertainment Group, had altered our lives in unfathomable ways. SureHaven had catapulted us to stardom.

For now, we had to play by their rules.

But soon, that would change.

I'd make damn sure of it.

"Finally." Simon, our production manager, groaned. He walked toward us, flicking through pages on his clipboard, and met us in the middle of the stage. "Let's get through this quickly." Simon spoke with military command and cocked his finger like a pointed gun. "We need to re-block the lighting that failed during 'Horizon' last night. Can't have Hunter singing in the dark, now can we?"

"Hell no. Light me up." Hunter shimmied over to his place on stage where he stood when we performed that song. He struck a "Staying Alive" pose with one finger pointed in the air, wriggled his hips, and held the mic to his lips. "Hit me."

The sound and lighting technicians at the control panel in the center of the auditorium set to work.

A beam of blue light shone down on Hunter. He gyrated, relishing the attention as the spotlights were reprogrammed. Even now, when it was just us and the crew, Hunter radiated electric energy. He was a born entertainer. The complete package with his baritone voice, seductive moves, and a lethal dose of Harry Styles charisma.

I couldn't drag my gaze away from him. Since freshman year, Hunter's good looks, charm, flirtatious teasing and banter had never affected me. He'd been like a brother. But once my dreams had started, everything changed. Mesmerized by the lights shining on him, I watched his every move. The sway of his hips. The slide of his hand over his chest. *Damn.* My body temperature jumped ten notches. He wore his black designer jeans the right way—snug and firm on his hips, molding over his perfect ass—not loose around his crotch like an advertisement for brand-name underwear. His gray cable-knit sweater stretched across his broad shoulders. What would it be like to bury my face against the wool? Feel his toned arms around me? Listen to his heart beat in time with mine? Then—as if he sensed me watching him—he turned and gave me a breathtaking, wicked smile.

Shit. So much for putting him out of my mind.

"Hey?" Kyle stepped in front of me. Flecks of amber flared in his dark eyes.

That was the warning I needed to get my head in the game.

Yep . . . Kyle was the reason nothing would ever happen with

Hunter. He meant too much to me. I wouldn't risk losing our friendship or everything we'd worked so hard for over some silly, in-my-dreams notion.

I stared down at my Old Skool Vans, unable to meet Kyle's gaze. I was afraid—afraid he'd see the truth. He'd see through my bullshit and know Hunter had starred in my dreams, not him. I didn't know why I'd been mumbling Kyle's name. I was probably calling out to him for help. To give me a good shake and slap some sense back into my head. I certainly fucking needed it.

"You in there, Gem?" Kyle waved his hand in front of my face. "Don't let him get to you."

Too late for that. Looking up, I drew in a deep breath to clear my thoughts. Determination to put this nonsense behind me set in. "I'm good. Let's do this."

But Kyle didn't budge. He just stood there, watching me. Intensity and intrigue, worry, and concern burned in the depths of his eyes.

His drilling gaze sent a shudder down my spine. He knew me better than anyone. Clasping my hand tighter and tighter around the cool metal of my mic, my palms sweated.

Shit. Could he tell?

"Come on, you two. Move," Simon hollered from the side of the stage.

Saved by Simon, I took my position between Kyle and Hunter. I clipped my mic onto its stand and Simon cued the backup band. It was time to sing "Horizon," my favorite song.

Hunter sang. Slow. Deep. With all kinds of sexy.

> *Don't care if we fly*
> *Don't care if we run*
> *Don't care how we're gonna get there*
> *Just gonna follow the sun*

Then Kyle's voice, smooth and enchanting, channeled into my ear monitors.

So, take my hand
We'll soar above the clouds
Follow our dreams
Never gonna touch the ground

I closed my eyes, licked my lips, stepped up to the mic, and sang.

Yee-yeah-ya. Yee-yeah-ya, Yee-Yeah, Yeah

We'll aim for the horizon
Don't know when we'll be home again
So baby, come on, come with me
Don't know where this road will end

Then the three of us sang in perfect harmony.

Let's aim for the horizon
Let's touch the stars
Sail across the oceans
Follow our beating hearts

With you by my side
We're gonna touch the sky
Gonna love you forever
'Til the day I die
'Til the day I die

Every time I sang this song, goosebumps shivered across my skin. I'd written the lyrics with Kyle on the plane to Los Angeles when we'd first signed with SureHaven. Our heads were full of dreams, and anything seemed possible. Now we live a life beyond our wildest imaginations.

I glanced at Kyle, then at Hunter. Both guys looked at me with nothing more than brotherly kindness and love. That was a good thing. That was the way it was supposed to be.

So why had my stupid head, my stupid heart, and my stupid

dreams changed the way I felt about Hunter?

Maybe I was just exhausted and needed a decent vacation—this tour had been fucking long.

Nothing could ever happen between us. Nothing. I had to lock my feelings away, once and for all. Because having a relationship with Hunter was insane, deranged, and totally inconceivable. And it would only lead to trouble.

I liked trouble.

But not the kind that could rip our lives apart.

Chapter 2

GEMMA

Every concertgoer crammed into Madison Square Garden screamed and cried, clapped and chanted. I stood at the end of the stage, closed my eyes, and clutched onto the backs of Hunter's and Kyle's sweaty shirts. Their arms wrapped around me in a tight embrace. For two hours, we'd entertained the crowd. We'd rocked the opening with "Live my Life", cranked out a heavy electric guitar set, ramped up the energy with a medley of hits, swooned everyone with a love ballad, then we'd closed with encores of "Rise Up" and "Escape".

Tour was done.

Twenty-four countries. Fifty-three cities. Eighty-seven shows. *Done.*

Pyrotechnics fired. Confetti cannons blasted. Streamers fluttered through the air.

With my heart pounding in time with the crowd's stamping feet, I tilted my head back and let the gold confetti brush against my face. The fans shrieked at the top of their lungs, "*Everhide . . . We love you . . . More. More. More*". The decibels reached dangerous levels, and the reverberation shook The Garden's walls. *So freaking cool!*

"We did it." I didn't know whether to laugh or cry or shout

for joy. Exhaustion ached in every bone in my body. Perspiration soaked my clothes. But adrenaline still hurtled through my veins. I gripped onto the guys' waists, not wanting to let them go, not wanting the moment to end.

"We nailed it," Kyle hollered and squeezed me tight.

"Time to party." Hunter broke our huddle and pumped his fist in the air.

Taking one last look across the auditorium, I soaked the atmosphere in as the guys and I waved farewell and blew kisses to the incredible crowd. We took one last bow, turned and raced off stage. We crashed into a wall of hugs and high-fives from our entourage. Escaping their clutches, I dashed to the dressing rooms for a quick shower, changed into my favorite leather pants, and rejoined the swarming backstage after-party. Time to celebrate. Chart-topping music echoed off the concrete walls. The crowd of ticket winners, friends, and crew was thick. Alcohol flowed like open faucets down everyone's throats.

It was going to be a big night.

I took a seat next to Kyle on an equipment trunk and downed Jack Daniels, matching him shot for shot. I prayed for the buzz to kill my senses. Because the minute I wasn't performing, thoughts of Hunter bombarded my mind and left me questioning my sanity. If this nonsense continued, I'd spend my vacation stretched out on a therapist's couch.

Maybe therapy was what I needed.

Kyle clinked his glass against mine. "Cheers—to the end of another tour. Gem, you were incredible, as always."

"So were you." I nudged my arm against his. "Best show ever."

"Here's to many more." Kyle downed his JD in one big mouthful, swallowed hard, and gasped. He tousled his fingers through his dirty blond hair and rubbed at his undercut. "Want another shot?" He grabbed the bottle of JD from beside him and waved it toward me.

"Hell yeah." I held out my glass for a refill and instantly downed it. The whiskey slid and burned down the back of my throat, igniting flames inside my chest. Just the hit I needed.

Being here with Kyle was the grounding I needed. He was my rock. My four-four common time. The constant in my life I could always rely on. The true friend I needed in this crazy world.

While Kyle was deep, thoughtful, and easygoing, Hunter was a ringleader—goofy, the jokester, the life of the party. But at some point during the tour, Hunter had moved from the brotherly-love category to the I-want-more category, and I had to move him back. I needed to restore balance.

Bring on vacation.

A bright flash near the stage caught my attention. Hunter danced with a group of three star-struck, college-aged girls, grinding his groin up against one of their slender bodies. They were laughing. Drinking. Stumbling this way and that.

He closed in on the stunning blonde. He slid his hands down the girl's hips, hovered his lips near her neck, rubbed his body up against hers. Like wisps of theatrical smoke snaking across a stage, jealousy crawled beneath my skin. It was always there these days—the dig, the pull, the niggle. But there it would remain. Tucked and hidden away. *Damn it.* Why couldn't I find someone who'd dance with me like that?

Someone like Hunter . . . but not Hunter.

He turned in my direction, his eyes shining brighter than a disco light. "You two need to get off your asses. Come and dance." His deep, husky voice projected like a megaphone over the top of the crowd.

"In a minute," I shouted over the noise. "After another drink."

"Okay. Love you." Hunter waved, barely taking a second to divert his gaze away from the girl twerking her ass in front of him.

"I don't know how Hunt does it." Kyle shook his head as he topped up my glass. "Girls flock to him like pigeons fighting over a French fry dropped in Central Park."

"You can't talk. Look over there." I pointed to a group of girls ogling Kyle and snapping photos. "You're just as bad. You can take your pick."

Kyle checked them out, umming and ahhing, taking his metered time. He downed his drink and shook his head. "None of those chicks do it for me." He swayed, bumping into my side. "But what about you?" Something was off in his tone. With a lackluster wave, he pointed to a few guys standing by the table twenty feet away. "Do any of them catch your interest?"

I wanted to laugh. *What? Someone other than Hunter?*

Unfortunately, no one came close. Not the smartly dressed guys by the drinks table. Not the guys dancing up a storm with my friends, Lexi and Kara. Not the guys checking me out, looking nervous and shy. Since my dreams had started, I'd found it harder and harder to find anyone as appealing as Hunter. He was the one who'd captured my attention, not some random, desperate unknown.

"Not yet. But you never know what might happen after I have a few more drinks." I stared vacantly at the people dancing, ignoring the weird vibe radiating off Kyle. I drew my shoulders back, refocused, and scanned the guys by the table once more. Maybe I should take someone home. Maybe another one-night stand would help clear my head.

But the emptiness in my chest grew heavier. Lately, I'd entertained the idea of having a boyfriend again. Someone who wouldn't tip off the paparazzi, or plaster naked photos of me over the Internet, or sell the story of our sex life to gossip magazines. Like my scumbag ex, Ben, had.

Fuck . . . I missed being in love.

That crazy high. The butterflies. Holding someone close each night.

But how was I supposed to let anyone get close after being burned? I'd learned the hard way that with life in the public eye, it was best not to have a relationship. Having a boyfriend was not an option. Simply a no-go zone.

That was the price I had to pay.

Kyle fidgeted, rolling his empty glass back and forth between his fingers. He swung and kicked his heels against the metal trunk, sending vibrations up my legs.

Something was definitely wrong.

"What . . . what if I had an alternative suggestion for you?"

Kyle's voice cracked and snagged, like a DJ scratching a vinyl. I hadn't seen him this pale since our first performance at Wembley Stadium in front of eighty thousand people. He turned and looked at me through his long dark lashes, but his gaze fell to my lips rather than meet my eyes. "What if . . . you'd consider . . . something totally crazy—"

"Hey." Hunter sprang in front of us. I jumped, spilling my drink all over my pants. He dipped and darted around, doing a weird jig in time to the loud music. "Stop sitting around. Come dance."

"Where do you get your energy from?" Kyle's short, sharp tone matched his icy glare.

I jerked my chin back. I hated seeing Kyle troubled by something, but now wasn't the time for deep conversation. Hunter was right. It was time to move. "You've gotta admit, Hunt's mood is contagious." I slapped Kyle on the thigh. "We'll talk later, I promise. But right now, let's dance." I jumped off the trunk and followed Hunter over to join the partygoers.

Music blared. Time ticked. More JD was drunk.

A lot more.

I jostled and jumped around in the middle of the crowd. People bumped into me from all sides. Hands touched my arms and back, and some guy with greasy hair and not much taller than my five-foot, four-inch frame spun me around. I went to move away, but he grabbed me around the waist with his gorilla-like hairy hands. His hold was tight. Too tight. I tried to wriggle free, but he wouldn't let go. My pulse shot skyward. Clenching my jaw, every muscle in my body tensed. I knew self-defense. I wouldn't think twice about dropping this dickhead to the ground with a quick knee to his groin.

Out of nowhere, Kyle appeared, grabbed the guy by the back of his shirt, and shoved him out of the way. "Time's up, buddy." He stood tall, like a protective shield between me and Mr. Hairy Hands. "Are you okay, Gem?"

"Yeah, thanks for that."

"Anytime." He stepped toward me, caught me around the waist, and drew me in to dance.

Placing my palms on his shoulders, I took a calming breath. Nice and slow. Just what I needed to regain my composure. In sync with Kyle, I swayed to the music.

Seconds later, Hunter edged in behind me. The back of my head hit his chest. His belt buckle nudged into my lower spine. With gentle strokes, he rubbed his hands up and down my arms, sending heat shimmering across my skin.

Damn, he feels good.

Kyle inched closer, leaving no gap between us.

The guys' warmth and delicious citrusy and spicy scents wrapped around me. The music took over. I closed my eyes and moved in time with them.

Sandwiched between Kyle and Hunter, I had all the support I'd ever need. Ever want. Ever desire.

They were my safe haven.

My solidarity.

In this crowded room, no one else mattered. No one would ever understand our connection. The rest of the world disappeared. It was just the three of us. Three *friends* having a good time.

But even for us, dancing this close wasn't normal.

"Found anyone that's caught your eye yet, Gem?" Kyle's low voice hovered near my ear. The sweet smell of JD heavy on his breath made my head spin. Gripping onto the lapel of his leather jacket, I tried to ignore Hunter behind me.

"No-pe." The P made a popping sound between my lips. "No one." The lie knotted in my gut. Wobbling on my feet, I lifted my chin. Kyle's dark eyes locked onto mine, and a wave of warmth flooded into my belly. *Hmm. Definitely too much JD.* Since coming offstage, I couldn't recall how much I'd drunk. Somewhere in the range between excessive and extreme.

Hunter slowly skimmed his hands up my arms and placed them on my shoulders. My skin tingled in their wake. I giggled, unsure whether his hold on me was to keep me balanced or himself upright. But he was too close. Just his touch sent a fever coursing through my veins. With a gentle brush of his fingers, he scooped my long hair away from the side of my neck. The rush of cool air eased my body temperature. But then he leaned forward. His long hair tickled my shoulder. His hot, whiskey-laced breath sent goosebumps skittering down my arm. Before I could move away, he pressed his lips against my flesh.

What the fuck?

My eyes widened. I froze.

Hunter never kissed me like that or danced with me like this.

Drunk. He must be drunk. I certainly was. But whatever this was, it had to stop.

Before I could step aside, Kyle shoved Hunter on the shoulder. Fire blazed in his eyes. "What the hell are you doing?"

"Nothing," Hunter snapped, still standing with his chest pressed flush against my back.

"Chill it, guys." I splayed my hands out to either side. There were too many people around. Too many cameras. Too many gossipy tongues. "I know there's enough alcoholic vapor in here to bottle and set up a brewery. But Kyle, don't be silly." I rubbed his arm, then reached over my shoulder and patted Hunter on his cheek. "Hunt's just goofing around. Aren't you, Hunt?"

Hunter stumbled and swayed to the left. "Just showing my appreciation. You're my leading gal." He planted a wet kiss on my cheek. My nose wrinkled. Wrinkled in a good way. In an *I-want-more* kind of way. In a heartbeat, his hands disappeared from my shoulders, only to reappear on my upper thighs. He swirled his fingers over my legs. His lips hovered dangerously close to my ear. "And I appreciate how you rock these leather pants."

The low rumble in his voice made my knees buckle. He shouldn't be talking to me like this. It set off all kinds of heat and alarm bells inside my system. Good. Bad. And everything in between.

"Yeah, well, enough of the appreciation." Kyle's lips curled into a snarl. "Don't be a jerk."

I closed my eyes and winced. Kyle's voice struck me like a bad note. He was right. With my headspace in a mess, being this close to them . . . close to Hunter . . . wasn't good. I needed to keep my wits about me and not do anything I'd regret.

Time to defuse the situation. Time to get some distance.

Peeling Hunter's hands off my legs, I took a step sideways. The guys glared at each other, their jaws tense. The air sparked like a live wire ready to zap. I couldn't work out whether they wanted to punch each other in the face or burst out laughing.

"You guys are awesome." I gave them a playful nudge on the arm. The last thing I needed was these two fighting. "I'm going to get another drink. You want one?"

"Nah, I'm good." Hunter winked at me, gave Kyle a cool smile, then turned. He skipped one foot behind the other and made a beeline back to his group of eager girls.

"Gem, I'll come with you." Kyle followed me toward the drinks table.

But as we broke free from the dancing crowd, Kyle caught my hand. "Hey . . . there's something I want . . . I need to talk to you about." His voice quaked with an unsettled edge. "Can we sit for a sec?"

"Sure. Let me grab some drinks first."

Kyle pointed toward the trunk we'd sat on before. "I'll meet you over there."

I collected a fresh bottle of JD and some glasses, wove and ducked around a few people, and made my way over to Kyle. I handed him the drinks to hold. But before I climbed up onto the four-foot-high trunk, Hunter called out.

"Hey everybody. Watch this."

I turned to see what was going on.

Hunter was on the stage, lying on top of an equipment trunk like it was a toboggan. He lay poised at the head of the ramp, ready to launch himself downward.

Hunter wasn't crazy enough to ride that thing, was he?

The crowd shuffled back and cleared the path. Laughter and shouts of encouragement filled the room.

"Go for it!" A drunk fan screamed.

"Hunter! Hunter! Hunter!" The crowd chanted.

My pulse thudded in my ears.

Yep. He is.

Like the crazed paparazzi in a high-speed pursuit, Hunter took off down the steep slope. I held my breath, worried he'd hurt himself. But halfway down the ramp, the trunk veered sharply and headed straight for me.

Oh shit.

Panicked, my chest tightened. My heart slammed against my ribs. With other trunks blocking my escape, there was nowhere to go. No time to move.

"Gemma. Look out!" Hunter yelled, waving his hand.

Rata-tat-tat-tat. The hunk of metal hurtled toward me.

Kyle cried out from above. "NOOOO!"

But there was nothing he could do.

I turned to brace myself, squeezed my eyes shut, and screamed. "ARGH!"

Hunter and the trunk crashed into my side, knocking the oxygen out of my lungs. *Oof.* But the caster wheel lock ramming into my shin like a butcher's cleaver chopping through solid bone was a whole new level of pain.

"FUUUUCK!" I cried.

My legs buckled, and I fell.

For a split second, the jaw-jolting thud of my head hitting the side of the trunk overpowered the excruciating agony in my leg. Sharp pain ricocheted down my neck and speared along the length of my spine as I hit the floor.

Through distorted angles and hazy vision, I registered the horror on Hunter's face. Kyle, ghost-white, appeared above me. His voice, nothing but a muffle in my ears. I wanted to reach out to them. I didn't want to feel the pain splintering like shards of glass through my bones. Didn't want to feel the cold, hard concrete beneath me. Didn't want to feel the warm blood trickling down the side of my face.

Unable to move.

Unable to register.

Everything went black.

Chapter 3

KYLE

Sitting at 3:07 a.m. in the emergency waiting room next to Hunter was not how tonight was supposed to end. My plans to tell Gemma how I felt, how much I loved her, and finally ask her out had turned to shit, thanks to Hunter. I was so angry and annoyed at him for interrupting us. So worried about Gemma. So pissed off at myself for not stopping the trunk in time. I clenched my teeth so hard I thought they might crack like rocks under too much pressure. My stomach cinched as visions of Gemma lying in pain, crying on the floor, filled my head. I should've paid more attention to what was happening around us, but I'd been so nervous, so caught up in sorting out what to say to her. I didn't see Hunter fly across the room until it was too late.

Fuck, I hoped Gemma was okay. I prayed her injuries weren't as bad as they'd looked.

I drummed out an erratic beat on my leg and watched the seconds tick by on the clock above the reception counter. Amie and Sam, my bodyguard, stood at the desk, exchanging heated words with the administration assistant. I threw them a hurry-up glance and slouched into my seat.

I hated hospitals. The smells. The sounds. The sirens. I'd spent too many hours between their walls. First, when my kid sister lost her fight with leukemia when she was thirteen. And second, when my parents were killed in a car crash two years ago, and I had to identify their bloodied, broken bodies. *Not fun.* Now, Gemma was here. The last place I ever wanted to see her.

She'd been with the doctor since we'd arrived. I turned to Hunter. "Fuck this shit. How much longer is this going to take?"

"We've only been here half an hour." Hunter held an icepack to his bruised cheek, his only injury from falling off the trunk. "Setting her leg is going to take a while." He lowered his chin and shook his head. "I can't believe it's broken. I never meant to hurt her." Anguish hung in every word. And so it should. She was our life.

"You're a fucking idiot," I snapped with too much bite. "Showing off like a dick. What were you thinking?"

"I wasn't." He mumbled. His shoulders sank two inches.

"No shit." I sneered. Hunter was my best friend. He had been since our first day in elementary school. Nothing would ever change that. But right now, I hated him for hurting Gemma. "Gem better be okay, because if she's not . . . I'll kick your balls up your ass."

"Thanks, bud. You always know how to make me feel better." He half-grinned, rubbing his cheekbone and moving his jaw around, up, and down. "Do you think I should get the doctor to look at my jaw? It might be broken."

"It's not broken." I puffed air through my nose. "There won't be any permanent damage to your precious face." But I could give him some. Maybe rearrange his million-dollar teeth. Give him another black eye.

"It fucking hurts," he moaned, pressing the icepack against his cheek.

I chuckled, low and soft. "It's a bruise, you pussy." If he wanted sympathy, he'd have to find it elsewhere. I honestly cared about him, but he wasn't badly hurt.

The hospital entrance doors slid open and in staggered a middle-aged man with a bloodied towel wrapped around his hand. After checking in with another assistant, he took a seat in the far corner. A couple of chairs along, a young woman sweated profusely as she vomited into a sickbag. Next to us, a group of college girls held ice to their male friend's gashed forehead. They'd all pulled out their phones to take snaps of Hunter and me. Yep, we attracted attention wherever we went.

Amie placed her hands on the counter and leaned toward the administration assistant. "We need to get the guys out of here or you're going to have a riot on your hands. Fans will storm this place at any moment. And trust me, you don't want that."

The flustered assistant stole a glance at Hunter and me, then met Amie square in the eye. "We're a hospital. Not a celebrity hideout." Her voice quivered like a cell phone on vibrate. "I can assure you; Gemma is in safe hands. Why not take the young men home? They can come back later in the morning."

From my seat six feet away, I was about to rush over and object, but Amie beat me to it.

"Pfft," Amie huffed and folded her arms. "That's not going to happen. Surely there is somewhere other than here where Kyle and Hunter can wait. We'll pay for a goddamn room if we have to."

The admin lady gaped. "A room? We're not a hotel."

I smirked. This assistant didn't know who she was dealing with. Amie always got her way.

Sam's deep James Earl Jones voice filled the waiting room. "Ma'am, I assure you, it's for the safety of your patients and everyone here. I'd be very happy to shove them into the janitor's closet if that's all you have available. But as you can see, these two are attracting a crowd."

I followed Sam's pointed finger to the group of about fifteen young girls hovering outside the entrance doors with cell phones poised in their hands. No one looked sick—or like they needed the emergency services of a hospital. I recognized three of the chicks from the after-party. *Shit.* Now was not the time for putting on smiles, having photos taken, and signing autographs for fans. Gemma was hurt. But I was sure they were just worried about her, too.

Chester and Mick—Gemma and Hunter's bodyguards—rose

from their seats nearby and shuffled closer to the doors. Wearing black tailored suits, with wired bugs in their ears and steely glares, they intimidated most people. They'd keep the fans away.

Hunter sighed and slumped in his chair. "This sucks. I hate waiting."

"You and me both." I nodded. "Let's hope she won't be much longer so we can get out of here."

I leaned forward and rested my elbows on my thighs. Hunter fidgeted with his watch and checked the time every few minutes. Just like I watched the clock.

Seeing the worry on Hunter's face gave me some solace. It was good to see him concerned about someone other than himself for a change. We loved wild parties, but like always, Hunter hadn't thought his actions through. It was all fun and games until someone got hurt. It shouldn't have been Gemma.

I lowered my gaze and stared at a scuff mark on the floor. It was funny how life changed. Months ago, I would've been right beside Hunter, dancing with those girls at the after-party. But easy chicks throwing themselves at me didn't do it for me anymore. The loneliness didn't do it for me anymore. The constant ache in my heart didn't do it for me anymore.

Tonight, I'd planned to put everything on the line for Gemma. I'd loved her as a best friend since high school, but my feelings had changed after my family's tragic accident. I'd tried to ignore the pull toward her by being with other girls, staying focused on the tour and hiding behind my public persona. I'd kept up the façade. But she'd taken hold of my heart. There was no one else. She was it. All I ever wanted.

During the tour, we'd shared some magical moments—we stayed up until dawn and watched the sunrise from hotel rooftops, the world disappeared every time she looked at me when we sang "Horizon", and the air came alive every time we wrote new music.

Did she feel the same way about me as I did about her?

I was sure she did.

I had to take the chance. I was tired of watching and waiting from a distance, hiding my jealousy when she was with other guys.

I was tired of not being hers.

Leaning back in my chair, I glanced in Hunter's direction. What would he think about me dating Gemma?

Probably nothing.

He'd probably crack a bottle of JD to celebrate.

But I'd thought long and hard about asking her out. I'd lost too much sleep contemplating the consequences. What if it didn't go as planned? I was risking everything—our music, our friendship, the bond I shared with the two most important people in my life. Losing them scared the hell out of me. Hunter and Gemma were like family. No . . . they *were* family.

But I had a connection with Gemma I could no longer deny.

The swing doors to the emergency ward flung open with a loud swoosh. The doctor we'd met when we'd arrived walked toward us in his blue scrubs. I jumped to my feet, rushed over, and met him halfway across the room.

"Is Gem okay?" My voice ran at a higher pitch than normal.

"About time, Doc." Amie folded her arms, stepping in beside me with Sam and Hunter flanking her.

"Gemma's fine." Dr. Fraser's voice drawled, set to super slow. "She's had five stitches to the cut on the side of her head, and the X-rays confirmed she has a fractured tibia. There was no bone displacement, so she didn't need surgery, but we had to give her a general anesthetic to set her leg in a cast." The doctor, with a playful glint in his eyes, turned his attention to Hunter. "I'm not usually open to bribery and corruption, Mr. Collins, but your offer of VIP tickets to one of your future shows was too tempting. My daughter will be ecstatic. She's a huge fan. So, I thank you in advance . . . and I've cast Gemma's leg in the color you requested."

"Awesome." Hunter pumped his fist and gave the doctor a friendly slap on the shoulder. "Thanks, man. You're a legend."

I shook my head at Hunter. "I don't want to be you when Gem wakes. She's *not* going to be impressed."

"Good thing we're in a hospital, right?" Hunter laughed, looking too pleased with himself. Oh, I couldn't wait to see Gemma's reaction. A tornado would be tame in comparison.

Dr. Fraser cleared his throat. "We're transferring her up to the private ward now. We want to keep her in for a night or two. She's very fatigued and suffering from dehydration. Luckily, it's the end of your tour. She needs a good rest."

"Can we see her?" My heart rate quickened. I'd waited around long enough.

"Yes, you can head up to Ward Seven." The doctor pointed toward the elevator bay.

Nearing a sprint, I took off with Hunter on my heels. Our security team and Amie were quick to follow.

After checking in at the nurses' station, I skidded to a halt in front of Gemma's room. Hunter shoved me in the shoulder, trying to open the door before me. I jabbed my elbow into his ribs, grabbed the handle, and rushed into the room ahead of him.

The nurse at the end of Gemma's bed jumped. Her eyes widened, and her mouth gaped.

"Oh, my God." The twenty-something-year-old woman covered her mouth, then placed her palm against her chest. "Hi. I'm Nicole. I'll be looking after Gemma. I'm such a huge fan. I couldn't believe it when I saw her name on the admission chart. I thought I was dreaming. Now . . . you're all here."

"Yes, we are." I brushed the nurse's comments off, hoping I wasn't being rude. I darted straight past her to Gemma's side. Clutching Gemma's hand, I leaned over and kissed the top of her head. "Hey, Gem. We're here."

"Babe." Hunter eased around to the opposite side of the bed and took her hand in his. "I'm so sorry."

With mascara racooning her eyes, Gemma stirred. Little whimpers and moans fluttered from her lips. Her eyes cracked open, and a sleepy smile inched across her mouth. "Heeey, guys."

"Alright, Hunter, I mean . . . Mr. Collins. Give the girl a moment." The nurse shooed him out of the way and headed around to his side of the bed to do her observations. But I didn't budge from my spot beside the IV machine. I wasn't moving until I knew Gemma was okay.

The nurse in her sky-blue scrubs peered into Gemma's face.

"Hi, sweetie. Do you know where you are?"

"Yeah. Hospital," she slurred.

"Yes. That's right. You're in Lenox Hill Hospital." She leaned closer. The ID badge hanging around her neck swung like a pendulum every time she moved. "Can you tell me your name?"

"Um . . . it's Gemmma. Gemmma Lonsdale." Gemma tried to prop herself up on her elbows, but the nurse placed her hand on her shoulder.

"Do you remember what happened earlier tonight?" Nicole shone a bright light into Gemma's eyes.

"Yeah, but are you trying to fucking kill me?" Gemma closed her eyes tight, her hand shooting up to cover them. Pain contorted her face. A shudder ripped through my bones. That light must have felt like an arrow being rammed into her eye socket.

Nicole, seemingly oblivious to Gemma's anguish, continued her observations. Blood pressure. Temperature. Pulse. I rocked on my feet, wishing the nurse would hurry and leave us alone.

Blinking her sleepy eyes open, Gemma reached up to touch the square-inch of gauze stuck near her temple. "Am . . . am I going to have a scar?"

"You've had five stitches," Nicole said as she pushed the blood pressure machine aside. "You'll probably have a small one about half an inch long, nothing to worry about."

With soft strokes, I swept Gemma's tangled hair off her brow and brushed my thumb across her worry lines, trying to erase them. "Hey . . . it's just another one to add to our battle-scar stories. Like this one." I pointed to the small scar line underneath my chin where Gemma had accidentally smacked me in the face with her guitar at one of our first gigs.

"It's going to be nothing like this one." Hunter traced the marks on his left forearm. The silver lines zigzagging across his skin were a constant reminder of the end of our first tour. In London, we'd partied hard. Gotten high and drunk. We were having a fucking wild time . . . Then Hunter fell through a glass door. He severed a tendon, had surgery, needed thirty-eight stitches. It was a night we'd never forget.

"And what about my leg?" Gemma tried to sit upright again, but the nurse wouldn't let her.

"Please rest, Gemma." Nicole patted Gemma on the shoulder. "You'll be fine. It's not a bad break. We'll talk about it after you get some sleep." Nicole fussed with Gemma's pillows and blankets, then moved to stand beside me. She flicked her fingernail against the clear tubing on the IV machine and placed a small plastic controller near Gemma's pillow. "This is morphine. It's set to automatically administer through your IV every four hours. If the pain gets unbearable, all you have to do is press this button two or three times. Okay?"

"Shhuuure." Gemma smiled a lazy smile.

I needed a shot of whatever Gemma was on to ease my worry and nerves. But at least she was okay. Maybe now, my blood pressure could come down.

The machine whirred, clicked, and administered a dose of morphine into Gemma's arm.

"Holy shhhhit." Her glassy eyes stared at the IV rammed into her skin. "This stuff is awesome. You should try some."

I squeezed her hand. She was so beautiful, even spaced out on drugs.

She swiveled her head toward Hunter. "Hey, don't beat yourself up about this. It was an accident. You know me. Shit happens. It's a few stitches. A broken bone. I'll be fine."

Then she turned to me, her gaze piercing right through to my soul. Could she see how much I cared for her? How much I loved her? That she was the one?

"Thanks Kyle. Thanks for being here." I strained to hear her soft voice and the muffled words that slipped from her lips. "I love you. And Hunt. And my guitar. And gnocchi. And ice cream. And—"

Chuckling, a grin tugged at the corner of my mouth. "Those drugs are really kicking in, aren't they?" I patted and rubbed her hand. "We love you, too. But you should get some rest."

"Yes. Let her get some sleep, Mr. McIntyre." Nicole spoke to me but her gaze remained glued to Hunter, even when she wrote on Gemma's chart. She went to place the folder in the pocket at the end of the bed, but she missed it. The folder fell to the floor with a smack. She rushed to pick it up, fumbled with it again before she finally slipped it into the holder. Her cheeks reddened, and she gave Hunter an awkward smile.

I just rolled my eyes and turned back to Gemma. Her eyelids were shut. Her breathing had deepened. Her long dark hair fanned around her face. I glanced at Nicole. "How long will she be asleep?"

Nicole placed her hand on her hip and gave me a *that's-the-most-stupid-question-in-the-world* type of look.

I realized my mistake. "Sorry," I mumbled. "We're just worried about her."

"That's very sweet. She's one lucky girl." Nicole clicked the top of her pen and stuck it in her pocket. "I'll get a cloth to clean her face quickly, then she needs a good rest before the next round of observations." Nicole disappeared into the private bathroom.

I hadn't taken in much of the surrounds when Hunter and I had rushed in. I'd been too focused on Gemma. But this was no ordinary hospital room. It was larger than most hotel suites we'd stayed in when traveling. And although I hated the fact that Gemma was in here, it was much better than hanging around in the emergency waiting area and the growing crowd of fans.

"Hey, Kyle." Hunter jutted his chin toward the door. "Are you going to talk to Amie and security about staying?"

"You can." I stretched my neck from side to side to release the lingering tension.

"Why me?" He straightened, jerking his chin back.

"I'm not leaving Gemma." I leaned my hip against the bed railing and stood my ground.

"Neither am I." He pulled a chair closer to the bed and took a seat.

I dropped my head back and stared at the ceiling. Of course he had to be stubborn. I just wanted him to leave. I wanted the nurse to leave. I wanted everyone to leave so I could be alone with Gemma. Be here when she woke up. "Just do it. You put Gem in here—you go sort everything out."

Hunter sucked in a deep breath. Hardness set in his azure

eyes. "Fine. I'll be back in a few minutes."

He pushed the chair aside and stormed toward the door, nearly bumping into Nicole as she came out of the bathroom. She stepped aside, but her gaze followed Hunter's ass as he left.

"Would you like me to get you a cold cloth? Or do you need to lie down for a bit?" I teased, pointing toward the long gray sofa by the window.

"No. I'm fine. I'm fine now." Nicole's cheeks burned bright red as she walked over to clean Gemma's face.

What shocked me though, was Hunter's behavior. Normally, Hunter would be all over someone like Nicole. Flirting and laughing and carrying on. But he'd ignored her. Maybe hurting Gemma had affected him more than I gave him credit for.

The nurse looked toward the door. "Hunter's just so . . . I'm sorry."

I yawned and covered my mouth. I'd heard it all before. *Hunter's just so good looking. So much better in real life.* Blah, blah, blah. I certainly had my fair share of admirers, but Hunter scored most of the attention. And he was welcome to it.

In high school, girls barely noticed us. We were the weedy, pimply, music geeks. Not the sports stars or part of the in-crowd. How things had changed now we were famous. Just a couple of kids from Montgomery, New Jersey, who'd gotten a lucky break.

Nicole jutted her chin toward the sofa. "Why don't you have a rest while Gemma's sleeping? It looks like you could use it. There's a spare pillow and blanket in the closet. I'll let you know when she wakes up."

"Thanks. I need to make a few quick phone calls, and then I'll do that. It's been a long night." I kissed Gemma's forehead, walked over to the window overlooking 77th Street, and glanced down at the growing group of photographers and fans on the sidewalk. I loved our followers, but they were crazy to stand out in the freezing cold.

After I made calls to Gemma's girlfriends and her mother, I stretched out on the sofa and glanced at my watch. Four a.m. With a heavy sigh, I covered my eyes with my arm. Since I'd come off stage, nothing had gone to plan. My moments alone with Gemma had been wasted, strangled by my nerves. I could perform in front of thousands of people without so much as a butterfly, but I couldn't tell Gemma how I felt about her when we'd been by ourselves. I was such a fucking idiot. I wouldn't let my jitters get the better of me again. I'd talk to her soon, with no more delays or interruptions. And hopefully, we could become something more than friends. God, I loved her. My mind raced again with what to say, but my adrenaline had run out. Exhaustion hit, and my eyelids grew heavy.

A quick nap was all I needed. Then I'd be ready. Ready for my world to change. I'd risk anything and everything for Gemma.

Even my heart.

Now all I needed was for her to wake up.

Chapter 4

GEMMA

Everything hurt. My head. My leg. My arm. Any attempt to move sent needles of pain stabbing through my entire body. What the hell did I do last night? Oh . . . that was right. The after-party. Hunter. The trunk. My leg. Panicked people, paramedics, nurses, doctors, X-rays, stitches.

The soft blip of a machine tapped a slow rhythmic pace somewhere beside me. Opening my eyes, nothing looked familiar. These were not my sheets. Not my pillow. Not my bed.

Fuck. I was still in the hospital.

I blinked away my grogginess. Hunter sat to my right. Machines stood to my left. Kyle lay stretched out asleep on the sofa by the window. The clock ticked on the wall above the door; it was a quarter to eight in the morning.

With fumbling fingers, I touched the gauze tugging at my temple. *Stitches.* Five, if I remembered correctly.

The IV in my left wrist pinched and pulled on my skin. White sheets, tucked across my waist, were as tight as a straitjacket. The warm blanket draped over my thighs was uncomfortable and heavy. The weight surrounding my leg had reality hit me like a taser.

Grabbing the remote beside my pillow, I raised the back of the bed.

"Gem. You're awake." Hunter leaped off the vinyl chair and clutched my hand. Dark stubble shadowed his face. "I'm so sorry. This is all my fault." His voice, barely above a whisper, was hard to hear over the trolley carts being pushed down the hallway. "I never meant to hurt you."

I closed my eyes and clenched my jaw to fight back the tears. I wouldn't let this accident get to me. I was strong. I wasn't a crier. Everything would be fine. But Hunter's pranks and games had gone too far, and I'd paid the price. A broken leg. A fucking broken leg. Right before vacation.

The smell of industrial-strength cleaner in the air churned my stomach. The ability to form saliva had vanished. My parched throat made it difficult to swallow. "I know you didn't, Hunt. It's okay. I'm okay."

"Doesn't make me feel any better." He lowered his gaze and tucked his long hair behind his ear.

"Hey . . . what happened to your face?" I pointed to the shiny black bruise underneath his eye.

"I hit it on the trunk when we crashed. I deserved more than this for putting you out of action for eight weeks."

"Eight weeks?" My voice jumped up a scale. "You mean I've got wear a stupid cast for eight weeks?" I ripped the blankets off my legs . . . and screamed. "It's PINK! Who the hell put a fucking pink cast on my leg?"

"Not me." Kyle jumped up from the sofa, grabbed a cup of water off the tray table at the end of the bed, and handed it to me. Somehow, he always knew what I needed.

I guzzled the water and handed the empty cup back to him. "Thanks. I needed that." Now I could talk without ripping my throat to pieces.

"You're welcome." He put the cup down, leaned against the bed, and rubbed the palms of his hands against his eyes as if trying to erase his tiredness. "You can thank Hunt for the cast. He bribed the doctor."

What? I dug my nails into the bedsheets. "I'll kill you, Hunt. I fucking hate pink."

"I know. That's what makes this so entertaining." He beamed, pulling up the sleeves on his sweatshirt to his elbows, revealing the small tattoo of our initials, GKH, on the inside of his left wrist. It had faded over the years, but it still meant so much. We each had one exactly the same, in exactly the same spot. *Friends forever . . . maybe.*

"Just you wait." I jabbed my finger at him as I spoke through tensed lips. "Vengeance will be sweet."

"I look forward to it." Hunter's eyes sparkled as he scanned my leg. "I think it looks sexy." He tickled the skin near the top of my cast. His soft circles and gentle strokes made the hair on my thigh stand on end. I flinched. Twitched. His touch was weird. And nice . . . but then, the air prickled.

Kyle glared at Hunter. His dark eyes had frosted over. The veins on his neck bulged. My blood pressure spiked like an ultrasound, and I slapped Hunter's hand away. He shouldn't be touching me like that. Had Kyle noticed Hunter's behavior, too? What was with Hunter lately? All touchy, feely. He wasn't the affectionate type.

But then Hunter's face turned serious as he stretched his legs out in front of his chair. His brow furrowed and his Adam's apple lurched. "Gem, there's something else we need to tell you."

"What? What else is there?" I tugged at the neckline of my ugly yellow hospital gown. My heart palpitations tapped against my ribcage. "It's my head, isn't it? There's something wrong after hitting it? Have I got some kinda permanent damage?"

Oh God. What if there was? What if the hit to my head was serious and I couldn't sing? Or play? Or had mobility issues? What would I do with my life? Music was all I knew. All I loved. All I ever wanted to do.

"No, no, it's nothing like that." Concern wedged between Kyle's eyebrows. "When you were under anesthetic, they couldn't get your leather pants off, so they had to cut them."

"They what?" I shot upright and slapped my hand against the mattress. "Goddamn motherfuckers! They were my favorite. I bought them in high school for twenty bucks in a thrift store. Can they be saved?"

Unable to look me in the eyes, Hunter and Kyle shook their heads, sucked in their cheeks, and tried not to laugh.

I slumped back against the pillows, glanced toward the ceiling and cursed again.

Losing those pants was worse than breaking my leg. I loved those fucking pants.

I'd worn them for our first big show. I'd worn them when we'd signed with SureHaven. I'd even worn them to bed.

"Where's the doctor?" My chin quivered. "I want to go home."

"Gem." Kyle clutched and squeezed my hand. "The doctor wants you to stay in for another night. He said you're too dehydrated and fatigued."

Of course I was. I'd just traveled the globe, hadn't had a decent sleep in months, and I'd drunk an obscene amount of JD last night. The throb in the back of my skull was a clear reminder of that.

"Can I sit?" Kyle pointed to the mattress beside me.

"Go for it." I straightened the sheets and the blanket over my cast and drew them up to my waist. He lowered his butt onto the bed beside my legs. Hunter moved closer on his chair, scraping it loudly against the floor. Then Kyle shuffled forward a few more inches, settling right next to my hip.

Okay, they were concerned about me, but they were both acting weird.

I grabbed the triangle bar dangling above my head and hoisted myself to sit higher on the bed. "Where's my phone? I need to call Kara and Lexi to cancel vacation."

Kyle reached inside his leather jacket and handed over my phone. "I've already called them. They're going to come in and see you after work tonight. Vacation is still on, but you'll be sitting on your ass in the cabin rather than snowboarding the slopes."

"That's not my idea of fun. But thanks for calling the girls." I took my phone and clutched it against my chest. What would I do without him? Kyle was the glue that stuck the three of us together. He kept Hunter's ego under control, kept my head out of the clouds, and kept us all focused on the music.

"Do you want me to cancel going to see my cousin in Seattle and stay with you instead?" Kyle picked at the frayed threads on the knee of his ripped jeans.

Hunter shook his head. "Kyle, you don't have to do that. Gem, why don't you come to Chicago with me? My folks and Jenny would love to see you."

I twisted the sheet around in my hands and stared at the knot I'd made. I loved these guys. But after being on the road for months, I needed a break. Especially from Hunter. I needed to get my head and my heart back under control so they wouldn't affect our work, our music, or our lives.

"I'll be fine, but thanks for offering. We need some timeout otherwise we might end up killing each other." *Oh wait . . . Hunt had already tried that.*

Kyle nodded, cleared his throat, and stared down at his hands. "I know. It was just a thought." He looked up at me from underneath his long lashes. "I . . . I also called your mom. Save you one time from dealing with her. I thought it was best to let her know what happened before she found out via social media and hounded you for details."

My chest tightened, and a bitter taste flooded my mouth. I wiped my hands on the sheets, smoothing out the wrinkles. "You shouldn't have bothered. I'm alive, so I doubt she'd be concerned. She wouldn't come home from her travels or men for anything less than my funeral or an inheritance." *Probably only the latter.*

Kyle scratched at the few whiskers he'd grown since he'd last shaved. "She was in a café or something when I called so it turned into a fiasco."

"What else would you expect?" My head sank deeper into the pillows. "How many times did she drop our name during the conversation this time?"

"In the five minutes I spoke to her, I think"—he counted on his fingers—"at least seven." Kyle put his hand up to his ear to mimic a phone. "*Oh! It's Kyle from Everhide. Everhide this. Everhide that. Oh no, I'm not coming home. Why would I? Victor and I have opera tickets. We've booked a cruise to Cyprus. Then we're going to Milan.*"

Kyle's impersonation of my mother's voice, complete with a perfectly nasal Fran Drescher pitch, brought a smile to my face, but tugged at the emptiness in my chest.

I'd always been nothing but an inconvenience to my mother. She craved social status and men, and I was often left to fend for myself when I was a kid. Janine had never supported my love of music, never paid for one guitar or piano lesson, and had never seen me perform. But when I became famous, Janine rode off my celebrity status like a Kardashian.

While it had broken my heart at the time, as an adult, I now understood why my father had left when I was twelve. He'd tired of my mother's shallow and cheating ways. I just wished, to this day, that he'd fucking taken me with him.

The door flung open with a whoosh and in walked Amie, with Kate, our publicist.

"Good. You're awake." Amie tilted her surgically modified nose into the air and swept her Emma Stone blonde bangs out of her eyes. Her voice filled the room with as much warmth and compassion as an ice cube. I expected nothing less.

To Amie, we were nothing but a money-making product. If the three of us weren't performing, making and releasing singles and albums, we wouldn't be bringing in the bucks. We'd signed her as our manager as part of our deal with SureHaven. Amie had become an instant friend; we'd hung out and made grand plans for success. But as we reached every goal, and the guys and I had become a multimillion-dollar business, Amie had grown a god-like complex and a bitchy attitude to match.

I couldn't wait to get rid of her when we signed a new contract with SureHaven. I counted down the days until that could happen. Until we could record a complete album of our own material, the songs the guys and I had written. It was how we were discovered and what we wanted for the future. It would happen. But until then, Amie was a part of our deal.

"Hey, gorgeous." Kate dumped her laptop bag and armful of belongings onto the small table in the center of the suite, ducked around Kyle, and gave me a hug. "Are you doing okay, sweetie?"

"Yeah, but the cast is already itching." I slid my hands underneath the sheet and scratched my skin at the top of my leg. *That's better.*

"Bec will come in and see you later." Kate's soft voice hovered with fatigue. It had been a long night for everyone. "She was going to grab an overnight bag of clothes and toiletries for you."

"Thanks." I ruffled my fingers through my hair. Yep, I really needed a hairbrush. Bec, our personal assistant, truly was a treasure.

"Right then, you three." Amie waved her fuchsia-colored talons back and forth between the guys and me. "We have a lot of things to cancel and reschedule. Kate?" Amie snapped her fingers at our publicist. "Are you ready?"

Kate sighed, flicked her long black ponytail over her shoulder, and took a seat at the table. She opened her laptop, cracked her knuckles, and wiggled her fingers above the keyboard. "Yep."

"Amie, we don't have to cancel anything." *Did we?* Doubt strangled my throat. "I can still sing. I can still play the guitar."

"I'm sure you could, but with a broken leg, your security, and safety are of concern, so we will restrict any unnecessary travel." Amie grabbed her cell phone out of her blue ostrich leather Birkin bag before dropping it onto the floor by Hunter's chair. "We'll have to cancel performing at the iHeartRadio Awards and the Kids' Choice Awards."

"Cancel iHeart?" Hunter pushed his chair back two feet from the bedside and slumped. "But it's the first time we've been asked to perform there."

I curled my toes underneath the bedcovers so tight they hurt. The guys and I had been looking forward to that show, and now the opportunity was gone. Next year, someone else will be hotter than we were right now, and our chance to perform will disappear.

Amie spun on the balls of her feet to face Hunter. "You want to go on stage without Gemma? Just say the word. I'll make it happen."

Hunter leaned forward, rested his elbows on his knees, and looked at me. The light in his eyes clouded over. He'd hate not performing; he'd be on stage every day if possible. But his lips drew into a reassuring smile, and he gave Amie a shake of his head. "Never. That's not an option."

"Just as I suspected." Amie's fingernails tapped against the screen of her phone. "But you guys can still fly out to LA to attend."

Kyle drew his brow into a pinch. "We don't have to go if you want to cancel—"

"No chance. You're going." She cut him off with a flick of her hand.

Everything became a blur as Amie and Kate reorganized our lives and schedules for the next couple of months. So much preparation had gone into getting ready for these appearances, and now it was erased by a few quick phone calls.

Stupid broken leg.

"What about the Billboards in Vegas at the end of May?" Hunter asked. "That's only two and a half months away."

"Gemma will be fine by then. Won't you, Gemma?" Amie cut me a cold look. That was nothing unusual. Not sure her face could move anyway, thanks to her Botox. "You're going to rest up and heal that leg of yours. Just because you're injured doesn't mean everything stops. We'll start the new album, run through the demos, go through marketing strategies and creatives, and hit the studio as soon as possible. You'll do interviews and local appearances as normal, but no performances until you're better."

Yep . . . It was all work and hardly any rest at all for us. Good thing I loved what I did. But I hated missing out on going anywhere with the guys.

"This sucks." I flopped back against the pillows. "Can't I do anything?"

"Yes. Get better," Amie snapped, turned away, and made another call.

Kate stretched her arms over her head. "That's everything we needed to cover for now. I'm going to head into the office and deal with these press inquiries before my inbox and cell phone go into meltdown. Gem, so far the gossip ranges from you collapsing on stage from a drug overdose to you nearly being killed in an accident and fighting for your life in ICU."

I puffed air through my nose and threw her a lopsided, understanding smile. "So, just your average, typical day at work, huh?" I'd had much worse gossip said about me than that.

"Seems like it." Light shimmered in Kate's eyes as she packed up her belongings. I liked Kate. She was cool.

"We'll be off then." Amie bent down, taking her sweet time to pick up her handbag, giving Hunter an eyeful of her cosmetically enhanced cleavage. And by God, did he ogle, like he wanted to crawl into her top and have a feast. My hands curled into fists beneath the sheet. Jealousy simmered through my veins. *Fuck. Stop.* Hunter wasn't mine. He could look. *But ugh! Amie?*

Amie rose and drew back her shoulders, enhancing her chest size even more. "If there are any other changes, I'll let you know." She gave us a catty smile, waved goodbye, and headed out the door with Kate.

Kyle shuffled around to face me. "That wasn't too bad. Only a couple shows canceled—otherwise, it's business as normal."

"Eight weeks will fly by. I'll make sure it does." Hunter winked at me as he played with his silver necklace.

"After vacation, promise me you'll come and stay at our place." Kyle glanced at Hunter for confirmation. He nodded without hesitation. Kyle dipped his chin, then turned back to me. "That way, you don't have to go up and down your staircase. We'll look after you until your cast is off."

Stay with the guys?

I drew in a long, deep breath, and my pulse quickened. I hung out at their penthouse all the time. I even had a room there. But I liked my condo. It gave me some separation from them—even if it was literally only around the corner. Right now, I needed distance, not upping my chances to witness Hunter parading around in nothing but his boxer-briefs. "Thanks, but I'm sure I'll be fine. Let's see how I handle crutches first."

"Okay." Kyle's stomach grumbled loudly. His hand shot up to rub it. "I think that's my cue. I need food. I'm gonna grab something quickly from the cafeteria. You want anything?"

"Nah, I'm fine." Even though my tummy ached, the thought of food made me feel ill. "I'll eat later."

"Okay. I'll be back soon."

But Kyle didn't move.

His dark gaze locked onto mine, making my skin prickle. Something still troubled him. We didn't get a chance to talk last night. I hated seeing sadness and worry lurk in his eyes. Whatever was bothering him, we'd sort it out—like always.

"When I get back, we need to talk," he whispered.

"Yeah. Okay." I guessed I'd find out what was going on when he returned. Clearly, he didn't want to talk about it in front of Hunter. That was a worry in itself.

"Hunt, want anything to eat?" Kyle asked.

"Yeah, sure." He stretched and rubbed the back of his neck. "Grab me a wrap of some kind. Thanks."

"Will do. I'll be back soon." Kyle stood, leaned over, and kissed me on the forehead. I smiled as tiny tingles shot over my scalp. Warmth curled down the back of my neck and settled in my chest. Why did that always happen? I was so lucky to have two guys care about me so much. He winked at me, then turned, grabbed his wallet and phone off the table, and headed out the door.

Hunter pulled the chair close and ruffled his fingers through his messy hair. Dark circles shadowed his eyes. Exhaustion was taking its toll.

"Why don't you go home and get some sleep?" I yawned, covering my mouth with the back of my hand. "I'll be okay here by myself."

"Maybe later. After lunch. But I want to talk to you about something first." He tugged at the neckline of his T-shirt.

"Sure. If I can stay awake." I wriggled my toes and shuffled about. Moving around this time wasn't too bad; the painkillers dulled the ache in my leg and the throbbing in my head.

"How's the leg?" Hunter rested his arms on the mattress, but when his eyes met mine, they darkened. The air became thick and heavy. It settled over me like a huge velvet curtain. My stomach flipped in acrobatic somersaults. He shouldn't be looking at me like that. Not with lust and desire and want.

Damn, these drugs are good. No . . . bad. Very, very bad.

"There's something I want to ask you." His voice croaked and cracked. That wasn't like him. "Something I've been thinking about for the past few months. I've thought long and hard about this . . . about you. You know I love you, right?"

Tension tugged at my temples. Had he noticed a change in my behavior and was concerned? *Shit.* "Same goes. I love you and Kyle."

Hunter's neck flushed, and he bobbed his head up and down in short, sharp jerks. "I know. But here's the thing." He sucked in a deep breath and straightened. "I was wondering if we . . . I mean you . . . would you . . . go out with me?"

What? I pinched my eyebrows together and jerked my chin back. *Go out?* "Yeah. Sure. No worries. The three of us will go out after vacation. Kyle's always up for something, but my leg will limit our options."

But Hunter closed his eyes and shook his head. "No . . . That's not what I meant. Gem, I want you to *go out* with me. Just me. On a date."

Oh shit. The blood drained from my face.

My jaw hit the floor.

A date?

Holy. Fucking. Crap!

I hadn't expected that.

What the hell was he thinking?

Chapter 5

GEMMA

My heart clambered into my throat. I blinked. Stared. Blinked again. "Wh-what did you say?" Maybe the morphine had affected my hearing because Hunter wasn't making any sense. I pinched my arm to make sure I wasn't stuck in one of my steamy dreams.

He covered my hand with his. "I can't stop thinking about you. I want you to be my girlfriend."

"Since when?" I drew my hand away and hugged myself tight. "Five minutes ago? After you stopped gawking at Amie's boobs?"

"She does have a nice set, doesn't she?" He grinned and slowly bobbed his head.

"What the fuck?"

"Shit . . . I didn't mean that." He winced and shuffled in the chair. "I'm sorry. This isn't going to plan. Gem, I'm serious. I want to go out with you."

"With me? Just me?" My voice went all soprano. My heart rate monitor blip-blip-blipped even faster. "How hard did I hit my head last night? Because you *do* girls, not girlfriends. You've never had a girlfriend . . . Not ever. Not even in high school."

"Diversionary tactics. They've all been practice so I could perfect my skills."

"You're nuts, Hunt." I fumbled around for the remote.

"Where's the emergency button? Quick—call the nurse and get the defibrillator. I think I'm having a heart attack. This is crazy talk. You can't say stuff like this to me. It would change everything."

"I know it will." He fidgeted with his watch.

There was too much at risk. Hearts and music and friendships were at stake.

"And what about Kyle?" Worry dug into my brow. Something about Kyle niggled the back of my brain and lurked in the depths of my chest. I couldn't figure out what it was. "We have to think about him and the consequences."

My head spun faster than a vinyl at 78rpm. *Breathe. Just breathe.* My hot dreams about Hunter weren't supposed to become a reality. *Were they?* My pulse strummed at speed and my stomach swayed back and forth. I stared at him, square in the eye, making sure my mind was clear and not fogged by any drug. There was no mischievous grin on his face, no playful glint flickering in his gaze.

Holy shit. He was serious.

"Kyle will be fine. Trust me." His voice never faltered. "He loves us and will support our decision."

I didn't share his confidence. We were a trio. Always had been. Inseparable. Backup band members, crew, and management would come and go throughout our lives, but the three of us had to remain united. Balanced. Even.

"I don't believe that." I squirmed around on the bed, trying to get comfortable. Trying to comprehend what he'd said. "Hunt, you're like a brother to me. You always have been. It would be too weird being with you."

"Gem, think about it." He took my hand in his.

I couldn't tell whose fingers trembled more—mine or his. Did he really have feelings for me? Really want *me*?

But it didn't matter. We could never work.

"We'd be great together." Warmth simmered through his azure eyes. "You've set a high benchmark, Gem. No one else compares with you. You're smart. Talented. Have a beautiful soul. You know me better than anyone else, even Kyle. I love spending time with you. You're one of the sexiest hot-as-hell girls I've ever met."

"But you're a boob guy." I couldn't get the exasperation out of my voice as I shimmied my hands in front of my flat chest. "I've got nothing."

"I've seen 'em." His eyes sparkled. "There's enough. Trust me."

I sank into the pillows, wincing and shuddering. Thanks to my ex-boyfriend, the whole world had seen me naked. *Asshole.*

But Hunter? Wanted to date me? How had I not seen the signs he was interested? I was usually super perceptive. I'd been so caught up in my head I'd been blinded and hadn't seen my feelings were reciprocated? *Holy shit.*

He squeezed my hand, sending my pulse up another notch. "No one gets me like you do, Gem. We have fun together. You don't put up with any of my shit. You keep me grounded. But I don't want to just be friends anymore. I'm crazy about you."

Goosebumps shot up my arm. He made my guarded wall warp.

"You're right about one thing." Worry dug into my forehead. "You're mental. What would we do if it didn't work out? What if we hurt each other? I couldn't live with that."

"I promise we won't ever let it get to that stage."

"You say that now." But everyone I'd ever loved had been hurt, or driven away, or broken by a failed relationship. Why would he be any different?

"Tell me something. Be honest." His smile was back-loaded with too much mischievous sexiness. "Have you ever thought about it? Thought about us together?"

Heat flooded my cheeks recalling my dream from yesterday. Hunter had been going down on me in the back of a limo, on our way to some grand event. It had been hot sex. Wild sex. Totally orgasmic sex.

Hunter licked his lips. My pussy quivered. *Oh boy.* What could that tongue do to me?

Shit!

I pulled my hand free and wiped my clammy palm on my stomach. "Of course, I have. I've even had some crazy dreams. But don't flatter yourself. I've thought about doing it with lots of people. Doesn't mean we should act on it."

Hunter rose, then sat down beside me on the bed. "Don't you want to see if what we have is something special?"

I closed my eyes to block him out of my mind, but no matter how hard I tried, I couldn't. Him, having feelings for me, changed the whole game. Would I regret not finding out if we were meant to be together?

Could he be the one?

He lived and breathed my world. He understood our everyday pressures. He'd been through every up and down with me. What could be better than falling for one of my best friends?

No. No. No. No. No.

"How can I believe you when you've never showed any interest before?"

"Yes, I have. Remember, New Year's Eve in Paris, watching the fireworks from our hotel balcony? I wanted to kiss you then. In Japan, after skiing on our day off, I came so close to telling you. Last night at the after-party, I wanted to dance with you more than anybody else. I want to sit up all night writing songs with you, like you do with Kyle. I want to spoil you rotten and have loads of fun."

My heart couldn't handle him saying all the right things. He had to stop. Stop right now. Because with each breath, I felt myself falling—falling for him.

"But last night you *were* picking up girls. You tapped some girl in our hotel suite here in New York three days ago. Amie's tits had you mesmerized a few minutes ago."

"Yeah, just some meaningless fun. But I'm done with that." Hunter drew my hand up to his mouth and kissed the back of it. His lips were soft and tender. His warm breath shivered across my skin. "You're probably analyzing every pro and con right now like you always do, but trust me, I already have. Stop over-thinking this and just be mine."

An *I'm-so-in-shock-I-don't-know-whether-to-laugh-or-cry* puff burst from my mouth. Twelve hours ago, I'd been cursing my dreams, begging them to stop, and had never wanted to risk our friendship and bond. Now, here I was in Alice's trippy Wonderland, and he was asking me out.

He nudged my thigh. "So how about it?"

My stomach flipped. Could we be more than friends? No one made me laugh like he did. He was the prankster, the adrenaline junkie, the charismatic standout in any room. On the other hand, he was a playboy. A huge flirt. And he had an ego the size of the Empire State Building. That was a worry.

"Is this another one of your jokes?" Red warning lights flashed inside my mind. "Don't go messing with my heart, Hunt, because this is serious shit."

"I wouldn't do that, Gem. Never. My intentions are honorable . . . but what I want to do to you certainly isn't." His eyes hinted at a whole lot of delicious mischievousness and sent a rush of heat to my core.

"Hunt, I'm scared. After what happened with Ben . . ." Tears stung my eyes.

"Ben was an asshole."

He wasn't wrong. "You love the spotlight like he did. I don't want what we do to be splashed across the Internet. I don't want interviews to be about our relationship. Out there"—I jutted my chin toward the window—"we're about the music, not our private lives."

"I agree. So we'll keep being together under wraps until you're ready. I know how much Ben hurt you. We've all been through our own scandals and scrutiny. But since then, we've learned how to deal with the paparazzi and reporters. We've had enough media training to handle anything. We can do this. I promise." He made it sound easy. Too easy.

Crap. Maybe dating him could work.

The warmth from his smile chipped away at the barrier cemented around my heart. Hunter's charm was like an intoxicating drug, totally addictive. And I wanted more.

I swallowed hard. I couldn't believe I was contemplating this. "I have to admit it, yes, something has changed between us. But I'm worried about Kyle. This could change everything. And I don't want that. If . . . and only if I agree to go out with you . . . there have to be some ground rules." My words came out firm and strong, taking me by surprise considering my nerves rattled like Halloween chains.

"Ground rules." A deep trench etched into Hunter's brow. "Okay, I'm all ears. Let me have them."

"This has come out of nowhere, so I need time. Time to make sure that you and I being together won't affect our work . . . or Kyle. I need to be sure that this *is* something special. We have to adjust, and so does Kyle. So, while I've got my cast on, there's to be . . . no sex."

Hunter's mouth fell open. "No sex?"

"I mean it. We need to do this without being influenced by fucking." *What the hell was I saying?* No sex would be ridiculously hard. Especially after all my hot dreams . . . and the things I'd heard and seen him do to other women. Fuck, it was going to be a long eight weeks.

"That's a harsh ground rule, Gem." Hunter raked his fingers down his face, then rubbed the back of his neck. "Are you sure about that? I can think of five different ways to make you orgasm without hurting your leg."

Heat coiled through my core. My thighs tensed. But no. I had to stand firm. "Five. That's all? With your reputation, I expected more."

"I'll gladly accept the challenge." He turned on an irresistible smile that made my heart flutter.

"I'm sure you would."

Eight weeks would give me enough time to see if being in a relationship affected the dynamic between us and Kyle. This had to strengthen us, make us better, and keep everyone happy.

"Two months?" Hunter scratched his jaw and wiped his hand across his mouth. "That's a long time, but okay. You're worth the wait." A touch of sexy glimmered in his eyes. "So, does that mean it's a yes?"

If I said yes . . . there was no going back. It scared the shit out of me to risk everything. But if I said no, I'd always wonder if he was the love of my life. The piece to fill the emptiness that lingered deep inside my heart.

Sheer terror, hope and longing spiraled through my mind. We'd been through so much together. We could survive anything. We had to. I inhaled slowly and nodded.

Hunter's face lit up like Broadway. "You won't regret this. I promise." He leaned forward and kissed me on the forehead.

It was funny. My skin didn't tingle like it had when Kyle had kissed me in the same place before. Surely I was just flustered and excited and definitely overwhelmed.

Hunter brushed his fingertips down the side of my cheek. "We're going to be good for each other, Gem."

He edged closer. His mouth hovered an inch from mine. His hot breath teased my face. *Oh wow.* My heart pounded like a drum. My eyes drifted shut. How many times had I dreamed of this moment? Too many. I'd lost count.

He pressed his lips against mine, soft and warm.

I placed my hand on his chest. His heart raced as fast, if not faster, than mine. His lips trembled against my mouth. But then . . . his long hair fell forward and tickled my face. His stubble scratched my skin like sandpaper. *Ouch.* We turned our heads in the same direction at the same time. *What the . . .?* Our noses butted and bumped together.

I'd never been so uncoordinated in my life.

Then . . . he stuck his tongue into my mouth.

What the fuck?

I pulled back and burst out laughing. "What are you trying to do? Gag me?" I licked my lips and wiped the corner of my mouth. "That . . . was the worst first kiss ever."

Hunter lowered his gaze and nodded. "Yep! Geez, Gem, I really thought you'd be a better kisser than that." He teased, but his eyes smoldered.

"What? Me?" I thumped him on the arm. "It wasn't my fault. You're the one who stuck your tongue in."

"True." He took my hand and kissed it once again. "We'll practice. A lot. I hope that kiss didn't change your mind."

I glanced over Hunter's shoulder. Through the glass panel on the door, Kyle appeared.

My heart beat faster than a strobe light.

Oh shit.

The handle turned.

Hunter squeezed my hand. "So, Gem, are you still keen to give it a shot?"

The door swung open.

Kyle stepped into the room. "Give what a shot?"

Chapter 6

KYLE

Two steps into Gemma's room, my pace faltered. Something had happened. The charge in the air made the hair on my arms prickle. Gemma gnawed on her bottom lip. A glassy sheen shimmered across her beautiful green eyes, but they were rimmed with redness. She wouldn't look at me. Had she been crying? What the fuck did Hunter do?

He sat beside her. On the bed. Close.

Too fucking close for my liking.

I dropped the chicken wraps onto her tray table and dragged another chair over to sit beside her, wedging it in between the bed and the IV machine.

"What's up with you two?" I didn't know where to look. Gemma's face had paled like she was about to throw up. Hunter just stared at her with concern knitting his brow.

"Do you want to tell him, or shall I?" Hunter brushed the tip of her nose with his fingertip.

She winced, shook her head, and closed her eyes.

Shit. Whatever it was, it wasn't good. Had the doctor visited while I was away and given her some bad news? What was going on? I pulled my shoulders back, bracing myself for the worst. "Tell me what?"

Hunter grinned like he'd just gotten a standing ovation. "I asked Gemma to be my girlfriend. And she said yes."

What. The. Fuck? The blow to my gut knocked the breath from my lungs. My heart lurched and splintered. It took all my strength not to keel over. *What?* "You what?" My eyes shot to Gemma, praying this was a sick joke. But she lowered her head and drew her arms tightly across her stomach.

Then . . . I saw it.

The nod.

Gemma's barely-there nod.

I wanted to disappear through the floor. "You're going out with Hunter?" The words burned my throat. "Please, tell me you're not serious?" Anger coiled through me like hungry flames in search of a forest to burn. Digging my fingernails into my kneecaps, I glared at Hunter. "Gem has a wet dream. You think it's about you, and suddenly you want to fuck her?"

"It's not like that." Hunter's pitch hit the ceiling. "Kyle, this has been brewing for months."

"Why didn't you tell me you wanted to go out with her?" A cold sweat broke on my brow. How could I criticize him when I'd never told him I had feelings for her, either?

Hunter shrugged. "Timing was never right. But you're cool with this, aren't you?"

I somehow forced air into my lungs, but a shudder ripped through me. The excitement plastered on Hunter's face was another sucker punch to my solar plexus. I clenched my jaw, my fist, and everything else humanly possible. Every muscle was like a stretched rubber band about to snap. I needed to focus on something, anything, to stop myself from planting my fist into Hunter's precious face.

The IV machine whirred. The nurses' muffled conversations drifted in from the corridor. A trolley cart wheeled past the door.

"I . . . I never saw this coming." My voice was surreal, not my own. I turned to Gemma and my world stopped. As she looked at Hunter, her eyes shone, and a glow radiated across her face. *Shit.* My heart split wide open. My stomach hit the floor. Lowering my chin, I slouched back into the chair.

Fuck.

I wanted her to look at me like that. Not Hunter.

I'd gotten it all wrong.

She had feelings for Hunter . . . not me.

Of all people. Why Hunter? My best friend. How could I watch him be with the girl I loved?

Gemma wrung the bedsheet in her hands. "I never knew Hunt felt this way about me."

"Me either," I mumbled.

In my fifteen minutes of absence, they'd become an item. My feelings were no longer relevant. Totally void. Obliterated. I could never tell Gemma how I felt. I'd never deny the two people I loved and cared about their chance at happiness.

But nausea churned in my gut. Acid burned up my esophagus and sent a bitter taste into my mouth. With true grit, I held my tongue. I wanted to say, *"Gem, pick me instead."* I wanted to say, *"No, you two can't be together."* I wanted to say, *"Gem, love me, not him."* But I swallowed the words swarming through my mind and told them what they wanted to hear. "You two will make . . . an awesome couple. Very cool."

"You're not upset?" Gemma tugged at the bandage on her head.

Was that disappointment in the depths of her eyes, or was it just wishful thinking on my part? What did she expect? For me to yell and argue and protest? How could I? I couldn't do that to my best friends.

"No." I turned to face the window being pelted with rain so she couldn't see my shattered soul. My broken heart.

"Thanks, bud. You're the best." Hunter's warm tone made my gut twist and sour. "I told you Kyle would be okay."

Me? Okay? Not even close. My jaw ached. My ears rang. The walls caved in around me. The air had become too thick to breathe.

I needed to get out of there. I needed space. I needed to escape.

"Um . . . I gotta go. Maybe home for a while." I leaped from my chair. It slid backward and banged against the IV machine. *Shit.*

Holding myself together, I stepped forward. I cupped Gemma's face and pressed my lips to her forehead. As I closed my eyes, I breathed her into every cell of my body. I savored the feel of her silky brown hair against my fingertips, the scent of her cherry blossom shampoo, the touch of my lips against her soft skin. "I'll see you later, Gem. Get some rest."

Then, with the speed of an Amtrak Express, I turned. I grabbed my wallet, my jacket, and my heart off the floor and rushed out the door.

I needed a bar. A bottle of Jack Daniels. And I needed them quick.

***

I burst out of the rear entrance of the hospital onto 76th Street and turned my face toward the pelting rain.

"FUUUUUUUCK," I screamed, long and hard. My voice ripped and burned my throat, cutting it like razors, until every ounce of breath had escaped my lungs. The sound echoed through the narrow street, ricocheting off the surrounding buildings. Birds, sheltering in the trees from the icy spring rain, scattered into the sky. Clutching my chest, I collapsed against the brick wall of the hospital. The cold droplets of water stung my skin, dripped from my hair, trickled down my cheeks, and slowly numbed my flesh.

I'd lost her.

Just like that.

I'd lost Gemma.

I'd missed out on my chance to tell her how I felt.

It didn't matter anyway. I'd made a huge mistake. I'd misread the signs—staying up all night writing songs with her in hotel rooms, talking until daylight broke when we should've been sleeping. Her hugs that had felt like she'd never wanted to let go. I'd been a fool, delusional, to think I had a chance with her. Thank God I didn't ask her out. It was obvious her interests lay elsewhere.

"Kyle?" Sam's hand appeared under my elbow. My bodyguard had tailed me, bolting from Gemma's room. "Man, you look like crap. What's happened?"

I shrugged him off. "Leave me alone."

"Put your damn coat on. It's freezing out here." Sam tugged his collar higher and avoided stepping in the muddy pools of water by the doorway. Up and down the street, soaking leaves drooped on the trees. Delivery trucks looked as if they shivered while waiting to be unloaded at the service entrance. Cars appeared miserable, left outside in the cold and dreary rain.

With a grunt, I slipped on my leather jacket and headed toward Lexington Avenue.

"Hey, man. Let me call the car to take you home," Sam called from behind.

"No. I need a walk."

"Are you fucking crazy? It's raining. It's freezing. Do you want to be swamped by the horde of fans that are staked out at the front of the hospital? You stand out like the Chrysler Building. I have to think of your safety."

"Fuck off." I stomped my Nike into a muddy puddle, splashing slush onto my jeans.

Fuck.

Fuck it.

Fuck everything.

I swung my fist through the air, picturing it colliding with Hunter's face, and kept walking. I needed to be alone. I needed to calm down. Because right now, I could only think the worst. I wanted to take every one of the priceless guitars in Hunter's collection and smash them to pieces. I wanted to grab every piece of music equipment in our home studio and destroy it. But most of all, I wanted to find every piece of paper, every lyric, every song I'd ever written about my love for Gemma and burn them.

Burn them all.

"Kyle, stop." Sam's voice only added fuel to my fire.

I turned, stormed back a few steps, and got right in Sam's face. "I need to go for a walk. Either you come with me or stay here." I shoved my hands into my pockets, spun on my heels, and headed along the street.

"I don't get paid enough for this shit," Sam growled. "Wait up. I'm coming."

I wasn't a complete idiot, so I avoided the hospital's main entrance on 77th. I wasn't up to facing fans and photographers.

Flicking up my jacket collar, I quickened my pace and headed along 76th, north along Third, and then slipped east onto 78th.

Local shops, salons, and laundry services lay at street level beneath tall apartment blocks. Expensive brownstones nestled in between the commercial chaos. I didn't know this part of the city well, but I needed to absorb New York back into my veins after being away on tour for so long. I needed her energy, her vibrancy, and her strength.

That was what I needed.

Strength.

Strength to lock away my feelings for Gemma. I had to dig deep, pour my heartache into my lyrics, and move on. *Somehow.*

The wet sidewalk muffled my footsteps. Keeping my eyes down, I ignored the world around me. I glanced up only occasionally in desperate search of a bar. There had to be one around here somewhere.

Out of nowhere, Sam threw his arm around my shoulders and pushed me sideways, knocking the breath from my chest. He shoved me through an open restaurant door and slammed it shut behind us.

"Sam, what the hell?" I shrugged out of his hold and shook the rain off my jacket.

"What's with you today?" Sam scowled, flicking his hand at me. "We've had a growing crowd tailing us. There's too many of them to keep you safe."

Fuck. I ripped my fingers through my wet hair and paced back and forth across the checkered black-and-white floor. "Sorry, man. I just wanted to go for a walk."

Some days, simple things were impossible.

Sam switched the sign on the glass door to "closed" and pulled the curtains across the front window before the guy standing at the front counter could object.

The young man's eyes bulged as big and white as the dinner plates piled up on the counter behind him. "Hey, what are you doing?"

"There's a riot heading this way. I did that for your own safety." Sam thumbed over his shoulder toward the door, then scanned the restaurant. "You got some other way out of here? All I need you to do is stay closed for half an hour. We'll compensate you for the inconvenience."

The Asian man's face paled. He nodded and pointed toward the kitchen. "You can leave via the back door. But . . . but . . ." He gaped at me and fidgeted with his apron. "Holy crap. You're Kyle McIntyre? From Everhide? Wow! I was at your concert last night. You guys are sick."

"Thanks, man. I hope you enjoyed the show." I feigned a smile, digging deep to find an ounce of professionalism. I'd have to deal with my hurt later once I was out of this mess. "I'm sorry about the intrusion." I hated causing problems, but then I looked around the vacant café—we hadn't interrupted any patrons.

His face lit with a wild smile. "I can't believe you're in my family's restaurant. This is so unbelievable. None of my friends at school will believe you were here when I tell them."

His excitement had no effect on me. I was dead. Inside and out.

Sam nudged me on the shoulder, pushed me toward a booth at the back of the yellow wallpapered restaurant, and took out his cell phone. "Sit, while I sort out a car to come and get us."

I flopped down onto the maroon-colored seat and turned to the waiter who'd followed. "What's your name?"

"Leon."

"What kinda food do you do here, Leon?"

The guy's mouth moved this way and that before he formed any words. "Um . . . Vietnamese. My mom and dad make the best Vietnamese rolls ever."

"Great." My belly rumbled at the thought and smell of food. I'd forgotten all about my wrap. Left untouched on Gemma's tray table back at the hospital. *Idiot.* "I'll have a serving of chicken rolls and bring some beef noodles for Sam. Better make them takeaway, please."

Leon nodded and scuttled out to the kitchen with our order.

"You got any liquor?" I called out to Leon.

Leon reappeared, pointing to the small collection of bottles in a cabinet at the back of the restaurant.

"Excellent. I'll have the bottle of JD . . . and a glass, please."

Leon rushed around faster than the Flash and placed them on the table before me.

"Thanks, man." I picked up the bottle and poured a shot. With only a quarter of the contents left in the bottle, it would barely make a dent in drowning my sorrows. But it was a start.

Sam eased into the booth seat opposite. The air squished out of the cushion as his backside settled. He waved at Leon, who lingered in the kitchen doorway. "Leon, do you have any tea? I'd love a cup of very strong black tea, please."

He nodded and disappeared.

I downed my shot of JD and didn't hesitate before pouring a second.

Sam crossed his arms, his broad shoulders nearly taking up the entire width of the booth. "So, you gonna tell me what's going on, or am I going to have to guess?"

"I don't want to talk about it." I stared at the amber liquid as I swirled it around in the bottom of the glass.

"Kyle, I've been your bodyguard for five years. I know something's happened. My guess is it has something to do with Gemma."

My gut twisted at the mention of her name. "She's fine," I muttered through clenched teeth.

"Doesn't sound like it. We've got half an hour until the car gets here, so start talking."

"About what?"

"You flinched when I mentioned her name. What's up?"

"Nothing."

Sam leaned forward. His eyes narrowed to slits. "I may be a quiet man, but I'm very observant. I've seen the way you look at her. I'm not stupid. You may have everyone else fooled, but not me."

Sam didn't break eye contact with me, not even when Leon placed a steaming cup of tea down on the table.

"Here you go, sir." Leon dipped his chin. "Tea. Hot. Strong and black. Your food will be ready in about five minutes."

"Thanks." I waved my drink at him. "Much appreciated." I may feel like shit, but I still had good manners.

Leon bowed excessively, then scuttled back behind the counter. He sat on a stool, pulled his cell phone from his apron pocket, and typed madly. Social media, no doubt.

Sam tapped his fingers on the tabletop. "Kyle, we could sit here all-day circling around the truth. Stop with the bullshit and tell me what happened."

The cool JD slid down my throat and burned deep inside my chest. I licked my lips and swallowed down a truckload of anguish. "Hunter happened. He supposedly feels the same way about her as I do and asked her out . . . and she said yes."

Sam frowned; confusion drilled into his face. "Hunter? Asked Gemma out? Damn. I had him nailed down to liking someone else."

He did? "Who?"

"Doesn't matter now."

Hunter wanting to commit to one person had me baffled. Hunter loved to play the field. He loved the girls, and the endless supply of sex. My head thudded, unable to process his sudden change of heart.

"What are you going to do about it?" Sam picked up his tea, blew on it, and took a sip. "Did you tell her how you felt? Are you going to fight for her?"

"What?" Exasperation hurtled through my veins. "No. I can't do that. And what's the point?" I clutched my glass so hard I thought it might shatter. "She looked so fucking happy. I couldn't say anything. If Hunter is the one, so be it. I'd sooner see her with him than with some loser from God knows where. She's all that matters." *Truth.*

I just had to get my heart to align with my head, and I'd be fine.

He raised an eyebrow. "So, you're just going to sit back and let some other man take your woman?"

"She's not my woman. It's not some other man. They're my best friends. Hunt and Gemma are the closest thing I've got to family. I can't jeopardize that."

"I know, man. I know. It's been tough on you since you lost your folks, but you deserve to be happy, too."

I was. Until today. *Fuck.* "Well, it's obviously not meant to be with Gemma."

Saying it aloud forced a vise to tighten around my chest. "I'll be fine after a few more drinks." I held up the now empty bottle and waved it toward Leon. "You got another one of these?"

Leon jumped off his stool so fast he knocked it over. He raced out to the kitchen and returned with a fresh bottle. He'd barely placed it on the table before I grabbed it, cracked the top open, and poured another drink.

Leon wiped his hand on his apron. "Your food's ready, too. I'll grab it for you." He zipped off again and returned with our meals.

Sam glanced at his watch. "We've got time. I'm gonna eat." Sam pulled out his box of noodles from the takeaway bag and inhaled the fragrant food. "Damn, this smells good."

My belly grumbled and gurgled. I'd eaten nothing since before the concert last night. *Yep.* I was starving.

"Enjoy." Leon bowed and backed away, returning to his stool behind the counter.

My mouth watered. I grabbed one of my Vietnamese rolls and took a bite. I mumbled over a mouthful, "Fuck. These are amazing."

"The noodles are sensational, too." Sam slurped on a noodle strand.

I reached inside my jacket and grabbed my cell phone to take a photo of the rolls. "Hey Leon, what's the name of this joint?"

"SpiceItUp Rolls. Why?"

"Are you able to feed a crowd of crazy people when we get out of here?"

"Um, yes, sir. Why?"

"If I post these online, this place will go nuts."

Leon's eyes lit up. "Really? You'd do that?"

I pointed at my rolls. "These are fantastic. The people of New York need to know about this place."

"Oh wow, thank you. Thank you so much."

I pointed to the cell phone trembling in Leon's hands. "Would you like a photo for your friends? Proof that I was here?"

Stunned, Leon bopped his head. "Yeah. Yes, please."

Sam chuckled, wiped his mouth on a napkin, and offered to take the photo. "Kyle, I think it's about time I got a pay rise and included 'photographer' as part of my job description."

I stood, placed my arm around Leon's shoulders, and smirked at Sam. "You get paid shit loads. Stop complaining."

"Not complaining. Just pointing out the facts." Sam's white teeth flashed behind a quick smile before he clicked away on Leon's cell phone.

After a few snaps, Sam's cell phone buzzed. "Car's here. Time to go." Sam packed our food away into the bag, ready to head off. "Thanks for your hospitality, Leon. What do we owe you?"

"Oh, no, no." He shook his hand. "You don't have to pay. It's on the house."

I sighed. While it was great to get free stuff wherever we went, I wanted to ensure we paid when necessary. Especially when it looked like this place could do with our business. I pulled out my credit card. "I insist. Plus, I'm taking the bottle of JD."

Leon hesitated, then ran over to the till and processed my payment.

Movement at the window caught my eye. Silhouettes of people hovered outside the curtains. Hands blinkered around the eyes of those trying to peer around the edges. The noise and squeals grew louder. Knocks tapped on the door.

"Time to go." Sam guided me through the kitchen, out to the alleyway and into the waiting car.

"That was the best food I've had in a long time." I sank into the leather seat and stretched out my legs.

"Certainly was," Sam grinned, patting his round belly as the driver took off. "But back to our unfinished discussion. What are you going to do about Gemma? Stop hiding your feelings, or that's only going to cause more problems. Tell her how you feel. Let her decide. If she chooses Hunter, so be it. But what if she chooses you?"

My chest ached. I shook my head and took a long drink straight from the JD bottle. I'd seen the look in her eyes. The way she'd looked at Hunter. There was no need for competition when I wasn't even a contender.

"She would've said no if she didn't want to be with him."

"If you can stand on the sidelines and watch the woman you love, be with someone else, without knowing if she has feelings for you, you're stronger than anyone I know."

"Guess that's the ultimate price of loyalty."

"I think you're a damn fool. But if you're going to get drunk over it, do it at home so I don't have to get your ass out of any more sticky situations."

"Deal." The whiskey slid down my throat, and reality sank in.

Hunter was with Gemma. There was nothing I could do about it. *Nothing.* I'd respect their relationship. Her happiness was key. I'd always be there for her, in whatever capacity, even if I'd never be more than just a friend.

A few more drinks were what I needed to pull myself together. In all this madness, there was one thing I was sure about—my friendship, my loyalty to Hunter and Gemma would never fail. I needed to find the strength to deal with this new situation.

Otherwise . . . how the fuck was I going to survive?

Chapter 7

The first signs of spring had hit the city. The trees in the park across the road from my condo in Tribeca were covered in new growth. The snow had disappeared. The sky was a brilliant blue. But the air still held a chill. After ten days of vacation in the mountains with my girlfriends, Lexi, and Kara, the freezing weather, drizzly rain, and exhaustion from the tour had finally caught up with me. Struck down with the worst cold, my whole body ached. My nose ran. My head throbbed.

After ducking into the pharmacy across the road to grab more painkillers for my leg and a fresh supply of tissues, I hauled myself along on my crutches, heading for home. Despite wearing a warm coat, beanie, and scarf, I shivered. The cold air burned my cheeks, constricted my lungs, and frazzled my brain. My reality was about to change. Hunter was due back from his vacation at any moment.

Hunter is my boyfriend. Hunter is my boyfriend. Hunter is my boyfriend.

Saying it over and over did nothing to settle my nerves. The mix of excitement and apprehension shooting through my veins didn't help either.

Hoisting myself along, I concentrated on my swing—crutches, legs, crutches, legs. My arms ached. I was fit from performing, but fuck this shit. I panted from the exertion.

"Gemma."

Shit. My breath hitched. I halted in the middle of the small paved park. The last thing I needed was to be swamped by fans. I scanned the crowd standing at the pedestrian crossing. No one glanced my way. I peered at the people sitting on the park bench. No one looked up from their coffee. But movement across the street caught my eye. Hunter jogged toward me. His azure eyes glinted in the sunshine, and a cute smile tilted his mouth. My heartbeat fluttered in an anxious but good way. *Yep. I can do this.* With his loose hair brushing the shoulders of his black sweater, and his jeans molding perfectly to his hips, his breath misted as he tucked his bare hands under his armpits and crossed the street. He jumped to a halt in front of me, wrapped his arms around my waist, knocking my crutches and shopping bag to the ground. Laughing, he picked me up, spun me around and placed me back on my feet.

"Hi honey. I'm home. Missed you." Lowering his head, he gave me a quick kiss on the lips.

My pulse spiked as I scanned the street. Did anyone see? Have a camera pointed at us? *Fuck.* Covering his face with my glove, I pushed him gently backward. "Don't kiss me out here, you idiot. We're not going public yet." Shuffling back a step, I tugged my beanie back into place, then rubbed my runny nose. "Plus . . . I have a terrible cold. And don't ever call me *honey*."

"You're right." He stubbed his boot against the ground. "Honey doesn't suit you. I'll have to come up with something else. How about . . . Shnookums?"

Groaning, I thumped him on the arm. "No pet names. Not ever."

"No names. Got it." He picked up my crutches and shopping bag. "You mastered these things yet?"

"Yep." I hooked the crutches under my arms and headed for the crossing. "But stairs suck. I have muscles I didn't know existed. My arms and shoulders ache all the time. I might have to take up the offer and stay at your place. Is that okay?" I'd thought long and hard about it. I'd struggled at home by myself. Staying with the guys would be easier . . . and it would help the three of us adjust more quickly. If I kept control around Hunter, everything would be fine.

"It sure is." He nudged his elbow against my arm and gave me a saucy wink. "I'll give you a massage later on to make you feel better."

Hmmm. With Hunter's hands on my flesh, I wasn't sure our no-sex rule would last very long.

"Maybe. But if I stay, it'll be in the spare room. Not in yours. I'm not ready for that. Not yet. You promised we could take this slow."

"I'm down with that, Gem. But can we pick up the pace? It's fucking freezing." He rubbed his hands together and blew on his fingertips.

"Sure." I zoomed along on my crutches. We headed down the laneway to his place, only one building and five hundred yards away from my own front door.

After the doorman let us in, we caught the elevator up to the penthouse. As I hoisted myself down the long hallway toward the open living area, my crutches squelched on the white oak floors. Video game noise blasted my ears and reverberated off the walls. Sun streamed in through the floor-to-ceiling windows. Hunter and Kyle's huge five-bedroom penthouse took up the entire tenth floor of the building and resembled a glasshouse rather than a private, cozy home. With its high-end security and electronic gadgetry, their place had more gizmos and tech than a hi-fi mega store.

Kyle sat sprawled out on the white leather sectional sofa, flicking and pressing the buttons on his game controller. His eyes were puffy, his hair was an unkempt mess, and he didn't even look up from playing his video game.

An ache lurched deep inside my chest. *Was he ignoring me? Why?* I shuffled around the furniture to sit next to him and dropped my shopping onto the floor. "Hey. I didn't know you were back early."

"I came home yesterday and went straight to bed. I've got the flu." Kyle coughed loudly. His chest rattled and rasped. God, we were like twins. Sick as dogs.

I patted his thigh. "I feel you. I've got the worst cold, too. Why didn't you call? I could've come over and we could've hung out together and shared a box of tissues." I lifted my cast onto the chaise and propped a cushion under my knee.

He shrugged. "I felt like crap. I wouldn't have been good company."

"Gem? Kyle? Latte?" Hunter called from the kitchen.

"Sure," we said together.

"Are you happy now Hunt's home?" Kyle's jaw tensed as his focus remained glued to the huge TV. He clicked and twisted the controller around in his hand. Explosions and gunfire boomed and reverberated through the sound system. Jet fighters and enemy attackers flew and spun across the screen.

"Yep." I grabbed a music magazine off the coffee table and flicked through the pages, not taking any notice of the contents.

"So why are you breaking out in a cold sweat?" he asked.

"I'm not." I turned another page of the magazine, jiggled and wriggled my toes.

"Yeah. You are. You're fidgeting."

Shit. I so was. I took a deep breath and glanced over at Hunter. I couldn't lie. "Dating him is just . . . going to be weird."

"Tell me about it," Kyle mumbled under his breath.

Hunter placed the lattes on the coffee table, fell on the chaise beside me, and rested his head on my lap. What the hell was he doing? Oh . . . yeah. Boyfriend stuff. I smiled and ran my fingers through his wavy hair. Okay, I could do this. Everything would be fine.

Then . . . I sneezed. And sniffled. And rubbed my watery eyes.

Kyle coughed and barked.

"You two are disgusting. I'd better not get sick." Hunter sat upright and shuffled to the end of the sofa. "Not sexy at all, Gem."

"You know you want me." With my runny nose and raspy cough, there was nothing seductive about my tone or my state of health. Diving into my bag, I grabbed the box of tissues I'd bought. I plucked one out and blew my nose.

Hunter wrinkled his nose and circled his finger through the air. "Not like that, I don't. But I know what I do want. And that's food. Want anything, sweet pea?"

"Don't call me that." I nudged him hard in the leg with my good foot. "But since you've offered, some bagels would be nice. The ones from the shop around the corner. And some chicken soup. Soup would be soooo good."

Hunter ran his hand up my thigh. A sparkle shimmered in his eyes as he crawled toward me and tried to kiss me on the lips. But I placed my hand against his face and laughed. Yep, kissing him was still too weird to contemplate.

Undeterred, he grinned and sat back on his heels. "Just because I'm your boyfriend now doesn't mean I'm your slave, woman!"

"While I've got this broken leg, you are." I pointed toward the kitchen. "Now, get me some food, manbitch!" It would be fun ordering Hunter around instead of having him telling everyone what to do.

But Kyle groaned and threw the game controller aside. "Okay, you two, there's gotta be some ground rules. There's to be none of this lovey-dovey shit while I'm in the room. Otherwise I'll move out. Maybe I should stay at your place, Gem? So you two can be alone."

"Go pack a bag, bud." Hunter waved toward the hallway.

"Don't be stupid," I glared at Hunter. This change would take all of us some time to get used to. We'd survived everything. Surely we'd make it through this. "Kyle, I promise. No sweet talk. If Hunt keeps this up, I'll be out of here before anyone else. Got it?" I had to agree with Kyle. Sweet talk made me nauseous.

"Fine." Hunter pushed up the sleeves of his sweater and stood. "I'll go order some food since our housekeeper's slack. Kyle, you right to keep Gem company?"

"Always have been." He sighed and rested his head back on the sofa.

The office door down the hallway clicked closed behind Hunter. I swiveled toward Kyle but the air between us was as thick as a barricade. That wasn't normal. He stared at the ceiling, then slowly turned his head toward me. His face softened, but his smile didn't reach his eyes.

Worry swam through my chest. I grabbed a cushion and cuddled it against my stomach. "What's going on? You said you were okay with me and Hunt. Is that not the case? I won't let being with him affect our music or our friendship. I promise."

Concern flickered in his eyes, but within a blink, it was gone. He shuffled toward me and hooked his arm around my shoulders. After a few deep breaths, the tension in his body eased. "You've nothing to worry about, Gem. I'm fine. It will just take some time to get used to."

"Tell me about it." I rested my head against his shoulder. "You know you're the best."

He rubbed his hand up and down my arm and cuddled me tighter. "I know."

Hunter's footsteps thudded on the floor. "Hey, lovebirds. Dinner, groceries, drinks, and bagels will be here within the hour." He slipped onto the sofa beside me and draped his arm across my waist. "Can you wait that long?"

"Sure." I leaned closer to Hunter and brushed my hand down his cheek. His soft stubble tickled my fingertips.

Another chill sliced through the air, and Kyle moved a foot away from me. With a steely mask drawn across his face, he picked up his game controller and zapped away.

I didn't want him to act like this. I didn't want to hurt him. But Kyle should be supportive. Understanding. Happy for us. I hadn't gone into dating Hunter blind. I'd known the consequences. I just prayed I hadn't made a mistake. Only time would tell.

Hunter's eyes locked onto mine, and he gave me a cheeky smile. He rubbed his hand up and down my sweatpants. He lowered his voice to a husky whisper. "How about that massage I promised before?"

Massage? My throat ran dry. I licked my parched lips. Just the thought of his firm fingers driving into my flesh made my blood pressure rise, my body tense, and my hands tremble. Was that sweat underneath the back of my hair? *Yep.* Drawing myself upright on the sofa, I inched away from him. "Maybe later. I need food first."

What the hell was wrong with me? I wanted to be with Hunter. All the dreams I'd had must have meant something. The shift from friends to lovers should be easy. The lines and boundaries that had never been crossed had to disappear. Once this flu was gone, I was sure that would happen. It had to. For the sake of my sanity if nothing else.

Chapter 8

KYLE

The flu had flattened me for four days, but the moment I'd felt better, I'd pounded out the miles on the treadmill in the gym on the building's ground floor. I'd pummeled the crap out of the punching bag until my knuckles hurt, had done weights until my muscles fatigued, and sweated it out on an exercise bike until my body screamed to stop. I'd never worked out so much in my life, not even when I was training for the tour. Exercise was the only thing that had taken my mind off Gemma. I'd found my coping mechanism.

I yanked off my saturated T-shirt and wiped sweat from my brow. As I hooked it around my neck, I headed up to my penthouse. I walked straight past Hunter sitting at the dining table, stabbing at the keys on his laptop. After dropping my towel and T-shirt on the kitchen counter, I headed for the fridge and grabbed an energy drink. I took a seat on one of the kitchen stools and downed half the bottle.

"What's eating you?" I jutted my chin at Hunter. "Did you get up early and Google yourself again?"

"No," he snapped, then grinned. Yeah, I'd caught him doing that more than once. "Not today. I couldn't sleep. I came out here and have been working on some lyrics."

"Here, let me see." I slipped off the stool, stepped over to the table, and spun the screen around. I scanned the words.

You don't look like someone who likes small talk
Let's get out of here and go for a short walk
Back to my place at the end of the street
And let's see where the night leads

Let me show you a good time
Let me kiss you all over
Say you'll be mine
How about forever?

My heart constricted into a tight ball. Was this a song about Gemma? That Hunter saw her as *his* forever? *Shit.* I struggled to breathe, but I focused on the raw, fast-paced electric beat that had formed inside my head. "I like 'em. Maybe we can work on them later."

"I know I'm not as good as you and Gem at songwriting, but I'm . . . so . . . frustrated. Being with Gem should be easy, but it's not. We should just . . . click. But that hasn't happened." Hunter's hands curled into claws, hovering them above his keyboard. "It's fucking killing me."

I puffed air through my nostrils. *This was killing him?* How could it be? How could *he* be frustrated? He had Gemma. "You have to give it time."

Hunter slouched in his chair. "It's been three weeks since I asked her out, and we haven't even properly kissed. She's been sick and pissed at me because we got photographed in the park when I came home the other day. And I forgot her mother is part of the deal."

"Yeah," I grunted. "I've heard Gem on the phone covering up your little mishap." After the loss of my parents, I'd encouraged Gemma to keep in contact with her mother, but lately I'd changed my mind. All Janine ever wanted was the gossip and the inside scoop on our lives. Luckily, Gemma never gave her anything. "You agreed not to go public. What were you thinking?"

"I wasn't. I fucked up." Hunter slammed his laptop shut and wiped his hand over his face. "I gotta do something for Gem. Now she's over the flu, I want to be with her. But she doesn't want to have sex of any kind—no fingering, no tongue-fucking, no nothing—not until she gets her cast off. She's worried about screwing up our friendship—and whether we can still work together. She's my girlfriend, and she won't even sleep in my bed. It's driving me fucking crazy."

I bit my lip hard, anything to stifle my laugh. Hunter not having sex with Gemma was the best news I'd heard in weeks. "Hmm . . . that must be tough."

"To top everything off, *I'm* struggling to cross the line with her. Half the time I feel like I'm trying to screw my sister, and that's so wrong in so many ways. I love her and want this to work out, but every time I get close to her, I freeze up. So does she. How can two people who want to be together do that?" But within one breath, his desperate tone turned mischievous. "I want to at least get to second base. Third would even be better . . . if you know what I mean."

Unfortunately, I did. I didn't want to picture Hunter going to second or third base with Gemma. Or any base, for that matter. "You're better with girls than I am. You figure it out." Was it wrong to secretly enjoy Hunter's pain? *Yes.* But I didn't want to be like that.

"This is different. I've never done the relationship thing before. So far, it sucks."

"So, why *did* you ask her out?" I winced, not sure if I wanted to hear the answer.

"Why does any guy ask a girl out? She's hot. She's fun. She's the best."

I stepped back from the table and leaned against the kitchen counter. Was that Hunter's way of describing the sparks that ignited in the air when she walked into the room? That the chemistry that drew you toward her was simply unexplainable? How no other girl existed anymore. That you'd do anything to make her happy . . . even if that involved saying nothing so she could date your best friend. *Crap.* Maybe that was just the way I felt about her, not Hunter.

I gripped the edge of the counter. "Gem's not some fling. Don't you hurt her. I swear I'll kill you if you do." My hands twitched like I was holding an invisible blade, ready to plunge it straight through Hunter's chest. I'd do anything to protect her. But I didn't want to lose my best buddy either. Somehow, I had to find a way to stop my destructive thoughts. My best friends were together. I had to accept that. I had to find a way to live in this new hell . . . somehow.

"Good to know you've got my back." Hunter smirked. "I just want to do something to break the ice between us."

"Then maybe you need to get your head out of your ass and think about what one does in a relationship. Take her to the movies, go out to dinner—surprise her with gifts."

But wait. That wasn't Gemma. If I ever had a date night with her, I'd take her out of the city, maybe to my beach house in Amagansett, sit under the stars and play guitar with her until dawn broke.

Hunter leaned back in the chair. "You think Gem would be into that kinda shit? A date night?"

Was Hunter a complete idiot? He should know what she liked.

"I guess there's only one way to find out." I shrugged my shoulder and sipped my drink.

"A date. Right." Stress crept into Hunter's voice. "That will involve security. A driver. A private dining room. I'll hit up Lexi. Ask her where to go. She blogs about restaurants. I can do that." Hunter dragged his fingers down his cheek, leaving red marks in their wake. "Fuck. There's so much to organize. And what if the paparazzi follow us?"

That was a constant issue. We were always followed. Gem handled the cameras most days, but was paranoid about having her privacy invaded. And rightly so after what Ben did to her. *Prick.*

The blood drained from Hunter's face. I hated seeing him suffer. I wouldn't let him drown. I cared about him too much . . . and Gemma. "Why not start with something simple? She's restricted in what she can do with her cast. So how about I take off tonight and catch up with Hayden so you could set up something nice in here?"

"Here?" Hunter sat two inches taller. "That sounds like a plan. I'll order in. We'll play video games. Do you think she'd like to play *Battlefront* on date night?"

"Hunt?" I shook my head and lowered my gaze. Was this a lost cause? "That is something you should already know after all these years."

"I should, shouldn't I?" He raked his fingers through his hair, then rubbed the back of his neck. "I just can't think straight. I haven't gone this long without sex in years; it's screwing with my head. Do you think I could change her mind?"

Gemma was so headstrong when she set her mind on something and rarely changed it. But I'd seen Hunter's charm in action and when he turned it on, I doubted even Gemma would be immune.

"That's between you and Gem. You never know your luck. Just . . . treat her right." I glanced at the skyline and tried to focus on something other than the sinking sensation swelling inside my stomach.

A police helicopter flew overhead.

A flock of birds dived past the window.

Taxis honked on the avenue below.

Whether Hunter and Gemma slept together tonight, it didn't matter. The inevitable would happen. *Fuck!*

"I could do with some luck." Hunter's shoulders slumped.

"If you're that frustrated, why not jerk off?"

"I've been doing that. It's not the same."

"No shit." I bobbed my head. Having Gemma sleep in the room next to mine added to my pent-up frustration.

Hunter rested his elbows on the table and dropped his head into his hands. "Date night. I can do this. Date night. Think. Think. Think."

I rolled my eyes and slammed my empty bottle down on the countertop. I didn't want their night to be a disaster. "Okay, let me help you out, because you're stressing over this too much. Her favorite food is gnocchi. Her favorite flowers are tulips. Video games should *not* be on the agenda . . . not at all. I'll leave the rest up to you."

"Thanks, bud. You're the best."

"Yep. I am." *But I didn't feel it.*

Hunter's cell phone buzzed on the table. Amie's name lit the screen. Hunter stood in a rush, scraping his chair against the wooden floor. "Amie. Hi. Hold on a sec. I'll go into the office." Hunter turned and walked backward. He tapped his hand over his heart, then pointed at me.

"Love you, too," I mumbled, and stared down at my running shoes. With a loud sigh, I grabbed an apple from the fruit basket and sat at the table.

This situation sucked.

But it was time to get rid of my anger, my hurt, and the dagger stuck in my chest. Maybe that was what I needed to do tonight. Go out and pick up some girl. Have a good time. And forget about my feelings for Gemma. Was that even possible?

Gemma's crutches squelched on the floorboards. She walked out of the hallway with a sleepy smile on her face. My heartbeat doubled. Her hair was a mass of tangled brown knots—exactly how I pictured it after a wild night between my sheets. Her green eyes shone with warmth—nothing like the hunger I struggled to hide from my roaming gaze. That was hard to do when she wore one of my old T-shirts—one I'd given her after our concert in Berlin a few months ago. It hung off one shoulder and barely reached the top of her thighs. All the blood in my body rushed to my dick. It twitched, hot and needy.

Yep. No chance of forgetting about her. Not ever.

"Morning." She leaned her crutches against the kitchen counter and stretched her hands up into the air. Bending side to side, her shirt rode upward.

I stole a glance at her blue and red stripy panties beneath the hemline. Now there was absolutely no way I could leave the room anytime soon. Wriggling on the chair, I focused on the wall behind her. I had to get my thoughts and body under control because

I couldn't react like this around her now that she was Hunter's girlfriend.

"Where's Hunt?" She scanned the living room and terrace.

"He's in the office talking to Amie." I bit into my apple and chewed.

"Oh . . . fair enough. What are your plans for today?" She hobbled around the kitchen, reaching into cupboards, opening the fridge, grabbing food, and bending over the drawer for a plate. Was she trying to torture me? She cut open a bagel, then spread cream cheese onto the bun. "We don't have anything on until our meeting at SureHaven tomorrow. Is that right?"

I finished another mouthful of apple, then dragged my gaze away from her. "No, that's in two days. Tomorrow we're catching up with Bec and Kate to prep for promo. Today is free. Would you like me to take you down to the river in your wheelchair this afternoon after we get some work done?"

"Sure. I'm going stir crazy in here."

So was I. Maybe a dip in the chilly Hudson River would do me some good and put an end to my body going into overdrive when she was in the room. I waved my almost finished apple at her. "But tonight, I'm out of here. I'm going to catch up with Hayden."

"Cool. Can I tag along?" She munched on a mouthful of bagel. "It's been ages since we've seen him."

"No, sorry. Tonight, I'm a one-man show." I'd never really gone out without Gemma and Hunter. Just the thought of not being with them created a huge vacuum inside my chest. Maybe this was how I'd cope. I'd let the void grow and grow, and let it consume me until there was nothing left. That sounded like a plan. I gnawed the last of my apple down to the core, taking every fiber possible. "I don't want to ruin the surprise, but Hunt has plans for you."

Gemma stopped, the bagel hovering halfway to her mouth. "Really? Like what?"

"I can't tell you. It's a surprise."

The color drained from her face. "Don't keep secrets from me. Not ever. Now tell me." She stuffed the bagel into her mouth, grabbed a coffee cup, and jabbed at the buttons on the coffee machine.

I leaped from my seat and headed into the kitchen to help. After her latte was brewed, I carried it over to the table and waved at her to sit. With the bagel wedged between her teeth, she hobbled over to me and sank into the chair. I rubbed her shoulders and kissed the top of her head. "In-va-lid."

She slapped me on the leg. "Thank you, but what is Hunt up to?"

"I've said too much. You'll be fine." I picked up my sweaty shirt and towel off the counter and walked backward toward the hallway. "I've gotta take a shower."

"Kyle? Wait. Spill it." Her eyes shimmered with worry. "You know I'll stress about it all day now you've mentioned it."

Shit. I was such a fool. I shouldn't have said anything. She'd fret to no end. I didn't want that. With a deep breath, I closed his eyes. "A date night. Hunt's planning a date night for you. That's all." And I'd be drowning my heartache, once and for all.

"A date?" She wrinkled her nose. "Where the hell is he taking me?"

"You'll have to wait and see."

"Shit. But you're taking me out first, right? To the river?"

Crap. "Yeah . . . but that's not a date."

But God, I wished it was.

Chapter 9

GEMMA

Holding on for dear life, I clutched onto the armrests of my wheelchair. At a run, Kyle pushed and zigzagged me along the Hudson River Greenway, past the people walking dogs, the joggers clocking up some miles, and the cyclists pumping their pedals. My stomach rolled when Kyle spun me around in circles, doing doughnuts on the pathway, tipping me sideways onto one wheel. Giggling, I squealed, "Stop." Tears stung my eyes; it had been weeks since I'd had such a good belly-aching laugh.

Catching my breath, I straightened my throw across my legs to keep the April chill away. It was so good to be outside.

After being noticed by a few fans and having photos, Kyle and I escaped the crowds and took shelter underneath a tree. As we sat on the bench, the kids in the nearby skate park zoomed around on scooters and boards, the wheels scraped and scratched against the concrete. I tugged my beanie down low over my ears and drew the zipper on my jacket up higher.

"Thanks for the heads up on what Hunt's planning for tonight." I nudged Kyle in the arm. "You know how much I hate surprises."

I'd barely seen Hunter all morning. He'd taken off before lunch and had been in and out of the apartment several times since, dropping off bags loaded with stuff. Every time I'd asked what he was doing, he'd made up an excuse of having more errands to run, swooped in to give me a kiss on the cheek, then had taken off again.

A night alone together would be good. I'd finally be able to break down the barrier around my heart. It had been nearly three years since Ben had betrayed me. It was time to feel again. But something niggled my insides. While I trusted Hunter with my life, could I trust him with my heart?

Kyle picked up a pebble, tossed it in his hand several times, then threw it hard against the tree trunk ten feet away. "That's why I told you—so you'd stop stressing. But considering you aren't supposed to know what he's doing, you could bail and come out with me and Hayden if you wanted."

That sounded like a good plan, but no. "Not sure Hunt would like that if he's going to all this trouble." I fumbled with the fringe on my scarf. "This is our first official date, and I'm nervous."

"Why?" Kyle jerked his head back.

In the park, a skateboarder jumped onto a rail, slid along it and landed perfectly before zooming across the way. It would be months before I could do anything like that again. *Stupid broken leg.* I wriggled on the seat, resting my cast up on my wheelchair. "Hunt's been with so many girls. I'm afraid I won't meet his expectations. I'm afraid if we don't work out, I'll end up just like Mom in one doomed relationship after the next. And then there's this . . . this weird tension whenever we try to be close. Like something is holding me back."

Kyle picked a dead leaf off the ground and shredded it to pieces. "I can't help you with this shit, Gem. That's between you and Hunt."

Confused, I shook my head. "But you and I have always talked about everything. Can't I talk to you about him?"

He stared toward the river, then lowered his chin. "You're my best friends. I'm not going to play middleman. I can't do that. Isn't that what your girlfriends are for?"

I slumped back against the bench. "I'm away so much. I don't know them like I know you. I trust you more than anyone." I'd always been able to talk to Kyle, but now my relationship with Hunter was a no-go zone. Why? I'd expected things to be awkward, funny and weird at first, but not a total barricade. Was this another concern to add to my list? I had to ensure things didn't get worse. My friendship with the guys meant more to me than anything else in the world.

"I'm always here for you, Gem. But please, I can't get in the middle of you two. I won't. I love the two of you too much."

"Okay. I love you, too." I had to hold on to his reassurance that everything would be fine. I understood where he was coming from. I had to respect his wishes. Maybe I shouldn't even go out with Hunter. No . . . wait. I had to see if the spark was real or just in my dreams. I'd be crazy not to.

"It's getting late. We better head back." He stood, but I grabbed his gloved hand and squeezed it. His gaze met mine and my heart stumbled, flipped and fluttered. *Ugh.* Nerves about tonight were killing me.

"Thank you . . . for everything. For telling me about tonight, for bringing me out here, for being honest with me." I pasted on a confident smile and slid into the wheelchair. I placed the throw over my legs. "Let's go so I can get date night over with."

"Gem, stop stressing," he chuckled. "Just have fun. You always do."

Here's hoping.

Kyle kicked off the wheelchair brake-lock and pushed me back to his place.

I headed straight into the spare room, showered in my en suite, and blow-dried my hair. Sitting on the edge of the bed, staring at the minutes ticking by on the clock, my palms clammed up. I hadn't been this nervous since singing live on TV for the Discovered-On-YouTube contest. Date nights were what couples did. Spending time alone was what you were supposed to do. *I can do this. I've spent hundreds of nights alone with Hunt before.* But . . . now things were about to change.

Had he forgotten about our no-sex rule? Was tonight about getting me into bed earlier than discussed? I dressed in sweatpants and a hoodie. My hands trembled. My head throbbed. Was I ready to sleep with Hunter?

As I pictured him naked, heat flushed my cheeks. His fair skin was flawless. He had abs like corrugated iron. Several tattoos including an intricate pattern of swirls on his upper left arm. I'd seen him prance around in his boxer-briefs when we'd changed outfits backstage, in cars going to places, hanging out in hotel rooms and here inside his home. I'd seen him naked, too—drunk, wasted, accidentally coming out of the shower, way too often. But now . . . I didn't have to turn a blind eye. *Hmm.* Would he be as good in bed in real life as he had been in my dreams?

He fucking better be.

Slowly, my nerves turned to excitement. Tonight was a step in the right direction. Pushing my fluster aside, I headed out of the bedroom.

There was no going back.

Nothing would ever be the same.

I had to do this.

Yep . . . It was time for date night.

Chapter 10

GEMMA

I half-sat on a kitchen stool and placed my cell phone down on the counter. Kyle jumped up from the sofa. Dressed in Levi jeans and a black button-down shirt, he seemed ready for his night out.

"You're wearing sweats?" He arched an eyebrow as he looked me up and down. Humor skipped through the depths of his dark eyes. "It's not very sexy for date night."

I brushed my hands over my thighs. "Geez, thanks. But not much else fits over my cast. And remember? I'm not supposed to know what's going on."

"True. But still."

"Are they that bad?" I glanced at my clothes. In my experience, guys didn't care what I wore. I could wear a burlap sack, and they'd still get turned on. And besides, I wasn't expecting to have sex. *Definitely not . . . well . . . maybe.*

"I'm joking." A smile played at the corner of Kyle's mouth. "You'd look good in anything or nothing. Trust me." But no light touched his eyes. He thumbed toward the hallway. "Um . . . I'm going to head out, so I'll see you later. Tomorrow . . . sometime."

Before I could ask about his plans, he turned, grabbed his phone and leather jacket, and fled for the elevator.

My stomach sank. Normally when he left, he'd give me a quick hug and a kiss on my forehead, but tonight, I hadn't gotten either. When the elevator doors pinged closed behind him, it was like someone had pulled the plug out of my daylight.

I was left alone.

For all of two minutes.

Hunter's footsteps echoed down the hallway. A different light turned on. My spotlight. My heart rate jumped from *largo* to *presto*. He entered the room wearing my favorite black jeans that sat low on his hips, a white T-shirt that molded to his toned body, and his hair was tied back into a man-bun.

I scraped my teeth across my lower lip. I jiggled my foot on the stool's rest. *Damn.* I could be in a lot of trouble here.

It was hard to play it cool when I knew he'd made plans. But what? I didn't know.

He stopped in front of me, and his smile broadened. He smelled of cinnamon and spice, making my head feel light and dizzy.

"Y-you look nice." I cleared my throat and kept my voice level. "Where are you going this evening?"

Hunter took my hand in his, kissed my palm, and entwined our fingers. "Nowhere. But I have plans. It involves you, me, dinner and later . . . my bedroom." His azure eyes sparkled with too much sexiness. He leaned in and hovered his lips a few inches from mine.

I placed my hand on his chest. His heart beat hard against his ribs. "Hunt, we agreed not to—"

"Fear not, babe. I'll remain true to our ground rules. No sex. I promise." Hunter pressed his lips against mine, then made a trail of the lightest, softest, most delicate kisses toward my ear. In his deep, husky voice, he whispered, "Unless you've changed your mind. I want you, Gem. Regardless of when it happens, it will be special. But I *will* wait until your cast is off, if that's what you want." He nibbled on my earlobe, sending goosebumps down my spine. "Do you want to wait?"

I closed my eyes. The vibrations of his hypnotic voice rippled through my body. Heat exploded in my core. In my mind, I was already half undressed and ready to peel off my panties. *Damn.* He was good.

Hunter may stay in control, but could I? His body begged to be touched, especially when it was within arm's reach.

I blinked, gathering my thoughts. "Wait . . . We agreed to wait."

Why had I come up with this stupid no-sex rule?

Band. Friendships. Kyle. Music. That was why.

But if Hunter kept this up, my rules might have to be broken.

"Okay." Hunter brushed his fingertip down the tip of my nose. "I have the whole evening sorted. Dinner will be delivered soon, so in the meantime, let me get you a drink."

Hunter did his best Channing Tatum, *Magic Mike* spin, complete with a seductive wink and shimmy of his shoulders before heading into the kitchen. I laughed, admiring his butt as he walked.

He dived into the fridge and pulled out a bottle of bubbles. "Champagne?"

My mouth fell open. "Krug. You bought Krug? That's eight hundred dollars a bottle."

"Only the best will do."

He grabbed the flutes from the cupboard and placed them on the counter. As he peeled off the bottle's foil and undid the wire, he winked at me. Then he twisted the cork. With a pop, it shot skyward and hit the ceiling. Champagne exploded everywhere. It sprayed Hunter's T-shirt, spilled over the countertop, splashed onto my sweatpants, and dribbled onto the floor.

"Fuck!" He dashed over to the sink with the bottle.

"I would have preferred it to be in a glass." I laughed, hobbled off the stool and flicked the champagne from my fingertips.

Hunter grabbed a handful of dishtowels from the drawer. He threw me one and wiped up the mess with the others. "That was not part of the plan. I'm so sorry." He looked me up and down, his face ashen. "Did you get wet?"

"A little, but I'm okay." I dabbed my pants and dried the stool.

"I saved half of the bottle, but there's another one in the fridge." He dumped the pile of wet dishtowels into the sink. "Let's try again, shall we?"

"Sure." I threw him my dishtowel and leaned against the stool.

Pouring fresh glasses, Hunter's hands shook like maracas at Mardi Gras. Was he going to spill the champagne again? Was he as nervous as I was? *Good.* That made me feel a touch better.

"Here's to our first date." Hunter clinked his glass against mine and downed half the flute in one gulp. He drank $800 champagne like it was bottled water, while I sipped and savored every mouthful. I didn't take the luxuries we could now afford for granted. Just over five years ago, the three of us had been living in the back streets of Montgomery, struggling to find our next gig, trying to establish a name for ourselves. Then we'd gotten our break. Skyrocketed to stardom. Many days still felt surreal. We'd traveled the world, had millions of fans, and we'd toured. We wore designer clothes, had bought beautiful homes, and had achieved our dreams. It had been an incredible ride. Losing our privacy, being betrayed, used and taken advantage of . . . not so much. But the three of us had grown stronger, smarter, wiser. We'd nearly done our time with SureHaven, and then we'd be on our own path, making our own decisions, giving the world *our* music. We'd get there. I knew we would.

"Right." Hunter placed his glass down and rubbed his hands together. "Let me get everything set for dinner."

I stayed put and drank my champagne while Hunter set the dining table. My heart swelled, close to bursting, when he decorated the center with a bunch of red tulips. *He remembered my favorite flower? Wow.* He even lit a vanilla-scented candle.

The intercom chimed, and dinner arrived.

"So sorry, Mr. Collins, for being late." The delivery guy apologized to Hunter at the elevator door. "It might be best to reheat the meals in the oven for ten minutes."

"Thanks, man."

Hunter returned to the kitchen and placed the foil trays into the oven. "This is bullshit. I ordered in so I wouldn't have to do anything in the kitchen. Now I've gotta be Jamie Fucking Oliver."

That made me laugh. "You're no Jamie Oliver. You can't cook."

"You're right." He circled his fingers through the air, then pointed at the oven. "But I can reheat. Shall we have some more champagne while we wait?"

"Yep. But let's sit on the sofa. It's more comfortable for my leg."

Settling on the chaise, I propped a cushion under my knee. Hunter handed me a fresh glass of Krug and sat beside me.

As soft music filled the room, we fell into banter and chatted about upcoming appearances, appointments, and meetings. We discussed the songs we'd been working on and the photoshoots we had scheduled in our calendar. Time disappeared, and my nerves dissipated. *Thank God for champagne!*

Two glasses of bubbles turned into three. But with no food in my stomach, the alcohol went straight to my head. I didn't tense all over when Hunter put his arm around my shoulders or played with my long hair.

"Wait." Hunter sat upright. "I almost forgot. I bought you something today." He dashed into the office and came back with a long, narrow black box tied with red ribbon.

My heart beat faster. I hadn't expected a present. "You didn't have to buy me anything. But thank you." I glided my fingers over the silky bow, fumbled with the tie, and opened the box. I stared at the woolen scarf and ran my fingertips over the soft cashmere. It was so fluffy . . . and . . . fleecy . . . and . . . nice for next winter. But purple and red check?

So. Not. Me.

I liked plain-colored chunky knits. I wouldn't hurt his feelings after the effort he'd gone to. *Oh, shit, I'd have to wear this ugly thing.*

Faking a smile, I leaned over and kissed him on the cheek. "Thanks. It's great."

His eyes shone. "Awesome. Amie helped me pick it out."

I hesitated, then placed the scarf on the coffee table. "You were with Amie today?"

"She came shopping with me. I've never done this dating thing before. I wanted to make sure I do everything right."

"You didn't need her help." A nerve twisted at the base of my neck. Amie's taste was radically different from mine. Hunter didn't need to go to all this fuss of buying expensive champagne, fancy food, and fine gifts for our night together. "I'm just happy to have some us time." No work. No paparazzi. No one else but us.

"Me too. But I want tonight to be perfect."

He drew me into his arms. I rested my head on his shoulder. All the effort he had made put a tiny dent in my guarded heart. I hadn't done anything special for him. Work commitments had kept us busy. Vacation had kept us apart. My health had kept me quarantined. But now that was behind us. It was time to bury my fears and put every effort into making this relationship grow.

But the smell of smoke filled the air. I wrinkled my nose and pulled out of Hunter's embrace. "Do you smell something burning?"

Hunter leaped from the sofa. "Oh fuck. Dinner."

He rushed into the kitchen and yanked open the oven door. Smoke billowed out and filled the room. The fire alarm shrieked to life. I covered my ears to block the sound. So much for relaxing. Hunter grabbed the oven mitts and threw the smoldering trays into the sink. After fetching the broom from the pantry, he held it above his head and reset the alarm.

"Shit." He tossed the broom back into the pantry and slammed the door shut.

Staring at the containers in the sink, his shoulders slumped. "Dinner's burned. I ruined your gnocchi."

I pursed my lips, trying not to laugh.

He jammed his hands onto his hips. "Now what do I do?"

"Just order in again." I shrugged like it was no big deal. But I was starving. And Hunter didn't need any more stress. "Or you know what? How about you re-heat the pizza that's in the fridge, leftover from yesterday?"

"Pizza? You'd want that?"

"Sure. Pizza with some more champagne sounds perfect."

"I go to all this trouble, and we end up eating leftovers." Hunter shook his head, grabbed the pizza from the fridge, and threw it in the microwave.

After burning his fingers on the plate and dribbling melted cheese onto the floor, he placed the food on the table. "Dinner is served."

"Excellent." I hobbled over to join him. But when Hunter took the first bite of his slice, pepperoni fell onto his white shirt.

"Oh . . . you've gotta be shitting me." He rolled his eyes and wiped at the stain, spreading BBQ sauce into a big smear across his chest.

I giggled and chewed a cheesy string into my mouth. Hunter looked even sexier, if that was possible, when he was in a fluster. "Hunt, don't worry. It's fine."

"Nothing's going right. I'm sorry."

I clutched and rubbed his hand. "There's nothing to be sorry about. So chill." But as I leaned back, I glanced out at the southern city skyline. I needed to take my advice. *Chill.* But it seemed impossible. Taking a breath, I took in the nighttime shrouding Lower Manhattan. Millions of lights lit building windows, and car headlights formed long strands of red and white on the streets below. I turned to Hunter. His eyes sparkled. Holding his champagne flute close to his lips, a smile curled at the corner of his mouth. That smile sent too much heat into my cheeks.

He placed his glass down, stood, and walked around to my side of the table. He bowed and held out his hand. "Would you care to join me for a dance?"

My heart skipped a beat. "Are you serious?" I blinked. "I can't dance with a broken leg."

What was he thinking? How could I dance? Was I supposed to just stand still while he gyrated against me? Visions of Hunter dancing with girls at after-parties filled my mind. My mouth ran dry. *Oh yeah . . .* I wanted to dance.

Hunter flapped his fingers for me to take his hand. "Are you going to trust me, or are you going to sit there all night?"

Regardless of how ridiculous dancing with a cast would be, I took his hand.

"I trust you with my life, Hunt." *Just not my heart.* Not yet anyway. "Of course I will dance with you."

The music changed. Ed Sheeran's "Perfect" wafted through the sound system.

How convenient for a slow song to come on?

Nerves flitted across my stomach as I hobbled toward the space in the center of the room. Hunter drew me into his embrace. I snaked my arms around his waist and rested my cheek against his chest. My head spun with the scent of his citrusy cologne. In sync with the music, we swayed from side to side.

His heart pounded in my ear. His jagged breaths were far from being Zen. Neither were mine. But I flicked the tension from my hands, glided them up the front of his T-shirt and linked my fingers behind his neck. I tilted my head back.

He widened his stance to avoid my cast. Bending down, he placed his forehead against mine. "I'm counting down the days until I can dance with you properly, Gem."

"Yeah. Me too." But this was nice. It'd be even better if the performing acrobats in my stomach disappeared. If I had a few more glasses of champagne, maybe horizontal dancing with Hunter would be an option. I teased my fingers through his hair. "I've seen the way you dance. I'm looking forward to it."

"Oh, really?" He wriggled his hips against mine. A rush of heat charged through every part of my body and tingled my toes. But then he stopped. His eyes darkened, and blue fire ignited in their depths. He stroked my hair, then cupped the side of my face. "You're so beautiful, Gem. Always have been."

My heart thudded and jumped toward my throat. My breath snagged in my lungs.

Oh God. This was it.

He was going to kiss me.

This wouldn't be some peck on the cheek, or one on the forehead, or a *see-ya-round* type of kiss. *This* would be epic.

His lips inched closer. His clammy palm trembled against my cheek.

I closed my eyes. Held my breath.

Then . . .

His lips touched mine.

Neither one of us moved. Neither one of us dared to breathe.

But his warmth enveloped me.

I'd wanted this. Had dreamed about this. Bring it on. Sucking in a deep breath, I parted my lips and returned his kiss. Our tongues touched with soft, warm flicks and playful teases. The taste of sweet champagne coated every kiss. While I wanted to take my time, Hunter wanted to race. Good thing I liked things fast, too. Our tender kisses quickly turned hot and fiery. I slid my hands down and curled them around his waist. Grabbing a fistful of his shirt, I drew him closer.

A guttural groan rumbled low in his throat. *Sweet.*

But . . . something was off. What was it? Was it just my nerves messing with my mind?

As we kissed, Hunter's hand wandered until it settled beneath my boob. Could he feel my heartbeat hammering like a drum? *Hell . . . the man on the moon could.* Grinning against my lips, he gently brushed his thumb across my shirt, over my hardened nipple. It took all my willpower not to slap his hand away, my usual reaction in the past. Ignoring his touch, I slid my hands downward and grabbed onto his tight, toned butt.

But his belt dug into my stomach. His hard-on pressed against me, firm and undeniable. I winced. Oh, that was weird. *But it's Hunter. My boyfriend.* What was wrong with me?

He tasted of champagne, which was nice. But his teeth kept knocking against mine, sending jolts and shudders through my molars. His tongue was way too zealous. I had to pull back several times to draw breath. To avoid bringing up my dinner.

Undeterred, he buried his hand in my hair and erased the gap between us. But his leg knocked hard against my cast. A sharp jolt shot through my bones and jerked my knee.

"Ow," I gasped, more from shock than from being hurt. Jumping back, I bent over, clutched onto my cast and wriggled my toes. *Ugh!* I'd do anything to scratch my skin. It tingled and itched. It drove me mad not being able to do so.

Hunter caught my arm. "Shit. Did I hurt you?"

"No." I shook my head and straightened.

He ripped his fingers through his hair. "I'm so sorry, Gem. I'm nervous. I've never been like this before in my life. I wanted tonight to be perfect, but it's been one nightmare after the next." He flicked his hand at me. "Or maybe you should've never said I was like a brother, because now I feel incestuous every time I want to touch and kiss you."

Still trying to wriggle my knee, I closed my eyes. Was that the issue? He was like a brother? Surely not. Softening my gaze, I looked up at him. "You goose. If it makes you feel any better, I feel the same way."

His shoulders sank two inches. The tension evaporated from them. "I'm glad it's not just me. I know this will pass. We'll find our groove." He grabbed my crutches and handed them to me. "How about we go watch a movie in my room? No funny business. I promise."

Spending the night next to him, feeling his arms around me, having his lips against mine, would be good. I could do that. And hopefully I'd get over this ridiculous *he's-like-a-brother* awkwardness once and for all.

"Of course, I'll come with you."

Hunter grabbed our cell phones and led the way down the hall. He opened the door, and I shuffled into his room. It was dark and smelled citrusy, just like him. City lights filtered in through the wall of windows, creating a kaleidoscope of colors on his electric guitar collection mounted above his headboard. As I propped my crutches next to the bed, I let out the breath I'd been holding. He'd picked up his dirty clothes off the floor, and he'd made his king bed—hopefully with clean sheets.

"Wow. You cleaned your room." *Impressive.*

"All for you, babe." He placed our cellphones on his nightstand.

After flicking back the bedcovers, he helped me onto the mattress and put a cushion under my knee.

I rearranged the pillows behind my head. "Are you happy now you've finally got me between your sheets?" We'd crashed or passed out in bed together before, but that had only ever been as friends.

Grinning, he dashed around to the other side and jumped in next to me. "That was my plan."

He kissed my cheek, then grabbed the TV remote off the nightstand. He switched on the huge flat-screen TV hanging on the opposite wall and selected the latest action movie.

I curled into him. The light from the TV shimmered across his face, highlighting his chiseled jawline. Tonight, even though everything had gone wrong, and our kiss hadn't been earth-shattering, I'd had fun. Possibly thanks to the champagne. As I traced the silver scar on Hunter's forearm, my thoughts skipped to Kyle. Where was he and what was he doing with Hayden? Drinking? Picking up girls? Having a wild night? I made a mental note to thank him for letting Hunter and me have this night together.

Hunter hooked his arms around me and kissed the top of my forehead. "I didn't think us being together would be so awkward. We'll get better with time and practice."

"I like practice," I whispered, trailing my fingers across his chest.

"Mmm. So do I. I can practice for hours."

He rolled me onto my back and kissed me. Slowly. Tenderly. Not as rushed. This time was a definite improvement. More control. More evenly paced. More lips. Less tongue.

He smiled against my mouth. "Much better."

"Much." I hooked the loose strands of his hair behind his ear, then kissed him again. He edged closer, our bodies aligning at a weird angle to accommodate my cast. But that didn't stop him from trailing kisses down the side of my neck, or stop the goosebumps from prickling my skin.

His warm hands wandered, touching my hair, my arm, my hip. Then . . . he found my breast.

I squeezed my eyes shut.

This is soooo weird.

But he can do this.

He's my boyfriend.

Boyfriends do this.

Hunter dipped his head and grazed his teeth over the top of my T-shirt and nipped at my peaked nipple. His hot breath burned through the thin fabric and shot across my flesh. Okay, I liked that. My heartbeat hit somewhere near 200bpm. I arched toward him, begging for more of his mouth on me. I circled my hands over his shoulders and down his back. The tips of my fingers dug into his skin and traced each muscle and groove. If Hunter kept this up, our whole no-sex rule could be gone out the door at any moment.

But then his cell phone vibrated with Amie's ringtone.

"Ignore it," I panted, clutching at his hair.

"Gladly." Hunter kissed his way down to my stomach, to the skin at the base of my shirt.

Now this was progress. I closed my eyes and sank deeper into the pillow.

The cell phone blared to life again.

And again.

And again.

"Why the fuck is she calling?" Hunter groaned and flicked his head back. "It must be urgent. I'll answer it and tell her to fuck off."

I slapped my hands against the mattress, puffed my hair out of my face, and glared at the ceiling.

Fucking Amie.

Hunter rolled over and answered Amie's call. "You better have a fucking good reason for this, because you know what you're interrupting . . . Are you kidding me? . . . We fly out tomorrow night? . . . Hold on . . . I'll go to the office." Hunter held his cell phone against his chest, leaned over, and kissed me on the head. "I'll be back in a few minutes."

He slid off the bed and disappeared out the door, leaving me alone and in a hot pool of fluster. But Amie's call had been a blessing in disguise. It had stopped us from getting carried away. Had stopped us from going too far. It was too soon to take that step.

Then Dwayne Johnson's muscled body filled the screen, all buffed, hot and sweaty. Guns and helicopters and chaos reigned havoc in the movie—just the distraction I needed.

But ten minutes later, Hunter still hadn't returned. The fire that his kiss had ignited had fizzled. Twenty minutes later, my frustration twisted tighter into the base of my neck. How could he talk to Amie for that long? Thirty minutes later, he finally returned and crawled into bed.

"Sorry, babe. Amie had urgent details about changes to our trip. Kyle and I are now leaving tomorrow for seven days instead of three. LA for the iHearts, then Dallas and Minnesota."

I hated the guys were going away without me. It would be the first time since signing with SureHaven we'd be apart for publicity appearances. "And I miss out. This sucks. Am I that much of a security risk?"

"Gem, no one wants you getting knocked about. Going on promo won't be the same without you."

"Too right." This leg better heal quickly.

Hunter hooked his arm around me again, kissed my head, then focused on the movie. As the credits rolled, my eyelids grew heavy. I melted against his body. His warmth. His touch. Being together would work. Nothing would ever come between us.

Nothing.

The elevator chimed.

And Kyle crashed into the hallway.

Chapter 11

GEMMA

I hobbled as fast as I could out into the hallway behind Hunter. Kyle sat on the floor, back against the wall, drinking straight from a bottle of JD. His eyes were red. His hair, a mess. My chest ached. *Holy shit!* What had happened?

Hunter groaned and hooked his arm under Kyle's. "Come on, bud. Let's get you to bed."

But Kyle shoved Hunter's hand aside. "Fuck off. Leave me alone." He hauled himself to his feet and stumbled down the hallway toward the living room.

I hadn't seen Kyle this drunk in years. Not since his parents died. But trying to talk to him was futile. After half an hour, I gave up and headed back to bed, leaving Hunter with Kyle sitting on the sofa in the dark.

I fell asleep somewhere around 1:15 a.m.

But a loud noise woke me early in the morning. Blinking my eyes open, I glared at the clock. 6:30 a.m. I rolled onto my back, stared at the ceiling, and swore. Why were beating drums and thrashing cymbals drifting down the hallway at this hour? I'd kill Kyle. So much for soundproofing. So much for using drum mutes.

I wiped the tiredness from my eyes, not able to recall when Hunter returned to bed after dealing with Kyle.

I rolled toward him. He lay with his bare back toward me, the black sheet draped lazily over his waist. But seriously? Could he sleep any farther away from me in this huge bed? It looked like he was about to fall over the side. His chest rose and fell slowly with each breath, the consistent rhythm a sure sign he was sound asleep. I ran my gaze over his perfect body, taking in his dark hair falling in soft waves on the pillow, his tattooed upper arm, the intricate detail of the guitar and snake wound together like a treble clef on his shoulder blade, and the small dip in his back. Hmm . . . maybe I could get used to waking up next to him every morning.

Rubbing my fingertips together, I reached out to touch him but stopped with my hand suspended in midair. Why did I find it difficult to touch him? Last night, the champagne had helped to break my inhibitions. When we'd kissed and had gotten carried away, it had felt good. Hell, I'd even gotten turned on. Who wouldn't? But there was a barricade I couldn't get past. I wanted to lose myself in him, but every time he came close, jittery nerves and stomach knots consumed me. Hunter was hot. Gorgeous. Sexy as fuck. So what the hell was wrong with me?

The thudding noise down the hallway pulled my thoughts away from Hunter. I peeled off the sheet slowly, grabbed my crutches, and snuck out of the room. As I made my way across the hallway toward the music room, the noise grew louder and louder. Clangs and crashes and chaos were barely muffled by the door. Kyle obviously had no regard for anyone trying to sleep. I was in the right frame of mind to tell him where to shove his drum kit.

I eased the door open and peered inside. I took a deep breath, ready to rant, but my heart jolted at the sight before me. Kyle sat thrashing away on the drums, striking at the cymbals, the snare, and toms. The sticks were nothing but a blur in his hands. His eyes were closed, totally lost in the beat. Sweat glistened and shimmered on his shirtless body; his muscles were pumped and strained. Veins protruded along the lengths of his arms like twisted cords and cables. His jean-clad legs struck the pedals. His lips moved, mouthing words I couldn't make out. My nose wrinkled at the reek of alcohol in the air; a near empty bottle of JD stood near his feet.

Kyle could play guitar, bass, and piano, all to perfection. While drums were not his specialty, watching him was awe-striking. His passion, unrelenting. Gone was the will to abuse him—I just wanted to watch him in action. I slipped into the room, shutting the door quietly behind me. I shuffled my way past racks of guitars and a pile of mics and power cords over to the digital piano and sat on the stool. Kyle seemed unaware of my presence, never faltering in his performance.

The beat was raw, angry, and intense. It was all over the place with no clear structure. But after a few minutes, it gathered an even rhythm, and I joined in, tapping my fingers against my thigh. Whatever Kyle was playing, I liked it. The power of the music struck me right in the solar plexus and charged every one of my nerve endings. It was like nothing I'd ever heard before.

The vibrant music consumed me and coursed through my body. As Kyle hammered out the beat, the notes appeared in my mind. The chords. The tempo. The melody. Flicking on the digital piano before me, I hovered my hands above the keys. First, I played a chord, then added in a note, then another, then another. Singing "dah-dah-dee-dah-dah," I fell in perfect sync with Kyle.

His eyes remained closed, shut tight. The muscles in his strained jaw ticked. He had to know I was there, but the music ruled the moment. That was how we wrote most of our songs together. The melody guided them. Words created them. Moments made them.

Just like now.

My hands glided across the piano keys in time with his drumbeat. Faster and faster we played. Wanting to capture the sound, I hit the record button on the keyboard panel.

But Kyle's strokes came louder. Harder. More aggressive. Loaded and heavy. I pulled my shoulders back, trying to avoid the crushing weight growing inside my chest. There was an element of pain in the beat that was almost too much to bear.

My lips parted, and my hand went to my chest. My heart raced out of control. It was one of the most moving pieces of music he'd . . . we'd ever created. But Kyle stopped playing. My skin prickled. He stared at me with cold, dark eyes. His chest heaved as he sucked in one panting breath after the next.

"What are you doing here?" He snarled, then bent down, picked up the bottle of JD, and drank.

"You woke me." I blinked several times to bring me back from the beat that had transported me away. "You haven't played the drums in months. That. Was. Incredible."

"It's nothing." Kyle took another drink and wiped his mouth on the back of his hand.

"How was your night out?" I glanced at the almost-drained bottle. "Still partying, I see."

"It was fucking fantastic." He slurred and swayed on the stool. "More importantly, how . . . was . . . yours?"

The frost in his tone caught me off guard. He'd never spoken to me like this. "Kyle, what's wrong?"

"Nothing's wrong. Everything's fucking great. Wonderful, in fact."

"It doesn't sound like it. Did something happen last night?" I asked. His chilling glare and ferocious vibe sent a shudder coursing across my skin. I rubbed my arm and wriggled on the stool. "Have I done something wrong? Has Hunt?"

A short, sharp laugh burst from his mouth. "Yeah. This has everything to do with you and Hunt. I didn't want to be here, listening to the two of you fuck all night. Was your date night amazing? All tulips and fine food and great champagne? Please tell me all about it. No . . . wait." He held up his hand. "I don't want to know. It's none of my goddamn fucking business."

Why was he acting like this?

His stinging words cut across my chest like razor-sharp knives. Tears stung the backs of my eyes.

"Too right, it isn't." I dug my fingernails into my palms. "But for your information, we didn't fuck all night. Not at all. We had dinner and watched a movie. I fell asleep in his room watching TV, you big ass."

Kyle stood and strode over to me. His boots thudded against the wooden floorboards. He stopped, bent down, and glared at me, just inches from my face. His bloodshot eyes burned with a raging fire. His drunken breath nearly knocked me off my seat. "You're trying to tell me, on your big romantic date night, nothing happened. Somehow, I don't believe you. If it was me, I wouldn't be able to keep my hands off you. And I'd make damn sure you'd still be in my bed."

My mouth fell open. My heart stumbled and lurched toward my throat. The hair on the back of my neck stood on end.

He'd what?

Holy shit! Where was this coming from? I shook my head, dazed and confused.

He straightened, reached over, and hit the replay button on the piano. Music filled the room as he froze. Goosebumps shivered across my skin.

Kyle's mouth curled into a wicked smile. He put the bottle to his lips and drank. I felt the whiskey burn my throat when he swallowed. He slammed the bottle down on top of the piano. His eyes bore into me, held me captive like a haunting melody. "I bet on my life you don't make music like that with Hunt. I know you don't. Only you and I will ever make music like that." Pain and anger sawed through his voice. "Tell me you didn't feel our connection. Tell me you didn't burn for more of it. Tell me you didn't feel one . . . single . . . thing."

My heart hammered against my ribs, but I couldn't move an inch. Couldn't breathe.

He held his arms wide. "Didn't think you could. Making music. Making magic. That's what we do. You and me." Fire flared in his eyes. Angry anguish spiked his voice. "You should be with me . . . not him." He stabbed his finger toward the door. Tears welled in his eyes as he grabbed the bottle of JD off the piano. Stepping back toward the doorway, he swung the bottle between his fingertips. "I'm so done. Done with this shit."

Kyle slammed the door behind him. I jumped in my seat. My whole body shook. My heart cracked. Nausea flooded my stomach.

What the hell?

My logical and rational thoughts kicked in. *Kyle's drunk. He's tired. He's still adjusting to me being with Hunter.* There was no way he could be jealous. No way. He would've said something to me if he'd had any issues.

But my heart didn't want to be rational.

Or logical.

I swiped away a tear that had fallen onto my cheek with trembling fingertips. My relationship with Hunter shouldn't be affecting Kyle like this. He'd said everything was fine. What the hell had just happened?

Fuck! This was all my fault. It wasn't ever supposed to be like this.

No . . . wait.

I was following my heart. I had to. Whatever this thing with Kyle was, it was just a bump in the road. We'd get through it. We always did. We had to for the sake of our band. Otherwise, I had no future with Hunter. Music was more important. It always would be.

I hated how things were different between the three of us. Different because there were hearts involved. Hearts and emotions and feelings. *Shit!* We'd never had to deal with these things when we were *just* friends.

What made it even harder was I didn't know what my heart was doing. It ached. It pummeled my ribs. It bled.

Kyle was my rock. I needed his strength. I hated seeing him hurt and shattered. Somehow, I had to make everything right. How was I supposed to put him back together when everything was a total mess?

Chapter 12

KYLE

I woke early in the afternoon. The hangover from hell pounded like a jackhammer inside my skull. My mouth was dry. My breath smelled like a dead animal. *Ugh!* I dragged myself out of bed, showered, and packed for my trip to the iHeartRadio Awards and some publicity stops. The whole time, visions of being in the music room at some godforsaken early hour with Gemma bombarded my mind.

I'd sensed her the moment she'd walked in. I always did. But fueled by alcohol, the power of music had possessed me. All my hurt, frustration, heartache, and pain had come out through the drumsticks.

I'd played until I had nothing left.

Numbness was all that remained.

But the look on Gemma's face was something I'd never forget. The shock in her eyes when I'd ranted ripped my heart in two. I'd never meant to hurt her. I wanted her to be happy. How stupid had I been?

Would she believe me if I put last night down to a drunken stupor? Probably not. But I had to deny everything. That would be best for everyone. Maybe last night was the therapy I'd needed to finally get things off my chest, to move on and stop dwelling on her.

Yes, it was time to move on.

I zipped up my suitcase and dragged it out into the hallway. Hunter had drilled the changes to our schedule into my liquor-laced brain last night. He'd even set my alarm. With half an hour to kill before the driver was scheduled to pick us up for the airport, I headed toward the kitchen. *Fuck.* Gemma sat on the sofa, working away on her laptop. Her eyes met mine, and a cold shudder ripped through my bones.

"We need to talk." Gemma's hard tone was like a sharp slap across my face.

I winced, opened the kitchen cabinet, and grabbed the bottle of Tylenol. "Where's Hunt?" Was there any way I could avoid this conversation?

"He's taking a shower." Gemma's eyes followed my every move. "You need to explain this morning."

I swallowed two tablets with a full glass of water and made my way over to the sofa. I slumped down next to her and stared at the ceiling. I wasn't sure I could explain what had happened. Alcohol combined with heartache and music was one lethal cocktail.

I took a deep breath, then turned my head toward her. "What about it?"

She shut her laptop and tossed it on the chaise beside her cast. "Why didn't you say anything to me? . . . About having feelings for me?"

"What are you talking about?" I winced, the throb in my head and chest unbearable. "Why? What did I say?"

Gemma repeated every word I'd said. But it was unnecessary because they were still crystal clear in my mind. I tried to find some glimmer of inner strength to beat down the truth. When would my lies finally harden my heart and stop it from aching? I didn't want to let this pain rule me anymore.

"Gem, of course I care about you." I wiped my hand down my face. "You know that. And yes, we connect when we play music. I don't ever want to lose that. I'm fine with you and Hunt being together." Denying everything would make this easier. Easier for all of us. It had to. It had to. *It had to.*

She wriggled on the seat. "I've never heard you play drums like that before. It was incredible and so intense. Then . . . when you went off at me . . ." Gemma's voice quivered, barely above a whisper. "I . . . I didn't know what to say."

"I'm sorry. I didn't mean to upset you." I rubbed her hand. "It was a long night, and I had way too much to drink. I got carried away playing."

"The music was mind-blowing." She wrapped her arms around her belly. "Kyle, I really care about you. But I'm with Hunt and struggling to make that work as it is. You're my best friend, and I don't want you to be jealous or upset or whatever the hell is going on with you. But if you want me to do something different, please let me know. I don't want any problems between us. You and Hunt will always come first. You've got to remember that."

"Gem, seriously. I'm fine. There's nothing to worry about."

"Good." Gemma smiled, but it didn't reach her eyes.

Guilt weighed down on me, pressing against my chest. From now on, I'd have to be more careful about what came out of my mouth. My two best friends were together, and I would *not* get in their way.

"Hey." Gemma nudged my arm. "I recorded what we played. We'll have to write some kickass lyrics for it when you get back."

My stomach lurched. Remembering the soul-crushing heartache I'd felt when I played was not something I wanted to do. Something I didn't want to think about. Not ever again. "Nah, it was probably shit."

Hunter stomped down the hall, dropped his suitcase by the elevator, and ambled over to the sofa. "I'm ready to go." He leaned down and kissed Gemma on the head. "See ya, babe."

I turned away, not wanting to witness any affection between the two of them. But seriously. No kiss on the mouth? Those two had the weirdest relationship I'd ever seen.

"Let's go, Kyle." Hunter straightened.

Not wanting to move, my stomach gurgled, and my head hurt.

"You look like shit," Hunter smirked. "You better not throw up on the plane again, like you did in Singapore."

The memory of rough turbulence on a hangover made a cold sweat break out on my forehead. "Let's hope it's a smooth flight."

"Now I'm glad I'm staying home." Gemma grinned, then glanced at the clock hanging on the wall. "You two better go. Don't have too much fun without me."

Hunter grabbed his wallet off the sideboard. "Promise. You take care of that leg."

"I hate that I'm not coming with you." She pouted and turned to me. "Come here." She beckoned me over with a wave of her hand. "I need a hug."

I sighed and shuffled over to her. She curled her arms around my shoulders and rested her chin on my shoulder. I breathed her in to every cell as I rubbed my hands across her back. "We'll see you in a week. Hope you miss us heaps."

"Yeah, I will. And just so you know, we're going to be okay." She whispered in my ear. "You, me and Hunt. Together forever. Always."

I buried my face in her hair and held her tight. Forever in hell was not my idea of fun. But I refused to let this come between us. Gemma meant too much to me. I was just too hungover to deal with anything else right now.

She gave me a peck on the cheek and drew away.

I flicked her long hair back over her shoulder. *So beautiful.* "There's no doubt in my mind, Gem. Together forever. Always."

Hmph . . . If I told myself that often enough, I might actually believe it.

Chapter 13

KYLE

After six days of a grueling non-stop publicity tour from LA to Dallas and Minnesota, my tiredness disappeared, and a new buzz hummed through my veins. I took a seat on one of the high-backed leather boardroom chairs opposite Gemma and Hunter at SureHaven Records on Madison Avenue. April sunshine filtered through the windows, casting rays of light onto the glass-framed photos of musicians and rock legends lining the wall. For the first time in weeks, I looked forward to something.

Today was demo day.

Time to work on our new album. New songs. New sound. New direction. This was what I needed to keep my mind off Gemma.

But even after three cups of coffee that morning, my concentration kept lapsing. I couldn't keep my eyes off her. She sported a new haircut. It was still long, hanging halfway down her back, but it was darker, gone from light brunette to dark chocolate. I wanted to bury my face against it, brush my fingers through it, wrap it around my hands while I . . . *I wished.* Gemma was stunning, but I had to rein in my ogling. It was time to get down to business.

I took a sip of my fresh coffee and skimmed over my emails and to-do list on my cell phone. "Are you two ready for today?"

Hunter leaned back in his chair next to Gemma, hooked his

feet up on the table, and took a selfie for his Instagram page. "Hell yeah. New songs here we come."

A nervous energy swirled in the pit of my stomach—I was eager to get the long day underway.

We were a few weeks off hitting the studio, but I couldn't wait. I loved recording. It was one of the best things about being a musician. Laying down the vocals, playing around with the music, being creative, and the good times we had were worth every minute of the long and grueling hours.

Gemma sat with her broken leg resting on another chair. Even in sweatpants, she was beautiful. But she fidgeted with her pen, her book, and her cast.

"Gem?" I lifted my chin toward her. "What's up?"

She tapped the end of her pen against her notepad at hyperspeed. *Tap, tap, tap, tap.* Then she stopped. "I'm sure the team here is going to give us some amazing songs, but we've written so much of our own incredible material over the past few months. What are our chances of getting more of *our* songs onto the album? Not their manufactured shit." Fire ignited in her eyes as she glanced back and forth between Hunter and me. "Are you guys honestly happy to continue collaborating with the same production team and the same songwriters again, and sing whatever tracks they throw at us?"

It was our dream to record an album full of our own tracks. But we had to see our SureHaven contract through to the end. "Gem, I love the stuff we've created lately. But we have to sit on those songs for now." I kept my tone steady, even though I wanted to gag her mouth when it came to this topic. I loved she wanted more, however, there was nothing we could do. "You know as well as I do, SureHaven owns us for now, and we can't do anything about it."

"I agree with Kyle on this one." Hunter swung his legs down off the table and rocked back on his chair. "Let's not piss 'em off."

Gemma jabbed her finger against her notebook. "We've made this company millions. They know we're talented. This album should be our material, not theirs."

"That's not going to happen," I sighed. "We may not write these songs, but we make them our own when we hit the studio. Today, we'll go through the demos and choose the ones we like. Don't go causing us any more problems."

Gemma had a go at the executive team every time we recorded. I doubted whether today would be any different. I'd usually rallied behind her, but not anymore. I had to focus on the only thing in my life that mattered now, and that was music. This contract with SureHaven was nothing but a stepping stone in our career. We'd known what we'd signed up for. In the scheme of things, a six-year, five-album contract wasn't a lifetime sentence. We couldn't fault SureHaven. They'd made us global superstars. We'd learned so much from them. We owed them our lives. So, for now, I had to keep Gemma's head out of the clouds and her mouth shut. "Once this album is done, we'll negotiate new terms and conditions for our future. We'll get creative control. I promise."

She tousled her fingers through her hair. "Can we at least discuss the possibility of using more of our own material?"

I loved it when she stood her ground. Loved her fight. Her passion. Her fire. It matched my own. But this was a fight we couldn't win.

"Come on, babe." Hunter rubbed her shoulder. "Kyle's right. Let it go. We get three of our own tracks on the album. You've gotta be happy with that. I don't care what they make us sing. I'd churn out nursery rhymes if I had to, as long as I get to perform. Although, I have to admit . . . I do like the age-group of our current fan-base over kindergarten any day."

Too fucking right.

"I'm going to kick your ass back to kindergarten." Gemma folded her arms and glared at Hunter, daggers shooting from her eyes. "Thanks for the support."

Hunter shrugged, undeterred by her disapproval. "Choose your battles, babe. We have to take it up the ass from SureHaven for now."

"I know . . . but let's change that." Challenge set in her tone. "We should talk to our lawyer. Richard can renegotiate new terms for us."

"Gem. Enough." I closed my eyes and rubbed my brow. God, I wanted to record our own music as much as she did. It burned inside me, hot and bright. But our hands were tied. "We've left it too late. We're too close to hitting the studio." I hated seeing the hurt in her eyes, but we had a job to do.

Hunter shot forward, rested his elbows on the table, and turned to Gemma. He lowered his voice, determination firing in every word. "Let's make sure these guys are left with no other choice but to give us everything we want after this album. Let's make them beg to do our will."

That was the plan. My efforts may be futile, but I'd call Richard tomorrow. I typed a reminder into my phone. I'd do anything to keep Gemma happy. A quick call to Richard wouldn't hurt. But it would take more than a miracle to change our current contract.

I looked up. An ache stabbed the center of my chest. Gemma had turned her chair around to face the window. She wiggled her toes peeking out the end of her cast and gnawed on the side of her thumb. I'd been so caught up in my heartache over the past few weeks, I'd failed to see she wasn't happy. "Gem, is this what's bothering you? Are you that miserable about making another album? Doing another tour?"

"Yes . . . I mean, no." She spun to face me. "I love what we do. Don't ever doubt that. Not ever. Music is life. But I struggle with wasting our talent and not being honest with myself . . . and as an artist."

Her words packed a low blow into my gut. When was the last time I'd been honest with myself? Seeing Gemma and Hunter together was no less painful than when they'd first gotten together. My feelings for her still simmered below the surface. Every day, I struggled with whether to tell her how I truly felt or just let it lie. I hated the constant knot twisting in my stomach. The way I was going, I'd end up with a fucking ulcer. How long could I stay silent?

Gemma and I shared the same ambition, drive, and goals. I was patient, though; she was a cannon, ready to fire. I loved that about her. "Gem, I understand that. I feel the same way. But for now, let's make this album the best it can be. We want a more rock-oriented sound this time. Focus on that."

Her brow furrowed as she stared at her notebook. She tapped her pen. Slowly, a small smile curled across her lips. "Yeah. I will."

"Good." Hunter grabbed the water jug and poured everyone a glass. "We haven't heard the tracks yet. I'm sure they'll be awesome. There'll be nothing to worry about." As Hunter handed me a water, he gave me a *please-change-the-subject* kind of look.

I chuckled and quickly scrolled through my emails to find the one I'd flagged. "Gem, when we were away last week, did you read the email from SureHaven? Grant Entertainment Group has put in an acquisition bid."

"Yeah, what's that about?"

Amie barged in without knocking. "How're my favorite rockstars?" She dumped her pile of folders onto the table, flicked her bangs out of her eyes, and jammed her hands onto her hips.

"We were discussing the Grant takeover bid." I pinned her with my gaze, trying to gauge her reaction.

"Oh, that." Amie swiped her hand through the air, dismissing our concern. With a flick of her fingers, she tugged on the cuffs of her business shirt. "If it happens, it happens."

But the hair at the base of my neck prickled. Something wasn't right.

"If Grant takes over, it's a good thing." Amie placed her hands on the table and bent forward, giving Hunter an eyeful of cleavage. Yeah . . . he looked. And smirked. I wanted to clip him over the head. Gemma was right here. He should only have eyes for her. Amie shrugged her shoulder. "It means we all stand to get what we want—new contracts, new deals, more market domination . . . And I like dominating."

A glint shimmered in her eyes. An evil smile curled across her derma-filled lips. A shiver shot down my spine. Amie was our manager and was supposed to be on our side, but her arrogance was getting harder and harder to tolerate. If she wasn't so good at what she did, I'd be looking for a new manager.

"We have a big day ahead of us, so let's get moving." Amie

collected her belongings and turned toward the door. "We're in Studio A. The sooner we get through the demos, the sooner we can get you into the studio, and the sooner we all make more money. Let's go."

Chapter 14

KYLE

Crammed into one of SureHaven's sound studios, I sat at the small oval table, taking notes, listening to demo after demo. Hunter lay on the leather sofa at the rear of the room. Gemma rocked on a chair by the control panel, sitting next to two of our producers—Zac and Tommy. Amie and Jeremy, one of the senior executives and head of production at SureHaven Records, sat across from me.

I kept my head down, concentrating on the raw tracks, acoustic guitar riffs, electric beats, and page after page after page of lyrics printed out before me.

"This would be so much easier if it was our own material," Gemma mumbled for at least the fourth time in the past hour.

I winced, then chuckled. Gemma never gave up.

Jeremy leaned back in his chair and folded his arms. "Got a problem with something, Gemma?"

"Yes. In the discussions we had about the direction of our new album, you agreed we could aim for a much grittier sound. But all these tracks are disco pop, R'n'B, or way too rappy. They're not us. If you'd listen to more of the songs we've written, you'd see they're exactly what you're looking for."

Jeremy inhaled; a wheeze rasped in his throat. His huge belly swelled like a street parade balloon. "I appreciate your input,

Gemma, but we know what sells. We've already invested a lot of time and money in producing and selecting these demos. And you *are* getting some tracks onto the album. I'd be happy if I were you."

"Yes, I am. But—"

"But nothing." Jeremy's voice cut through the air like a guillotine. "You're talented musicians. You wouldn't be signed otherwise. I'm sure you're well aware that a lot more goes into marketing an album than just writing a catchy tune." His tone hardened even further. "Do you have issues with your current contractual obligations, Ms. Lonsdale?"

I stopped doodling on my paper. Jeremy had never been so cold, blunt, and short with us before. He usually loved our music, the suggestions we made, and the changes we wanted to the demo tracks so we could make them our own. But today he was as harsh as the Great Basin Desert.

Jeremy leaned forward and jabbed his finger against the table. "We've some of the best songwriters and producers in the country wanting to work with you, but if you don't want to do that, there are many other artists out there,"—he waved his hand toward the door—"who'd be willing to take your place."

My heart lurched against my ribs. Was Jeremy threatening us? Why? Where was this coming from? He'd been our advocate and had been part of the A&R—Artists and Repertoire—team who had signed us before he moved into production. Was he just having a bad day? Whatever the case, our lives at SureHaven depended on Jeremy more than anyone. He held too much power and could influence the CEO's decisions with a click of his fingers. With the three of us wanting to negotiate a new contract soon, I didn't want to get Jeremy off-side.

It was time to intervene.

I swiveled to face Gemma. "Gem," I whispered harshly. "Not now. Please stop. Now's not the time for this discussion. And you know that."

She opened her mouth to protest, but I shook my head sternly. Worry flashed across her face. She sucked in a deep breath, pulled her shoulders back, and gave him a subtle nod.

"Sorry, Jeremy." Gemma's lips twitched. Her fists clenched in her lap. "I'm not upset with our contract. Everything's fine."

Gemma's lies stabbed my gut. The past few months had been nothing but lies. But this was work, and we had to bend to SureHaven's demands for a while longer.

"I just haven't liked any of the demos we've heard so far," she said, tucking her hair behind her ear. "Let's hope we can find some tracks we all agree on."

"Excellent idea." Hunter groaned, sat upright on the sofa, and stretched his arms over his head. "Next track. Hit it."

Zac, one of the producers, pressed play on the control panel.

A *bob-diddy-bop-bop* song blared from the speakers.

"Oh, come on. That's not us." I cringed at the sweet poppy tune. "It sounds like 80s disco."

"Kyle, it's a demo." Jeremy tugged at his shirt collar and stretched his neck from side to side. "You can add your own edge to it when you hit the studio. But at the end of the day, we need to produce something that sells."

"We understand that." I pointed at the lit-up panel. "But that was fucking terrible."

Gemma threw Jeremy an *I-told-you-so* glare, and Hunter nodded in agreement.

Zac played the next track.

"Ew . . . that's even worse." Gemma shuddered but mimicked the high notes perfectly, like Sia singing "Chandelier".

The next rap song made Hunter slice his hand back and forth in front of his neck to cut the track before it finished.

I chuckled, low and deep. The three of us were so in tune when it came to music. It was the one thing we never failed to agree on.

We heard two more songs that got a tick for further consideration.

The next track, "Light Up the World," was one of ours, and one of my favorites. The first few notes played. Goosebumps tingled my arms. My heartbeat quickened a fraction. I'd written this song with Gemma late one night after a rehearsal. We'd just been out to an old warehouse in Newark, to practice on the stage that had been constructed for our world tour for the first time. With the backdrop shaped like the Manhattan skyline, LED projection screens and lights flooding the risers and platforms, the three of us had been so excited and couldn't wait to perform in front of thousands of fans. We'd captured the feeling.

My gaze met Gemma's. That strange pull between us hummed through the air.

She smiled, clapped, and her eyes sparkled. "I love this song." She reached over in front of Tommy and turned up the volume on the control panel. She stood and sang. Her strong, bold voice filled the air.

> *When the night*
> *Comes over me*
> *I see your light*
> *Strobe to the beat*

For someone so petite, she could pelt out a tune. She transformed into a shining light when she performed. Everyone fell transfixed, completely under her spell. Maybe that was just me.

> *I hear your heart*
> *Pound next to mine*
> *Just take my hand*
> *And move in time*
>
> *With me, with me, with me*
>
> *So let me make*
> *Love to you tonight*
> *You call my name*
> *It feels so right*
> *Together, we'll light up the world*

My skin tingled with every word she sang. This song was exactly how I felt about Gemma. That I could do anything with her by my side. With a beaming smile, she motioned for me and Hunter to join her. We rose to our feet and glided over to stand beside her. In perfect sync, we sang:

Like the sky
Full of stars
You shine so bright
And steal my heart

You showed me how
To breathe again
Just take my hand
And feel my skin

Touch me, touch me, touch me

So let me make
Love to you tonight
You call my name
Everything's all right
Together, we'll light up the world

There's no place I'd rather be
Than here with you
Standing next to me
Together, we'll light up the world

At the end of the track, my heart boomed. Laughing, I high-fived Gemma and Hunter. That was wicked. This was what I had to focus on. I may never have Gemma in my bed, but I would always write incredible songs with her. That was what would drive me. Music was the key to surviving.

"Nailed it." Hunter pointed his fingers at Jeremy's face.

Jeremy grinned with a *we're-going-to-make-so-much-fucking-money-it's-insane* look smeared across his face. Amie gazed at Hunter with a smile curling across her lips. Zac and Tommy held their breaths, waiting for Jeremy to speak.

Jeremy leaned back in his chair and stroked his graying goatee. "I think it's fair to say I like that track."

"Yes." Gemma pumped her fist in the air. "Kyle, we did it. We got one." She flung her arms around me and gave me a big hug. Warm air enveloped me, tying me to her with invisible threads. Her cherry blossom scent filled my senses. For a split second, that pause between two heartbeats, the rest of the world didn't exist. Just her and me. I didn't want to move, didn't want to breathe—I just wanted to stay in this moment forever. Music would always connect us. Bind us. She would always be my reason for living. Always.

I kissed the top of her head. "Perfect." Just like she was.

Jeremy tapped his knuckles on the table and cleared his throat. "We haven't got all day."

Chuckling, I nodded and stepped out of Gemma's embrace. Time to get back to business. I turned to Zac. "Right. Next track."

After eight long hours of discussions, arguments, tracks being played and replayed, jotting down pages of notes and scribbling suggested lyric changes, we'd come up with thirty songs to take into the studio in four weeks.

That was when we'd work our magic and make the songs our own.

Gemma stood and stretched her arms above her head. Hunter yawned, and I rubbed my tired eyes.

"Great job, everyone." Amie massaged her shoulders, then waved her red manicured nails at the three of us. "But before we call it a day, there are a few quick items on my agenda I need to discuss."

"I'll leave you to it." Jeremy stood and shook our hands. "I have a flight to catch. Kyle, Gemma, Hunter, let's make another cracker album." After collecting his belongings, he left the room with Tommy and Zac.

Gemma and Hunter fell into chairs beside me. It was only seven o'clock in the evening, but all I wanted to do was go home to bed.

"First," Amie crossed her long legs and swiveled on her chair from side to side. Holding her tablet, she swiped her finger up the screen. "I've scheduled the rehearsals for your performance at the Billboard Awards. It's four weeks away and will be held in Vegas. Gemma, let's pray your cast is off in time."

"I had a checkup and X-ray last week. I'm on track to get it off in three weeks. But what if it's not? I can't jump around on stage."

"You'll be fine, babe." Hunter patted her thigh.

"I'm counting on it." Amie didn't even bother to look up from her tablet. "We've also received the final set designs to work with. You're the headline act, opening with "Escape"."

"Cool." I rubbed my hands together. "Escape", our party anthem, was full of energy and always got the crowd pumping. But then I stopped and grimaced. "We usually perform that track running around the stage. Can we change that to accommodate Gem's leg?"

"It's our biggest hit off our last album." Hunter's tone went up a notch and turned in my direction. "It won't be the same if we just stand at the mics and sing."

"Gem may not be able to walk properly by then," I snapped.

"He's right, Hunt." Disappointment clouding Gemma's eyes. "Even with physical therapy, it will take a while to regain my strength."

Hunter jerked his chin back. "You won't need that."

"Yes . . . I will." She glared at him.

"Hey," Amie interjected. "The choreography will be worked out during rehearsals. I just want to get the three of you back on stage, performing as soon as possible."

"Me too." Gemma mumbled as she leaned back in her chair. "At least someone here gives a shit."

I smirked and shook my head. I doubted if Amie cared. Her only concern was to make sure we were playing and bringing in the bucks.

"One last thing," Amie placed her tablet down, and folded her hands on her lap. "Tonight, at ten, I'm going to see a new band play called Pina. SureHaven are interested in signing them, and they could be a potential support act for your next tour. I know it's been a long day, but I've got a spare ticket. Who'd like to come?"

"I'll go," Hunter replied.

My head snapped in his direction. Hunter barely had time to draw a breath before he'd responded. Ping-ponging my gaze between Amie and Hunter, my skin crawled like a thousand spiders were scuttling down my spine.

What was with those two lately? The looks. The gazes. The small smiles they exchanged. I'd noticed them during our trip last week, hoping I'd been imagining things. Was there more to their flirtatious comments over morning coffees, the arm nudged when they talked, the sitting close to one another? Surely not. I rubbed my weary eyes, trying to erase my irrational thoughts. This outing with Amie was business. Just business. There was nothing more to it than that.

I gathered up my gear and stuffed it into my backpack. "Fine by me."

"Well, I'm out." Gemma packed her things, grabbed her crutches, and got ready to leave. "I'm nothing but a security hazard with my leg still in a cast. You go, Hunt."

I kept my eyes on Amie and Hunter. They exchanged barely-there glances and tiny smiles. Amie's cheekbones bore too much color, and Hunter had that predatory glint in his eyes. My stomach clenched. I prayed my concern was the work of my overactive imagination. But until proven otherwise, I'd be watching those two like a lion stalking its prey. Because Gemma was and always would be my number-one concern.

Chapter 15

GEMMA

In the guys' penthouse, I stretched out on the chaise and closed my eyes. It was only eight o'clock in the evening, but it felt like three in the morning. The long day at the studio had left me bone tired, and with Hunter getting ready to go out with Amie, frustration pummeled my brain. Why would he rather go out with Amie than spend time with me?

"Here." Kyle handed me a JD on ice and flopped on the sofa beside me. "Are you happy with all the songs we selected today?"

Hell yeah. SureHaven had come through with some incredible songs. They always did. I was excited to give each track our touch. But not having an album comprising our material would always be a thorn in my side. "Yeah. I am. I can't wait to work on them and make them our own once we hit the studio."

"We always do." Kyle twisted his glass in his hand. "But something about Jeremy was off. Normally he's chill, but today it was like he was ready to kick us out the door."

"Yeah, he's never made us feel disposable before." Jeremy's bluntness and threats did nothing to ease the knots digging into the back of my neck. Was the pending Grant acquisition of SureHaven causing issues we were unaware of? SureHaven had been invested in us since we'd signed. Our talent had captivated them. Our success was thanks to their phenomenal marketing, their reach, and their business expertise. I had to remember that and not push their buttons every time we met. But if I'd waited for Kyle and Hunter to make things happen, I'd still be sitting in Kyle's garage back in New Jersey trying to land our first gig.

Before we won the SureHaven contest and took on Amie as our manager, I—with help and encouragement from Claire, Kyle's mom—had always been the one to chase gigs, enter contests, and pushed the guys toward our dreams. And I'd continue to do so until we got what we wanted.

For now, our contract had us on a leash. We'd signed our life away temporarily. But that didn't stop me from having itchy feet.

I downed a mouthful of JD, then rested the glass on my leg. "Hopefully, Jeremy was just having a bad day. But you know me, I like to stoke the fire, and I'm always wanting more."

"Don't you already have everything?" Kyle's sharp tone caught me off guard.

"What's that supposed to mean?"

"Well . . ." He shrugged. "You have music, we have another record to work on . . . and you have Hunt. What else could you possibly want?"

I threw him a saucy smile and slapped him on the thigh. "An album of our own music." But I'd had enough talk about albums and contracts and songs for now. "It's getting late. It's time for me to head home." Yawning, I covered my mouth with my hand. When the boys went away on promo, I'd moved back into my place. The stairs were a struggle with crutches, but I'd managed. I'd survived on takeaway food, had relied on my housekeeper to clean up my mess, and my girlfriends visiting to keep me company. "Hunt's going out. You're tired, and so am I."

Kyle crunched on a piece of ice. "Why don't you stay for dinner? I'll cook, then walk you home."

"That would be nice." I sank deeper into the sofa, unable to find the energy to move just yet. "Let's order in."

"Nah. I want to cook. I need to do something to help wind down after a big day."

"I love your cooking." I softened my tone. "You used to come over to my place and we'd whiz up a storm. We haven't done that in ages. I miss that."

His chest rose and fell with slow, rhythmic breaths as he stared into his glass. "Things are different now, Gem."

My stomach sank to the floor. "I know. But it shouldn't be. What about when we sang our song today? That was awesome, right?"

For me? It had been nothing short of electric, like an amplifier thudding at full power. Had he felt that energy? Our connection? How strong our friendship was? When we sang a song we'd written together, it was as if no one else existed. Not even Hunter.

Why was that?

I wanted to feel that captivating vibe with Hunter. To have that creativity and passion and power take over me when I sang with him. But maybe my bond with Hunter was and would always be different. Hunter was fun. Goofy. A barrel of laughs when we performed. Kyle was . . . all soul.

He turned to face me, and a cool smile slid across his lips. "Yeah, singing 'Light Up the World' was amazing." His reassuring tone put me at ease. "We put Jeremy in his place, didn't we?"

"We certainly did." I patted his thigh and gave it a rub. How lucky was I to have two amazing guys in my life and make music every day for a living?

Shoes clicking on the floorboards echoed in the hallway. Hunter strode into the room, tying his black necktie. My body temperature jumped a few degrees. *Yep.* My chemistry with Hunter differed completely from mine and Kyle's. Hunter smoldered, dressed in a charcoal suit and black paisley shirt. But a hard twang struck my heartstrings. I should be the one going out with him for the evening, not Amie.

"You're spruced up." I scanned him up and down. "It's a bit much for going to see a band play, isn't it?"

"Amie and I will grab a bite to eat before we check out the band. So . . . *voila.*" He spun around, showing off his threads. "Do I scrub up okay?"

"You know you do. But seriously?" I jerked my chin back, feeling left out. "When are we going to go out to dinner?"

"I'd love to take you out. Are you ready to face the paparazzi and cameras and media frenzy? You know I am."

Shit. Worry slammed into my chest. Fear strangled my throat. If the paparazzi found out I was with Hunter, they'd trail our every move like they'd done when I was with Ben. I wasn't ready to have my private life splashed across the Internet again. Not yet. "Can . . . can we wait until my cast is off?"

Hunter swept toward me and kissed me on the cheek. "Of course we can. Don't stress." As he stood upright, he slapped Kyle on the shoulder. "Bud, you okay to look after my paranoid girlfriend?"

"Why wouldn't I be?" Kyle grunted and finished his drink.

"Just checking." Hunter's cell phone buzzed in his pocket. He grabbed it and glanced at the screen. "Amie's downstairs. I've gotta go. I'll be home around midnight. Don't wait up." With a skip in his step, he headed for the elevator. "See you tomorrow." He waved over his shoulder and disappeared through the doors.

I slumped against the sofa and sighed. I missed running around and going to events with the guys. Being locked up at home or here at the guys' place was sending me stir crazy. Damn broken leg. I had three weeks until the cast came off. That couldn't come soon enough. As I hugged a cushion to my chest, my belly grumbled.

Kyle chuckled. "Is that your way of telling me you'd like me to cook dinner?"

"Mmm. Yes, please."

"How about I make gnocchi?"

"You know that's my favorite. But you can only cook on one condition."

"What's that?"

"I help you."

"You sure can."

Kyle stood, grabbed my hands, and pulled me to my feet fast. He was too strong, too quick. I overbalanced. Stumbled forward.

And collided with his rock-solid chest. His hands shot onto my hips to steady me. My palms flattened against his pecs.

My head spun from the rush.

"You got your feet, Gem?"

"Yeah." Giggling, I lifted my chin and met his dark eyes, glistening with warmth. As I sucked in a deep breath, a blanket of calm air wrapped around me. His heart beat rhythmically beneath my hand, like a mechanical metronome. A comfortable silence lingered for seconds, but it could have gone on for hours. He was the best friend a girl could ever have. Smiling, I tapped his chest and took a step back. "Sorry for being clumsy. Thanks for your help."

He closed his eyes and pinched his eyebrows together, then he nodded. "Um . . . yeah. Anytime." He handed me the crutches, skirted around the furniture, and headed over to the kitchen. "Come on. Let's cook."

Did he have to walk so fast? What was with him lately? Loping along, I hobbled after him. "So, Chef? What can I do to help?"

Kyle opened drawers and pulled out pots and pans, cutting boards, knives, and utensils, then a mixture of ingredients from the pantry and the fridge. "Would you like to peel the potatoes?"

"That would be right." I propped my crutches against the counter and play-punched him in the arm. "Give me the worst job."

"You offered to help." Grinning, he dumped the bag of spuds in front of me.

"What sauce do you want with it?" He opened the fridge and scanned the shelves. "Tomato and onion, creamy garlic . . . no, wait . . . there's no cream. Tomato and garlic it is."

Side by side, we fell into making gnocchi, working together like rhythm and harmony. As we laughed and goofed around, Kyle made the sauce. I peeled the potatoes, washed them, and put them into the pot to boil.

Grabbing the onions and a knife, I diced away. But halfway through the first one, my eyes stung. Burned. Blazed with fire. *Fuck!* Tears streamed down my cheeks, blurring my vision and all sense of direction. "Kyle. Quick, I need a dishtowel." I flapped my hands in front of my face. "I can't see."

"Here, will these do?" He ripped paper towels off the roll and thrust a bunch into my hands.

I buried my face in them and wiped my eyes. *Ow!* Blinking the tears away, I glanced up at him through my wet lashes.

"Are you okay?" He rubbed the top of my arm. But the combination of humor glinting in his eyes and concern flicking across his face stirred something strange deep inside my belly.

Something . . . new. Something strange.

Something that tampered with my heartbeat.

What was that?

"Hey." He stepped in closer, leaving less than half a foot between us. With the softest touches, he brushed his fingertip down my cheek and swiped a tear away. "You forgot one," he whispered.

Oh . . . Did I?

He traced along the line of my jaw and teased his thumb in slow, sensual circles near my lips. His gaze never left mine.

My eyes fluttered shut. His touch was like silk gliding over my skin.

Shit. My heart jolted. Panic seized my throat.

Oh God. What was I doing? What was he doing? Was he going to kiss me?

No.

No. No. NO. NO. NO!

My eyes shot open. The golden flecks in his eyes had darkened to a dangerous level, but within a blink, it was gone.

I jerked my chin away from his touch and turned toward the counter. My breath shuddered through my lungs. Vertigo hit, and I wobbled on my feet.

Kyle wouldn't kiss me.

No way.

My mind was messing with me . . . again. "Um . . . thanks for the paper towels." My voice snagged in my dry throat. I swallowed hard. "Let's get this gnocchi on. I'm starving."

"Yep." Kyle dashed over to the stovetop and stirred his bubbling sauce. "Me too."

I sniffed loudly and wiped my watery eyes once more. I picked up the knife and continued to chop the onions.

The buzz from Kyle's touch had rattled me. It was nothing like I'd ever experienced with Hunter. Why not? I wanted Hunter to make my body hum.

I hacked at the onion lying on top of the cutting board, pulverizing it into a mash.

Now more than ever, I couldn't wait to get my cast off. I was sick and tired of being hindered by my broken leg. The lack of sex had messed with my brain. My no-sex rule was ridiculous. It was the reason I was struggling to connect with Hunter. The reason he'd kept his distance. We were afraid of turning each other on and going too far. Well, enough was enough.

No more stupid rules. Decision made. I'd stay here tonight.

The minute Hunter came home . . . he was mine.

He was due home at midnight.

I glanced at the wall clock.

In three and a half hours . . . we'd be getting it on.

Fuck yeah.

But first . . . I needed food.

Chapter 16

GEMMA

After devouring the divine gnocchi, I sat at the kitchen counter and downed another shot of JD. My foot jiggled against the footrest. I glanced at the wall clock for the hundredth time that evening.

Making dinner with Kyle, cooking, eating, and cleaning had only taken one and a half hours. Hunter was due home in two. Why was the clock moving so slowly?

The anticipation of long overdue sex was killing me.

Maybe watching TV would help pass the time.

Sliding off the stool, I grabbed my glass and placed my crutches under my arms to head over to the sofa. Struggling to carry my drink and coordinate the crutches, I stumbled, wobbled, and spilled my JD. My crutches crashed to the floor with a bang.

"Shit." I wasn't sure if my hands were shaking from my lack of coordination or from my mounting impatience and apprehension waiting for Hunter to come home. "This is so frustrating. I can't do anything myself."

"Here." Kyle rushed to my aid, picking up my crutches. "You should've asked. You know I'll help."

I handed him my glass, snatched the crutches from him, and hooked them under my arms. My head and heart pounded. Butterflies had turned into bats in my stomach. I hated waiting. I wished Hunter would hurry and get home. "I hate being useless."

"You're not totally useless. Just somewhat." Kyle's smile betrayed him.

In situations like this, when I had pent-up energy to burn, there was only one thing to do.

Play music.

Hard music.

Rip it up on my guitar for the whole of Tribeca to hear.

"Why don't I top up our drinks and we go belt out some tunes?" Kyle jutted his head toward the music room.

Cracking the tension from my neck, I stretched it from side to side. Kyle always knew exactly what I needed. It wasn't TV, it was music. "That. Sounds. Perfect."

"I'll see you in there."

I shuffled down the hallway into the home studio. Taking a seat at the desk covered in computer equipment, monitors and mics, I stretched out my aching leg. As I scratched my skin above the cast, a handful of pages covered in Kyle's scribble caught my eye. I smiled, wondering what lyrics he'd been working on. Many things we jotted down never amounted to anything, but I always loved to read his words. I grabbed the top few sheets and scanned them.

But I stopped at the second page. Deep-cutting, crossed-out lines dug into the paper. The date in the top right-hand corner was from last week when he'd been in LA.

> *When I'm with you, I'm no longer broken*
> *You know how I feel, even when words aren't spoken*
> *Feel my heart beat, my love for you is so strong*
> *You and me, girl, we're meant to belong*
>
> *I get lost in your gorgeous eyes*
> *Your smile so bright, I lose my mind*
> *My heart beats only and just for you*
> *I've searched the world, no one else will do*

I flicked to the next page.

You hold my heart
In your hands
Dance with me
I'm your man
When the light
Hits your face
It takes me to
Another place

And the next. The paper shook in my hand.

When I see you with him
I don't know where to begin
It breaks my heart every time
Knowing every day you should be mine

So take this shattered piece from me
'Cause without you, I cannot breathe
The ache inside runs way too deep
This smile I wear is too hard to keep

I want your kiss, I want your touch
Can't you see, Can't you see, Can't you see
That I love you so much
It hurts like hell to live and breathe
'Cause in this world, you're all I need
Can't you see, Can't you see, Can't you see
That I love you so much

What's it going to take to make you mine
I've loved you for all of time
I'd treat you better than he does now
Give me the chance, I'll show you how

My heart squeezed and squeezed, tighter and tighter. My lips trembled. Tears stung my eyes as I read page after page after page.

He'd lied to me. Kyle had lied.

He'd said he wasn't upset or jealous about me being with Hunter. But here it was, in black and white. I was usually intuitive. Why hadn't I seen this? Just how deep did his feelings run for me?

A cocktail of hurt, fury, rage, love, worry and concern blended inside my chest. He was my best friend. I hated I caused him all this pain.

The door swung open and in he walked, carrying drinks.

I stared at him, struggling to piece words together. "What's all this?" The pages quivered in my hand.

He placed the drinks on the desk and snatched the sheets from me. "Nothing. It's just some crap I was working on the other day. I meant to throw them out."

"Kyle—"

"Gem, please." His whipping tone cut me off. "Forget it."

No way in hell. I shot back the JD and slammed the glass down. "You've told me several times, even before you left for LA, that you were okay with me and Hunt being together. That you weren't jealous or upset. Was that all bullshit? Because these lyrics tell a completely different story."

"What the fuck makes you think they're about you?" He stuffed the pages into his folder and threw them onto the floor by the door.

"Aren't they?" No more lies. "If they aren't about me, who are they about?"

"Fuck, Gemma." He ripped his fingers through his unruly hair. "They're just words."

"No . . . they're not." Our songs were never *just words.*

He groaned. Tensed his jaw. Stared at the ceiling. Then he lowered his chin, met my gaze, and anguish burned in his eyes. "What do you want me to say, Gem? Yes, they're about you. Yes, it's how I feel about you. Yes, I mean every word. But what fucking difference is that going to make? You're my best friend's girlfriend." He placed his hand over his heart. "You're . . . and I truly believe it . . . my soul mate. That will never change. But the thing is, at the end of the day, you're not mine. You're Hunter's. So somehow, I have to learn to live with this fucked-up situation, now, don't I?"

My heart cinched and cracked. The pain in his voice and the agony in his eyes made me keel over. Kyle liked me? Really liked me. Why had everything in my world gotten so fucked up? It was never supposed to be like this. If he had feelings for me, he should've said something sooner. Not that it would've changed anything, but we could've talked it out and dealt with any issues, not letting them fester.

Straightening, I dug my fingernails into my palms to keep a clear head. To be mindful of his feelings. "Yes. I'm sorry this is fucked up. I care about you so much. I love you as a friend. But I'm with Hunter. And plan to be for a very long time. So, we have to deal with this."

"I am. I *will* be fine," he hissed through his teeth.

"I can't believe you lied to me." My heart struggled to beat. "Don't ever lie to me again."

"Yeah, well. Shit happens," he snapped.

He picked up his electric guitar, plugged it in, and strummed at the steel strings with so much force I thought they were going to break.

"Let's play." His voice sliced through the air and stabbed my soul.

He churned out the opening riff of AC/DC's "Thunderstruck". It charged the air, and fueled the fire lurking beneath my skin. Kyle's fingers raced across the strings, over and over again. The *ne-er ne-er ne-er . . . nah ah ah er ah ah ah . . . thunder* music taunted me into a challenge.

Bring it.

I ripped my hairband off my wrist and pulled my hair back into a tight ponytail. I hobbled over to the rack, grabbed my guitar, and hooked the strap over my shoulders. As I struck the strings, the sound reverberated through the amp.

Kyle's gaze locked onto mine.

The air between us zapped.

Oh . . . it was on.

With wild eyes blazing, we played.

The crazed noise bordered on deafening. The vibrations in each stroke charged through my body like an electrical storm. I attacked each fret, dueling note for note as Kyle stood opposite me. He played high; I played low. We matched chord for chord, struck riff for riff. If we'd held swords, this would be a fight until death or surrender.

AC/DC turned into Santana, which morphed into Bon Jovi, then Five Seconds of Summer before we hammered out our own rock tracks. Neither of us said a word. We just played—played and let the music vent all that had to be said. Felt. Conveyed.

Three hours disappeared. Kyle flicked his head. Droplets of sweat flew from the tips of his hair. Perspiration trickled down my spine. Wet strands from my ponytail clung to my neck. Our shirts stuck to our sweaty bodies. My heart pumped hard, but my callused fingers never faltered.

But by one a.m., my body screamed at me to stop. Puffing and panting, I placed my guitar down. I'd lost track of time, and Hunter still wasn't home.

"I'm done." I wiped off my sweaty brow on the bottom of my T-shirt. "I'm gonna call it a night. It's late. I'm going to shower and crash here." I grabbed my crutches and hobbled for the door. But I stopped and turned back to Kyle. His shoulders slumped as he mopped the sweat off the floor with a towel. Music had always gotten us through everything. I prayed it wouldn't fail us now. I leaned against the doorjamb. "Kyle . . . are we okay?"

"Yeah, Gem. Always."

Pity I didn't believe him.

The elevator pinged down the far end of the hallway, and Hunter stumbled in.

"Kyle?" He hollered at the top of his voice. "Kyle? You up?"

There was a loud thud against the wall.

I moaned. "Great. Hunt's drunk. We better help him."

There went my grand plans for what I wanted to do when he arrived home. Not that I was in the mood anymore. Not after my run-in with Kyle.

I shuffled into the living room. Kyle followed close behind.

Hunter lay face down on the sofa with his head turned and buried deep into the cushions. His jacket hung half off his shoulders. His hair fell loose around his collar. He reeked of whiskey and cigarettes.

"That's my boyfriend," I mumbled under my breath. "Hunt, you awake?" I nudged him on the shoulder. He groaned but didn't roll over. Had he passed out? That wasn't like him. He could drink a bottle of whiskey and not be this intoxicated. The band must have been really good . . . or really bad . . . or getting wasted was the only way to survive an evening with Amie. Either way, I was jealous of missing out on a big night. I glanced at Kyle. "Should we try to get him into bed?"

"Nah. Fuck him." Kyle chuckled and shook his head. He flicked his hand at Hunter. "He can stay there. Let him sleep it off. Wouldn't be the first time he's passed out on the sofa."

"True." I shrugged. "Well, I can't move him. So he's staying put." Turning to Kyle, I rubbed his arm and gave him an *I'm-sorry-for-everything* small smile. "Hey . . . thank you for tonight. For dinner, the music and for finally being honest. Somehow, we'll work things out. I'm just not sure how yet. Jamming with you was awesome and one of the most incredible sessions I've had in months. It was nice to let off some steam. You're the best—don't forget it."

Hurt flashed in his eyes, and my insides curled. My casual saying suddenly took on a different light. How cruel were those words to him? I closed my eyes. "I'm sorry. I didn't mean—"

"It's okay, Gem. Let's call it a night." He stepped away, turned and headed toward his room.

After showering and brushing my teeth, I crawled into bed in the spare room and drew the blankets up to my chin. I rolled onto my side and tugged the pillow under my head. Before I turned the nightstand light off, I stared at the photo hanging on the wall—the three of us at the Grammys. That night, Hunter had played up to the photographers, waving, smiling, loving the attention. I'd stood in the middle, being blinded by hundreds of flashing cameras. And Kyle . . . looked at me. With a beautiful smile drawn across his lips, and his arm tucked around my waist, he'd held me close, protecting me.

I shut my eyes. A gazillion thoughts of Kyle raced through my mind. My heart struggled to find peace. I hated hurting him. Discovering he had feelings for me made me feel special and loved, but also shitty and awful and like the worst person in the world. But what could I do?

I was with Hunter. I wanted to see if what we had was real, was love, was meant to be.

I was committed to that. I'd never wanted to cause problems between the three of us, but I had. If our friendship was as strong as I believed it to be, we'd survive. I had to see this through.

I wanted Hunter in every possible way.

With all my heart and soul, mind, and body, I wanted to be his.

Things may not have gone to plan tonight, but tomorrow was another day. I hoped Hunter didn't have a hangover in the morning. We needed to be together. We'd go to my place so we could be alone. Away from Kyle. Yes, that was the plan. Butterflies flapped and fluttered in my stomach. Yep . . . with no rules in place, it was time to take my relationship with Hunter to the next level.

Chapter 17

KYLE

I sat on the leather armchair, plucking away at my acoustic guitar. Hunter lay on the sofa opposite me, still passed out from last night. The soft music tinkering through the air was the only thing that kept me calm, controlled, restrained. But when Hunter stirred, my notes grew louder and louder. Two buttons were missing from Hunter's shirt. Red scratches crossed his chest. Lipstick smeared his stubble.

What the fuck happened last night?

Hunter better have a damn good explanation or these strums would turn to swift blows into his guts.

My fingers slipped on the strings, sending a piercing screech through the air.

"Do you have to do that here?" Hunter groaned, rolled, and sat upright. He rubbed his bloodshot eyes, ran his fingers through his mass of tangled hair, then swiped a hand over his pale, blotchy cheek. "What's up your ass this morning?"

"You tell me?" I snapped with venom. I put my guitar on the floor and glared at him. "What did *you* do last night? Better tell me everything before Gem wakes up."

"What are you talking about? I went to see the band with Amie. And the way my head feels, I guess I drank too much." Hunter's voice didn't falter, but his concern-filled gaze darted toward the hallway.

"Then why are your buttons missing—and what's with the lipstick on your face?"

What little color was left in Hunter's cheeks drained away. His mouth moved, but no sound came out. He wiped his fingers over his lips and rubbed at the corners of his mouth.

"Were you mobbed by fans? Or did you screw someone behind Gem's back?" I clenched my fists, my knuckles turning white. "I said I'd fucking kill you if you hurt her."

"I didn't sleep with anyone," he mumbled.

"If I recall correctly, you don't wear lipstick either." Anger churned through my veins, ready to explode and scream like Slipknot.

"Shit." Hunter tugged at his shirt collar and closed his eyes. His brow furrowed with deep grooves. "Amie kissed me." His hand shot up to stop me from speaking. "Before you go off the deep end, it was nothing. Just a drunken, one-time, will-never-happen-again, goodnight kiss when the driver dropped me home."

"What the hell?" Fire blazed through my tone. I didn't care if I woke the entire district. "She's our manager. What were you thinking? What . . . about . . . Gem?"

Hunter flinched and buried his face in his hands. "I fucked up, okay? Don't say anything. Please. I beg you."

"The hell I won't." I jumped to my feet. I turned and stared at the traffic heading down Sixth Avenue. Tension coiled from my toes to the base of my neck. How could Hunter do this to Gemma? I should've known better. Anyone who batted an eyelid in his direction was always going to be a temptation.

Hunter needed a lesson in self-control. I was a fucking master at that. It's all I'd done for weeks. Music and working out were the only outlets that had helped me keep a grip on the way I felt about Gemma. But now she knew. It hadn't changed anything. But I still loved her. And I wouldn't let anyone hurt her. Especially Hunter.

I spun around and jabbed my finger at him. "Tell Gem or I will. We made a pact to never tell any lies because that's when problems start. We've always been honest with each other. Remember?"

Hunter huffed, throwing a cold smirk in my direction. "Speak for yourself, bud."

I balked. I blinked. "What's that supposed to mean?"

"Kyle, I'm not blind. I know how you feel about Gem. I know you love her."

My knees buckled. The sharp edge in Hunter's voice speared my heart.

"But she's my girlfriend." Hunter's gaze burned me. "I trust you around her. Always have and always will. I love her too. I really do. No one gets me like she does."

My throat constricted, and my pulse whooshed in my ears. Hunter was more observant than I realized. I swallowed hard, struggling to speak through my strained jaw. "Then prove it, Hunt. I mean it. If you love her anywhere near as much as I do, you wouldn't be doing any of this shit." I pointed toward Gemma's room. "Tell her about last night or I will."

"Tell me what?"

Gemma swung out of the hallway on her crutches.

An ache tore through the center of my chest. *Crap.* I didn't want to cause problems or see Gemma get hurt but protecting her was my priority.

Her eyes shone in the morning light. She was already dressed for the day in clothes she'd kept in the spare room. Her oversized T-shirt hung off one shoulder. Her sweatpants were rolled at the cuffs. An old sock of Hunter's covered the bottom of her cast and she had on a running shoe on the other foot. No doubt she was about to head home.

Fuck, I never wanted her to leave.

"What's up?" She smiled, rocking on her foot.

"Gem." Hunter shot to his feet and kicked his shin against the coffee table. "Ow. Fuck."

"You goose," she giggled. She mustn't have heard my conversation with Hunter.

Placing my hands on the back of the armchair, I dug my fingers into the leather. Hot blood surged through my veins. As I glared at

Hunter, my voice sliced through my teeth. "Tell her."

"Guys?" Worry crept into Gemma's tone as her gaze darted back and forth between us. "What's going on?"

Hunter gave me an evil glare. "Asshole."

There was no way Hunter would get away with this. This wasn't about wanting to break them up. No way. I'd never do that. It was about being honest. A friend. Loyal to the core. Gemma had to know. The knots in my stomach twisted tighter. Would Hunter ever forgive me? Would Gemma ever forgive Hunter?

Would we survive this fucking mess?

I had no idea—but there was only one way to find out.

Nausea flooded my gut. "Hunt, last warning. Tell her."

Hunter lowered his head. "I fucking hate you, Kyle." *No, he didn't.* He pivoted to face Gemma. He let out a shaky breath as his shoulders sank three inches. "I . . . I kissed Amie last night."

Fire exploded in Gemma's eyes. "You fucking did what?"

Chapter 18

GEMMA

A blaring sound, like a thousand New York taxis honking their horns, exploded inside my head. "You . . . you kissed Amie?" I stared at Hunter, swaying on my crutches. Bile bubbled up my throat, burning my chest. "What kinda kiss? A kiss on the cheek? The lips? Or you made out like mad ferrets?"

Hunter's face paled as his gaze fell to the floor. "I guess . . . ferrets. We were drunk. Things got out of hand."

Jagged breaths charged in and out of my lungs. *Oh. My. God. He kissed Amie. That fucking bitch.*

I froze. A feverish chill washed over me, numbing all my senses.

I couldn't think.

I couldn't breathe.

Shit. Shit. SHIT!

I needed fresh air.

Hunter splayed his hand across his chest. "Gem, I swear it was a stupid mistake. It meant nothing."

He stepped toward me, but I held up my finger. "Don't. Just don't, Hunt."

My vision blurred. My head pounded. I had to get out of there. Get out quick. I charged down the hallway and pressed the elevator button. The doors opened, and I slid inside. On Level 2, I headed out onto the building's pool deck. My crutches were a blur as my arms worked in overdrive. I stormed past the line of sun loungers and folded umbrellas and reached the far end of the lap pool. I fell onto the bench underneath the huge potted tree and threw my crutches onto the ground.

There was no one else around. I had the place to myself. And somehow . . . somehow, I had to process what Hunter had just said . . . *Done.*

He'd cheated on me.

With Amie.

Was it just a kiss, or was there more to it?

Fuuuuck!

Tears welled in my eyes as a sharp laugh burst from my chest. I stared up at the leaves rustling in the breeze. Was I kidding myself to think Hunter would stop his womanizing ways for me? Even though he'd promised to do so.

I couldn't tolerate cheating. It was what had driven my father away from my mother. I'd seen it ruin too many people's lives.

The door at the far end flew open. Hunter rushed out. Half way to me, he slowed. He'd changed into a faded red T-shirt and jeans. Good, otherwise he'd reek of *her.*

"Gem?" His anguish punched my soul.

I didn't know what to think. To feel. I just sat there shaking my head.

He fell onto his knees in front of me.

"I don't know what to say other than I'm sorry. I'm so fucking sorry." Devastation deepened his voice. "I mean that with all my heart. I never meant to hurt you. Being drunk was no excuse."

"You promised me." My voice quivered in my throat, and a tear escaped, catching on my cheek. "You said you'd change."

He squeezed my hand resting on my lap. "I have. But I fucked up."

"With Amie?" I could taste acid on my tongue. "Of all people, you had to kiss her? I can barely tolerate being in the same room as her. And you . . . you kissed her."

He slammed his eyes shut. His Adam's apple lurched. "It was drunken stupidity. That's all."

My jaw tensed. I'd heard this drunk excuse too much lately—first from Kyle, now from Hunter. "Be honest. How far did you go?"

"We just kissed. I swear." Hunter crawled closer. "She tried to get all over me, but I stopped her. I didn't fuck her. This whole lack-of-sex thing between us is frustrating the hell out of me, because I want to be with you, and I'm not."

My eyes widened, and fury licked through my veins. "So, this is somehow my fault?"

"No." He winced. "No. Not at all. It's mine. Please, Gem, I'm begging you." He edged between my legs and cupped my face. "It won't happen again. You're the one I want. I care about you too much to lose you over a stupid kiss."

Tears blurred my vision. "Hunt, this is too hard. We're not working. Being with you should be easier than this."

"It will be." He brushed my damp cheek with his thumb. "With us being apart for vacation and travel, I admit, the last few weeks have been difficult. But you get your cast off in three weeks, and everything will be back to normal. We'll be fine. Give me a chance. Give *us* a chance."

I pulled away from his touch, unable to meet his gaze.

My chest ached.

It would be so easy to walk away. Right now.

Just say it's over.

Hunter stroked the side of my head. "I'm yours. Please don't quit on me."

His words tugged hard on the chords in my heart. *Fuck.* He'd played his ace. My mother was a quitter. So was my dad. When times had gotten tough, they'd walked away. I wasn't like that. I'd committed to Hunter. Was this just the first rough patch in our relationship? Should we work through it?

But cheating? How could I ever trust him again? Was this the final straw where I had to cut him loose, so it wouldn't affect our band anymore? I couldn't risk our friendship over this. Or was it too late and too much damage had been done? So much for taking another chance on love. All it had done was cause problems.

Hunter's eyes locked onto mine; their usual sparkle gone. "I will do anything to make this up to you. Name it. I'll do it."

Sweet revenge swirled through my mind. "Can we fire Amie?"

"What?" Hunter jerked his chin back.

"If the three of us agree . . . she's gone."

"Shit." He sat back on his haunches and stared at the deck. "Are you serious?"

Getting rid of Amie had its appeal, but she was a damn good manager. It would be hard to replace her, but I was over Amie's tyrannical ways. And now she'd made out with Hunter when she knew we were together. "Yes, I am. If she makes one wrong move, she's gone. If you so much as smile, spit or fart in her direction, I'll rip your balls out through your throat."

"I do like my balls where they are." He placed his hands on my thighs and rubbed them up and down. "Gem, please forgive me. How many times do I have to say I'm sorry before you'll believe me?"

As I stared at the pool's surface rippling in the breeze, I searched my mind for a way forward. We'd been through so much together, so much pain and heartache, so many good times and laughs, highs and crazy adventures, we should be a perfect match. We just needed to find our spark. It was there somewhere. It *had* to be. It just needed time to flourish. Hunter was right. We couldn't lose what we had over a kiss. Like him, I wanted us to work. But if he made out with someone again, there'd be no more second chances.

"I trusted you." I stabbed my finger against his chest.

"And you can." He took my hand in his and entwined our fingers.

Filling my lungs with air, I reinforced the protective shield around my heart. What Hunter had done hurt like hell, but it hadn't broken me. Nowhere near it. Ben and my mother had done more damage to my heart than Hunter ever could. With him, here on his knees, begging for forgiveness, I had to believe him. He'd never done anything like that before, nor had he been struck down with crippling guilt. Hunter had never regretted anything, but this had gotten to him. That was huge.

But I wasn't naïve, either.

"You hurt me, Hunt. Don't ever do that again." I wiped my wet lashes with the back of my hand. I prayed for the unease in my stomach to settle. It hadn't gone away since I'd played with Kyle last night. I'd wanted to avoid damaging the bond I'd shared with the guys, but now we'd all been scarred. *Fuck.* Things had to get better. I hoped everything would calm down in a few days. "Have you talked to Kyle? About us? He's not handling us being together."

Hunter shook his head. "No, I haven't. But he'll be fine. So will we. He cares about you and has promised to turn me black and blue if I ever fuck up again."

I ran my fingers through Hunter's hair, the soft strands slipping through my fingertips. "He won't get the chance, because if you do, I'll beat him to it." I clutched a handful of his hair and gave his head a gentle but *don't-fuck-with-me-again* shake.

"You won't ever have to. I promise." He took my hand in his and kissed it. "I'll make everything right. You have my word. So . . . are we good?"

I'd been asking myself the same question over and over again. I wanted us to be good. Wanted everything to be perfect. But there were two sides to every story, and I'd yet to hear Amie's. "Let's take it one day at a time."

"I'm down with that."

He leaned in and wrapped his arms around me. I rested my head against his shoulder and circled my hands over his back. No tingles or sparks skipped across my skin. A gazillion doubts swirled through my mind. Was I crazy to give him another chance? Probably. But I wasn't a quitter. There was only one way forward. One way to reset things with Hunter. One way to put this behind us . . . I had to talk to Amie.

Chapter 19

GEMMA

Smoke came out of my ears. For two days, Amie had avoided me. But during our rehearsal break for the upcoming Billboard Awards, I refused to let her escape. As Amie entered the warehouse's bathroom, I stormed after her on my crutches. I shoved the door open. It crashed against the wall and rattled the paper-towel dispenser hanging near the basin.

"You can't avoid me forever, Amie." The concrete walls amplified my voice. I shuffled forward and jabbed my finger toward her face. "All morning, I've put up with your shit and your flirting with Hunt. I'm not blind. Did you seriously think you'd get away with what you did the other night?" My blood boiled through my veins. "It stops right now. Stay away from him. You know we're together."

Amie washed her hands and flicked the water onto my feet. "Oh, I see. You think I'm in the wrong? Let me guess. Hunter said it was all my doing. I was the one who kissed him. Right? So, I guess this is from someone not enjoying themselves." She tugged down the collar of her Ralph Lauren shirt and pointed to an ugly love-bite on her neck.

What the fuck? That wasn't from *just a kiss*. A spear of pain shot through my ribs. I swayed on my crutches as dizziness swam through my head. But I wouldn't give Amie any form of satisfaction.

"Don't turn this around. You shouldn't have even gone near him."

"True." Nonchalance slid through her bitchy tone. "But it was fun."

Gripping the handles of my crutches, my knuckles turned white. "I don't care. Hunt's mine. Go lay your claws into someone else."

Amie shrugged one of her bony shoulders. "Hunter's not boyfriend material. He was put on this planet to fuck. You, of all people, should know that." She wiped her hands on a paper towel and threw it in the bin. "Get over it. Now . . . let's get back to rehearsals." Amie opened the bathroom door. "We have to sort out what we're going to do with you on stage, since you can only hobble around like a cripple."

I clenched my teeth, resisting the urge to throw myself at Amie, bitch-fight her to the ground and punch that smug smirk off her face. "Good thing my injury is only temporary. Unlike the mess you've done to your face." I wriggled my finger at Amie's eyebrow lift, cheek implants, and puffed-up lips. "That shit's permanent."

Shoving past Amie, I jabbed my crutches against the floor and hurried over to the practice area. I took my position in front of my mic. Every muscle in my body ticked with tension. My head ached and throbbed.

Kyle and Hunter came over. Worry lines formed deep creases in their brows.

"What happened?" Kyle asked. "We heard you shouting."

"Amie and I had a few words about what happened the other night." I whipped my head around to face Hunter. Ice frosted my words. "By the whore-mark on her neck, looks like more than a kiss went down. Is there anything else you're not telling me?"

Guilt spread like seeping tar across Hunter's face. "No . . . I'm sorry—"

I cut him off with a wave of my hand. "Enough. I don't want to talk about this anymore."

How could I ever trust him around Amie again? For work or

just hanging out. He'd seemed genuine in his regret and in wanting to make things work. But how could we move forward when I'd worry and question every move? *Ugh!* Why did relationships have to be so complicated? Stuffing my frustration aside, I took a deep, calming breath. I had to focus on our music, not Hunter. I dropped my crutches on the floor and grabbed my mic. "Let's get this rehearsal over with."

But all afternoon, I struggled through the session. My voice was off. My leg ached. My mind was elsewhere. Something about Hunter and Amie didn't sit right. My intuition was in overdrive but gave me no clear answer why. Would I ever forgive and forget what happened? And if not, at what point did I say enough was enough?

***

The doctor made the last cut with the saw, grabbed the spreader, and cracked the cast away from my leg. Finally, the hideous pink cast was gone. I grimaced and wrinkled my nose. All the muscle tone in my calf had vanished. My flesh drooped around my bones. My skin was pale and yellow.

"That's gross." But then I scratched my skin, swirling and scraping my fingernails over my shin. *But damn! That's so fucking good.*

Kyle and Hunter stood beside me, peering at my leg.

"You'll need a spray tan, Gem," Hunter nudged his elbow against my arm.

"Sunshine on the pool deck might be better." Kyle gave me a cool wink.

That option sounded better than a spray tan.

"Some sunshine would be good. Your skin color will return in a few days." The doctor reassured me as he discarded the cast into the trash can. "But your leg is very weak. Get some physical therapy. Don't overexert yourself. No running. And you'll have to wear a moon boot until you get your strength back."

"Are you serious?" I groaned, but anything would be better

than wearing a cast.

"I'm afraid so." The doctor dipped his chin as he pulled off his gloves. "For about a month."

"Great." I flopped back onto the pillow. At least a moon boot would be easier to move around in.

With my new black, slim-line moon boot in place, I hobbled out of the hospital with the guys and into our waiting car. Hunter edged in close to me and wrapped his arm around my shoulders. He nuzzled into my ear and lowered his voice. "At least this boot can come off."

Oh shit. My chest tightened. My palms sweated. Now with my cast off, there were no rules in place. Since the Amie-incident, we hadn't ventured any further in the bedroom. But now . . . was I ready to do so?

The past three weeks had disappeared in a blur. They'd been tough emotionally and physically. Long days had been devoted to rehearsals, and even longer hours had been spent on rebuilding my trust in Hunter. He'd come with me to dress fittings and helped me select several outfits for up-and-coming events. Fashion was his forte, so that part had been fun. He'd taken me on walks, to the spa, and out shopping. He'd borrowed a friend's speedboat, but he'd had more fun gunning it across the water than being with me.

The worst thing about Hunter's newfound attentiveness was that everything seemed to be an effort. The constant niggle at the base of my neck never eased. Nothing felt genuine. Any affection between the two of us disappeared whenever Amie entered the room.

Surely, I was overthinking things and had nothing to worry about. I had to push my worries aside. We had rehearsals for the Billboard Awards to perfect. We headed to Las Vegas in three days. And somehow, I had to cross one long-overdue bridge. After the awards, I had to sleep with Hunter. That would be a good thing . . . right?

***

The drive out to the airport had been slow. The flight to Las Vegas, long. The full-dress rehearsals for the Billboard Awards had been fun. Catching up with friends, other artists, the presenters, and joking around with the TV crew backstage, had me hyped for tonight's show. In a few hours, I'd be back on stage. The adrenaline was already pumping through my veins.

On the outskirts of Las Vegas, at a mansion owned by one of the SureHaven executives, the guys and I were getting ready for the awards. For the past two hours, Carla—our makeup artist, hairdresser, and miracle worker—had preened, plucked, and transformed me into red-carpet glamor.

Margo—our stylist—had dressed me in a stunning Ellie Saab black halter-neck jumpsuit, accessorized with my moon boot. In front of the mirror, I smoothed my hands over the shimmering fabric and drew my shoulders back. My straightened hair, smoky dark eyes highlighted with glitter, bronzed cheeks, and bold red lipstick gave off a sexy siren vibe. I loved it and felt like one, too. Turning this way and that, I made sure my ass didn't look too big in this outfit. *Nope. All good.* I rose onto my toes. "I hate not being able to wear high heels. I'll look like a midget next to Kyle and Hunt." This would be a first, walking a red carpet in flats. I'd wanted to wear my new gold-jeweled Roberto Cavalli stilettos, but they were at home, tucked away in my closet for a few more months until my leg was better.

"You'll be fine." Margo's eyes shimmered as she handed me a pair of dangling diamond earrings to put on.

Carla quickly fussed with my hair one last time and doused it with another cloud of hairspray. "There. Off you go."

"Thank you. Love your work, as always." I kissed Margo and Carla on the cheek, then leaned forward to grab my clutch off the bed. But my hand shot up to my chest. I winced as my skin pulled. "Ow! Shit, Margo. Did you have to use so much tape to stick me into this thing?" Margo had used so much Hollywood tape my chest would get a full waxing when I changed to go on stage.

"Yes." Margo shrugged, unapologetic. Her tone remained level as she raised a fine eyebrow. "Unless you want a wardrobe malfunction for everyone to see?"

"Ah . . . That would be a no." I didn't need more photos of my naked boobs to cause another Internet meltdown. Once had been enough. I grabbed my clutch and clip-clopped out of the room.

I'd made it halfway down the staircase when the guys turned toward me. They sat on the sofa in the living room, dressed in snazzy suits. A cheeky grin touched the corner of Hunter's mouth. Kyle's eyes shimmered as he nodded.

"Stop gawking. Both of you." I snapped, but heat rushed to my cheeks. Their reaction was the only compliment I'd ever need.

Hunter leaped from his seat, rushed over, and kissed me on the forehead. "You look amazing." His gaze traveled down the front split of my top, nodding his approval. "You'll be the hottest chick on the carpet. Guaranteed."

High heels clicked on the marble floor tiles. Hunter's hand dropped from my waist as he took a step to the side. Amie, Bec, and Kate entered the room.

My mouth fell open as I glared at Amie. *What the fuck?* Amie normally dressed head to toe in Ralph Lauren. She'd discarded her usual conservative business attire for a pair of skinny white leather pants and a sheer top with a plunging neckline. *Had Margo gotten to her?*

Amie's outfit looked like something I'd wear on stage— definitely not her usual style.

Kyle's brows pinched together. His lip twitched into a sneer. He didn't like Amie's new look either. But Hunter's reaction . . . was the complete opposite. His eyes darkened to a stormy blue, sharp and hungry, like a tiger on the hunt. There was no hiding the fact he liked what he saw.

My heart shrank, and an ache filled the space. With a flick of my wrist, I slapped him on the arm with my clutch. "Hey . . . You said you only have eyes for me."

"I do. I was looking, not touching." Hunter threw me a cheeky smile and headed out the door.

"Have a great time. See you later." Bec shooed us on our way.

My mind rattled as I slid into the limousine and took the seat behind the driver. Had I been a fool? Was there something going on between Hunter and Amie? I wanted to stop having suspicious thoughts every time she was around, but something kept digging and gnawing away at my insides. Amie took the seat next to me. *Ugh!* I pressed my clutch against my stomach and edged as far away from her as possible. Kate, Kyle, and Hunter sat opposite while our security guards took the back seat.

The limousine took off down the hillside and headed for The Strip. By the time we hit the freeway, my excitement to walk the red carpet, meet the fans and perform at the awards had kicked in. But it was quickly shot down when Amie dropped her pen and leaned forward, giving Hunter another eyeful of her tits. His eyes darkened, and one corner of his mouth twitched into a smile.

A shard of ice stabbed my chest, and a cacophony of white noise exploded inside my head. Hunter had never looked at me with that much fire blazing in his eyes.

Shit. I clasped my clutch so hard I thought the buckle would snap. For weeks, Hunter and I had tried to navigate our relationship. Make it work. But nothing had changed. I'd tried to convince myself that things would get better once my cast was off.

But it wouldn't.

Not after seeing this.

I swallowed hard, my throat dry as the desert. I didn't want to be like my mother, who used men and jumped from one relationship to the next. I didn't want to give up when things got tough. But being with Hunter wasn't about social status, or money, or chasing a lavish lifestyle. It was about taking a chance on love. But the flame had never ignited. I'd cried enough tears and had fought for long enough. We'd hurt each other enough. Before things got worse, I had to end things. While disappointment and failure hung heavily in the pit of my stomach and hurt my heart, I wasn't broken. Far from it. I'd discovered we were friends. Just friends. Nothing more.

I couldn't stay with someone when there was no spark. I wanted magic. That buzz. That high.

Over the past few weeks, maybe my subconscious had

prepared me for this moment. I'd found the strength to admit the truth.

Hunter and Amie were into each other. The vibe between them was unavoidable. Undeniable. *Un-fucking-believable!*

I filled my lungs with air and closed my eyes. Kyle would've never acted like this. He would've never cheated or even looked at anyone else. Kyle would never . . .

Oh . . .

Oh shit. A wave of warmth washed over me and settled in my chest.

Kyle.

Kyle?

What the hell?

My heartbeat quickened as my mind spun faster and faster. But then . . . a blanket of calmness settled over me. The knots that had been embedded in the base of my neck for weeks disappeared. Was it the realization that Hunter and I were over, and I no longer had to fight for something that wasn't there?

Or was it something else?

Something that made me feel light for the first time in months.

And why couldn't I stop staring at Kyle?

Chapter 20

GEMMA

The limousine turned off Frank Sinatra Drive onto Park Avenue and made its way toward the T-Mobile Arena. *Kyle? Wow. Damn. Holy Shit.* I'd had enough emotional upheaval to last a lifetime, but clearly the universe wanted to inflict more. I didn't know what to make of the craze spinning in my head. But first things first. I had to deal with Hunter . . . after the show. I wouldn't break up with him before a televised event. What if he got upset? I cared about him too much; I wasn't heartless. Plus, there were too many ears, eyes, and cameras around for that kind of private conversation. We didn't need our personal lives splashed across the Internet.

The car slowed to a crawl and joined the long queue of limos inching along the road to the venue. Barricades on the streets kept screaming fans at bay like caged wild animals.

"Gem?" Kyle nudged his knee against mine. "Are you okay?"

"Yeah." A small smile curled across my lips. "I am. I really am." *Hopefully. Kinda. Yes. Maybe.* I'd be on edge until I talked to Hunter, but I could pretend everything was good for a few more hours.

The limousine eased to a halt at the front of the red carpet. Sam, our head of security, flung the door open, letting the roars and screams from the crowd flood inside.

"Gemma. Kyle. Hunter. Everhide."

The chanting wove its magic. Electricity skipped through my veins. Pulling my shoulders back, I sat two inches taller and pasted on my smile.

Hunter slid out of the car first and made his way over to the fans. Kyle was next, and I followed. It was catty, but as I passed Amie in my moon boot, I stomped on her toes . *That's for stealing my boyfriend, bitch!* I held no hard feelings, but her pained grunt filled me with a petty but worthy sense of satisfaction.

Feeling lighter, I looked up.

Kyle stood waiting for me. *Dark eyes. Handsome suit.*

He held out his hand . . . and smiled. "Gem."

Oh . . .

My pulse quickened. Butterflies fluttered in my stomach.

I slipped my hand into his . . . then *zap*.

The electric shock coursed through my entire body. A light exploded inside my head, my heart, and my soul. Heat rippled across my skin, and my knees buckled.

What the hell?

His touch . . . *oh wow* . . . his touch.

I curled my fingers around his. *What the hell just happened?*

"Gem? Are you okay?" He held me steady.

I shook my head, unable to take my eyes off him. It was as if the world around me had dissolved, and I stood on center stage with no one else around but him.

Kyle was there for me. Always. Where was Hunter? Off playing it up to the crowds, being adored by the fans.

Kyle was always by my side.

How had I not seen that before?

"Did . . . did you just feel that?" I whispered.

"Feel what?" Shards of gold flickered in the depths of his beautiful espresso eyes.

I glanced at our clasped hands, questioning if I'd imagined things. *No. I didn't.* My skin still tingled and hummed. But the screams from the crowd and camera flashlights snapped me out of my bubble. It was time to move. "Um . . . nothing. I'm okay."

"Do you need help?" Concern hovered low in his soft tone.

"No. I'm fine." *Not even close.* "Let's go."

We headed over to the barricades and worked our way down the line of fans. Hobbling along on my moon boot, I had selfies with the crowd, signed autographs, and said hello to some regular celebrity-meeting junkies. Even a few of the "Ringers,"—members of our biggest fan club—were spotted in the sea of faces.

The Award's production crew, with oversized lanyards hanging from their necks, ushered the three of us along to keep the program on track. After several interviews and a blinding number of photographs, we entered the arena. Security escorted us through a series of doorways and corridors into the backstage area and took us to our dressing room. Hunter had ripped off his suit jacket and unbuttoned his shirt before the door had shut.

Carla and Margo stood ready to dress us and touch up our hair and makeup.

Stepping in behind the modesty panel, I ruffled and scrunched my fingers through my hair, teasing it back to life. I undid all of Carla's red-carpet hard work in a few seconds flat. Then I unbuttoned my halter top. I held my breath and ripped the fabric and Hollywood tape off my chest. "Fuuuccckk." Rubbing my skin, I glanced down at the side of my breast. *Ow!* A strip of red raw flesh burned, but it wasn't bleeding. *Thank goodness.* I grabbed my performance outfit off the hanger. I pulled on my new leather pants, refitted my moon boot, and shimmied into my silver sequined top. *Oh yeah.* This was much more comfortable. I walked out from behind the screen and checked out the guys in their leather pants and button-down shirts, and with their freshly messed up hair. *Nice.*

"Fuck, we're hot." I laughed as I gave them a hug.

But when Amie walked in and threw Hunter a flirtatious wink, it was the reminder I needed to end things with Hunter as soon as possible.

After a quick hair and makeup touchup, the guys and I put on our in-ear monitors and connected our transmitters. We ran through vocal warmups, then high-fived and hugged each other.

"Let's nail this gig." I hollered as we followed a crew member out of the dressing room. We headed behind the constructed stage and past elaborate props. Ducking our heads under a low metal bar, we made our way via torchlight to the hydraulic platform that would lift the three of us onto the main stage for our performance.

The atmosphere buzzed all around us. My heartbeat thundered against my ribs. Performing alongside these guys was what I was born to do. I didn't want to think about Hunter and Amie. Didn't want to think about having to end my relationship. And didn't want to think about that spark I'd gotten from Kyle. But every time I looked at him, even my toes tingled.

It was showtime. Time to put my crazy thoughts aside. I grabbed my mic from Eddie, one of the stage crew members, and stepped onto the platform, followed by the guys. But just when we were in position, Hunter stole the platform's remote control from Eddie.

Eddie's eyes widened, and the color drained from his face like he was about to have a heart attack.

"Hunt, no," I snapped. I wasn't in the mood for his antics today. Normally they were fun and made me laugh, but nope, not tonight.

Hunter bounced and jumped beside me, shaking the remote around in his hand.

"Silence," Jon, the other crew member, placed his finger over his lips. On the small TV monitor beside him, the auditorium lights dimmed. The people in the mosh pit and balconies roared and waved their arms. Jon's eyes stayed glued to the monitor as he spoke into his headset. "Prepare for telecast."

I checked my balance on the platform and closed my eyes. *"Leg, please be okay. Please be okay."* I wriggled my toes to make sure it wasn't aching too much.

No, it is fine.

All I had to do was walk to the front of the stage and sing. Hunter and Kyle would strut around the set and play it up to the crowd.

"We are live in . . . ten . . . nine . . . eight." Jon flicked some switches on the control panel. My heart pounded as I gripped my mic.

"Give me the remote." Eddie mouthed to Hunter, sweat beaded

on his brow.

Hunter shook his head.

Ugh! I knuckled him in the ribs. I loved mucking around with the guys before a show but knew when to draw the line. Hunter never did.

"Seven . . . six . . . five . . . four," Jon counted down.

"Please." Eddie held up his hands, begging. Jon's eyes widened.

The audience chanted our name. "*Ev-er-hide!*" Clap, clap, clap. "*Ev-er-hide!*" Clap, clap, clap.

But Hunter kept dancing around on his spot.

I gripped my mic tighter and tighter, resisting the urge to smack him over the head with it.

Would he ever grow up?

Probably not.

But I had.

I wanted so much more than he could ever give.

Falling into place, the guys turned face forward. I faced the back.

"Three . . . two . . . one . . . go . . ." Jon cued with a point of his finger.

"Welcome to the Billboard Awards." The booming voice of the host filled the auditorium above. "Opening tonight's show . . . please welcome onto the main stage . . . EVERHIDE."

I put on my in-ear monitors, blocking out all sounds from the screaming crowd above. The electric guitars and heavy drumbeat from our backup band on stage sprang to life and filled my head.

Hunter pressed the button on the remote, then tossed it to Eddie, who collapsed in relief. The platform rose, and I looked up. The stage trapdoor above us opened, and we rose higher and higher. Blue and red spotlights zigzagged across the stage. Lasers darted back and forth. Fog billowed across the floor.

"*Here we go,*" Kyle mouthed.

I squeezed his hand and raised my microphone to my lips. It was time to get this party started, and what better way to do that than with our number-one hit song, "Escape."

I licked my lips.

Swallowed.
Then sang, hitting the first notes perfectly.

Come escape, come escape, come escape with me

The weekend's here, just moments away
I'm gonna pick you up, we'll be on our way
Driving in my car, with you by my side
Let's head up north, enjoy the fast ride
Come escape, come escape, come escape
With me

The week's work is done, let's get out of this town
Gonna take you away, nothing'll slow us down
Let's escape the city, leave the lights behind
Gonna drive real fast, gonna blow your mind
Come escape, come escape, come escape
With me

We're gonna turn the music up, so everyone can hear
We'll dance all night, party 'til the morning light
Let's call up the girls and bring in the guys
Let's drink lots of liquor, and have a great time
Wanna feel the music beat, feel your body overheat
Next to mine, next to mine
Come escape, come escape, come escape
With me

Getaway. Gonna party. Every day.
Oh baby ... escape with me

***

After arriving home at five a.m. and crashing by myself, I woke up at midday. I blinked and rubbed my sore eyes. Plucked and pulled clumpy black mascara from my eyelashes. *So much for the makeup remover.* My head throbbed, and my mouth was drier than the Nevada desert after drinking too much champagne. But we'd won awards for Top Group, Top Radio Song, and Top Touring Artist. The hangover was fucking worth it. We had more trophies to add to our collection of Grammys, Brits, VMAs, AMAs and other awards.

But during the excitement and celebrations last night, I hadn't had the chance to talk to Hunter. People, parties, and the paparazzi had made it perfectly impossible.

I'd get the chance on the plane home.

I quickly showered and waited in the front room of the house while Bec, Kate, and Amie rushed around, organizing everyone for the trip home. After the long night, everyone dragged their feet.

I slid onto the stool in front of the Steinway grand piano, ran my fingers over the cool ivory keys, and tinkered. I stared out the bay window at the end of the room and looked across the desert valley toward the Vegas Strip.

Memories of the after-party drifted through my mind. Hunter had flirted with nearly every female present. What caught me by surprise was it didn't bother me. But what did was my awareness of Kyle. And what was I going to do about it? All night, his eyes had been on me. All night, I'd watched him move, smile, and dance. All night, I'd found myself drawn to him from wherever I was in the room. That touch of his hand before the awards had triggered something inside me. I didn't understand it, but whatever it was . . . I wanted to explore it, examine it, and experience it over and over again.

I pressed down on the keys and sang random words. I kept my voice soft, barely above a whisper.

> *You broke down my walls*
> *Shot me down*
> *Made me fall*
> *Held me up*
> *Stole my heart*
> *With just one look*
> *Just one smile*

Just one touch

I chuckled as heat rushed into my cheeks. Changing chords, something different unfolded beneath my fingertips. I glided my fingers over the ivory keys. *Hmm. I liked this.* This tune had potential. I liked the melody I'd created if nothing else.

"Hey."

I jumped, striking down heavily on a chord. Kyle stood in the doorway, leaning against the doorjamb. *Shit!* How much had he heard?

He strolled over, sat down on the stool next to me, and put his arm around my shoulders. I rested my head against him and inhaled his earthy scent.

"What were you playing?" He planted a small kiss on the side of my head.

My heart beat a touch faster as tingles spiraled down my spine. "Nothing serious."

"It sounded good. Show me the chords again." He took his phone out of his pocket and hit record.

"Um . . . okay." I straightened and slid my fingers over the keys, humming the words in my head to recall the tune.

"You were singing before. What were the lyrics?" Kyle watched my fingers glide.

I shrugged. "I don't remember." *Liar.*

He switched off the recording and nudged my arm. "It sounded nice, whatever it was."

"Thanks." I nudged him back. I wanted to talk to him about everything that was hurtling through my mind. Ask him what he thought. Find out what it all meant. But footsteps approaching killed the moment.

"Hey, lovebirds." Hunter staggered into the room, rubbing his eyes. "Remind me never to drink champagne again."

"Don't drink champagne again," Kyle and I said in unison. We laughed and bumped our arms together.

The low wattage humming across my skin was impossible to ignore.

But whatever it was, it had to wait. I needed to talk to Hunter.

"Come on. The driver's waiting." Hunter jerked his head toward the door and headed outside.

On the drive to the airport, everyone nursed sore heads. Once we settled onto the plane, Hunter pulled his cap over his bloodshot eyes, curled up in a blanket, and went to sleep.

Feeling the love? Not. I guessed talking to Hunter had to wait until we got home.

Tomorrow . . . on my birthday.

Chapter 21

KYLE

I ambled upstairs, going from room to room, opening the windows in my Amagansett beach house. Hunter stomped around below, taking dustcovers off the furniture. I shoved open a shutter and filled my lungs with fresh air. The hot, late-May sunshine glimmered on the surface of the calm ocean, and gentle waves crashed lazily onto the shore beyond the grass-covered dune. My Long Island shack was nothing like the surrounding mansions or Hampton homes that lay half an hour away, but this old, three-bedroom wooden house with its shingled roof was the only thing I had left of my family.

Every time I came here, the memories flooded my mind. Swimming and playing football on the beach with my cousin Kade. My baby sister, Emily, building sandcastles before she'd gotten sick. Playing board games and guitar on the deck with Mom. Fishing with my father before he'd gotten drunk and turned into an asshole.

After I finished school, my parents had left the nightmares of New Jersey behind them and moved here to live permanently in our vacation home. But one rainy night when they were traveling to Manhattan to see me perform, a truck ran a red light, and they were gone.

That was two years ago.

It still seemed like yesterday.

For months, my life had been a blur. I'd hit the bottle hard and couldn't recall what had happened from one day to the next. I didn't think I would've made it through the loss of my family if it weren't for Hunter and Gemma.

Maybe that was why I'd been so scared of asking Gemma out. Scared to love her more than I already did. Scared of losing her to something worse than my best friend. But I'd sooner live in this nightmare than not have my best friends by my side.

In the master bedroom, I opened the last window and let the sun warm my face. It was good to be back at the beach, away from the city and work and the media. Hunter had promised Gemma a party—tonight was all about her. And what better place than the beach to celebrate her twenty-fourth birthday?

"You want a beer?" Hunter hollered from the kitchen below.

"Sure do." I stepped toward the door and stopped, smiling at an old family photo on top of the dresser. I ran my finger over the faded photograph of my family on the beach. Mom held on to her big floppy hat. Dad held a beer in one hand and a football under his other arm. I pulled bunny ears behind my sister's head.

"Miss you," I murmured.

"I'll be out on the deck," Hunter called out again.

"Coming." Putting my brave face on, I made my way down the stairs and headed outside. I tugged my baseball cap lower and sank into the sun-bleached wooden deckchair next to Hunter. I grabbed the beer, took a sip, and adjusted my sunglasses. "What did you buy Gem for her birthday?"

Hunter scratched at his stubble. "A new acoustic guitar. Hers is so old and crappy. It's about time she got a new one."

"You're out of your mind. She loves that thing." Hunter looked at me blankly. "It was her dad's. She'll never part with it. I wouldn't ask Gem to give that up, even if my life depended on it."

"Nah, she'll love this new Fender."

Hunter sounded confident, but I wasn't convinced. Gemma's old acoustic was her favorite. She often brought it over to our place when we wrote songs and loved the way it sounded.

"What about you?" Hunter tilted his chin toward me. "What did you buy her?"

"Nothing much." I shrugged my shoulders. "Just a necklace." But it wasn't just a necklace. I'd thought long and hard about what to buy her. Something unique for someone so special.

"Really?" Hunter wrinkled his nose. "Gem doesn't wear much jewelry, so good luck with that."

I smirked and nodded. *Yeah, but I know Gem better than you do.*

Hunter checked the time on his watch. "Catering's due to arrive in half an hour. Gem shouldn't be far off. It's going to be a huge night."

"Cheers to that." I clinked my beer bottle against Hunter's.

A loud knock struck the front door as it creaked open. I glanced over my shoulder. Gemma and her friend's voices chimed through the house. "We're here."

I sprang to my feet before Hunter, charging through the door to greet them.

*****

Gemma

By nine o'clock, loud party music shook every wall in the house. With a JD in hand, and my moon boot on, I danced and sang at the top of my lungs with Kara and Lexi in the middle of the living room. Over forty friends surrounded us, celebrating my birthday.

I ran my hand underneath my hair and lifted it to cool my neck. Sensing Kyle watching me, I couldn't help but smile. I spun around and met his gaze. He was sitting on a stool at the kitchen counter, chatting with Hayden. I waved, ignoring the flutter inside my stomach. Since Vegas, in the car and on the red carpet, everything had changed. How had I not seen what was right in front of me? I'd never felt like this before, and I did not know what it all meant.

I had to find out, but one daunting task remained. I needed to talk to Hunter.

With travel, lack of sleep, and party preparations taking up the hours since landing back in New York, I hadn't had a moment alone with him.

Pulling my gaze away from Kyle, I searched for Hunter. He sat on the faded floral green sofa in the far corner . . . next to Amie. They were laughing and joking and talking into each other's ears. But there was no flare-up of jealousy in my stomach, no raging anger in my blood, no ache in my heart.

Just relief.

I couldn't hold out any longer. There'd never be a right time to talk to him, so now was as good as any. I finished my drink and excused myself from my friends. Weaving my way through the crowd, I made my way over to Hunter and stopped directly in front of him. He didn't look up, so I kicked his foot.

"Gem." He jumped an inch away from Amie. Guilt riddled his face.

"Can I steal you for a moment, please?" I kept my tone cool and ignored Amie.

"Sure, babe."

I held out my hand and dragged him to his feet. We headed down the hallway to the laundry and closed the door behind us. Letting go of his hand, I turned and jumped up to sit on top of the washing machine.

Hunter's eyes filled with seductive mischievousness. He stepped forward, edged between my legs, and nuzzled my neck. "Mmm. You want to do it here? I'm down for that."

I rolled my eyes and let out a *you've-got-to-be-kidding-me* groan. Grabbing a fistful of his long hair, I yanked his head away.

"Stop. Can you be serious for a moment? Don't you think it's about time we were honest with each other?"

Hunter paused, lowered his head, and stared at the ground. "'Bout what exactly?"

"You and me." My stomach cinched like an industrial cable tie. I faced another failed relationship. Just like my mother. But I shook the comparison aside and swallowed the bitter taste in my mouth. "We're not working. We never have."

Hunter grabbed the washing machine beside my hips and closed his eyes. "Gem, don't . . . It's your birthday."

"That's exactly why I'm talking to you. I want to be happy, and I'm not. Have I got this wrong?" I held my breath, hoping I hadn't misread the signs.

"No . . . no, you haven't." Breathy relief filled his voice. He opened his eyes and relaxed his broad shoulders.

"It's okay." I placed my hand on his shoulder and gave it a rub. "It's been brewing for a while."

He nodded.

"Our spark never evolved into anything more. We gave it a shot, but it's not happening." I tilted my head to the side and wrinkled my nose. "You've got a thing for Amie, haven't you?"

Hunter stepped back and wiped his hand down his face. "Gem—"

"Hunt? It's alright. I wanted to slap the shit out of her when you first kissed. That really hurt. But I don't think anyone, not even me, will stop you two from getting together." The truth stung, but it wasn't unbearable. "You don't look at me like you look at her. I don't know what you see in her. She's thirty-three, but whatever. Maybe our pathetic attempt at being a couple did some good. It's shown us who we're meant to be with. Maybe that's why we never slept together—we never had that connection."

"Oh . . . we connected." Hunter raised one sexy eyebrow, and the suggestive glint in his eyes sent heat rushing to my cheeks. We'd certainly had some hot and steamy make-out sessions, but we'd never crossed the line and gone all the way.

"We had some fun, but it's over." I stuffed away the remnants of my disappointment, drew my shoulders back, and pointed at the door. "Go. Find Amie. Don't keep her waiting any longer."

His eyes sparkled in the bright fluorescent lights. He hadn't looked that happy in months. He lunged forward, clutched my face, and kissed me on the forehead. "Thank you." He fell back a step and placed his hands on my knees. "You're really okay with . . . with Amie . . . with me?"

"Yeah. It hurts a little, but I'll be fine."

Hunter nodded and lowered his chin. "I really wanted us to work, Gem."

"I did, too."

"You're sexy as hell, and I really wanted to get into your panties," he said, matter-of-factly, then grimaced. "But I couldn't get over the fact that you're like a sister to me. You're my Gem. Always will be."

Hunter *was* like a brother to me. A big goofball brother who'd always be there to have fun with.

"Well, lucky for me, my panties will remain unexplored territory by you." I jutted my chin toward the door. "Go . . . have fun. But Hunt . . . Promise me one thing. Please be careful. I don't trust her."

"I will," he nodded, tapping his fingers against the doorjamb. "But hold on. Wait a sec." He eased toward me, circled his finger through the air, and a cheeky smile quivered across his lips. "Let's backtrack. What did you mean when you said something about working out who you should be with? You weren't just talking about me. So, spill."

I pursed my lips as heat rushed up my neck.

Hunter grabbed my thighs and squeezed them. "Please tell me it's Kyle."

I gaped, struggling to form words. "How . . . how did you know?"

"You two have always had this insane, incredible connection. It's grown over the past few months, knocking anything and anyone out of contention. I always hoped our friendship, although different, was as powerful as that and would evolve into something hotter, but it never did."

I stared at my trembling fingers resting in my lap. "It's hard to comprehend. Like you and me, we've been friends forever. I risked everything to be with you. I wanted you. But all we did was hurt each other. Finding out how Kyle felt about me was hard. I never wanted to upset him. Was even more terrified of losing him. We kept having these intense moments that rattled me—when we cooked, played music, hung out. I wished I had them with you. But they never happened. I kept seeing you with Amie. I kept fighting for something that wasn't there. Then . . . in Vegas, everything clicked into place. Everything changed. Now . . . all I see is him. I haven't talked to him yet . . . so please don't say anything."

"I won't. And I'm sorry, it was the same with me and Amie. The moment I was with you, I noticed her. It did my fucking head in." Hunter hooked his finger beneath my chin and lifted it. "I never meant to hurt you, Gem. That was . . . and will always be . . . my biggest regret. For that, I'm truly sorry. I hope you and Kyle find a way through this mess and can be together."

"Yeah. Me too. But that's enough breakup talk." I play-punched him in the arm. "Go. Find Amie."

"You're so freaking amazing." He swooped in and hugged me tight. "I love you . . . but like a sister."

The door flew open, and Kyle filled the doorway. His eyes widened, and the color drained from his face. "Shit. Sorry, I didn't mean to barge in. Hunt, the guy organizing the bonfire, is here."

Kyle shrank back a step, but Hunter reached out and stopped him. "Bud, great timing. I'm out of here. She's all yours." Hunter kissed me on the cheek and took off down the hallway.

Kyle leaned against the doorjamb. Disappointment clouded his eyes. "You did it in the laundry? Really?"

I shook my head. "No-pe."

"What's he so happy about?"

"We broke up."

Kyle blinked rapidly and stammered. "You . . . what? He broke up with you on your birthday. I'll fucking kill him."

"No need. I broke it off . . . Well, it was mutual."

"Oh. Are you okay?" He held out his hand and took a step toward me. A mix of concern and elation swirled in his eyes.

"Yep. I'm relieved. And so is he." I hopped off the washing machine. I needed a moment to breathe. Clear my head. Move forward.

I'd finally ended things with Hunter. That had been long

overdue. *Done.*

"Are you sure everything's fine?" Kyle inched closer and rubbed my arm.

The fire that sparked in his eyes turned up the tempo of my heart rate. Was my future with him? The night was still young. Anything was possible. And I couldn't wait to see where things went. But I needed to get out of this laundry. I took his hand and headed for the door. "Yes. Absolutely. But before we head down to the beach for the bonfire, I'm gonna need another drink."

Chapter 22

KYLE

In a daze, I followed Gemma out of the laundry, down the short hallway, and into the crowded living room full of drunk partygoers. She'd broken up with Hunter. I didn't know whether I wanted to jump for joy, hug her, or take her in my arms and kiss her. Maybe all of the above. My heart thudded so loudly I could hear it over the pumping music. The blood rush to my head certainly wasn't from alcohol.

Gemma grabbed a cup and the bottle of JD off the top of the upright piano, poured a straight shot, knocked it back, and poured another.

"Want one?" She waved the bottle at me.

"Yep."

We clinked cups and drank. The whiskey burned like wildfire in my throat and stomach. But fuck, that felt good. I let out a shaky breath. Right then and there, I wanted to tell Gemma how I felt. But damn it . . . She'd just broken up with my best friend and probably needed time to get over him.

Pouring another drink, my hand trembled. I didn't know what to do or say to her, but I knew one thing for certain: I wouldn't lose her again.

The blaring music cut.

"Hey, everyone," Hunter's voice boomed from the doorway that led outside. "Let's head down to the beach. The bonfire's started."

The crowd cheered, grabbed drinks, and headed out over the dune. I hung back by the piano with Gemma, watching everyone leave. When the last of the partygoers stepped out the door, she took a step to follow, but I caught her arm.

"Can you wait a sec?" I struggled to swallow. Struggled to draw breath.

"Sure. What's up?"

The air grew thick and heavy. Touching her skin made my fingers quiver. Why did she have this effect on me? "Before the day disappears, I have to give you your birthday present. Can we go onto the deck?"

"Yeah." She nodded, took my hand, and led me outside.

We sat facing each other on the cushioned bench. Everything seemed surreal. The gentle breeze wafting through the air. Waves crashing on the beach. The sky filled with millions of stars. And Gemma, here with me . . . the most surreal situation of all.

My heart pounded at a million miles an hour. I wanted her. But did she feel the same way about me? She'd denied having feelings for me before. I wasn't sure my heart could handle it if she rejected me. Was there a way I could find out if we had a chance at being together without making a fool of myself? Maybe my gift might give me a sign.

"It was so busy this afternoon I never got the chance to give you this." I dug my hand into my shorts pocket and pulled out a black velvet pouch.

"I was wondering when I'd get something from you," Gemma slapped and shoved my knee. "You've kept me hanging all day."

She bit her lip as I placed the pouch in her hands. She tugged the cords open and tipped the necklace into her palm.

She froze, staring at the square gold pendant and chain shimmering in the light. Was that a good sign, or a bad one?

"You've got it upside down." My voice snagged in my throat as I turned it over in her hand.

"Oh, my God!" She splayed her hand across her chest. "It's staff lines, a treble clef, and G Major." She brushed her fingers over the metal, examining the cut-out lines and the intricate gold embellishments.

"I had it custom-made," I stuttered, unable to gauge her reaction. "Do you remember—"

"The first song we ever wrote together at school was written in G-Major. I still have the piece of paper we wrote 'All Wound Up' on in a plastic sleeve at home."

She looked up at me. Her beautiful green eyes glistened with tears.

"You like it?" I asked, wiping my clammy palms on my thighs.

"I love it. It's the best gift ever." She flung her arms around my neck and hugged me tight. I closed my eyes, squeezed her close, and absorbed the feel of her in my arms.

"Hey, Gemma?" Kara called from the edge of the sand dunes fifty yards away. "You coming, or what?"

Gemma pulled away and wiped her eyes. "In a minute. We're on our way," she hollered to Kara, then turned back to me. "Here, help me put it on."

She dropped the chain into my hand and spun around. After fumbling with the clasp several times, I secured it around her neck. She re-faced me and played with the pendant. The necklace was perfect. It hung exactly at the bottom of the dip in her throat. Just as I'd intended.

She glanced up at me from underneath her long eyelashes. My skin prickled. I could almost see the current of energy hovering between us. I felt it . . . everywhere.

"Come on," she whispered. "We better get down to the beach."

She patted my thigh, went to stand, but I caught her hand.

My heartbeat thundered in my ears. "First . . . there's something I need to know." My voice scratched my throat, not coming out cool, calm, and collected like I'd planned.

"What?" Gemma settled onto the bench, her knee brushing against mine.

I stared across the seagrass-covered dune, up toward the

lights shining in the neighbor's house half a mile away. My stomach flipped like an Olympic gymnast. "Why did you and Hunt break up?"

She lowered her gaze and picked at the frayed hemline of her denim shorts. "It wasn't working. And . . . I had my suspicions he liked someone else."

"Amie?"

Her head whipped up. Disappointment glazed her eyes. "It was obvious, wasn't it?"

I nodded. "Ever since that night, they went to see the band together. Are you upset about ending things with him?"

"To be honest . . . No, I'm not. It took us some time to realize we're just good friends. It's another relationship failure on my part. Do you think I'm going to end up just like my mother?"

"You're *nothing* like your mother."

"God, I hope not." She half-smiled as she tucked her hair behind her ear. Her emerald birthstone earrings sparkled, just like her eyes. She softened her voice. "I hope something good has come out of it, though. Being with Hunt made me see things that were right in front of me the whole time in a different light."

Was it wishful thinking to think it was me she was talking about? My vocal cords tightened like the strings on my bass guitar. "Did . . . did it have anything to do with me?"

"It had everything to do with you." Her voice was barely audible over the waves crashing in the distance.

Hot air rushed into my lungs. If my heart beat any louder, she'd hear it thump, thump, thump.

She rounded her shoulders and rubbed her arm. "When we were in Vegas, I'd decided to end things with Hunt, but we didn't get the chance to talk. Then, at the awards show, something unexplainable happened. It's crazy, but I got a static shock from you when you helped me out of the car. Everything changed in that moment. Everything became clear. For the first time in months, I knew what I wanted—it wasn't Hunt." A small smile touched her lips. "Everything I was fighting to find and have with him, I already had with you. You're my rock. It's taken me far too long to realize that."

A lump caught in my throat. It took me a second to grasp the magnitude of what she'd said. I reached for her hand and entwined our fingers. My palms tingled, feeling her silken skin beneath my callused fingertips. "That moment you had in Vegas happened to me a few months after my parents died. I couldn't explain what happened, but suddenly, I couldn't exist without you. But my grief consumed me. I got so lost, depressed, and drank way too much. Then we were back to recording and touring. I bottled everything up inside, didn't want to fuck with our friendship. Then Hunt happened. I didn't want to cause problems, so I lied about how I felt, kept my distance, and tried to stay out of the way." *Most of the time.*

She shook her head. "Don't do that anymore. I've made so many mistakes along the path to getting here, but now . . . you're all I see. I'm sorry being with Hunt hurt you. Is there any chance you'd be able to forgive me?"

I smoothed my hand over her hair and swept the loose strands behind her ear. "I'm crazy about you. So, I guess there's only one way I'll be able to forgive you. And that is . . . be mine."

Concern etched her brow. "I've just broken up with Hunt. Does that bother you?"

I didn't care if she'd broken up with Hunter five minutes, five hours, or five months ago—it was in the past. "No. No, it doesn't." My gaze fell to her gorgeous lips—lips I'd dreamed about tasting for years. "So, is it a yes?"

I held my breath. Waves crashed on the shoreline. People's high-pitched laughter wafted up from the beach. Crickets chirped in the grass beside the deck.

Gemma's gaze softened.

Her mouth curled into a smile.

She bobbed her head. "Yeah . . . I'd like that."

That was all I needed.

My heart soared through the clouds, pounded my ribs. "Then there's only one thing we need to do before we go down to the beach."

"And what's that?" Her eyes glimmered in the soft light.

"Something I should have done a very . . . *very* long time ago."

I cupped the side of her face, leaned forward, and touched my lips to hers. Time stopped. My heart hammered harder and faster. The world around me disappeared. Kissing her was everything. Everything and more. Soft. Sweet. Tender. Warm . . . Divine. She parted her lips and kissed me back. Heat shot over my skin. The whiskey on her lips warmed my insides. The scent of her floral perfume filled my head. Her touch ignited my soul. *Fuck yeah.*

As my eyes drifted shut, I teased my tongue along the seam of her mouth, then flicked it into her mouth to taste hers. To explore, savor, and cherish her. Her kisses, soft at first, became hot and hungry. She buried her hands in my hair, tugged on it and had my body craving more of her touch. More connection. More of her.

Control. I had to keep control.

Slow things down.

But *fuck*! . . . I was kissing Gemma. After endless months of agony, I was finally with her. I caressed her cheek, smiled against her lips, breathed her in. I ran my hands down her bare arms just to make sure I wasn't dreaming about her once again.

She yanked on my T-shirt, pulling me closer. Her fingernails scraped across my back, scratching my skin. *Fuck.* She could rip my clothes to shreds if she wanted to. The low murmur and hum deep in her throat turned me on and made my body ache . . . ache to have her.

Heat scorched my lips. She kissed me like she knew exactly how I liked to be kissed. Just a little tongue, a lot of touching and tasting. If I'd known she kissed like this, I would've done this years ago. Before Ben. Before the tour. Long before Hunter.

But *shit* . . . This was mind-blowing and crazy and perfect. There was no need to rush. Catching my breath, I rested my forehead against hers. "Gem, I'm yours. Have been for a long time."

"Shh." Her voice enveloped me like a warm embrace. "Kiss me again."

She edged closer, resting her leg on top of mine. She brushed her hand through the back of my hair and drew me toward her. My lips found hers again. Our tongues united, feeding off each other, shooting goosebumps down my arms.

Hmm. So fucking good. Her hands were everywhere. In my hair. On my back. Running over my shoulders and chest. Every time she moved, my fevered blood rushed south. My body temperature approached dangerous levels. My heart exploded with more passion than a stadium full of screaming fans. How was I supposed to maintain control when she felt so incredible?

She trailed her fingertips across my stomach, then skimmed them around my waist. *Fuck. That tickled.* I flinched and wriggled, not wanting to lose connection with her lips. She giggled against my mouth and slipped her hand underneath my T-shirt. "I love that you're ticklish."

"Don't be mean." I grinned, catching her hand.

The blaze from the bonfire peeking over the dunes caught my eye.

Shit. Time to stop.

Time for the beach.

But she clambered onto my lap, straddled my hips, and kissed me again.

Fuck!

All my good intentions disappeared. My heart was in freefall, not wanting to pull the ripcord to stop the adrenaline surging through my body. There was no way I could hide the effect she had on me. My cock grew harder and harder within the confines of my board shorts. Curling my arms around her, I pulled her closer. Her petite frame molded perfectly against my chest, intensifying the heat between us. Trying to keep my wits, I ran a line of kisses down the side of her throat. I licked and nipped, tasting the salty ocean on her skin as her pulse throbbed beneath my lips.

She was so perfect. So beautiful. Everything I'd ever wanted.

But damn it.

It was her birthday.

People were waiting down at the bonfire.

Summoning all my inner strength, I dragged my mouth away from hers. She panted, catching her breath. Her gorgeous lips glistened. Her eyes blazed with heat. It was impossible to look away.

"We need to get down to the beach." I struggled to find my voice as I hooked the shoestring strap of her tank top back onto her shoulder. It had slipped off during our kiss.

She barely nodded, traced my lips with her fingertips, and showed no sign of moving. "Whatever this is between us, I don't want to screw it up. Let's take it slow. Okay?"

"Yeah. Absolutely." But I clenched my jaw, trying to will away my hard-on and put out the fire in my blood. I could do slow. I'd go at whatever pace she needed to. Slow was way better than nothing. If I could kiss and touch her like this, I'd be fine. "Whatever you need, Gem. But I swear, I'm not going anywhere. Other than with you, down to the bonfire."

I lifted her off my lap, stood and gave her a *thanks-for-the-hard-on* smile. I held out my hand, but she glanced at my crotch. Then she looked up at me . . . Wildfire swirled in her eyes.

She stepped forward and grabbed the front of my T-shirt.

"I've changed my mind. I don't want to go slow." Her tone was low and hot. "Fuck the bonfire. Take me to bed. Now."

Chapter 23

GEMMA

Kyle's kisses had ignited something deep inside me, and I didn't want to switch it off. Standing in the middle of the deck, I clutched his shirt, drew him closer, and kissed him, long and hard and deep. Kyle dipped his knees and picked me up like I weighed no more than his Fender. I hooked my legs around his hips and my arms around his neck. He carried me into the house, dodged furniture, and tables, and headed up the stairs.

The moment Kyle gave me the necklace, I knew my heart belonged to him. When he said he was still crazy about me, everything fell into place. I'd thought I'd need time to get over Hunter, but that wasn't necessary. We were barely together. So why wait? Why go slow? Everything about Kyle felt right.

At the top of the stairs, I yanked at the back of his T-shirt, even before he placed me down inside his room. He gave me a wickedly sexy and devilish grin, reached over his shoulders, and tugged the shirt off. *Damn.* I couldn't keep my hands still. I glided them over his chest, his stomach. Touching every muscle that rippled in the soft light, added to my hunger.

My fingers trembled as I ripped off my moon boot. I couldn't go fast enough. Kyle kicked the door shut, tore back the bedcovers, then turned to me. He raked in a deep breath, his shoulders rising high, then lowering. His eyes, dark and smoldering, held me captivated. He stroked his calloused fingertips softly against the side of my cheek. "Gem, are you sure about this?"

I ran my hands around his waist. His skin blazed beneath my touch. His muscles tensed when I tickled him. I liked that. *Sweet torture.*

"Absolutely." I gently pushed him back onto the bed and mounted his hips. Flicking my hair to one side, I leaned forward and kissed him.

He cradled my head and buried his fingers in my hair. Shivers shot across my skin. His tongue entwined with mine in a perfect rhythm of touching, tasting, and teasing. A sexy murmur erupted in his throat, sending heat rushing through my veins. Since Ben, I'd only had sex with guys for fun—no emotional attachment. My heart hadn't entered this vulnerable territory for almost three years. My whole body shuddered—scared, excited, and totally intoxicated by Kyle. With each passing second, I felt myself falling . . . falling hard and fast.

I wriggled my hips against his, rubbing against his hardness. Heat ignited in my core. I wanted him . . . now. Shuffling backward, I trailed kisses down the side of his neck, across his chest, and over his stomach. His muscles flexed and quivered beneath my playful nips and kisses. At the top of his board shorts, I undid the tie and yanked the Velcro open.

"Gem, slow down."

"Kyle, I haven't had sex in nearly ten weeks. I need you naked . . . Now." I tugged his shorts lower.

His eyes flared with fire. With no hesitation, he raised his hips so I could wriggle off his shorts and boxer briefs and toss them aside. My heartbeat jumped, ogling him naked. His dick was rock hard. His chest heaved. His bronzed body was toned to perfection.

He grinned, sat up, and drew me onto his lap. His lips pressed against mine. "You are going to be the death of me if you look at me like that."

"Okay . . . but fuck me first."

He took a deep breath and held it. His gaze locked onto mine.

I brushed his hair away from his eyes. "What's wrong?"

His eyes smoldered like glowing embers. "Nothing. I just never thought we'd be here like this."

I silenced him with a kiss. We could talk later. But right now, I needed action. I wrapped my arms around his shoulders, crushing my chest against his. The air sizzled and sparked.

He grabbed the bottom of my tank top and pulled it over my head. His hand followed his gaze down to my push-up bra. He cupped my boob gently. Goosebumps skipped across my skin.

"Not much to play with, is there?" Giggling, I shrunk an inch back from him.

"More than enough." He slid his hands around me. With nimble fingers, he freed the bra clasp, and tossed the flimsy garment onto the floor.

He dragged his thumbs over my peaked nipples, tweaked them, then dipped his head, and took one into his mouth. *Oh yeah.* Arching toward him, I knotted my hands in his hair. He circled and flicked his firm tongue around my bud, nipping, licking, sucking. I moaned. My head fell back. Heat rippled through my body and tingled my toes.

I needed more. He didn't disappoint.

He gave equal attention to my other breast. His warm, wet tongue was pure magic. But I tugged on his hair and drew his lips back to mine. With each taste, our kisses grew hotter and harder and deeper. Dizziness spun through my head. As his feverish flesh pressed against mine, waves of heat coiled through me and pooled between my legs. I needed him. Wanted him. I could stay like this forever . . . connected to him . . . if it wasn't for the growing ache in my shin. "Kyle? I'm sorry. We have to move. My leg's hurting."

He snaked his hands around my hips, rolled me to one side, and lay me down on the mattress. But rather than lie on top of me, he sat beside my leg. He slid his hands over my calf muscle and gently massaged it. "Is it hurting too much? You want to stop?"

"Hell no." That was the most ridiculous thing I'd heard all day.

"Good." He threw me a breathtaking smile and crawled his way up the bed, kissing across the arch of my hip, over my stomach, up to my breasts, my throat, and back to my lips.

I grabbed onto his shoulders to draw him over me, but . . . he didn't move.

A devilish glint shimmered across his eyes. "Nah-ah. Your shorts? They have to go. That okay?"

I nodded as his fingers glided down my body, leaving a fiery trail in their wake. He fumbled with the button on my shorts, popped it open and agonizingly, slowly, painfully, lowered the zipper.

He brushed his fingers against my panties. Everything between my legs tensed, ached, anticipated.

"Want me to go slower?" Kyle's breathy voice hovered near my ear.

"No. Faster. Definitely faster." I clutched onto the bedsheets, resisting the temptation to tear my shorts off to speed up the process.

Kyle shuffled down the bed, eased off my shorts and panties, and tossed them aside, knocking over the bedside lamp. He chuckled softly. "Now we're wrecking the furniture . . . Nice!"

He crawled up the mattress and stretched out beside me. He edged in close, nudging his cock against my abdomen.

My fingers trembled, begging me to touch him. As we kissed, I ran my hand over his arm, his hip, his butt, his thigh, and up toward his groin. Raking my short fingernails gently through his pubic hair, I teased and tickled him. He squirmed once again.

"I never realized you were this ticklish." I smiled against his mouth. "It's like I'm torturing you."

"I think I can handle this type of torture."

"Good." I curled my hand around his rock-hard cock, stroking him as I circled the head with my thumb.

He moaned, murmuring through his teeth. He grabbed my hand, drew it away, and entwined our fingers.

"Gem, that's really good. But believe me when I say I won't last long if you keep doing that."

"Okay then. Touch me."

The corner of Kyle's mouth curled, full of predatory hunger.

My body hummed all over when his fingers headed between my legs. My eyes fluttered closed, my muscles clenched in eager anticipation. He teased and tickled the inside of my thighs, nudged my legs wider and made his way higher. He eased two fingers between my folds, circled and rubbed my clit, then dipped them inside me. He pulsed and drove and fucked me with them. *Oh yeah. So damn good.*

I gripped his shoulders and rocked toward his touch. My God, I was going to explode. I blinked my eyes open. He loomed before me, his eyes smoldering with hot desire.

"You like that?" he whispered. I didn't miss the strained control in his voice, the tension in his body, the need for more . . . of me.

But I could hardly breathe. My mind was nothing but haze. All I could do was nod. Pant. Beg for more.

"You feel so good." He rubbed me, teased me, stroked me. "So wet, so . . . mine." The possessive tone in his voice fed me like an aphrodisiac.

"Kyle." My voice was nothing more than a faint murmur. I was close. Too close to losing my mind. "Enough." I grabbed his hand. "I want you inside me . . . Now."

Faster than lightning, Kyle dove into the nightstand drawer, grabbed a condom, and rolled it onto his shaft. He edged his way in between my legs. Taking his weight onto his elbows, he hovered over me. His erection teased my opening.

My heart skipped against my ribs. *This was it.* I cupped his face, breathed him in, and wrapped my legs around his.

His gaze locked onto mine. "I want you so bad, Gem."

"Same."

As he crushed his lips against mine, he rocked his hips and nudged his cock against me. Slowly, he entered me. First an inch, then withdrawing, then sliding his sleek hardness all the way in.

My eyes widened, and shivers shot up my spine. *"Oh . . . wow."*

He froze.

"Sweet Jesus, Gem." He closed his eyes. His heart pounded beneath my touch.

"You okay?" I kissed the hollow of his throat, the side of his pulsing neck, then nibbled on his earlobe.

"Yes. I am now."

Then he moved, thrusting into me with a steady, rhythmical motion. A low groan rumbled deep inside Kyle's throat. The reverberations coursed through my veins and teased my nerve endings. I tightened my legs around him and rocked my hips to get deeper penetration. Every time he drove into me, my body craved more.

My core clenched tight. I ran my toes through the soft hair on his legs. "Damn, you feel good."

He thrust into me hard. Kissed me fiercely. Touched me sensually. Made my body hum. Every time our eyes met, his were full of so much adoration my heart faltered. I wanted to remember this moment. Our bodies were connected. Our hearts beat as one. This had changed something deep inside me. Maybe Kyle was right. We were soulmates. And now we were united.

I brushed my fingers down the side of his face. "Please tell me this feels right."

A slow smile touched his lips. "This is better than right. We're made for each other, Gem." He drove deeper into me, making my hips pulse. "But holy shit. When you rock against me like that, it makes me lose my mind."

"What? Like this?" I tilted and rolled my pelvis up against him.

His body shuddered, his cock throbbing inside me. He buried his face into the pillow beside me. "Yep."

"What if I do it again?" I snaked my hands around his shoulders and rocked my hips once more.

Kyle's head flicked back, and his face tensed. Seeing Kyle turned on like this had a profound effect on my heart—like it would never operate properly again without him.

"You're so bad." A sexy smile played across his mouth. He ran his hand down my side and over my leg. He hooked his palm underneath my thigh and lifted it up beside his hip. "Guess that means you're in trouble." He kissed me and thrust into me, gentle and deep, then hard and fast. Each drive sent shockwaves jolting through my system. He didn't relent.

My breath quickened, panting against his lips. I couldn't get enough of touching his body, kissing him, or tasting his mouth.

My hands gripped his hips. Blood whooshed in my ears. His hot flesh, glistening with sweat, sizzled against mine.

Kyle drove hard into me and hit that sweet spot deep inside. *"Oh . . . yeah. There."*

We moved as one. Panting. Rocking. Kissing.

His breath seared my skin as he trailed a line of hypnotic kisses toward my ear. "I love you . . . so fucking much."

My eyes flew open. The most intense orgasm ripped through me. My back arched, a bolt of energy shot up my spine and tingled the base of my neck. My body quaked beneath his.

My heart beat like a boombox. "Wh . . . what did you just say?"

He moaned and thrust again. Again and again. His heart thundered against mine. Then . . . he stilled. His body convulsed and shook with its own release.

I didn't want to move. The rush of blood left my head in a spin.

His gaze softened as he smiled. "I love you, Gem." The weight in his voice cinched around my heart. "Have for a long time."

Tears swelled in my eyes, and I drew him in to kiss. He curled beside me on the bed, pulling me into his arms. I rested my head against his shoulder and smoothed my hand over his chest, feeling the racing beat of his heart.

He loved me. Really loved me.

How did he survive seeing me with Hunter every day? If what I felt right now was love, I was in serious danger. Because if I ever lost this, I didn't know what I'd do. Music wouldn't be enough to help me survive losing this.

"Going slow didn't last long," I giggled. "Guess we got carried away."

"I'm not complaining." He hugged me tight and kissed my forehead.

"Neither am I." As I lay wrapped in his arms, a warm breeze wafted through the open window. I breathed in Kyle's spicy scent and traced lazy swirls over his chest, circled his nipples, and tickled his happy trail. I was beyond content, but painful thoughts lingered. "I'm so sorry about everything. About Hunt—."

Kyle placed his finger over my lips. "I don't ever want to think about Hunt when I'm lying here naked after making love to you. It's in the past. All I care about right now is that you're with me. I'm yours. This is our future."

"Maybe you're just the rebound guy." I injected a dash of cheekiness into my tone.

"Oh, rebound, you say." He flicked the sheet into the air, crawled on top of me and nestled between my legs. "Let's get this straight. I'm no rebound. I'm yours forever. There's nothing else to it."

My heart leaped as he kissed me. I felt like I was floating five thousand feet above the ground. I never wanted to look down, because if I fell from this high, my shattered heart would never mend.

Chapter 24

KYLE

I woke lying naked next to Gemma, her back to me. The navy-blue sheet draped over her waist as she snuggled it against her chest. Her gorgeous brown hair fell in long, soft waves halfway down her back. The mid-morning sun streamed in through the window and glowed golden on the tip of her shoulder. I had to rub my eyes to make sure I wasn't dreaming.

Playing dot to dot, I counted and memorized the location of the eleven tiny freckles on her back.

"You're going to have to stop doing that," she said in a sleepy voice.

"Stop what?" I shuffled closer, swept her hair to the side, and kissed the small of her neck.

"Watching me."

I curled my arm around her. "Just had to make sure last night was real."

"It does feel like a dream." She entwined her fingers with mine and kissed my hand. The touch of her lips on my skin sent a shiver up my arm. "Kyle . . . about last night—"

I closed my eyes and swallowed hard. Tightness gripped my chest as I braced for the worst. "What about it?"

"Being with you is incredible, but do you think we can keep it between us for now?"

Oh . . . That all? Phew. But . . .

I kissed along the line of her shoulder. "That may be hard, considering we have a house full of people downstairs."

Her body flinched. "I know. It's just that—"

"Gem, I won't say anything. It's surreal to me, too."

I'd bottled my feelings for her for so long, it wouldn't be an issue. I'd seen how hurt she was after Ben couldn't keep his mouth shut in interviews about their relationship. I'd take us being together to the grave if that was what Gemma wanted.

"Thank you. You're the best." Gemma rolled toward me and kissed my lips. She threaded her hands through my hair, and my dick sprang to life. Making love to Gemma twice last night had blown my mind. I'd gladly do it again, but if she didn't want all our friends to know we were together, we had to stop. I ran my hand down her arm, over her hip, and gave her a playful slap on the thigh. "Gem? You are very tempting and hard to say no to, but you have to go back to the city to help Kara today. And I can smell bacon cooking downstairs, which is calling my name."

"Kara will wait. Bacon can wait. I want to fuck you again."

"Hmmm." I moaned against her lips. "If you insist."

After another wicked orgasm and a quick shower, we dressed. I followed Gemma downstairs. My legs wobbled. Some distant memory flickered through my mind . . . I'd said she wouldn't be able to walk if I ever made love to her, but in fact, it looked like it was the other way around.

Kara—Gemma's best friend and a rising fashion designer— stood at the stove, flipping over-cooked strands of bacon in a pan. She glanced up, dropped the tongs, and rushed to Gemma's side. "What happened to you last night? You disappeared. Hunter told me you two broke up. I couldn't find you. Then I couldn't find Kyle and knew he'd be offering you a shoulder to cry on."

Oh . . . there was no crying. Pursing my lips to contain my grin, I walked past the girls standing in the middle of the kitchen and headed toward the bacon to finish the cooking . . . or save what was left of it.

"Kar, I wasn't upset." Gemma stole a glance at me. Her cheeks flushed red. "There was no crying involved."

I winked at her as I loaded the bacon into a dish and placed it on the counter next to the pan of broken fried eggs and the basket of bread rolls. Cooking definitely wasn't one of Kara's strengths. I grabbed a few plates and constructed breakfast sandwiches.

"What do you mean, there was no crying?" Kara grabbed a plate and squirted barbecue sauce onto her sandwich. "You broke up with Hunter. On your birthday. He's an asshole. Aren't you upset?"

"No." Gemma shook her head, smiled, and grabbed a sandwich. "I'm good. Real good. Thanks to Kyle." She bumped her hip against mine.

"You're welcome." I nudged my arm against Gemma's elbow and took a bite of my sandwich.

Kara's mouth fell open. Her eyes widened. She looked at me, then at Gemma, and then back again.

"Oh. My. God." Her voice went all Nicki Minaj, loud and high-pitched. "You two got together last night."

"Shhhhh." Gemma's finger shot up in front of her lips. "Keep your voice down."

Like Gemma, I glanced through the archway into the living room, where sleeping bodies sprawled across the floor, the sofas, the chairs, and even outside on the deck.

"How dare you, Kyle?" Kara's tone may have been menacing, but the brightness on her face told a different story. "How dare you take advantage of Gem when she's upset?"

"She wasn't upset. Trust me." I mumbled over a mouthful of sandwich and grinned.

"He's right." Gemma's eyes sparkled as she nibbled on a piece of crisp bacon. "Kar, Hunt and I were doomed from the start. But with Kyle . . . it's different. This feels right."

Kara put her sandwich down, jumped up and down, and clapped her hands. She leaped forward and hugged us. "Yay. About fucking time. Hunt was so wrong for you, Gem. But this"—she waved her finger back and forth between them—"is so good."

Warmth spread across my chest. *Yeah . . . it is.*

Now I had Gemma, I'd never let her go. Not ever.

A creak on the staircase stole my attention. Hunter's loping steps neared a skip. A mischievous glint blazed in his eyes and a devilish smile curled across his lips. Yep, there was no doubting what he got up to last night . . . not when Amie followed him with an air of defiance plastered on her face.

What did Hunter see in her?

"Morning." Hunter opened the fridge and grabbed a bottle of nearly empty orange juice.

"Wow, Hunt. It didn't take you long to get over me." Gemma winked at him, cocked her head to one side, and licked bacon grease off her fingers. "Hope she was worth it."

The evil glare she threw at Amie made me chuckle. Amie just sneered. Not sure her face could move any more than that.

Hunter hooked his arm around Amie's shoulders and drank the juice straight from the bottle. He wiped his mouth on his shirtsleeve and waved the bottle at Gemma. "Looks like it didn't take you long to get over me, either."

I froze, holding a slice of bacon an inch from my lips. I glared at Hunter, ready to defend what had happened between me and Gemma last night. It was special, not some lusty hookup.

"Guess so." A smile beamed across Gemma's face. She picked up her sandwich and took a big bite.

I let out my breath. Thank God there were no hard feelings between Gemma and Hunter. I loved how they could joke about what happened.

"Well, that's just great." Kara dusted crumbs off her fingertips onto the kitchen counter. "You all had sex, and I didn't. Because my boyfriend is at some fashion show without me. Guess which one of us is not happy this morning?" She glanced at her watch. "Shit. Time's getting away from me. Gem, eat up. We gotta get going. Or . . ." She waved her finger at us. "Are you going to find some other way back to the city?"

I chewed my mouthful of food to hide my smile.

"Wow . . . subtle, aren't you, Kar?" Gemma bobbed her head,

then shook it.

But Gemma didn't miss a thing, slapping me on the wrist for trying to steal a piece of bacon off her plate. I leaned in and kissed her on the cheek, but she quickly pulled away. The warning flashing in her eyes was like a stab to the chest. Did I have to stop doing the natural gestures I'd done for years? No more kisses on her forehead, her cheek, or the side of her head when others were around. Damn, this wouldn't be as easy as I'd thought.

Gemma wiped her fingers on a napkin, scrunched it into a ball, and dropped it on her plate. "Kar, Lexi and I promised we'd help you sort beads and buttons and stuff out at your work today. Unless . . ." Gemma turned to me, a sheepish smile played on her lips. "Kyle needs me to stay and clean up?"

The way her cheeks flushed when she looked up at me from underneath her long eyelashes made my heart skip a beat. If she stayed, I'd want to take her back to bed, and nothing would get done. It sounded like a fucking fantastic plan, but now that Gemma's leg was better, we'd be jumping back into work and traveling soon. She wouldn't get much time to see her girlfriends. "Gem, go have fun with the girls today. The cleaners will be here after lunch. Hunt and I will come home once everyone has left, and the place is in order."

"You sure?"

I nodded and leaned against the counter. "Yeah, we've got this."

As Amie grabbed a plate and made herself a sandwich, she glanced at Hunter, Gemma, and me. "Oh . . . We've had a slight change in schedule. I got an email from the executive team when we were in Vegas. They want to release another single off your last album. 'Rise Up' is a huge hit with the fans, so they want you to shoot a video clip. We'll meet with the production crew on Tuesday, stylists on Wednesday and fly to Hawaii at the end of the week to film."

"Whoa." A dull ache throbbed at the back of my skull. "Why weren't we involved in the emails or have a say in this? We're supposed to hit the studio for the new album."

"I know, but this is out of my control." Amie didn't look up from making her sandwich. "I've worked my ass off with the marketing team getting this organized and have secured an interview with *Entertainment On-Show* to promote the single. A journalist will fly out from LA and meet us at the resort."

"That's great." I rubbed at the ache in my brow. *Entertainment On-Show* was one of the largest entertainment networks in the country. They'd hardly given us any coverage before, so this was huge. "But you've known about this for days. Why is this the first time we're hearing about this? We've had no emails. No calls. No texts. No meetings."

Amie flicked her hair back, looking down her surgically modified nose. "Sorry, Kate and I had to make this happen. We can't knock back opportunities like this."

Hell no.

"So are we doing a promo tour for the single?" Gemma winced and closed her eyes, as if bracing herself for the answer. I knew where she was going with this. The three of us wanted to work on our next album more than anything. We wanted to see the end of our contract sooner rather than later.

"Yes." Amie's voice lacked any element of emotion. "Three weeks. We'll visit a few cities here in the US and the UK. Kate's scheduling the dates. We'll postpone hitting the studio until after that."

Muscles seized along the length of my spine. There it was . . . the delay. "This is bullshit." I fired up. "This is not what we wanted. We can hit the studio after filming. We'll easily get a few tracks laid down before promo."

"No can do." Amie shook her head. "You'll have photoshoots and back-to-back interviews, ready for the release."

Hunter clenched his fists, turned to Amie, and lowered his voice. "Why didn't you tell us . . . me . . . about any of this?"

Amie gave Hunter poor-puppy eyes and patted the side of his cheek. "We were too occupied with other things to talk business."

Hunter's sneer slowly morphed into a lopsided grin. The tension in his shoulders disappeared as he wriggled his eyebrows. He snaked his hands around Amie's waist, clutched her ass, and nuzzled into her neck. "Oh, yes, we were."

I puffed air through my nose and shook my head. How could he go near Amie? She'd withheld information from us. Hadn't fought for what we wanted. That was unacceptable. Inexcusable. But now Hunter was fucking her, how could Gemma and I make him see we needed a new manager? *Ugh!* We'll deal with that later. Tomorrow. Soon.

"Guys, this is shit." Frustration dug into Gemma's brow as she placed her hands on the countertop. "This wouldn't have happened if I hadn't broken my damn leg. I know the execs can pull this shit, but why now? Why when we're so close to hitting the studio?" She tilted her head to the side and glared at Amie. "Or is there something else you're not telling us? Has the album delay got anything to do with the Grant takeover of SureHaven?"

"I'm just following orders from up the food chain." Amie shrugged. "SureHaven wants to capitalize on your hit. We all make money out of this, so it's a good thing."

The hair on my arms prickled. We'd been kept out of the loop, and that wasn't right. Amie was up to something. Gemma had sensed it weeks ago, and that had triggered my suspicions. The way Amie brushed off conversations, the way she never directly answered a question, the way everything was so blasé didn't sit well with me anymore.

Kara wiped her fingers on a napkin. "Guys, it sucks recording is delayed, but you love video shoots and promo. Own that." Then she folded her arms and pouted. "I just can't believe you're going to Hawaii again. Without me."

Hunter leaned over the counter and ruffled Kara's hair. "We already have a stylist, sweetheart."

Kara swatted his hand away. "What makes you think I'd want to work for you anyway, asshole? I'm a designer, not a stylist."

Damn. I loved Kara's sass. And loved she didn't take any of Hunter's crap.

"Okay, enough, you two," Gemma placed her plate on the sink. "We better get going, Kar. You find Lexi, and I'll grab my gear."

I followed Gemma upstairs and sat on the bed while she dug

through her overnight bag.

"Gem, what's wrong?"

She grabbed her toiletries bag, ripped out her toothbrush and paste, and pointed them at me. "Amie shouldn't let SureHaven get away with this delay. She knows it's not what we want. I don't trust her anymore." She headed into the ensuite, wet her toothbrush and brushed her teeth.

"Neither do I."

She rinsed and wiped her mouth on a towel. "I don't want to delay recording. I want this contract with SureHaven to be over and done with."

"Me too." I leaned forward and rested my elbows on my knees. "We can't get out of our deal, but I wouldn't say no to getting rid of Amie."

"That's going to be hard." She dragged her feet out of the bathroom and tossed her toothbrush into her bag. "Hunt's really into her."

"Why?" Confusion pummeled my brain. But I knew better than anyone you had no control over who you fell for . . . or when.

"Trust me. I asked the same question."

"Well . . ." I caught her hand and drew her onto my lap. A small smile slowly inched across her lips. My heart somersaulted against my ribs. My future was different now. It had new meaning and purpose. Gemma was mine. That was everything. "If we have put up with Amie for Hunt . . . and deliver one more album . . . we're gonna suck it up and have fun, like we always do." I tucked her hair behind her ear, brushed my fingertips down her jaw, traced the fine line of her chin. "The best part about releasing another single, going on promo, then hitting the studio and doing another tour is that you and I will be together. And we can do what we did last night on repeat, every fucking day."

"Hmm." She ran her hands over my shoulders and linked her fingers behind my neck. "I'm looking forward to that."

"So am I." I leaned in and kissed the side of her neck. Her pulse quickened beneath my lips. I liked having an effect on her. Smiling, I made my way up to her ear, over her cheek, and down to her mouth.

"I have to go." She threaded her fingers into my hair and tugged on it. Drawing me forward, she kissed me again, flicking her tongue into my mouth and moaning. *Fuck*. My dick throbbed hard. Her breathy voice swept across my lips. "Shit. Kara's waiting."

"She can wait." Our mouths reconnected. The taste of peppermint toothpaste sweetened each touch of her tongue against mine. Her kisses were sensual and soft, then hungry and hot. Too hot. More of my fiery blood headed south. Running my hands around her hips, I drew her body closer to mine. She smiled and wriggled. A groan rumbled somewhere deep inside my throat. My want for her spiraled higher. Dizziness swam through my head. Electricity coiled along my spine.

I wanted more. More of her.

"Kyle? I'm sorry. We have to stop." Catching her breath, Gemma broke our searing kiss. Desire burned in her green eyes as she placed her palms on my thundering chest. Sparks zapped the air.

"Yeah. Otherwise the whole house will know we're together. You don't want that, right?"

"No," she pouted. "Not yet."

"Okay." But fuck . . . I wanted to get naked with her again.

Until that happened, I had to keep in control. Had to slow it down.

Slowitdownslowitdownslowitdown.

But not for long.

I kissed her lips and helped her to stand. "So . . . would it be okay if I come over to your place tonight?"

"I'd like that." Gemma tugged on the front of my T-shirt. "How's seven? Don't call, just come."

Still in freefall, I never wanted to come back to the ground. Being with Gemma was everything I'd ever wanted. Nothing and no one would ever tear us apart. Not ever.

Leaning forward, I hovered my lips an inch away from hers. "Can't wait. I'll be there."

Chapter 25

GEMMA

Kyle arrived at 7.01 p.m. I hated he was late. *Not!* I barely let him take two steps inside my front door before I'd torn off half of his clothes. Shirts and board shorts, shoes and underwear were scattered across the floor by the time we reached my sofa.

The next few days followed a similar ritual. Daylight hours were spent at meetings, nights were spent with Kyle. *Hot fun.* And at the end of the week, in the pouring rain, I arrived in Maui, Hawaii, with the guys, our entourage, and production crew, ready to film a video clip.

As I walked into the private three-bedroom villa I'd be sharing with the guys, I dropped my tote bag and placed my guitar case in the middle of the floor. I ripped open the organza curtains that led onto the timber lanai and looked over the crystal blue plunge pool and beautiful gardens. Everything was getting a solid soaking of rain. This wasn't your typical Hawaiian shower that disappeared within the hour. This was set in rain, and showed no sign of clearing anytime soon.

"Gem, want a beer?" Hunter called from the kitchenette.

"Hey, I'll get her a drink." Kyle dashed for the fridge and opened the door. "She's my girlfriend now. Remember?"

"Dude. It's a fucking drink." Hunter splayed his hands out wide and stepped out of the way.

"I don't care who gets me a beer. Just hurry up about it." I met Kyle halfway across the room and stabbed my finger against his chest. "You behave." I took the beer from him. Having Kyle rush to wait on me though, was kinda cool.

"Always." He gave me an innocent smile and kissed me on the forehead.

"This villa's huge. It's a waste, isn't it?" Hunter cracked open his beer and strolled over to the sofa. "You two will share a room, and I intend to be with Amie whenever I get the chance."

I wrinkled my nose. "First, when have you cared about where we stay as long as it's five-star, and second, I really don't want to think about you tapping Amie. Ever."

"Why?" Hunter laid his arm across the back of the sofa and gave me a playful smile. "Are you having regrets we broke up, babe?"

I choked on a mouthful of beer. "God, no. Never." My time with him had been one crazy chapter in my life. Despite the drama and heartbreak, he'd helped me take a chance on love and opened my heart again. Now I wanted to look forward to the future, not dwell on the past.

Kyle flicked the cap off his beer bottle at Hunter, then sat down beside him. "You had your chance with Gem. Let it go."

"Why? Are you afraid she's going to come crawling back to me?" Hunter's eyes shimmered with cheekiness. "She'd have to do it on her knees."

"Ew." I sat on the sofa opposite the guys. "There will be no crawling. Ever."

But Kyle glared at Hunter. "Don't talk to her like that." The sinister edge in his tone made the hair on my arms prickle. I wouldn't have these two fighting over me . . . again.

"I'm just having a dig at you." Hunter laughed, punching Kyle in the arm. "You two belong together. While I have no regrets about being with Gem, I'm sorry I caused a hurdle on the way to the inevitable."

I glanced at Kyle. Yeah, we were good. My heart swelled, filling my chest as he winked at me.

"Hunt, it's behind us. Can we just move on?" Sighing, I slumped onto the sofa. *Yep, over it. Time to move on.*

"Already have." Hunter raised his beer. "Gem, you'll always be my number-one girl. Kyle, you'll always be my best bud. I swear to you guys, nothing will ever come between us again. Not even someone like Amie. She's nothing but some fun for now."

Hunter may have acted flippant, but he'd fallen for Amie hard. I wasn't convinced that was a good thing. I cared about him a lot and didn't want him to get hurt.

"Time for another beer." Kyle leaped from the sofa, headed toward the fridge, and grabbed three fresh bottles. When he returned, he sat down next to me and grabbed his beeping cell phone out of his pocket. He read the message. "Shit. It's Kate. We have to go meet with her and review everything for our interview tomorrow with Gerard What's-His-Face."

"No time to rest, right?" I drained my first beer, stood, and grabbed the fresh bottle. "Come on, guys. Let's get this over and done with."

Another day. Another interview. Easy.

***

Torrential rain battered the roof as I walked out of the bedroom in Kate's villa, glammed up in a designer T-shirt and jeans. I made my way over to the guys and Bec, our PA, standing off to one side of the room. Carla followed me and fussed over my flat-ironed curls while Kate and Amie ordered the three *Entertainment On-Show* crew around, telling them where to put things. The sofa had been pushed back against the wall for our interview. Warm lighting hung from stands, silver deflectors were in position, boom mics dangled overhead, and two video cameras had been mounted on tripods.

"Ready?" I stretched from side to side after sitting for too long, getting my hair and make-up done.

"Always." Kyle rocked on his heels.

"This will be a piece of cake." Hunter flicked his hair back. "We've done this a million times. There's nothing we can't handle."

Kate walked over to us, stepping over cables and power cords, and ducking under a deflector. "You all set? We rehearsed your responses yesterday, so you should be fine. This guy from *On-Show* is new, but he knows the rules for being here. As always, questions about your personal life are off limits."

"Can we have some fun with him if he's a freshman?" Hunter's eyes glinted as he rubbed his hands.

I giggled. *So Hunt.* I loved it when we took control and direction of interviews, especially with inexperienced journalists and reporters who got nervous and tongue-tied around us.

"Oh, this guy's experienced, just new at *On-Show*," Kate warned. "So watch yourselves."

The door to the villa swung open, and in walked a short man in a beige suit and black button-down shirt. His balding head shone in the bright lights, and his beady eyes surveyed the room. He strolled into the center of the room as if the world operated on his time schedule.

"Great," I mumbled under my breath. "This guy will give you a run for the title of Mr. Arrogance, Hunt."

"He's no challenge." Hunter straightened to show off his full six-foot, two-inch stature.

"We've dealt with reporters like this before." Kyle rubbed my back but quickly drew his hand away. "Let's get it over and done with."

Kate led us over and introduced us to Gerard.

"Hello." I shook Gerard's weak hand before taking a seat between Kyle and Hunter on the black leather sofa. Hunter grabbed a cushion and stuffed it behind his back, elbowing me in the ribs. I grunted and slapped him on the arm. Kyle shuffled an inch closer, his leg brushing up against mine. The contact reassured me that everything would be fine.

Gerard sat on an armchair off to the side, crossed his legs, and rested his leather-bound notebook on his thighs. His wrist hung over the end of the armrest, his nails well-manicured and polished. With a snap of his fingers, he demanded herbal tea from one of his crew. If he was trying to channel Graham Norton, he was doing a fine job, but too diva-ish for my liking.

With a tug on his shirt collar, Gerard cleared his throat and ran over the interview outline. Once everyone was ready, the questions and cameras rolled. Five minutes passed with the usual pleasantries like, "What did you do after the tour?" and "How's your leg, Gemma?" before the line of questioning deepened.

"You're here shooting the film clip for 'Rise Up,' an *amazing* track off your album. Is it true you're giving all the proceeds to the Children's Leukemia Research Foundation?" Gerard tapped his pen against his notebook.

"Yes," Kyle dipped his chin. "We've been big supporters of raising money and awareness of leukemia since my sister's death from the disease nine years ago."

I didn't know how Kyle kept his emotions under control when asked about his sister, or how much this song meant to him personally. My heart hurt every time we talked about Emily. I'd loved her and missed her every day.

"Did you write the lyrics, Kyle?" Gerard looked down the bridge of his nose.

"It was a collaboration. Gemma and I wrote it with Deeno Clark. He's a sick producer, and we were stoked to work with him."

"Were you involved, Hunter?" Gerard clicked and spun the pen around in his fingers.

Gerard's constant pen-tapping niggled at the base of my neck. My hand twitched, wanting to grab the pen and throw it across the room . . . or spear him in the eye with it.

"Nah." Hunter smoothed his hands over his jeans. "But it's a wicked song to sing live. We're looking forward to doing a promotional tour when it's released."

"How does that make you feel when Gemma and Kyle are off writing songs without you?" Gerard's tone took a sharp turn. I wriggled in my seat. This question wasn't on our list. While we were happy to ad-lib and go with the flow, something in Gerard's tone and attitude set off an alarm inside my head.

"It doesn't faze me." Hunter never missed a beat with his quick responses. "We work on different tracks with different people. We mix it up and get to work with the best in the industry."

We certainly did. We'd learned so much. But I was itching to work on our own material. That would happen . . . soon.

Gerard turned over a page of his interview agenda but didn't even glance at it. His eyes locked onto me, and a crooked grin inched across his mouth. The hair on the back of my neck stood on end.

"The three of you obviously get on very well." He arched an inquisitive eyebrow. "Gemma, how do you cope with hanging out with two of the best-looking guys in the business?"

I smiled and took an even breath. This question wasn't on our agenda either, but this one I could handle. I'd been asked this question a hundred times before. "It's tough, but someone has to do it. I've known these two guys since high school. They're my ride or die. Our friendship means the world to me."

"Hmm. I bet it does." Gerard gave that pause—that disbelieving pause we'd all heard before. Gerard poked his pen in the air . . . at me. "Can you honestly tell me you've never had a romantic relationship with either Kyle or Hunter? Can you sit there and tell me that all the photos and rumors flooding the Internet are idle gossip?"

What the fuck?

I glanced at Kate. She stepped forward. "Gerard." Her tone was acidic. Ice hardened her gaze. "This line of questioning is inappropriate. If you wish to continue, I'd take an alternate route. I'm not sure your boss would like a call from me canceling this interview."

Gerard held up his hands. "My apologies. But if it's such a touchy subject, there must be some truth to it."

"You wish." I smirked and shook my head. But my pulse pounded against my temples. I dug my fingernails into my palms to stop myself from flying forward and socking Gerard in the face. *Breathe. Just breathe.* This guy was pure asshole.

"Gerard, stop wasting our time," Kyle snapped. "Get on with

your interview, or we walk."

"This is obviously a sensitive topic, Kyle." Gerard leaned forward. "I've seen several photos online of Hunter and Gemma together over the past few months. Is there something going on with these two you're not happy about?"

Kyle laughed and brushed his hand over his thigh. "There is nothing going on between Gemma and Hunter. I can assure you of that."

"You're quick to defend. Do I detect a hint of jealousy? Or are you the one with Gemma?" Gerard's eyes glistened and his wicked grin widened.

Kyle shook his head. "No. I'm not with Gemma." His tone remained calm, level, unwavering.

Damn . . . we had good media training.

But my throat ran dry. We'd all deflected the truth in front of the cameras before, but the ease with which Kyle had done it sent a chill through my bones.

He'd done this for me. Because I was a fucked-up mess. Paranoid. And wanted to protect what we had. We had so little privacy. Was it wrong I didn't want our new relationship to be in the headlines? No . . . no it wasn't. *Fuck Gerard.*

Kyle continued without missing a beat. "I'm pissed off that you're more interested in our love life than the cause we're trying to raise awareness of."

Gerard rubbed the side of his cheek. "Don't get me wrong, I think it's great what you're doing for sick children, but why do you never discuss your relationships? There are rumors flooding the Internet, and I want to uncover the truth."

My mind sifted through my focusing techniques. I tried to visualize a pinpoint of light. Tried to breathe evenly. *In. Out. In. Out.* But nothing worked. All my self-control vanished. Rage shot through my veins, bursting like the banks of a flooded river. I leaned forward and gave Gerard a frosty stare. "There's nothing going on between us. We're the best of friends. Why can't you or anyone else in the media accept that? Are you just a prick trying to create unwarranted gossip to sell your stupid magazines? We're tired of defending ourselves. Tired of telling you the truth over and over again. It's exhausting. I'm done. This interview is over." I jumped off the couch and stormed toward the door.

"Gemma, get back here now," Amie called out.

Ignoring Amie, I rushed out the door and stormed across the lawn over to the main resort pool. I turned my face skyward and let the heavy droplets splatter my skin. The warm summer rain was welcoming, but didn't cool my boiling body temperature.

I paced back and forth along the edge of the pool, venting. "The nerve of Gerard. How dare he ignore our interview rules? He'll never do it again. He's blacklisted forever. What was he trying to achieve? I don't care who he works for. He's a fucking dickhead. Asshole. Rampant motherfucker."

But wait. My overreaction wasn't about Gerard. It was about Kyle.

Nausea swayed through my stomach. I'd hated he'd lied. For me. *Fuck.*

"Gem?"

I stopped pacing and turned. Kyle strode toward me. His black T-shirt clung to his toned arms and shoulders. Rain dripped from the tips of his short hair and his dark eyes flooded with concern. "You okay?"

"No. I'm not. Who the fuck does that guy think he is?" I flicked my hand toward the villa.

"He's a jerk. We sized him up before the interview started. You can't let him get to you, otherwise he's just going to write bullshit about us."

I pressed my clenched fists against my head. "That's not why I'm upset."

He took a step closer, keeping a careful three feet between us, aware eyes from the villa would be on us. "Then what is?"

My hands shook as I wiped the rain from my face. My heart ached, and tears threatened to fall. "It's the first time we've lied about being together, and I wasn't prepared for how that would make me feel. It was shit, by the way. Hit me harder than expected. We've covered for each other so many times before, but this was different. Weird. Wrong. But we're right. I mean that. I just need to get my head straight. I want to protect us for as long as possible."

"Gem, I want that too. Lying sucked, but I'd lie under oath for you. You're all that matters." He gave my arm a quick rub. "I want to hold you right now, but that prick's photographer is standing in the doorway with his telescopic lens pointed at us." He stuffed his hands into the front pockets of his jeans. "Gem, I don't want a media fiasco surrounding us. Like you, I want to keep what we have private. We're still new, finding our feet, navigating our way forward. I don't want the paparazzi following us every second of the day. So . . . we've got this. We'll keep our relationship under wraps for as long as possible. I promise. You and I, and a handful of close people, are the only ones who need to know the truth. Fuck everyone else."

God, he melted my heart. I sniffled and rubbed my nose. "True. But you have to admit, it was so much easier when we were just friends."

"Yes, but life changed." His gaze softened. "Gem, we're together and we're good. You can say whatever you have to in an interview to keep those journo-pigs off us. But what you need to know is when the cameras are off, the doors are closed, we're alone, at home or with people we trust, I love you and I'll always be there for you. I'm yours."

I pursed my lips and nodded. He always said the right thing. Always calmed me. In the heavy rain, my long hair hung in droopy curls down my back and clung to my face, neck, and T-shirt. "Kyle, I so want to hug you, but that prick is watching, and it pisses me off. I can't believe I let this Gerard-fucker get to me."

"Hey." Hunter came out of the villa and jogged across the lawn underneath a green golf umbrella. "You two done? Amie and Kate want you back inside. They've given Gerard a good revving. Everything should be fine now."

"I need a few more minutes." I dug down deep to regain my composure. This wasn't my first horrid interview. I'd be fine in five minutes . . . maybe ten. Fifteen tops.

"Gem?" Hunter play punched my arm. "Don't let that jerk

upset you." A cheeky grin slid across his mouth. "I loved how you stormed out on him, though. That was fucking brilliant."

Smiling, a small sense of satisfaction rippled through me. *Yeah, fuck Gerard.* "That's the first time I've walked out on an interview. Bound to happen at some point in our lives, right?" I wrung out my shirt. Pointless, considering we were still standing in the pouring rain.

"Yep. But Gerard deserved it. Why don't we put that asshole in his place?" A goofy grin spread across Hunter's face. His eyes shimmered like his brain ticked in overtime with ideas and options. "Gem, you're still upset, so there's no way we're going back into that interview today. Amie can deal with Gerard." He jutted his chin at Kyle. "Gem needs alcohol and some fun, and I've got the cure."

Intrigue set in Kyle's eyes. "What did you have in mind?"

"Gem? You game?" Hunter's eyes sparkled; a sure sign he already had a plan.

"Always." I nodded, placing my hands on my hips.

Hunter threw the umbrella into the garden, dipped his shoulder, and grabbed me around the waist. He tossed me over his shoulder and ran toward the pool.

I squealed and laughed. "Hunt. No. What are you doing?"

Without breaking stride or his hold on me, he leaped into the air and jumped into the pool.

Warm water and bubbles swirled around me.

Breaking above the surface, I laughed and wiped my eyes. "This wasn't what I thought you had in mind."

"You were already wet." Hunter flicked water in my face again.

"Why . . . you—" I swam toward him, placed my hands on his shoulders and pushed down hard, dunking him under the water. He swam away from me and resurfaced.

"Hunt, you crazy son-of-a-bitch." Kyle chuckled and waved from the edge of the pool. "Come on, let's go get a drink."

I swam to the edge of the pool, struggling in my wet clothes. Kyle held out his hand to help me out. I grabbed it, put my foot against the edge of the pool, and pushed backwards. Kyle lost his balance and plunged into the pool beside me.

"Is this what I get for trying to be nice?" He grinned, flicking the water out of his hair. His eyes glistened and dimples formed at the sides of his mouth. "We'll see about that." Kyle dove toward me.

I squealed again and tried to escape, but Hunter caught my ankle. The three of us splashed and charged and dunked each other under the water. I hadn't laughed so hard in ages. Playing around like this was the medicine I'd needed. It reinforced the fact our friendship was unbreakable.

"Hunter. Gemma. Kyle. Out of the pool. Now!" Amie shouted from the side of the pool, waving her umbrella and pointing her finger. "We have an interview to get through, and you're acting like immature teenagers. Get. Out. Now."

"No. Sorry, Amie." Kyle ran his fingers through his wet hair, leaving tousled trails in their wake. "We're done for today."

"That interview was shit." Hunter swam up to the side of the pool and rested on his elbows. "Gerard's a dick. Tell him he needs to pull his head out of his ass if he wants to come on the video shoot tomorrow, or you can send him back to LA."

"This PR opportunity is huge. Don't fuck it up. Now, get out of the damn pool." Amie seethed.

Hunter tapped his hand on the edge of the pool. "Not going to happen. Gem's done. We're done." Hunter pushed off the side and swam back to where I stood in the chest-deep water next to Kyle.

Amie pointed her finger to the ground. "Hunter, get over here now."

"Later, Ames." Hunter turned to us. "That swim-up bar over there is open. How about that drink? Let's go."

With a salute to Amie, Hunter dove underwater and headed toward the bar. Amie swore, turned, and stormed back toward the villa.

I turned to Kyle. "Can you believe Hunt just did that? He hates confrontation."

"I know." Kyle trailed his hands through the water. "Maybe him sleeping with her is a good thing after all. It will keep Amie in her place."

"We can only hope." I closed the gap, leaving only a foot of distance between us. I wanted Kyle's arms around me. Wanted to float like honeymooners over near the pool's infinity edge or kiss him underneath the waterfall. But I couldn't do those things without making the headline news . . . or letting him into my guarded heart. Both scared the hell out of me, but I'd face them when the time was right. "Hey . . . I'm sorry about today. I'll be prepared for the next interview."

"Think nothing of it." Kyle brushed the tip of my nose with his fingertip. "We all have our good and bad days."

I reached underwater and tugged on his T-shirt. Damn, he looked good. All wet. And hot. All . . . mine. "I so want to kiss you right now."

"Please don't tempt me." He lowered his voice. The seductive tone rippled through my entire body. "There's nothing in the world I'd like to do more, but we're too exposed out here." I let go of his shirt and swam back a foot. "How about we have a drink with Hunt, then head back to our villa? He'll have to have some serious make-up sex with Amie, so we'll have the place to ourselves."

Alone time. I liked that. "One drink, then let's give that spa in our room a workout."

I glanced toward Kate's villa. Gerard stood by the window with his arms folded, watching us. Next to him, his photographer had his camera in hand and the long lens pointed at us. *Assholes.* I smiled and flipped them the bird, then swam toward the bar with Kyle.

Tomorrow, I'd have my emotions in check and be more prepared to take this dipshit Gerard head-on. I'd get through the day with Hunter and Kyle by my side. Gerard would go home with nothing but a professional interview—not about my relationship with the guys, but about our music and to raise awareness and money for Kyle's leukemia foundation. It was a cause close to his heart. Mine and Hunter's too. We'd loved Emily like a sister. We'd get through Gerard's questions. Shoot footage for the video clip. Head home.

We'd do this . . . together. Like always.

But first . . . I needed that drink.

Chapter 26

KYLE

I raised my arm and rolled my shoulder, trying to loosen my stiff muscles. After two days of filming in Hawaii, every muscle ached from pulling on cables and hoists. On the first day of our shoot, we'd flown to the Big Island to film on the lava fields. Yesterday, we'd headed to Kauai to film at Wailua Falls. After Gerard and his team left, we went ziplining at Koloa. *Fucking awesome fun.* But now I paid the price. Everything hurt.

Staggering out of the bathroom, I heard voices and the soft strum of a guitar coming from the living room. I ambled toward the door, opened it, and stopped in my tracks. Gemma sat next to Hunter on the sofa. They leaned into each other, the sides of their heads touching. Gemma had her old guitar propped across her lap and plucked softly at the strings. Hunter sang too low for me to make out any words.

I snapped my eyes shut and swallowed the bitter taste tainting my mouth. It had been months since I'd sat curled up on a sofa and played music like that with Gemma. I didn't realize how much I'd missed it until seeing them in the zone. Sure, we'd played music nearly every day. We'd jammed, rehearsed, and performed. But that wasn't the same as creating . . . sitting in the quiet with a guitar and letting the music or a feeling guide you. It was how we usually wrote all our songs.

But my hands twitched. I hated waking up without her beside me. I didn't like the knots tightening in my stomach as they sat close together. I cursed under my breath, wanting to kick myself for letting my jealousy flicker to life. Hunter and Gemma were friends. Best of friends. I knew that. This feeling was unjustified . . . *Right?*

Drawing my shoulders back, I walked over to them, leaned in, and gave Gemma a lingering kiss on the mouth. Hunter didn't flinch. Yeah, that cleared my mind. I sank my ass onto the coffee table and curled my hand around Gemma's bare leg. "Morning. You guys working on something new?"

"Maybe." Her smile, bright like the morning sunshine, stirred my dick to life. How could it not when she wore one of my old T-shirts, and nothing else that I could see? *Yep, instant boner.* "Listen to this. Hunt, sing." Gemma nudged Hunter on the side and strummed a few notes.

Hunter licked his lips, swallowed hard, then sang.

> *How could one night with you*
> *Change my whole point of view?*
> *Love used to be a game*
> *But now I'm not the same*
>
> *You've taken my heart by its strings*
> *And turned me upside down*
> *Is this something wicked?*
> *Is this love that we've found?*
>
> *Because my mind's all hazy*
> *And I'm feelin' a little crazy*
> *Whenever you're around*
> *My heart leaps and bounds*
> *If this is love, if this is love*
> *Oh, baby, please*
> *Lay it on me*
> *Pile it on, stack it high*

Oh yeah
Give it to me

"Wow." I blinked. "That's cool. I love the beat. You guys wrote that this morning? That's awesome."

"Yep." Gemma slipped her fingers along the steel strings. "Hunt came up with the chorus. I've been tweaking the tune. We've just been killing time, waiting for you to get your ass out of bed."

"I needed sleep. It's been a big few days. Aren't you sore after ziplining?" I rolled my shoulder again.

"Nope." Gemma shrugged.

"I fucking ache all over." Hunter sat upright and stretched. "There's only one cure for stiff muscles, and that's sex. I'll leave you two to it and go find Amie."

"Didn't you stay with her last night?" I rubbed my tired eyes. He'd gone to her villa after we'd had a drink at the bar. I hadn't heard him come back to our villa. But then . . . I'd been with Gemma, and we hadn't been quiet in the spa or the bed before we'd fallen asleep.

"No. She was working, so she kicked me out. But I think she needs a morning wake up call from *moi*." Hunter stood and headed for the door. "I'll be back here in two hours to leave for the airport. Have fun." He waved over his shoulder and headed out the door.

The second it closed, I fell onto my knees in front of Gemma and shuffled across the shag-pile rug to steal another kiss. "I missed waking up next to you. I thought after the video shoot, ziplining, and some wicked sex, you wouldn't be able to walk."

She set her guitar aside. "I did struggle and had to crawl out here on all fours."

I chuckled, ran my fingers along her necklace, then tugged at the neckline of her shirt. "So . . . this is where my shirts keep disappearing to."

"Do you want it back?"

She grabbed the bottom to lift it, but I stopped her and sat back on my haunches. "I like you wearing it. It makes me horny."

She narrowed her eyes and raised a sexy eyebrow. "I like you being horny."

"Good, because I think I'm going to have this problem for a long time."

She broke out singing softly.

> *I make you horny, horny, horny*
> *In the morning sun*
> *I never, never, never*
> *Knew I turned you on*

"Hmm . . . I don't think that song will make the cut somehow."

"No. Me either." She ran her hands up my arms. "I'm sorry if my playing woke you. I couldn't sleep. All these new lyrics and tunes are jumping around in my head, so I thought I'd come out here and write some down."

"Do you want me to join you?"

"Sounds perfect."

Gemma picked up her guitar and strummed away while I dashed into our room to grab my guitar.

When I returned, Gemma hummed with her eyes closed. Her cheeks were rosy pink. Her lips glistened as a small smile curled across her mouth. We'd had so many early morning starts, so many moments waking up in the same multi-room suites on the tour, but this morning was different. She was different. And I couldn't work out why.

Taking a seat beside her, I kissed her on the cheek.

"Gem, there's a strange vibe coming off you this morning. I think it's a good one, but I'm not so sure." My heart beat with caution. "Does it have something to do with Hunt?"

"God no." She shook her head. "It has nothing to do with him. But he was the one who pointed it out."

I sucked in a sharp breath. "Pointed out what?"

She leaned over and kissed me softly on the lips. "Can we not talk about this now?"

"So you can talk to Hunt about why you're acting all weird, but not me?" *Shit.* I didn't mean to snap, but my insecurity flared.

"It's nothing."

"Then tell me."

Her cheeks flushed as she bit her lip.

Her silence unnerved me, prickled my skin.

I stared at my hands, not knowing whether I was hurt, disappointed, or petrified by what she wasn't telling me. My only comfort was that she kissed me again.

"Alright." I plucked my guitar loudly. "We don't have to talk if you don't want to."

"It's not that." She swiveled toward me. Her knee brushed against my thigh. "After everything that happened with Gerard and our horrid interview . . . I want you to know . . . I'm scared. Scared of lying. Scared of how I'm feeling. Scared of the world finding out about our relationship before we know what it is."

My heart lurched. How could I put her mind at ease? I placed my guitar on the floor and entwined my fingers with hers. "Gem, I'm the same. I'm terrified this bubble will burst. I'm scared of how much I love you. Scared of losing you. Everything is so new and fresh and crazy. We need time for things to settle."

She ran her fingertips down my cheek and kissed my lips. "I know. Now . . ." She picked up her guitar. "Let's write some tunes."

I pushed the coffee table out of the way. I grabbed some of the throw cushions and made myself comfortable on the floor. Picking up my guitar, I plucked away in time with the tune she played.

"What do you think about this?" she asked, then sang.

After making love all night
This feeling is oh-so right
I'm dancing on cloud nine
Won't you let me be your valentine?

I shuddered. "Dear God, no." Lyrics swirled around in my head as I tweaked a tuning key. "What about something like this?" I strummed a few chords, slowed them down, then played a gentle romantic riff. Gemma stopped playing and gazed at me. A spark skipped in the air. With a smile, I lowered my voice and sang.

I'll be your drug, I'll be your fix, I'll be your ecstasy
Feel me charge up through your veins, I'll be your everything
No need to rush, no need to speed, no reason to fly
I'll be the one for you, I know I'm willing to try

You have my heart, my soul, you are, the air that I breathe
Just give me one chance, why don't you come be with me?
No need to rush, no need to speed, no reason to fly
I wanna love you every day 'til we die

Wanna touch your face, kiss your lips, and feel your skin
I'm so hot for you, I don't know where to begin
No need to rush, no need to speed, no reason to fly
I know you want me, I see the look in your eyes
I love you so much, I should have known
My heart is yours and so is my soul

"Wow." Her eyes glassed over, and she touched the necklace I'd given her. "That's beautiful."

"You like that?"

"Yeah. A lot."

I put down my guitar and crawled over to her. I curled my hands around her ankles and ran them up her silky-smooth bare legs. Taking her guitar, I placed it on the floor. The shirt she wore had ridden up to reveal her black lacy boy-leg panties. The glimpse gave me an instant hard-on.

"You should not wear clothes like this around Hunt."

"Why not?" She jerked her chin back. "I always wear stuff like this to bed."

"Because it's so fucking sexy."

I slid my hands up along her thighs and dipped my head to follow them with kisses. I shuffled between her legs, edging them wider, and worked my way upward with the softest touches. Her smooth flesh was warm beneath my lips.

"You think your old shirt is sexy?" Gemma ran her hands through my hair.

Nearing her groin, I lifted her shirt and blew my hot breath across the front of her panties. "On you . . . definitely."

She didn't stop my advances. Nuzzling my nose against her panties, I breathed her in. I nipped and tugged on the lace. Her eyelids fluttered closed, and her hips pulsed. She let out a soft moan, sending a hum coursing through my body.

I loved that doing this made her putty in my hands. I traced along the top of her panties, tickling and brushing her smooth belly before following the squiggly line of flowers in the lacy fabric downwards. At the bottom edge of her panties, I hooked my finger through the crotch of lace and tugged the stretchy fabric aside. My cock throbbed, eager to plunge inside her.

But not yet.

I wanted to taste her. Lick her. Make her melt.

I kissed her smooth, waxed skin. The scent of her arousal hit me, and I was a lost man. I pulled the fabric farther aside and ran my tongue up her slit. Her body jolted. A gentle whisper escaped her mouth. "Kyle."

"Yeah?" I did it again, this time tasting her saltiness. I swirled my tongue around her warm, swollen bud. Fire ignited in my stomach. My blood rushed through my veins. I wanted more. But damn, her panties were in the way.

"Had enough, Gem?"

"Nope. Not yet."

"Good."

I sat back, grabbed the waistband of her panties, and tugged them down her legs. I tossed them onto the floor. Shuffling back between her thighs, with her bare before me, I lowered my head. Her legs fell wider apart, giving me full access. I slid my finger through her slit and dipped into her wetness. My mouth and tongue took possession of her hot clit.

Her hips pulsed against my licks, nips, and sucks. The rolling '*mmm*' sounds in her throat spurred me on. I gently drove my finger in and out of her. Her warmth slick on my fingers and the taste of her on my tongue made my dick ache for action. But he could wait. Her pussy was too fucking perfect.

Gemma's legs curled around my back. Her muscles strained. Panting, she clawed at the edge of the sofa. Applying more pressure to her clit, I tasted and lapped her sweetness.

My heart thundered against my ribs. Her hips rocked in sync with my rhythmic motion.

"Kyle," she moaned and tugged my hair.

I flicked my tongue against her clit and fucked her with two fingers. God, she felt so good. Tasted divine. Yep, I'd found Heaven.

Her thighs trembled. She arched. Tensed. Then shuddered. "Oh, fuck, yeah." Her body quivered and quaked. I kept licking and kissing her, letting her ride out her orgasm until she couldn't take anymore.

She pulled on my hair, drew me upward, and kissed my lips. "Damn," she panted against my lips. "You can do that to me anytime. But right now . . . I want this off." She clawed at my T-shirt and yanked it over my head. I discarded my boxer shorts, ready to crawl onto the sofa, but Gemma slipped down onto the floor beside me. She pushed me back onto the rug, straddled my hips, and guided my cock inside her.

"Fuuuck." My jaw and every muscle in my body tensed. I thrust into her and moaned. Buried in her hot wetness, my cock was as stiff as a steel rod. *So fucking good.*

Gemma hovered over me. Kissed me. Rubbed against me. "We won't get a lot of songs written if we keep doing this."

"Consider this research and inspiration." I tilted my hips, burying myself deeper inside her.

She moved with me, up and down, slowly. Steadily. *Sweet Jesus!* Gemma riding me was so fucking hot.

Slipping my hand underneath her shirt, I cupped her silky breast, massaged it, and tweaked her peaked nipple. She rode me harder.

"Do you like me fucking you?" She brushed and teased her lips across mine.

"I think that's an understatement." I moved my hand, threaded it underneath her hair, and cradled her neck. I kissed her with all that I had. "I love everything about you."

She drew back a fraction. Her heart pounded against mine. A small smile played across her lips. "That's good . . . because I love you, too."

My heart jumped, soared and boomed against my ribs. Warmth, electricity, and sunshine flooded through my entire body.

Nothing would ever top this feeling.

Gemma. Loved. Me.

She drowned any form of response from me with a kiss . . . a long, deep, hot tongue-entwining kiss. Her hips drove against me, hard and fast. I thrust into her deeper and deeper. As she closed her eyes, her breaths came in short bursts. She clenched around me. Touched me in all the right places. Unable to maintain control, I exploded, spilling my release into her. A guttural groan burst from the depths of my throat. "Fuck." Coming had never felt so good. Riding out every blissful wave, I held onto Gemma's hips. Drove into her. Thrust hard.

"Oh yeah. There." Her voice came out in breathy pants as she rubbed against me. Her body shuddered. Her insides throbbed around me. She stole the air from my lungs with a fiery kiss.

Heat enveloped us. Our hearts pounded. As we caught our breaths, she steadied her pulsing hips, then collapsed on the floor beside me.

I pulled her into my arms and kissed her on the forehead. She placed her hand on my chest. My heart still raced beneath her touch.

She tilted her head back and scrunched her nose. "So . . . I let it slip, didn't I?"

I couldn't control my grin. Her words from before still rang in my ears. "What slip?"

She slapped me on the shoulder. "The L-word. Hunt said it was obvious and told me to stop denying it. So here I am, taking his advice, and not denying anything."

"Hmm. Hunt and advice don't seem to mix," I chuckled. "But I'll make a note to thank him."

"How did we avoid this for so long?" Her fingers trailed across my chest and circled my nipples.

"I guess . . . fear." I combed my fingers through her long hair. "I was afraid of losing you if things didn't work out. But they have. And I couldn't be happier." I ran my fingertips down her cheek. *So beautiful.* "Wouldn't it be nice to stay in this bubble forever?"

"I'd like that very much." She pressed her lips against my neck, licked my throat, and made her way toward my mouth . . . but then her phone rang.

I reached up and grabbed it off the coffee table. "Bubble's burst. It's your mom."

"What the hell does she want now?"

"Let's find out." I swiped the screen and put it on speaker. I lowered my voice, pretending to be serious. "Hello, Janine."

"Kyle? Where's Gemma?" she barked.

"She's here, right beside me." I kissed her cheek.

But the color drained from Gemma's face.

Oh shit.

"Sorry," I mouthed.

Gemma nodded, tapped my chest, then ripped the phone out of my hand. "We're writing songs, Mom. What's up?"

Hmmm. But we weren't on a video call.

I swept my hand over Gemma's naked chest, cupped her breast and ducked down to take her nipple in my mouth. She slapped me hard on the back.

"How come I don't hear any music?" Janine asked.

I launched off the floor, straddled Gemma's waist, and grabbed my guitar. I struck the strings softly, eyeing Gemma's naked body beneath me. Yeah, I could write a song about this.

"Music, Mom. Can you hear that?" Gemma giggled and ran her hand up my leg.

I set the guitar aside, leaned forward and whispered in Gemma's ear, "I'm going to shower. I'll leave you to it."

"Okay," she mouthed. "So Mom, why did you call? . . . No, Mom . . . We've had this conversation already. I'm not with Hunter—"

I headed into the bedroom and shut the bathroom door behind me. I turned the shower on, stepped under the steamy water, and let the hot spray rush over me. Trust Janine to ring at an inconvenient time. She was no doubt trying to suck the latest gossip from Gemma. She never called for any other reason.

For as long as I've known Gemma, her mother has never shown her an ounce of love and has never supported her music. Janine did nothing but use Gemma, used her name and her fame, to flit through social circles. Gemma hung onto her relationship with Janine by a fine thread. I didn't know how much longer it would last. Too many times, Gemma had been hurt by people who were supposed to love her—her dad, her mom, Ben . . . even Hunter. I promised to change that. Promised not to hurt her. Gemma had grown into a beautiful, strong, confident woman. She had flaws and issues like we all did. But they didn't matter. I loved her with all my being. She needed to know and understand how much she meant to me, how much I loved her unconditionally, and I'd do whatever it takes to prove it.

Chapter 27

KYLE

After three weeks of traveling, visiting London, Los Angles, San Francisco, Chicago, and Miami, to promote our single, I arrived back in New York with Gemma and Hunter. Tonight was our last promotional gig—a live outdoor performance at the Rockefeller Center. We arrived at rehearsal just after one. I grabbed my bass guitar off the rack and headed over to my mic. I waved to the screaming fans leaning out of windows, jumping on balconies, and lining up outside the secure audience area.

I adjusted my microphone. *The Late Night Show* production crew and technicians, our backup band, and support team were all in position for rehearsal. All except Hunter and Gemma.

They laughed and joked around at the back of the stage. On their own sweet time, they strolled toward the front, play-punching each other's arms. Halfway to the mics, Hunter grabbed Gemma in a headlock and ruffled her hair. She squealed and tickled him in the ribs.

I twisted the microphone stand between my hands and stretched my neck from side to side to release the tension. But it didn't work. Nothing did. Over the past three weeks, during every performance, every show, and every interview, my suspicions about Gemma and Hunter grew. It simmered through my veins like a slow-release toxin infecting my blood.

I shouldn't worry. Gemma spent every night in my bed. But I didn't know how to get rid of my jealousy. I'd never seen Gemma and Hunter get along so well. They'd written some incredible new songs together. They were more affectionate toward each other than they'd ever been before, not even when they'd been dating. And the hardest thing not to notice was the looks they exchanged. The flirty gazes. The air kisses. The warm smiles.

Ugh!

"You guys done?" My sharp, acidic tone slid through my clenched teeth.

Hunter released Gemma from his headlock and smacked her butt. "Move that ass. Go."

"Yep." Gemma tied up her hair with her hairband, grabbed her guitar, and hooked the strap over her head.

Hunter lifted his chin at me. "What's wrong with you, bud?" He picked up his guitar and headed to his mic. He put it on, plugged it in, and ran his fingers down the neck, filling the air with an electric twang.

"Nothing." I tugged on the cord of my in-ear monitors.

But everything was wrong. Why the hell couldn't Hunter keep his hands off of Gemma?

"Good. Let's get rehearsal over with." Hunter turned to his mic, circled his finger in the air, then pointed at our sound and lighting engineers sitting patiently at the control panel. Cue to go.

Lights shone. Cameras moved. Our backup band played the intro to our song, "Black Book." The music filled my in-ears. I stomped on my phaser pedal, strummed my bass, and Hunter took to the mic.

I've got a little black book
Full of all the girls that I know
But you're on top of the list
You're what I need when I'm feeling low
I'm looking for a good time, don't need a long time
I'm looking for a good time, don't need a long time

The three of us hit perfect harmony in the chorus.

I wanna call you
Come on over
No need for small talk
Coz you know what I'm after
Let's hit the bed sheets
Wanna make you sweat beneath me
Wanna make love to you all night
Until the morning light
You're the fix that I need
You're all I need to breathe
Oh baby, you're what I need
I need
Need right now

Gemma slayed her guitar, then sang.

I've got a little black book
Of all the boys I could call
But you're on top of the list
You're all I need to hit the floor
I'm looking for a good time, don't need a long time
I'm looking for a good time, don't need a long time

I loved singing this song. It was fun, flirtatious, feisty. Lost in the beat, I strummed and rocked the rhythm on my bass. Bobbed my head in time with the beat. But when I looked up, Hunter gazed at Gemma like she was the only one in the world. My heart faltered. Nausea flooded my gut.
Fuck.
Hunter was still into Gemma. Was she still into him?
I gripped the neck of my bass so hard my knuckles ached.
Gemma was mine. Not Hunter's.
Mine.
On the side of the stage, Amie glared icy daggers at Hunter. I

could feel the Arctic chill from here. She folded her arms and drew her shoulders back. Had she noticed the vibe between Hunter and Gemma, too?

Then Gemma missed her high note.

What? She never missed a note.

She coughed, touched her throat, and kept singing. But she missed the cue to change positions with me.

"Cut." I sliced my hand in front of my throat, pulled off my guitar, and strode over to her.

"What's eating you? We've played this song one million, five hundred and seventy-three thousand, four hundred and twenty-three times."

"Four . . . I've played this song one million, five hundred and seventy-three thousand, four hundred and twenty-four times."

"Then what's the problem?" My voice went up several notches. "You're not focused. You missed our moves. What's going on?"

Her eyes darted around the stage. She glanced at Hunter, her feet, then rocked back and forth on her Vans.

A pinch formed between her brows. Anguish crept across her face.

I stepped in close, turned my back on everyone, and lowered my voice. "Gem, tell me?" Afraid of the truth, my throat constricted like someone had seized me around my jugular and squeezed hard.

She shook her head. "It's my mother."

"Your mom?" Not what I'd expected, but her mom was a handful.

"She keeps calling. I've tried to ignore her, but she hasn't stopped."

"Okay." But my mind couldn't let go of her with Hunter. "So why were you goofing around with Hunt?"

"What?" Confusion flashed across her face. "We weren't. We were just being normal."

Shit. Were they? Nausea pooled in the pit of my stomach. Why did I think the worst? That wasn't like me. I had to kill my jealousy before it caused problems.

Gemma groaned, reached inside her jeans pocket, and pulled out her vibrating cell phone. She showed me the caller ID. *Janine.*

"I should've turned the damn thing off." She winced, staring at the screen. "Shit. I'm sorry. Give me five minutes. I'll give her a quick call to make sure it's not an emergency."

"Sure." I rubbed her arm. I'd been a dick and needed to get my shit together. "Want some emotional support?"

"Yeah. That'd be nice." She set down her guitar, walked over to the far side of the stage, and stood behind the tower of speakers to make the private call.

"Gem?" Hunter strode toward her. "What's up?"

"It's her mom." I stepped, blocking his path to Gemma. "She just needs to call her." The more distance I kept between the two of them, the better. I raised my hand to the crew and the band. "We need five minutes." They replied with mumbles and grumbles and turned to talk among themselves.

Hunter glanced at Gemma. Worry drifted across his eyes. "Is everything okay?"

"I'm not sure. I'll get to the bottom of it. You stay here." I left Hunter standing in the middle of the stage with fans hollering at him through the secured fence. He turned and blew them kisses. Yeah, he was in his element.

I joined Gemma behind the speakers.

"Mom, I'm in the middle of rehearsal." She put the call on speaker so I could hear the conversation, then picked and scratched at the *fragile* sticker on the nearby equipment trunk. "What's so urgent? Is there an emergency?"

The waiting crowd was loud, but the noise coming through the phone was insane. Was Janine in the middle of a wild party?

"Yes, it's an emergency." Janine's hysterical voice wailed through the phone. "Are you with Kyle? I saw the photos."

Photos? What photos?

"Are you shitting me?" Gemma tilted her head back and paced. "I've walked away from rehearsal thinking there's an emergency, but all you want is gossip. For fuck's sake, Mom. I don't know what photos you're talking about."

"The ones of you and Kyle in Miami two days ago." Janine's voice skipped with excitement. "At a restaurant and then walking down the street. Kyle's got his arm around you."

Gemma froze. Her hand trembled. Her eyes squeezed shut.

Fuck . . . Miami.

My throat ran dry. After we'd performed, the band, Amie, Kate, Bec, and half a dozen other people on our team had gone out to dinner at Estefan Kitchen. We'd drunk too much and had to be escorted by our security team down the street to our cars. But a thick pack of paparazzi had swarmed us. They'd shoved cell phones and cameras in our faces. Flashing lights had blinded us. People had jostled around us, blocking our path. The photographers called out our names, yelled questions. Concerned about Gemma's safety, I'd put my arm around her shoulders to protect her. Chester and Sam, our bodyguards, cleared the way, and I'd dashed to the car with Gemma. Hunter and Amie had followed close behind with Mick.

Being pursued and photographed by the paparazzi wasn't a fun part of our job. Gemma had suffered anxiety for years, thanks to being ruthlessly hounded by the wolves. Miami had been bad. It had taken hours for her to settle. And going by the stress embedded in her brow, Janine had sent it skyrocketing again.

"*Shit,*" Gemma mouthed and clutched her hair. She winced, but kept her voice cool and calm. "There's nothing to tell, Mom."

My gut cinched. *Another lie.* Over the past few weeks, we'd become experts at hiding and lying about our relationship. On the one hand, I hated it. I didn't want to lie and wanted the world to know I was with Gemma. But it was kinda fun keeping everyone guessing.

The loud pop of a champagne bottle blasted through Gemma's phone.

Gemma rolled her eyes. No shock Janine was drinking. "Where are you, Mom?"

"I'm in Nice, having a late dinner with a bunch of girlfriends." Janine cackled down the phone. "Baby girl, is Kyle there? Maybe *he'll* tell me what's going on."

"Janine, I a*m* here. We *are* in the middle of a rehearsal." I gripped the side of the equipment trunk to steady myself and my voice. "We have to go. Is there any *other* reason for your call?"

Janine sighed heavily, then let out a long moan, and sighed again. Gemma sneered and shook her head, clearly not impressed with her mother's melodramatic ways. "Well, yes. Gemma . . . Victor and I are getting divorced. I filed the papers last week."

"You what?" Gemma closed her eyes and massaged her temple as if trying to erase the tension. "So, is that why you're having a party? You're celebrating another divorce?"

"I see no need to wallow." Janine's pompous tone was enough to boil anyone's blood. Especially Gemma's.

"Yeah. You don't seem upset." Sarcasm laced Gemma's words.

"Oh, I am." *Bullshit.* "You don't know what it's like being the mother of someone famous." Janine's woe-is-me attitude struck a nerve in the back of my neck and twisted the knots even tighter. This woman was unbelievable. "Victor hated all the attention."

Gemma gripped her phone so hard her knuckles turned white. "Mom, you could easily go about unnoticed, but you're the one who craves attention. I've seen you twice in the past two years; don't blame *me* for screwing up your fourth marriage."

"How can I not?" Her voice scaled upwards. "How will I find someone who'll put up with *you* as my daughter? All the fame, the news . . . the celebrity life I constantly have to put up with."

What the hell?

"Janine, that's enough," I snapped. "Don't talk to Gem like that. She's done nothing wrong."

"Oh, what would you know, Kyle?"

"If you don't like Gem's life, stop riding off it, and stop calling her."

"Oh no. I can't do that. I'm her mother." She tried to lay on the guilt trip but failed to make an impact.

"Then act like one." Fire licked my tone. Janine wasn't mother material. Gemma owed her nothing.

"Kyle, it's okay." Gemma rubbed my back. "Mom, enough. Sorry for being nothing but a disappointment. Sorry there is no gossip for you to spread. Sorry, I won't join your pity party. I gotta get back to rehearsal. Bye."

She ended the call, collapsed back against the speaker, and sank to the floor. "What the fuck is wrong with her?"

I squatted beside her and rubbed her knee. "Gem, this has to stop. I don't like seeing you upset. I'm sorry I used to say you should keep in touch with her. But I've completely changed my mind and have scrapped that idea."

"How can you say that after—"

A hollow ache flared in my chest. "My mom was nothing like your mom. My mom loved and cared for us. I don't think Janine is capable of that."

"But what can I do? She's my mom."

"She may be by blood, but not by nature."

"She makes me feel like shit." Gemma wiped a tear from her cheek. "She rides off my fame, then blames me when things go wrong. Why? What have I ever done to her? Nothing I do is good enough for her. Whoever I'm with will never be good enough. She doesn't want to be a part of my life. Never has. She doesn't give a shit about me. All she wants to do is gossip and find the next man with a big wallet. How can you be with me knowing what she's like?"

"Because I've known her for years, and I don't care what she thinks. And I know it's hard, but you need to do the same. She's not worth it, Gem."

"She's the only family I've got."

"No, she's not." A heaviness pressed against my chest. I knew what it was like to have a shitty parent. My dad had been a drunk, abusive asshole for most of my teenage years. I survived thanks to Gemma, Hunter, and my mom. My mom was fucking awesome, full of love and kindness. Janine possessed none of those qualities. "You've got me and Hunt. We're your family. We're the ones who count. And I'll be here for you no matter what. I promise."

But unease swayed in my stomach. I closed my eyes and swallowed hard. Now was probably not the best time to bring it up, but with all the lies being told over the past few weeks, I'd lost sight of the truth. I had to know what was going on with her and Hunter to calm my overreactive mind. "But Gem . . . are you having second thoughts? About me? I've seen the way you and Hunt have been acting during promo. Are you questioning our relationship? Do you think you made a mistake? Do you still want him?"

"What? No." She clutched my hand. "Don't be stupid."

"The two of you have been getting along so well, I thought—"

"Kyle . . . stop overthinking things." She gave me a gentle shake. "We're just happy. Really happy. He's getting laid. And so am I. I love being with you."

I sucked air hard into my lungs, alleviating the ache lodged inside my chest.

"You're not jealous, are you?" Gemma stroked the side of my face. "Please don't be. You've nothing to worry about. I'm yours."

I caught and kissed the back of her hand. "That's good to know."

"You really should talk to Hunt more." Gemma said as we stood. She dusted off her hands on her jeans. "Isn't it obvious? Hunt's fallen for Amie in a big way. It's strange to see him act like this. But I think he's actually in love with her."

"Holy shit." My mouth fell open.

"Yeah, I know, right?" Her eyes widened as she nodded.

So that was what was wrong with Hunter. That explained a lot. The doe eyes. The stupid look on his face. The song lyrics. I pulled my shoulders back. The huge dark cloud that had been looming over my head disappeared. I wrapped my arms around Gemma and gave her a big hug.

She squeezed me, then stepped back and smiled softly. "What was that for?"

"I love you." Relief flooded through me. My superstitions could end. "And don't worry about your mom. We'll survive anything and everything together. Even her."

A chill ran up my spine. I turned. Amie stormed toward us.

"This is taking longer than five minutes." Amie clapped her hands. "Time's up. Back to it."

"Sorry, it was my mom." Gemma stepped out from behind the

speakers.

"Oh, how sweet?" A double dose of sarcasm dripped through Amie's tone as she fluttered her fake eyelashes. "Now, get back to rehearsal."

"On our way." I nodded and followed Gemma back to our mics.

Hunter came over and gave her a hug. "Everything okay?"

"Yeah, thanks." Gemma patted his chest.

But the warm smile that passed between them stirred the embers of my jealousy. *Shit.* I needed to get rid of my insecurities. I wanted to believe wholeheartedly that she was mine. How could I erase my fear of losing her? She was my life, my future, my forever. Buying her a ring was out; she didn't believe in marriage. Not after her mother's track record. Could I write her a song? Hell, I'd already written over two hundred about her. So, what would put my mind at ease?

Time . . . I had to give us time.

"Okay, lovebirds." Amie stepped between us. "Whatever issues you have, get over them. This rehearsal has taken too long. Gemma, do you want to bring the song down a key if it's a struggle?"

Gemma's face reddened, and she shook her head. "No fucking way. I can do it. You know I can. I just needed a minute." She grabbed her water bottle and downed the entire thing.

"Fine." Amie gave her a curt nod. "I have to go into the office for a quick meeting. So sort your shit out. Finish this rehearsal." She turned to leave but stopped after taking one step. She snapped her fingers, swung around, and pointed at Gemma. "Don't make plans after the show. Once we've finished at eight-ish, I'd like to take you out to dinner. Just you and me."

"What?" Gemma jerked her chin back. "Why?"

But Amie ignored her, walked off the stage and disappeared.

I gaped, just as stunned as Gemma was. What the hell did Amie want?

"What the fuck?" Disbelief lit Hunter's eyes as he held his arms wide.

"I don't know. You tell me?" Gemma threw Hunter an evil glare. "I hope she doesn't want to become my BFF just because you're sleeping together."

Hunter puffed air through his nose. "I can't see that happening. But dinner?"

"Yeah . . . with just me?" Gemma wrinkled her nose. "Why does she want to do that? What the fuck does she want?"

Chapter 28

GEMMA

"SureHaven wants you to go solo."

I choked. Coughed. Whiskey burned the back of my throat and shot up into my nose. My eyes widened. "They want me to what?"

"Go solo. Hunter and Kyle can continue on as a duo." Amie's monotonous tone deadpanned against the other loud conversations in the busy Indian restaurant. She swirled her olives around in her martini. "SureHaven wants to offer you a sizable advance, and a two-album deal with an option. They'll give you one hundred percent creative control. Your music. Your lyrics. Your own branding. That's everything you've ever wanted."

Holy fuck! I closed my eyes. My heart pummeled my ribs. My pulse screamed in my ears. The smell of Indian spices and Amie's words made my head spin like a tornado.

"Stop!" I shot my hands up to cover my ears. "I don't want to hear any more. It's a hard no. Not without the guys. You'll never break us up. Not ever."

"Gemma, you could have the most amazing career as a solo artist. You could be the next Taylor Swift or Beyoncé." Her cold eyes sent shards of ice splintering through my veins.

Solo? Never. "I don't want to go solo. Why can't we as a band get the same deal? Creative control is what we want."

Amie shook her head. "Everhide is a product. A money-making machine. The guys, as a sexy duo, will be easier to market. A much more successful formula."

I clutched at the ache in my chest. "A product. We're not a product. SureHaven doesn't own us to that extent, and they never will."

"The boys can keep the name. But we want to open discussions with your lawyer. We want the three of you to see that this is a positive move."

"How is this positive?" I ground my teeth, keeping my voice low so no one around could hear. I peered over my shoulders to make sure no one was listening. "You know I'm with Kyle? Going solo would separate us for lengthy periods of time. I don't want to do that."

"Of course I know you're together." Amie's lips twitched. "We've been covering your asses for ages. If all that emotional bullshit is your thing, you've found your man. He's as tragic as a Shawn Mendes song."

My blood boiled, hotter than my Indian curry. "You wouldn't understand the connection we have. He's caring, and kind, and has a beautiful soul." I waved at the waiter for another drink, then looked Amie square in the eye. "SureHaven's not going to break us up, so deal with it." My voice dialed upward. "Get us the deal we want, not this lame bullshit." Diners turned with how-rude looks on their faces. Undeterred, I inhaled sharply, about to give Amie another ear bashing, but I stopped short. I blinked. New thoughts bombarded my mind. "Holy shit. Is this to get me away from Hunt? Are you threatened by me?"

"Don't flatter yourself." Amie folded her arms. "This has nothing to do with Hunter. He's nothing but a bit of entertainment."

"He's what?" My stomach cinched. "You know, he really likes you."

Amie shrugged one shoulder. "Not my problem. I made it clear to him from the start it was nothing but sex." She leaned forward, the devil shining in her eyes. "We don't date. We don't stay over at each other's places. We fuck. That's it."

My fuse blew. "You're such a fucking bitch."

"No, I'm a businesswoman. I'm here to discuss your future. That's my job. I'm not here to talk about Hunter."

I shook in my seat. "Fuck you and fuck your business. We're done." I downed my JD, grabbed my purse, and dashed toward the mezzanine stairs.

"Gemma?" Amie called after me. "We've more to discuss."

"Go to hell." I didn't even look back over my shoulder. I stormed down the stairs. Chester, my bodyguard, opened the front doors, and guided me outside to my waiting car. I slid into the back seat and rubbed my aching leg. I shouldn't have worn my four-inch Gucci pumps. But they looked so fucking good.

Dylan, my driver, took off.

"You sick, Gem? You look feverish." Chester asked from the front passenger seat.

"No." I shook my head. "Just side effects from having dinner with Amie."

"I can see how that would make you ill. She's like a bad oyster in the belly."

"You got that right."

The city streets blurred as we headed home. My palms sweated and my mind raced.

Fuck Amie. Fuck SureHaven.

I grabbed my cell phone from my purse and called Kyle.

No answer.

I called Hunter.

No answer.

"Hey?" I tapped the back of the driver's seat. "Dylan, can you drop me off at Kyle's, please?"

He nodded, but Chester raised his bushy eyebrows and gave me a cheeky grin. "You two are getting cozy."

"Yeah." I slumped back in the seat. "Or forming a coup to get rid of Amie."

Hunter and Kyle will be livid after I told them what had happened.

I raced into their penthouse, but no one was home. For the

next hour, I paced the floor, drank JD, and fired off a dozen texts to Kyle and Hunter. I changed into an old black T-shirt and a pair of denim shorts I'd kept in my drawer in Kyle's room. In the ensuite, I ripped a brush through my hair, ready to dash out and search the local bars and late-night cafes to find them. My phone buzzed on Kyle's bed. I raced out of the bathroom, stubbed my toe on the bed, swore like a trucker, and answered the phone.

"Hey? Where the hell are you?" I rubbed my throbbing toe, fought back the tears welling in my eyes and glanced at the alarm clock. 10:07 p.m.

"Baaaabbbbyyyy. Wheeerrre aarre you?" Kyle's drunken slur blended with the blaring music in the background.

"I'm at your place. I've been trying to call you."

"I went out for a few drinks. I'm in Brooklyn. With Hayden. At some bar . . . in Brooklyn. On some street . . . in Brooklyn. So we're . . . in Brooklyn."

"I got it. You're in Brooklyn."

"Brooooklyn."

"I need you to come home." Panic seized my throat, and my mind spun at a hundred miles an hour. "I need to talk to you and Hunt. Now."

"Wherrrre's Hunt?"

"Isn't he with you?" I stared out the window toward Brooklyn.

"Nooope."

"Shit."

"Gem, what's up?"

"Just come home, please."

I tugged on a handful of my hair. Where could Hunter be? Hopefully, he wasn't at Amie's, waiting for her to come home. "I'll keep trying to find Hunt." The elevator pinged. Hunter's footsteps echoed in the hallway. "Oh, wait. He's home. Kyle, please get here as fast as you can."

"I'm coming. Stay away from Hunt . . . I'm coming . . . home . . . now . . . I'm on my way."

I rushed out of Kyle's room and met Hunter halfway down the hallway. I flung my arms around him, buried my face in his chest, and held him tight. "Thank God you're home."

"Shit, Gem. What's happened?" Worry slid through his voice as he hugged me and rubbed my back.

"Were you at Amie's?" I wanted to scratch that bitch's eyes out. "Did she tell you?"

"No, I've been out with the guys from the band. What's up?" Hunter smoothed his hands over my hair, but there was no way I could calm down.

"It's not good." I shook my head and slipped out of his arms. "I'll tell you everything once Kyle gets home. He's been out with Hayden in Brooklyn."

"You're making me nervous." He rubbed the center of his chest. "If I have to wait, I'll need a drink."

"Me too. I'll make 'em." I spun on my toes and headed toward the kitchen. My hands trembled as I poured the JD, spilling some onto the counter. I handed Hunter a glass. He sat on the sofa. I paced the floor, sipping my JD, waiting for Kyle to come home.

I tapped my fingernails against the glass.

Mumbled under my breath.

Paced even more.

Hunter poured us another drink.

I kept walking, unable to sit still.

An hour passed.

"Gem? Stop. I can't handle this anymore." Hunter leaped up from the sofa, headed to the kitchen, and refilled his glass. "You're as strung out as a priest in a whorehouse. What the fuck's wrong?"

I sighed, slumped my shoulders, and sank onto a kitchen stool.

Hunter folded his arms and rested his hip against the counter. "I promise I'll act surprised or excited or however you want me to act when Kyle gets here. Don't leave me hanging like this. You're killing me. What's happened?"

My stomach flipped and twisted into knots. My palms sweated around my glass. Maybe telling Hunter the news first was a good idea; he wasn't as emotional as Kyle. And he needed to know what Amie had said about their relationship. *Shit.* I licked my lips and swallowed the hard lump lodged in my throat. "It's about my dinner with Amie."

"I gathered that much. What happened?" A deep crease formed between his eyebrows.

"A lot." I downed a mouthful of whiskey and slammed my glass on the counter. "I know you like her, but I don't. I've tolerated her for long enough. I can't work with her anymore. Not after tonight." I took a deep breath and dialed down my tone. But there was no way to sugarcoat the blow. "Hunt, she's using you. She said you're nothing but a fuck to her. She doesn't view what you have as a serious relationship."

Hunter lowered his gaze. His shoulders slouched. He snatched up his glass and downed his JD. He swallowed hard and knitted his eyebrows together. "She really said that?"

"Yep."

He wiped his hand down his face and nodded slowly. "Shit. Okay. Um. Thanks. But I'm a big boy." He lifted his chin, but the shine had disappeared from his gorgeous eyes. "I think I can handle Amie."

"You sure? You okay?"

He poured another JD, then placed his hands on the counter, leaning over as if he'd had a blow to the guts. His hair curtained his face.

My heart sank at being the bearer of bad news. And there was only more to come.

"Yeah, I'll be fine. Thanks for the heads-up on Amie." Hunter nodded and tilted his head to the side. "But that wouldn't have stressed you out like this. There's something else bothering you. Please tell me."

Kyle was taking too long. He still wasn't home. It had been over an hour since I'd called him. I swiveled my glass on the countertop and jiggled my leg on the footrest. The news gnawed at my insides and ate at my chest.

Shit.

"SureHaven wants me to go solo." I blurted, unable to contain the shitty news anymore.

Hunter choked, coughed, and dribbled JD down his shirt. His

eyes widened. "They fucking what?"

Shit. I should've waited for Kyle.

"I said no. I'd never do that."

"Oh, thank Christ." Hunter flattened his hand against his chest. "I was about to have a heart attack."

"Please don't."

"But . . . hypothetically . . ." He grimaced. "If you went solo, what would happen to Kyle and me?"

"They want you to continue as a duo." I made quotes in the air. "A more marketable product to please the female population."

"We're already fucking hot."

"I know." I bobbed my head. "But I'm not leaving you guys. Not ever. I stormed out of the restaurant before I could listen to any more of Amie's bullshit. And there was a lot. Believe me."

"Wait—what exactly did they offer you?"

As I relayed the details to Hunter, the color drained from his face.

"Fuck, Gem." His eyes glassed over, and his shoulders sagged. "Are you sure about this? Creative control is what you've always wanted."

Tears stung my eyes. "No, it's not. I mean . . . yes, but not as a solo artist."

I'd never considered a solo career before. Was I stupid for throwing away a great opportunity just to stay loyal to my best friends? *No. Never.* I already had an incredible career with them.

Hunter swiped his hand over his chin, then rubbed the back of his neck. "I bet this was Amie's idea, wasn't it? There's something going on at SureHaven that's to her advantage, and she's not letting us know what it is."

"I don't know what's going on, but if I went solo, there's no fucking way she'd be my manager." Acid dripped from my tongue. "She's not supporting us anymore. I'm sick of her, and I honestly think we should fire her."

Hunter stared into his glass and swirled the whiskey around. I'd never seen him look so crushed. "You really want to do that?"

"Yeah . . . I do." I softened my tone. He was hurting, and I hated that. But Amie had crossed too many lines, and no longer cared about us as a band. "Hunt . . . I'm sorry. You can still see her if you want to, but she can't manage us anymore."

"See her? No fucking way. And if she's trying to break us up, she can go to hell. Music comes first. Always." His azure eyes flooded with concern. "But do we still come first? Our band? Be honest with me, Gem. Now she's planted the seed for going solo, can you walk away from your dream?"

My mind was like a thousand-piece orchestra playing out of time. But doubt never played a beat. Going solo wasn't an option. "It's *our* dream to get creative control. After one more album with SureHaven, that dream will become a reality. I know it will. But there's no way I'm leaving you and Kyle. You're stuck with me. Forever."

"Thank God for that." Hunter stepped around the counter and held his arms wide.

I slipped off the stool, hugged his waist and rested my head against his chest.

He wrapped his arms around me and rubbed my back in slow circles. "You had me fucking worried for a sec, Gem. You make this crazy life of ours fun. It wouldn't be the same without you." He placed his chin on top of my head and stroked my hair. "Nothing will ever break us apart. I promise."

I closed my eyes, and a tear escaped down my cheek. "Yeah. Nothing."

The elevator door chimed, and Kyle stumbled into the hallway.

Hunter kissed me on the forehead and took a step back. Kyle stormed toward us, red rage burning in his bloodshot eyes.

"You." Kyle jabbed a finger at Hunter. "Get your hands off Gem. Now." He spat each word through clenched teeth.

Hunter raised his hands and stepped back. "What the hell is your problem?"

"Don't be stupid, Kyle." I jammed my hands onto my hips. I didn't need this shit.

"You think I'm blind?" Kyle staggered, waving his finger between me and Hunter. "I saw the way you two looked at each other all day. I've put up with your shit for weeks. You want Hunt back, Gem? Is that what this is?"

"What?" My knees buckled. I stumbled back a step, my ass connecting with a kitchen stool. Why was he being so cruel? "No."

"Kyle, you fuck-knuckle." Hunter flicked his hand at Kyle. "There's nothing going on between me and Gem."

"Bullshit." Redness crept up Kyle's neck like a nasty rash. "You had your chance. It didn't work out. So, what? Now you want another shot?" Fire flared in his eyes. "When you two were together, I stood back, regardless of how I felt about Gem. I never crossed the line. I respected you. But no, not you. The minute I'm out of the room, you hit on her again."

I couldn't believe what I was hearing. After talking to Kyle this afternoon, I couldn't understand where this jealousy was coming from. "Kyle, stop. I was upset. We're just talking."

He shot air through his nose. "That wasn't talking. Next time you want to be alone, don't call me, begging for me to come home."

Every word was a harsh blow to my solar plexus. I tried with all my might not to take them to heart. He was drunk. That I could handle. But I'd never had to deal with jealousy before. It had infected him like a crippling disease.

"Enough." Hunter shoved Kyle hard on the shoulder. "Get your head out of your ass. There's nothing going on."

But Kyle ignored him. Swaying, he edged closer to me. His whiskey-laced breath was like fire against my face. "You want Hunt? By all means, go for it. Go fuck his brains out. But I'll be no part of it. I'll not be part of this game. I'm not into sharing."

"Kyle, please stop." Another tear slid down my cheek. Kyle's face contorted with pain and rage. I reached out to comfort him, but he brushed my hand aside.

"Listen, you shithead." Hunter yanked Kyle away from me. Kyle staggered back a foot but regained his balance. "Gem's upset after her dinner with Amie. *You* need to listen."

"Listen to what?" Veins bulged in Kyle's neck like sinewy, snaking vines. He spun to me and searched my face. "What? What is it?"

I trembled and swallowed hard. Saying it out loud still felt like a surreal dream. "Amie . . . SureHaven . . ." My voice quivered and quaked. " . . . want me to go solo."

Kyle stumbled forward, his hands catching hold of the counter's edge. With a guttural growl, he picked up my glass of JD and hurled it at the pantry door. Glass shattered and fell into a million pieces across the floor.

Shuffling back a few steps, he sank to his knees. "Solo? No. Gem. No."

My heart lurched so hard it felt like every one of my ribs cracked.

"I said no." I reached out and touched his cheek, but he turned his head away.

Kyle?

He buried his face in his hands, dragging in loud, raspy breaths. Then he looked up at me. His eyes, swollen and dark. "Why?" His lips twisted. "Why did you say no? Maybe we *should* take a break from each other."

"No," I cried. "I don't want that."

"Never." Hunter eased forward.

But Kyle's icy stare sent a chill down my spine. "You're the one who is career hungry. The one with all the talent. Maybe you should do it. Go. Fucking. Solo."

My heart shattered. I didn't know where to look—out the window, at the JD trickling down the pantry door, or at Hunter, who was in as much shock as I was. "Kyle, do you hear yourself? You want us to break up? Go our separate ways?" I shot forward onto my knees before him. I stared into his red eyes, searching for his soul, his sanity, his sensibility. "No. We're together forever."

"Oh, come on," he snarled. "The three of us have never fought this much in our lives. Maybe we've run our course."

I reached out to touch him, to calm him, but he pushed my hand away.

My soul cried.

"I don't believe that for a second." My tone never wavered. "We've had some big changes over the past few months, navigating relationships and work. But we've survived. We always get through everything together. We always do."

His eyes bore into me, but his light d gone out. His jaw ticked with tension. "Maybe not this time, Gem. You've fucked around with Hunt. You've fucked around with me. You've fucked around with everyone to get what you want. Now you've got it, you can leave. You're just like your mother."

My chest seized. I froze on my haunches. Kyle just tasered my heart.

"Asshole." Hunter's fist flew downward and socked Kyle in the cheek. "Don't you ever talk to her like that. You shithead."

Holy fuck! I clutched my hair. Hunter had never hit anyone, not since Kyle's dad in high school.

Kyle was upset. He'd gone too far.

But he'd gotten one thing right.

I *was* just like my mother.

Feverish chills washed over me as I rose to my feet. Numbness consumed my mind. I backed toward the hallway, unable to feel the floor beneath me. "No, Hunt. Kyle's right. He's absolutely right. This is my fault. I fucked up everything. I'm so sorry. I gotta go."

I turned and raced toward the elevator. My feet couldn't carry me fast enough. On the ground floor, I charged out of the building . . . and ran. Ran and hobbled and jolted along as fast as my aching leg would carry me. With tears streaking down my face, and my heart in pieces, I disappeared into the darkness.

Chapter 29

KYLE

I pounded my fist against the elevator. She was gone. Gemma was gone. *Fuck!* What had I done? I curled my arms, covered my head, and slumped against the doors. Pain throbbed in the back of my skull like I'd been struck with an electric guitar. Every breath hurt. Every muscle ached. My heart screamed.

Hunter stormed down the hallway. "Good one, dickhead." His bitter tone was nothing compared to how broken I felt on the inside. "What were you thinking? You just lost the best thing that ever happened to us."

"You were all over her, asshole." I jabbed at the elevator button again and again. I had to go after her. I had to.

"I was not. I was giving her a fucking hug. Like I always do." Hunter grabbed me on the shoulder and pushed me toward the kitchen. "Get in here and sober up."

"I'm not that drunk. I haven't been gone that long. I'm more pissed off at seeing you together."

"Whatever. But you're not going after her like this. Don't be stupid. You'll only make it worse. Move it."

I trudged out to the kitchen and fell onto a stool. I stared at Hunter through stinging eyes, searching for signs of guilt on his face. But there were none. No shifty eyes. No beading brow. No jittery hands. He grabbed a bottle of water from the fridge, the bottle of Tylenol from the pantry, and slammed them down on the countertop. "Take these. Drink this."

I swallowed two tablets with mouthfuls of water.

Hunter stood opposite me, arms crossed, eyes as cold as an arctic frost. "You're the biggest idiot I've ever known. What the fuck happened to you?"

"Pier 115 happened." My shoulders slumped.

"What? Gem said you were in Brooklyn. With Hayden." Puzzlement flashed across Hunter's face. "How did you end up in Jersey?"

I downed more water, then wiped my mouth on my T-shirt. "We hit Pier 115, then headed to Brooklyn. We'd just gotten to some bar and had ordered drinks when Gem called."

Hunter tilted his head toward the clock. "You took your sweet time getting home. We waited for ages."

"Yeah. I saw you two waiting." The image of Gemma in Hunter's arms burned worse than ever before. Worse than when they were a couple. Because now Gemma had total control of my heart, and I'd never felt so betrayed. Betrayed by my best friends.

"For the hundredth fucking time, there's nothing going on between me and Gem."

I slammed the water bottle down, splashing water over the counter. "Then explain rehearsal. The way you looked at each other—"

Hunter threaded his fingers into his hair, grabbed a handful, and pulled it. "Bud, you're insane. You're concocting all this shit inside your head. Yes, I had something on my mind today, but it wasn't Gem. It was Amie."

"What?" I jerked backward. "She offered you a solo career, too?"

"No." He grimaced and scratched his chest. "She just . . . fuck . . . I couldn't get her out of my mind. Couldn't stop thinking about being with her. It drove me fucking crazy."

I laughed, one of those *you've-got-to-be-kidding-me* type laughs. "If you've fallen in love with her, then you're definitely mental."

"I'm going to plead temporary insanity. After what Gem told me tonight, I'm done with her. I thought what Amie and I had was serious, but it's not. It fucking sucks. But she doesn't give a shit about me, or anyone else for that matter. So before I end up a head case like you, it's over."

I closed my eyes. Vertigo swam through my brain. "But you and Gem—"

"For the last fucking time . . ." Hunter clipped me over the head. "Nothing. Is. Going. On. With. Me. And. Gem."

I drew my shoulders back. Holding my breath, I stared at him. The frustration and anguish burning in his eyes hit me harder than his fist.

Fuck! That was what I needed.

I slumped and buried my head in my hands. "Everything is so fucked up."

"You've fucking lost it, man."

"No. I haven't." *Okay . . . maybe.* "I've just never felt like this about anyone before. I get so protective and jealous and defensive. I know you care about her—"

"You're fucking right. I care about her a lot. I love Gem like a sister. And like you said to me when I was with her, I'll beat the shit out of you if you hurt her." He pointed his finger at my cheek. "Consider that shiner on your face the first warning, because you acted like a real fuckhead tonight."

I shrank three inches. Hurting Gemma was the last thing I ever wanted to do. "What the hell have I done?"

"You've made a huge mess, that's what. You're going to have to suck it up real hard to make it up to her. If that's even possible."

The thought of losing Gemma crushed me. I couldn't lose her. I'd fight for her until I drew my last breath.

"Hunt? What . . . what if she wants to go solo? We can't stand in her way."

"I thought that too. For all of two seconds before she shot me down for being an idiot. She doesn't want to go solo. We don't have to worry." Hunter held up his wrist, showing me his tattoo, the

GKH inked on his wrist. "We're Everhide forever."

I rubbed my identical ink. "We've been with SureHaven for five years. Maybe it's time we let Gem go."

Hunter slapped me on the top of the head again. "Do you hear me? We're not breaking up."

I swallowed hard, hurting my dry throat. "I don't want that. But she never wanted being involved with you . . . or me . . . to affect us as a band, but there's no denying it has."

"It's affected *you*." Hunter stabbed his finger against the counter. "Gem and I were smart enough to walk away from each other before I fucked things up even more. I never intended to fall for Amie, but I did. And Gem fell for you. She's yours. You love each other. Seeing you together doesn't bother me. In fact, I think it's awesome. I don't know how you're going to fix this shit, but you fucking have to."

I blinked. And blinked again. I was a complete and utter moron. Hunter's hounding finally got through. I needed some harsh reality. I rubbed my tattoo again. The thick fog in my head finally cleared. "You're right. I'm sorry. I've fucked up so much." I raked my fingers down my face. "I get so crazy, caught up in my head. I hate being insecure. That's not me. I'm just so into her. She's my life. I'm terrified of losing her."

"Then why the fuck are you still sitting here?"

"Shit . . . I need to find her. Find her now."

***

I rushed back to my building from the skate park near the Hudson River. Stress pounded in my head. I'd been searching for two hours and couldn't find Gemma anywhere. Not at her apartment, Kara's, Lexi's, or any of our regular bars and cafes. Not by the pool or on the rooftops of our buildings. Nowhere.

She'd left her phone at my place. That made me even more anxious. I prayed she was okay.

Where could she be at two o'clock in the morning?

A memory hit me—a distant past conversation. I halted in

my tracks. She'd told me once about a place she liked to go. To be alone. The old pier.

God, I hoped she was there.

It was too far to go on foot. I needed a car.

As I jogged down the lane to my building, a taxi pulled up outside. I broke into a run, hoping it was Gemma. But I slowed to a walk when Amie stepped onto the curb. The cab took off.

"What the hell are you doing here?" I snapped, walking toward the door.

Amie pulled her shoulders back. With too much makeup on, a low-cut blouse, and a tiny skirt, she'd give any Hollywood hooker a run for their money. "I've come to see Hunter."

"He doesn't want to see you."

"I'm sure I have something to offer that will change his mind."

"What? You going to make him an offer to go solo, too?"

An evil smile slid across her face. "Ahhhh. Gemma told you." She took small, slow steps toward me. "You know she's the most talented. You know she could go far. You know she could be a mega-star."

Amie wasn't telling me anything I didn't already know. But the mega-star thing? We were already a huge global success; how much bigger did Amie envision? Was it even possible? "Tough. She said no."

"I can give her everything she wants." Amie tilted her nose into the air.

I stood my ground, but my guts felt like lead. "Why are you trying to break us up?"

"Money."

I puffed through my nose. "Don't you make enough off of us already?"

"What can I say? I'm an ambitious woman and want to see a fellow female be a success."

The cockiness in her tone made me spit. "Bullshit. You don't give a fuck about Gem."

"I do if I make money out of her."

"Get the fuck out of here." I pointed down the street.

"I came to see Hunter, not you."

"I'm not letting you in. Hunt doesn't want to see you. And Nick, the night man, won't let you in either. If you want sex, go work the avenue up at Times Square."

A sly smile slid across her lips. "If I can't see Hunter, then you'll do for a bit of fun."

"No fucking chance."

"You sure about that?" She arched an eyebrow and slid an inch closer. "If Gemma won't go solo, maybe you will. You and me. We'd make a great team. We're both business-minded." She placed her hands on my chest, but I grabbed them and held her back. She leaned in and tried to kiss me, dipping and darting, aiming for my mouth, trying to break through my hold.

I didn't want to hurt her, but I was way stronger than she was. She had no hope in hell.

"Get your hands off me." I pushed her back, not wanting her foul, filler-filled lips, or her horrid hands anywhere near me.

"I could change your mind if you give me the chance." She grabbed my shirt and tried to kiss me again. My clenched fists shot up between us, stopping her. Her venomous mouth hovered an inch from mine. "Come on, Kyle. Let's have some fun."

"Fuck off." My voice dripped with disgust. "You're pathetic."

In the distance, Gemma walked around the corner into the laneway. She froze. My heart lurched. *Fuck!* What must this have looked like from where Gemma stood? With Amie clawing at me?

"Gem, wait," I called, pushing Amie aside.

But Gemma took off at a run.

I raced down the alleyway. "Gem, wait!"

As I reached the street, Gemma had hailed a taxi a few hundred yards away. She jumped in and sped off around the corner.

"Fuck!" I roared and punched the air. Why was nothing ever easy?

I scanned the street. No taxis. Just my fucking luck. I sprinted back home, entering through the garage to avoid Amie at all costs.

Upstairs was shrouded in darkness. I flicked on the hallway light, headed straight for Hunter's bedroom, and bashed on the door twice before charging in.

"Give me your keys." I held out my hand.

"What?" Hunter jolted from his sleep and rubbed his eyes. "No. Get the fuck out of my room."

"I couldn't find Gemma. I searched everywhere. I just figured out where she would've gone and came back here to get your car. But Amie turned up downstairs. Your wonderful girlfriend tried to kiss me. Gem came back, saw us, and took off." *Ugh.* The thought of Amie touching me made my skin crawl. "I need to go get Gem."

"Great. Catch a fucking taxi. Call an Uber."

"No, I can't wait that long."

"You've been drinking. You know better than to drink and drive."

"I'm sober. I swear. It's been over four hours since I've had a drink. You know I'd never get behind the wheel if I was drunk. Not after—" Not when my parents were killed by a drunk driver. "Just give me your keys, or I'll just take them."

"You need to buy your own damn car."

"One day, but right now, I need yours." I searched the top of Hunter's drawers for the keys.

"Hang on a sec." Hunter wiped his eyes again. "Where's Amie? You didn't let her up here, did you?"

"No. I wouldn't let her in. She's a real number." I sifted through his junk drawer, searching underneath condoms, cufflink boxes, pens, paper, and hotel lotions. "I told her you didn't want to see her. After tonight, I don't want to deal with her ever again. She's fucking gone."

"Whatever." Hunter tugged his sheet up and pulled his pillow underneath his head. "Now fuck off."

"Give me your keys."

"No. I love my car more than anything."

"If I put a scratch or even a mark on it, I'll buy you a new one. Promise."

Hunter grunted. "I'll hold you to that. They're in the other top drawer."

I yanked it open and grabbed them. "Thanks, man. Don't wait

up."

"I'm not. I wasn't." Hunter turned away.

I paused at the doorway and spoke over my shoulder. "What do you want me to do about Amie? When I came in, she was still downstairs."

"She can stay there. Don't let her in."

I grinned and took off.

In the garage, I jumped into Hunter's electric blue Ford GT supercar and turned it on. I revved the engine a few times, sped out of the garage, and flipped the bird to Amie on the way past. Planting my foot on the accelerator, I headed for the West Side Highway. I prayed Gemma was on the old pier. I had to make everything right. I had to. I hit the highway and headed north. To Gemma.

Chapter 30

GEMMA

I dangled my feet over the edge of the pier and stared into the black waters of the Hudson River. It was quiet. No constant hum or bustle from daytime boats and ships and ferries. The only sounds around were the murky waters lapping softly at the pylons below and the odd scurry of traffic filtering along the West Side Highway. At 2:33 a.m., I had Pier 97 all to myself. A temporary escape from the craze of Manhattan behind me. No concerts, stages, or bright lights. No fans or cameras. No Hunter. No Kyle.

I wiped my wet eyelashes and closed my eyes. I let the warm summer air seep into my skin. Every muscle in my chest ached. Kyle had turned out to be like everyone else who'd said they loved me. He was the first person I'd trusted with my whole heart in a long time. But he'd gone and broken it. Broken it with his jealousy. His cruel words. His lack of trust.

Damn him for having this power over me.

Drawing my legs up, I wrapped my arms around them and rested my chin against my knees. More tears slid down my cheeks. How did I let things get so bad between Kyle, Hunter and me? In the past few months, there had been way too many fights, too many arguments, and too many broken hearts.

It was time to put an end to it all. The consequences terrified me. Why couldn't everything go back to the way it was before? Before Hunter. Before Kyle. Before my dreams had started. So I wouldn't ruin relationships like my mother did.

The throaty rev of a car engine roared behind me. I knew that sound. My heart raced faster than that car could go. Gravel crunched beneath fat tires. Headlights streamed around me. Everyone in Manhattan knew that car. I knew he'd be concerned about me, but he didn't have to come and get me. And how had he known where I'd be?

Exhaustion seeped into the marrow of my bones. I couldn't even be bothered to turn around.

He killed the engine. The door swooshed open, then closed. Footsteps drew closer but stopped a short distance away.

The air prickled around me. Electric energy. Heat swirled through my veins. *He* shouldn't be affecting me this way. There was only *one* person who made my body react like that. And that person wasn't here.

"Hunt, I'm fine." I stared straight ahead. My eyes focused on the black nothingness in the distance. "You didn't need to come and get me."

"Gem?"

Shit. I whipped around. My heart jumped into my throat. "Kyle? I thought you were Hunt."

Wariness hooded Kyle's eyes. A few yards away, he held out his hand like he was trying to approach a wild cat. Yeah . . . I might scratch his fucking eyes out.

"What are you doing here?" My voice sliced through clenched teeth.

"I've been looking for you for hours. Then I remembered you liked coming here when you needed time alone."

"Yes. You're interrupting. Go away."

"Please let me explain everything." He took a small step toward me. "I didn't kiss Amie. I swear. I'm sorry for not trusting you and Hunt. Seeing you in his arms drove me crazy. I was jealous and said some *really* stupid things I regret. I'm trying my best not to fuck everything up between you and me, but it's all I seem to do. I never meant to hurt you."

"Yeah, well. You did." I shot to my feet, dusted the dirt from my hands, and stormed past him. "If you won't leave, I will."

Kyle caught my arm. "Please, Gem. Give me a chance."

Hurt licked like fire through my veins. "Why? Why should I?"

"Because I love you."

He tugged me forward and tried to wrap his arms around me. I pushed back hard against his chest, breaking free from his hold. "Don't fucking touch me." I pointed my finger at him. "Not after what you said. Not after you've had Amie all over you. I can smell her foul perfume on you." My skin crawled with a thousand ants, and bile churned in my gut.

He sniffed his shirt and scrunched his nose. An animalistic growl rumbled deep in his throat as he gnashed his teeth. He ripped off his shirt, screwed it up, and hurled it into the river. "I fucking hate Amie so much. I want that whore out of our lives."

I gasped. Not at him for tossing his shirt into the river. Not for agreeing with him about Amie. But at him standing before me— faded blue jeans, toned arms, ripped body glowing golden in the soft lights. The body I'd loved, had kissed every inch of, and knew better than my own. But it was also the one who knew how to break my heart.

Kyle's chest heaved, his hands clenched by his sides. "Why is she doing this to us?"

His voice, loaded with sadness and pain, buckled my knees. But the damage was done. Amie had won. She'd caused a rift between the three of us. There was no way back from this. She'd infected Hunter with her poison, sunk her teeth into Kyle and frozen my heart.

"She wants me out of the way so she can have you and Hunt all to herself." Just saying the words left a bitter taste in my mouth.

"That's bullshit. That's not going to happen." Kyle paced back and forth, then stopped a few feet in front of me. "Forget Amie. Forget about everything for a moment." He closed his eyes, took a deep breath, and then looked at me again. His dark eyes bore into me with such intensity I couldn't draw breath. "Is going solo what you want to do?" His voice was chillingly calm, but fear flickered in his eyes.

"No. Going solo was never an option until I saw you with Amie." My chin quivered, and a lone tear fell onto my cheek. "Do you have feelings for her? Because if you do, I'd have to leave. I'm not like you. I could never watch you be with someone else every day. My heart couldn't bear it. The thought of leaving you and Hunt kills me. Traveling and being on stage without you guys would be horrible. Facing the fans without the two of you wouldn't be possible. I hate the prospect of that being my future. But I'd take it—take it any day over seeing you with her."

My jaw ached. Tears stung my eyes, but I wouldn't let another one fall. I didn't want him to see me broken.

Like I did after Ben, I had to find the strength to lock my heart away and rely on the only two things that got me through everything: myself and my music.

"Gem, I'm not fucking Amie. She came to see Hunt. I wouldn't let her in the building because he didn't want to see her. That's when she threw herself at me. I pushed her away. I swear that's what happened. I love you. Only you." He shot forward and wrapped his arms around me. I tried to wriggle free but couldn't. He held me tight.

"Let me go." I pounded my fists against his bare chest, his arms, his ribs. He just stood there and took every blow.

Then, my tears exploded.

My body shuddered and collapsed in his arms. I pressed my face against his chest and sobbed, crying against his beating heart.

"Please . . . let me go." I wished he had chest hair so I could tear at it. I wished I didn't have blunt fingernails so I could scratch him. I wished he didn't smell so fucking good. Every attempt to free myself was useless. With every move I made, he held me closer. Tighter. Harder. "Kyle. Stop."

"Not until you hear me out."

"Why? You didn't listen to me about Hunt."

"I was a total ass. I'm so fucking sorry. Please believe me. I wasn't with Amie."

He rested his head on top of mine. His heartbeat thundered in my ear.

Why was he doing this? Why wouldn't he let me go? His hold never slackened. It only made me cry more. More tears. More heartache. More pain.

Fuck.

I couldn't fight anymore. Not with him. I collapsed against his chest and rubbed my salty tears into his flesh. "That's the problem, Kyle. I believe you. But it's not just Amie . . . it's everything. Too much has happened." Too many other issues had driven daggers through my heart. "I hate that this has happened. I hate you don't trust me. I hate we fight all the time. I never wanted having a relationship to affect us as a band, or our friendship, but it has. It's caused nothing but problems. I should've never gone out with Hunt and should've never fallen for you. *I* fucked us up. I hate myself for that." So much for taking a chance on love. All it ever did was hurt. I should have known better. "I live for our music. Our band. I want to fix us, but I don't know how. Maybe Amie's right. We've achieved so much together. Maybe it *is* time we went separate ways. Maybe we should go back to just being friends." *Was that even possible?*

Kyle stroked my hair and rubbed my back. "We can't do that, Gem. I love you too much."

I didn't want to hear those words. Not anymore.

I sniffled loudly. My whole body trembled in his arms. I swallowed the bile burning up my throat and fought the nausea sickening my stomach. "But you said I was like my mother."

"I wish I could take that back." He stroked my hair, running the long strands through his fingers. "I really do. I was hurting. It was a cruel low blow. Please forgive me." He slackened his grip, only to take my face in his hands. He wiped my tears away with his thumbs. "I know you're scared and think you'll end up like her. But I know you won't because you're a fighter. You're stronger than you think. I know tonight is all my fault. Not yours. I'm the one not worthy of your love right now, not vice versa. I'll do whatever it takes to make it up to you. Don't walk away from me because it got ugly between us. I don't want to lose you. I won't lose you. I love you. I love you so much it fucking hurts."

I squeezed my eyes shut. "Please stop saying that."

"I can't. It's the truth." He cupped the side of my neck. "I hate seeing you like this. I want to kiss you and make everything right. But not out here, not where someone might see us. I want to show you how much I care about you. Take away all your pain. Put the pieces of you and me back together."

I shook my head. "I'm not sure you can."

Kyle was my rock, my titanium. But knowing how easily he could hurt me had left me shaken to the core. How could I trust him with my heart ever again?

He placed his forehead against mine. "Please let me try. Please?"

I just stood there. Could I do this?

"Gem?" He softened his tone. "Answer these three questions. Answer them honestly. That will determine everything. Can you do that for me?"

Shit. He'd let me hit him, swear at him, accuse him of cheating . . . and yet he was still here. Not walking away. Not turning to leave. Not running in the opposite direction.

I rubbed my wet nose. I didn't think he could say anything to make things better. There was no light at the end of this tunnel. But I had nothing to lose. I drew in a deep breath and nodded. "Okay."

The smallest of smiles tugged at the corner of his mouth, but worry still clouded his eyes. He placed his hands on my arms and gave them a gentle rub. "Question one: why did you break up with Hunt?"

Why? A dull ache thudded deep inside my head. I rocked on my Vans and lowered my chin. Kyle knew the answer. I'd told him about Las Vegas. About the moment he'd helped me out of the car, when my hand had slipped into his, and everything had clicked into place. My strong feelings for him, which had always simmered beneath the surface, had flared to life. I'd noticed everything. How protective he was, how he looked at me, how my skin tingled when he touched me. And more than anything, how we connected through music. That moment in Vegas was the moment I woke up.

A lump formed in my throat. I looked up into his hopeful face. "I broke up with Hunt because of you."

A spark of light flashed in his eyes, and he squeezed my arms. "Question two: what's the best song you've ever written and why?"

I jabbed my finger against his chest. "You know it's 'Horizon.'" I didn't even have to think about that one.

"Mine too." He caught my hand, holding it against his chest. His eyes ignited like flame to kindling. "Why?"

I closed my eyes, sifting through my memories. "It was the start of everything. We'd worked so hard. We'd gotten our lucky break. Hunt was off flirting with the flight attendant. But you and me? We sat on that plane, absorbing and savoring every second. We captured the feeling and the excitement of our dreams becoming a reality. I never wanted to forget that moment, where I was and who I was with . . . I was with you."

"We've reached beyond the stars . . . together." He circled his thumb over the back of my hand. My skin tingled. Dizziness swam through my head.

Why was he asking these questions? What did this have to do with anything?

"Question three." His eyes darkened, pinning me to the spot. "In the past six months—hell, I'm even going to go out on a limb here and say ever—what was your favorite moment? The one that stopped your heart, then a beat later, it burst to life. The one that changed your world forever. The one you know you can never go back on because nothing will ever be the same."

My breath hitched. My pulse quickened. My hand shot to my necklace—the one he'd given to me for my birthday. Our first kiss. Our first night together. The first time he whispered, *"I love you."* Waking up next to him in the morning, and nearly every morning since that night, had changed my life.

There was no Amie. There was no Hunter. If everything else disappeared, all I needed was Kyle. He was my heartbeat. My four-four common time. The only constant element in my life.

Somehow I found my voice. "My . . . my birthday. With you."

"Same. We've won awards, conquered the world, and live and breathe music . . . but that night tops everything we've ever done."

"Damn you." I slid my hands around his neck and kissed him . . . kissed him hard. He wound his arms around me and crushed me to his chest. His tongue danced with mine, stealing the oxygen from my lungs. My heart raced against his. Blood surged through my veins. There was fight left in me. For Kyle. I couldn't exist without him. "I love you so much."

"I know, Gem. I feel the same way about you."

"I'm sorry for causing all this mess."

"I'm sorry for causing more. But let's just put all this crap behind us. Please?"

"Yeah." I curled my fingers through his hair and kissed him, but he groaned against my lips.

He took my hands and stepped back. "Gem? We can't kiss like this out here. There could be someone watching. Let's go home."

A shiver ran up my spine. *Shit!* He was right. I glanced back toward the highway and over at the neighboring pier, but I couldn't see a single soul. Not one.

"Well then . . . you can take me home on one condition." I held out my hand. "I drive. Hunt has never let me drive his car. I won't tell if you don't."

His eyes glinted as he pulled the keys from his pocket and tossed them to me. "Your wish is my command."

We sank into the leather bucket seats and closed the doors. Kyle leaned over the center console and kissed my lips. "I've told you how much I love you." He trailed featherlight kisses along my jaw, down my neck, then nibbled on my earlobe. "Now . . . I'm gonna take you home and show you. We have a lot of making up to do." His voice hummed with a whole new level of seductiveness.

I tilted my head to the side to give him better access to my neck. "If I went solo, and had to tour by myself, your kisses are what I'd miss the most."

"Oh, I can think of a few other things I'd miss." His breath, hot and heavy on my skin, sent goosebumps down my arm.

"I would definitely miss these." His hand slid underneath my T-shirt and cupped my breast. He tugged the edge of my bra aside to find my nipple. Smiling, he dipped his head and nipped my boob through the fabric.

I grabbed his hair and pulled him back to my lips. "That all?"

"I'd miss your thighs, too." He brushed his lips against mine. His hands drifted downward over my legs. "I love kissing up the inside of your bare skin, knowing where you want me to go."

"And where's that?" I scissored my fingers into his hair and tugged on it.

He tickled up my inner thigh, crossed my shorts, then pressed against my crotch.

My insides quivered. "Kyle . . ."

"Yeah?"

I pushed him back into his seat, crawled over the console, and straddled his lap. "You can't sit there half-naked in front of me and touch me like that. It turns me on too much."

A devilish smile inched across his lips. "So let's go home."

"I won't make it. I want you. Now." I kissed and tugged on his bottom lip. "No one can see through the tinted windows." I flicked my hair back and hit my head on the low roof. "Ow. Shit. This car is ridiculous."

"Gem, this car clocks two hundred and ten miles per hour." Heat blazed in his eyes as he rubbed my head. "I can have you home and naked in two minutes. Stop."

But I didn't want to stop. I ground my hips against his. His cock pressed hard against my crotch through his jeans. I clutched the back of his head and drew his lips against mine. Touching him ignited my body. But he sat rigid, not willing to play. Gliding my hands over his shoulders and bare chest, I tickled him in the ribs. "Is that a stop, I really don't want this? Or stop . . . Please don't stop?"

Want for him blazed through my core. I slid my hand over his steely abs. With a wicked smile, I popped the button at the top of his jeans, and lowered his fly and boxer briefs. I took his hard, hot, heavy cock in my hand.

"Fuck. Please don't stop." Golden shards shimmered in his eyes. A low, sexy rumble echoed deep in his throat. His hands knotted through my hair, and he pulled my lips to his.

My heart skipped. *Yeah . . . he is mine.*

Kyle's hands shot under my shirt and unhooked my bra. I worked my fingers up the sleeves of my T-shirt and removed it in a perfect "Flashdance" style. Kyle's eyes widened as I tossed it on the driver's seat. "Gem, you never cease to amaze me."

He lifted my shirt, dipped his head, and took my nipple in his mouth. He flicked and circled his tongue over one bud, then the other. I arched my back, begging for more.

Reaching down between us, I wrapped my hand around his cock. I stroked him up and down, and ran my thumb through the seam, circling around the head.

"I love it when you touch me." Kyle found my lips again, his tongue entwining with mine. The fire between us was so hot it made it difficult to breathe. His soft hands cupped my neck, knotted in my hair, and roamed my skin. His hips pulsed, thrusting his cock against my touch.

So good, but I wanted more.

I tapped his shoulder. "Take my shorts off."

"How? I can't fuckin move in this car."

"Shit. Hold on." I unzipped my shorts, turned around on his lap, kicked off my Vans, and eased my shorts and panties free. They joined my bra. In nothing but my T-shirt, I shuffled around and re-straddled his lap. I slapped my hand against the fogged-up passenger-side window. "We're steaming it up in here."

"We are hot together." Kyle ran his hands over my bare thighs, then looked down one side of the car seat, then the other. "Fuck. Hunt obviously did not have sex in mind when he bought this thing. The seat doesn't move. My knees are killing me. Wait . . . I can lower the back."

The leather seat shot backwards. I fell forward over the top of Kyle. Laughing, we kissed and wriggled and shuffled about to get comfortable.

"You're lucky I'm small . . . and flexible." I rubbed my pussy against Kyle's cock protruding from the top of his half-undone jeans and boxer briefs.

"Yes, I am." He lifted his hips beneath me and tugged his jeans lower. "Now come here." He grabbed me around the hips and guided me into place. He teased my opening with his cock. As he kissed me, his fingers made their way between my legs. He circled and stroked my clit, teasing me with torturous strokes. "You're so fucking wet. Do you have any idea how much that turns me on?"

"Yeah. But I want you inside me." My body needed to be connected to his.

He took hold of his dick and guided it into my pussy.

I lowered onto him. First, just an inch, then a bit more, and then I took his full length. My toes curled. Heat rushed up my spine. Tingles pooled at the base of my neck. "Much better."

He cupped my cheek. "God, I love you."

My heart thundered with as much horsepower as the car's engine. "I love you."

He crushed his lips against mine. His hands curled underneath my hair and rubbed the back of my neck.

I smiled against his mouth as I rode him, gentle and slow. Steady and deep. But when he rocked his hips, I picked up the pace.

He grabbed my ass and tugged me forward, hard against him. Thrusting, he penetrated me deeper. The car seat squeaked in protest, but I didn't slow down.

"Gem, like that. Don't stop." He panted and closed his eyes. Sweat beaded on his skin. Pleasure and pain danced across his face.

I grabbed onto the car seat near his shoulder. My thighs quaked as I rode him, but I didn't stop. I wanted him. All of him. Every fucking inch.

He rubbed my clit with his thumb, circling and swirling in gentle strokes. But I needed more. "Touch me harder. Just a little . . . harder."

Kyle's thumb offered more friction. My insides clenched. A guttural groan escaped me. My orgasm ripped through me, coiling through my veins and shuddering through every cell in my body.

"God, I love it when you do that." His breaths came sharper and shorter, his lips curling into a wicked smile. "I love making you come."

As I caressed his face, my breath rushed against his. I drove my hips down toward his. He pulsed and rocked and thrust into me. His body jerked. And jerked again.

I giggled. "Same."

"Fuck." Grinning, his head jolted back against the seat. His body quaked against mine. I slowed to a languid rhythm as his cock throbbed inside me. I stroked his face, pushed his hair out of his eyes, and kissed his cheeks, his eyes, his nose, and his mouth.

"I love you," I whispered and smiled as his heart raced beneath my hand. "Don't ever doubt it, never forget it."

His eyes smoldered as he smoothed his hand over my hair. "Gem, I love you with every cell in my body and all my soul. And although I do like make-up sex, let's hope we never have to do this again."

"True." Fire still burned in my cheeks. The blood rush to my head had left me giddy. "And although it was good, we'd better get dressed and go home." I shuffled back into the driver's seat and pulled on my panties and shorts.

Kyle chuckled and did up his jeans. "I can't believe we just had sex in Hunt's car."

"Me neither." I straightened in the seat, turned on the ignition, and revved the engine. "He'd fucking kill us if he found out. Better not mention this to him."

"No. Better not."

I blasted the air conditioning to clear the foggy windows. Something shiny on the opposite pier caught my eye. While the walkway was lit with dim lights, darkness covered the shed. I could make out the railing at the top of the pontoon, but other than that, I couldn't see anyone or anything move.

Maybe it was the car headlights catching on something metal. But a shiver ran up my spine. My skin prickled. I squinted, looking harder into the blackness, but still couldn't see anything.

I clipped on my seatbelt.
My heart hammered against my ribs.
My palms sweated as I clutched the steering wheel.
Shit. Shit. Shit.
Had someone been watching?

Chapter 31

KYLE

"Don't answer it."

Not wanting to wake up, I refused to let Gemma out of my embrace to answer her cell phone vibrating on my nightstand. Drawing the bedsheets over us, I nuzzled into her neck, her soft hair brushing against my face.

"Okay." She hugged my arm tighter against her chest and entwined her fingers with mine.

But Gemma's phone buzzed again. And again. Then my phone rang too.

I flopped onto my back and grabbed my phone to turn it off. But seeing Kate's name on the screen at 7:04 a.m. made me think twice. Had we forgotten to be somewhere?

I thumbed the screen to answer the call and held my phone against my ear. "S'up, Kate?" I yawned and pulled my arm out from underneath Gemma. It was dead, full of pins and needles, but holding her had been worth it.

"What the hell did you two do last night?" Kate's voice fired out of the speaker. "You. Gemma. Pier 97. You're on every goddamn gossip and entertainment site across the Internet. *Gossipline* broke the story, and they're having a field day."

I shot upright. Nausea flooded my gut. "They what?"

"Kyle?" Gemma rose to sit beside me, tucked her arm around my back, and kissed the tip of my shoulder. "What's wrong?"

"Shit. Gem, get up." I scrambled out of bed and grabbed my boxer briefs off the floor. "We got photographed last night. We have to see what we're dealing with and come up with a plan."

Gemma froze, clutching the sheet against her chest, and stared into the distance.

Kate shrieked through my cell phone. "This is great. Just fucking great. You've got interviews all this week. They're going to eat you alive."

My stomach sank. My pulse rang in my ears. *Fuck!*

"I'll talk to Gem," I said to Kate. "I'll call you back soon."

I threw my phone on the bed, yanked on my underwear, and eased in beside Gemma. Her face had paled and held a green tinge. Her eyes had clouded over like a bleak winter's day as she drew the sheet up to her chin.

"Gem? We haven't seen the photos." I kept my voice calm, but my insides were in knots. I should've known better than to get carried away last night. But fuck . . . Gem was just too tempting. I rubbed her back and kissed her forehead. "Don't panic. It can't be that bad."

"I think I'm going to be sick." She wrapped her arms around her stomach and rocked back and forth.

"Gem. Breathe. Let's go check things out on my laptop."

She winced but nodded.

We scrambled to get dressed and headed out to the living room. I opened my laptop on the dining room table and waited for it to load.

Hunter mumbled as he trudged out of the hallway. "Why the fuck is Kate trying to call me at this hour?" He dragged his feet toward the kitchen and ruffled his hand through his hair. He grabbed a cup and hit the button on the coffee machine. "What the hell does she want?"

Gemma's shoulders slumped as she stared at the laptop screen.

My fingers trembled as I typed in my password. "Gem and I

got photographed last night."

"Doing what?" Hunter grimaced as he grabbed the milk from the fridge.

I Googled my name.

Across the screen, every feature story, headline, and dark, blurry image was of me and Gemma on the pier. Pictures of us fighting. Hugging. Kissing. And *shit . . .* in Hunter's car. *But wait.* I peered closer. The only things captured of us in the car were the steamed-up windows and Gemma's hand pressing against the glass. There was nothing more incriminating than that. *Thank fuck.*

But Gemma's hand shot over her mouth. Hunter joined us and loomed over my shoulder, sipping coffee. My hand shook as I clicked on the lead article by *Gossipline*, the tabloid giant claiming the scoop. The three of us read the article.

> *Kyle and Gemma from Everhide are HOT for each other and sizzle under the stars.*
>
> *Kyle McIntyre and Gemma Lonsdale, two of the three lead singers in the world-dominating pop–rock band, Everhide, have had us all fooled. For years, they have claimed to be nothing more than friends, but last night the duo was seen in the early morning hours on Pier 97.*
>
> *At first, the two singers seemed to have an argument, but matters quickly turned as they kissed and made up, and . . . got steamy inside Hunter Collins's car.*
>
> *Speculation about the trio's friendship has always been rife, and now we have evidence they are clearly more than friends. Sources tell us the couple have been together for more than a month since they ventured to Hawaii to film the video for their latest single "Rise Up".*
>
> *Millions of fans worldwide will be devastated to learn these two are off the market.*
>
> *We can't wait to see what happens next with this fiery new*

couple.
#Everhide #RockstarRomance #KyleandGemma #KyGem
#MoreThanFriends #BustedBigTime

Fuck.

Gemma sank into the chair beside me and trembled. "Shit."

I clutched her hand and gave it a reassuring squeeze. "Hey. It's okay. We'll deal with it." How? I had no fucking idea. Gemma didn't want to go public with our relationship. Neither did I. I wanted to protect her from public scrutiny, not create it.

Hunter clipped me on the back of the head—hard. *Ow!* He'd done that way too much in the past several hours. "You fucked in my car? Not even I've done that . . . no . . . wait . . . yes, I have. I think her name was Mandy, or Mindy, or something like that. But that's not the point. You had sex in *my* car." He shoved me on the shoulder. "You'd better not have left cum stains on the seats."

"I think we have more important things to worry about than that, Hunt." I sneered at him, then turned to Gemma. "Hey? These pictures? . . . They're not that bad."

Hunter leaned over, peered at the screen . . . and laughed. "Come on, Gem. These are fine. You're not butt naked like you were with Ben. Your tits aren't all over the Net again."

She winced and chewed on her thumb. "Everyone's going to assume Kyle and I had sex in your car."

"You *did* have sex in my car." Hunter pointed at the screen, then slapped me on the back. "Dude, you owe me some new wheels. You said not a mark. You two have gotten yourselves into a tight corner with this one. I can't wait to see how you're going to get out of it."

Gemma rubbed at the furrows digging into her brow. "What are we going to do?"

So much gossip had been published about the three of us over the years. It had never bothered me when it involved someone I didn't know or didn't care about. All the one-night stands, the hot encounters, the kisses with strangers at parties, and the wild rumors had never mattered. There was little or no truth to most of the stories, and my heart had never been involved. But now . . . this was different. This was about me and Gemma. I hated seeing her stressed, and I never wanted to humiliate her. Not after Ben.

I'd do anything to make this right.

"Gem?" I squeezed her hand. "We can deny it or be honest. Or say we were drunk. Or that I was with someone who looked like you. I'll take all the heat if you want me to. But whatever we decide, we need to get our story straight."

"Yes, but it's not just about covering things up. Last night was crazy. One minute we're on the brink of breaking up, the next . . . this happened." She flicked a finger toward the image of Hunter's car on the screen. "We have a lot of shit to sort out. I want to do that in private, not with the world breathing down our necks. We're still new. Still finding our feet. And still a clear fucking mess."

"But we're a good mess." I swiveled toward her and swept her hair back over her shoulder. "Gem, you know me better than anyone. I'll work on my crap. I promise. Last night we proved we can work through anything. We're still together. If anything, we're stronger."

"Oh, puh-lease." Hunter headed toward the coffee machine and made another drink. "You're going to make me vomit. You two are seriously fucked up. Just admit to being together. No one will care."

"No." Fear and worry swam through Gemma's eyes. "I'm not ready."

"Why not?" My heart wobbled. "The news is out there, so let's own it. It's not how I would've liked to have gone public, but the media has been saying shit about us for years. Denying it could only make things worse."

"Yes, it could. But I don't want to come out via a sex scandal. We'll do it on our terms when the time is right, not thanks to some gossip. We need time for things to settle. For you not to be jealous. For us to be secure and comfortable about going forward."

"Gem, I'm yours." I cradled the back of her neck and gave it a rub. "Nothing's gonna change that."

She closed her eyes and nodded. "Good." She slid her hand up my thigh and curled it around my leg. "I just want some time. To fall more in love with you. To be with you. To be certain something like last night never happens again. Please?" she pleaded. "I'm not going anywhere either. We'll get through this. I promise."

"Yeah." I dipped my chin. "We always do."

"Thank you."

Her cell phone buzzed on the table. She glanced at the screen and groaned. "Fuck. This is another reason why I don't want to say anything." She picked her phone up and waved it at me. "No surprise. Guess who?" She swiped the screen and put it on speaker. "Mom, how are you?"

Shit! I winced. *Yep. I understand. Totally.*

"How do you think I am?" Janine's shrill voice filled the room. "The Internet has gone crazy. Pictures of you and Kyle are everywhere. Is that you two having sex in Hunter's car?"

My gut cinched and hit the floor. We'd made world news in less than five hours. Seriously, didn't people have better things to do?

Gemma slipped out of the chair and paced beside the table. "Mom, no—"

"Just tell me." Excitement quaked in Janine's voice. "Is it true? I have to know. Tell me everything."

Gemma dragged a hand down her face. Her shoulders slumped. "Why, Mom? So you can run and tell your friends?"

"Yes, they'll be dying to know what happened." Janine's callous voice sent a chill through my bones. "Gemma, you'll never last in the music business if you can't handle the gossip."

The shimmer faded from Gemma's eyes. All emotion drained from her face as she stared at me. My skin prickled. I knew what was coming. I hated it, but we needed to get Janine off our case.

"Mom?" Gemma held her phone in front of her. "Kyle and I aren't together." She gave me an *I'm-so-sorry-I-have-to-lie* look. "It's all bullshit. Kyle and I were fighting, not making out."

My heart hit the floor. Why did it struggle to beat? Was it

because we fought? *Certainly.* Was it regret for putting myself and Gemma in this situation? *Definitely.* Was it because I loved Gemma so much I didn't care who knew we were together? *Absolutely.*

"Oh, baby girl," Janine whined. "Well, that's boring. When are you going to get yourself a boyfriend, so we have something fun to talk about? It's been ages since you've hooked up with someone hot and hunky. You need to stop thinking you're better than everyone else and find someone who'll take care of you."

A stab of pain shot through my chest. No wonder Gemma was afraid of love when Janine was like this. I clenched my fists on the table to stop myself from lunging forward, snatching the phone from Gemma, and telling Janine to go to hell.

"I don't need anyone to look after me." Gemma clutched her necklace, rubbing her thumb over the gold pendant. *Yeah . . . Gem had me.* "I can take care of myself."

"Fine. But I want to know what happened between you and Kyle. These photos have a story behind them, and I want to know what it is." Janine's voice carried way too much delight. "You can tell me all about it when I come to New York in a few days' time. I'd love to catch up when I fly in from Rome."

Panic flashed through Gemma's eyes. "You're coming here? Why? You never want to see me. If it's just for some gossip, forget it."

"Oh no. I haven't seen my baby girl for ages. And I'm being interviewed by a magazine." Janine boasted, light and flippant. "For some mothers of famous daughters feature. They're paying all my expenses and putting me up at the London Hotel. Will you meet me there for brunch on Sunday?"

I shook my head and folded my arms. There it was. Janine wanted to be seen with Gemma at a trendy restaurant.

"Why can't you come to my place?" Gemma stared at her cell phone.

"Oh, no. You must come to The London," Janine insisted. "Their brunch is amazing. You could bring Kyle with you."

Gemma groaned. "Nice try, Mom. But no. There will be no Kyle. And no Hunter." I glanced at Hunter who pouted like a schoolboy.

He loved any form of attention. But Gemma shook her head, then sighed. "I suppose I can come. Send me the time and I'll put it into my schedule."

"Will do," Janine said. "Send my love to the boys. Bye."

Gemma ended the call, came over, and sat on my lap. I wrapped my arms around her and hugged her tight. "Gem, don't go if she's going to upset you."

"Too late for that. But I haven't seen her in almost two years. I'll go. It'll be fine."

"Guys, Janine is the least of your worries." Hunter leaned against the counter and slurped his coffee. "We've got a week full of interviews coming up, and whether you like it or not, you two are going to be the number-one topic. So, we'd better go see Bec and Kate and get your story straight."

Chapter 32

GEMMA

I clung onto Kyle's hand. His fingers fidgeted with mine. The limousine made its way steadily along the narrow street leading up to the studio's entrance. Tonight, we were guests, live on the *Jimmy Royson Late Night Show*. This was our first interview since Kyle and I had been photographed on the pier two days ago. My stomach was more tangled than a box of power cords.

The sidewalk near the studio swarmed with screaming fans waving posters of all colors, pictures, drawings, and magazines in the air. The car windows offered little protection from the shrill cries and the blinding camera flashes.

"Another day at the office." Hunter waved out the window, but without his usual energetic vibe.

This interview wouldn't be easy for any of us.

"Everything will be fine." Kate gave me a reassuring smile. "We've run through and rehearsed how to handle the questions during the interview."

"Idiots." Amie tapped her nails on the back of her cell phone. "I've no sympathy for you, Gemma. Or you, Kyle. You should've known better."

I let go of Kyle's hand and wiped my sweaty palm on my jeans. Amie was right. I couldn't blame Kyle for any part of what had happened down at the pier. This was my fault. I was the one who'd kissed him. The one who'd crawled onto his lap in the car. The one who'd seduced him. Like always, everything had consequences. This one had landed us neck deep in shit. But we had constructed a solid story. We were good to go.

I was certain none of this would've happened if it wasn't for Amie. The three of us had agreed her days were numbered, she just didn't know it yet. Her recent power play would be our ammunition to take the heat off Kyle and me. Bitch didn't care.

"Amie, it's a good thing we have you to take the spotlight off us." I snapped with acid on my tongue.

She fluttered her false eyelashes. "Unlike you, Gemma, I'm not afraid of the truth."

Amie's words stung. I'd been lying and denying and covering things up for months. But being with Kyle . . . everything was different. He had more of a hold on my heart than I originally thought, and that terrified me. Terrified me in a good way. I just needed more time to be certain we were solid.

"We're here." Kate grabbed her purse, hooked it over her shoulder, and shuffled forward on the seat. "Let's get this over with."

Our bodyguards were the first to move. Sam slipped out of the front seat. Chester and Mick rushed over from the car in front and opened the door of the limousine.

For twenty minutes, Kyle, Hunter, and I worked the crowd. We posed for photos, snapped selfies, signed autographs, and ignored reporters shouting unwanted questions. We were then ushered into the green room to kick back until we were due on set. Rehearsals for the show earlier in the afternoon had gone off without a hitch. But I had a niggle at the base of my neck that wouldn't ease—a superstition to be prepared. I poured myself a third JD and knocked it back to settle my nerves.

"Gem, you ready?" Kyle clinked his glass against mine.

"No. You?"

Kyle's eyes glinted as he chuckled. "Not exactly."

"I'm sorry for getting us into this mess."

"It's not all on you, Gem. I played my part. This will blow over in a couple days. It always does. Just know that I love you and we'll get through it. Together."

The show's producer walked in, fitted us with lapel mics, and led us out to the main studio. Four telecast cameras stood positioned on the floor out front. Sound booms and lights hung overhead on trusses. The live audience sat huddled in tiered rows. Jimmy, with his thick bushy eyebrows and cheesy smile, sat behind his desk, engaging with the crowd. His famous orange sofa waited for its visitors.

I took a deep breath to settle the nausea pooling in my gut. *Here goes nothing.* I gave the guys a quick hug. "Love you. Let's do this."

Jimmy hollered and clapped. "And now I'd like to welcome our special guests for this evening." Jimmy pointed his hand toward us standing just off set. "None other than global rock sensation, Everhide. Please welcome Gemma Lonsdale, Kyle McIntyre, and Hunter Collins."

The audience erupted, clapping, screaming, and whistling. I followed Kyle and Hunter onto the studio set. Somehow, my feet cooperated.

I took a seat on the sofa between Hunter and Kyle, making sure I was sitting right in the middle, not closer to one than the other. I feigned a smile in Jimmy's direction and rested my hands on my lap. The JD had kicked in. A lazy buzz warmed my veins. Yep, I was good. The first interview after any gossip was always the worst. I was ready to get this over and done with.

"It's great to see you again. Can you believe it's been just over twelve months since you were last here?" Jimmy sounded genuinely pleased to see us, but we knew better. During rehearsals, he'd said he hadn't been looking forward to following through on his directive from the show's producers and executives. The pressure was on to address the rumors. He'd assured us he'd maintain his professionalism. That was why we'd agreed to come on his show. We'd run through questions and practiced. But when live, in front of an audience, things didn't always go to plan.

"It's great to be back," Hunter said, resting his arm along the sofa behind my head. "Last time we were here, we announced our world tour."

"That's right." Jimmy nodded. "Your third tour, *Endless Road*, was amazing. Did anyone here see the show?" He waved a finger toward the audience.

The crowd erupted with cheers and claps, but that did nothing to settle my nerves.

"And you've recently finished a promotional tour for your single 'Rise Up' to raise awareness for leukemia. Great cause, by the way. Is there anything else interesting you've been up to this summer? It has been a particularly *hot* and *steamy* one, hasn't it?" Jimmy grinned and loaded his words with cheeky innuendo as he tilted his head at Kyle.

Sweat trickled down the back of my neck.

"Yeah, the balmy nights have been tough." Grinning, Kyle shuffled around in his seat. The touch of his arm against mine was the sign I needed that all would be okay. A few more minutes, and the interview would be over.

"Hmm . . . your idea of tough must be very different from mine." Jimmy's eyes glinted. He pursed his lips and tapped his cue cards on the table. "Because the three of you have heated up the headlines lately. Some have been good. Some of them bad. Some days, I can't keep up with it all. Firstly, Hunter, I don't want to disappoint any of your female fans, but is it true that you're dating Amie, your manager?"

Hunter leaned forward and grabbed the glass of water off the table. "We had a thing for a while, but it didn't work out." His tone was full of nonchalance—impressive, considering how cut up he was about Amie. He sipped his water, then moved back onto the sofa.

"You win some, you lose some." Jimmy seesawed his hands in the air as if balancing something in the left, then the right.

Whoa. Jimmy brushed over Hunter's sexcapades without biting or digging deeper. We'd come up with some playful remarks during rehearsal, but Jimmy skipped them all. Why was that? Was it because Hunter had so many girls no one cared anymore? *Shit.* Maybe . . . just maybe, I should take some notes from Hunter about being honest about my relationship. *Fuck.*

"You're back on the market then?" Jimmy asked.

"I'm always available." Hunter gave the audience a flash of his charismatic smile, sending everyone into a frenzy of squeals and whistles.

"And what about you two?" Jimmy leaned forward onto his elbows. His eyes darted from Kyle to me. "What is going on?"

I let out a nervous laugh and shook my head.

Kyle inhaled deeply and rubbed his hand down his thigh. "Not much. It's just been business as usual."

"Damn . . . I'm in the *wrong* business then." Jimmy smiled, showing off his overly bright, white teeth, then quickly reset his poker face. "Come on, we've all seen the news . . . So what's the deal? You're young, you've had a late night, lost a shirt, let off some steam, got caught parking on a pier—"

"Well—" I grimaced.

Jimmy held up a placating hand. "Look, I don't want to embarrass the two of you. We've all seen the photos. I'd be surprised if anyone hasn't. And, like me, I'm sure there are many concerned fans out there who just want to know if everything is okay. Because one moment on the pier it looked like you were ready to kill each other, then . . . well . . ." His eyebrows wriggled. "Did Hunter's car have no air-conditioning?"

My pulse thundered in my ears. But I sat still, completely unmoved. Any form of reaction would only create more speculation. Thankfully, my years of media training kicked in. I inhaled. Slowly. Calmly. Deeply. I focused on the red light on the wall behind Jimmy's shoulder . . . and let the lies roll off my tongue. "Hunter's car is fine. It's *great* to ride in . . . I mean . . . great to drive." I made a bit of fun at my expense, but the heat in my cheeks was real. "But this is one of those situations where not everything is as it seems."

"She's right." Kyle stretched out his legs and ran his hand over his thigh. "The other night, we had a huge fight about work. She was upset. I was drunk. Things got ugly. We made up . . . Yes, I stupidly kissed her to say sorry . . . but that really didn't go down well. Gem got mad. We got in the car. Argued some more. That explains the steamy windows . . . and my black eye. She clobbered me one." He pointed to the bruise on his cheek from Hunter swiping him, not me. He continued without hesitating. "We drove home. I woke up with a huge hangover. I apologized, and we're best friends again. That's it."

"Wow." Jimmy held out his hand and waggled a finger between us. "So . . . you two. You're good?"

"Absolutely." I nodded and nudged Kyle in the side with my elbow. "Good as ever. Sometimes we just need to let off a little steam. The other night, we just let off a lot. It was weird, because we rarely fight." I laughed, ignoring the perspiration running down my back. "But to set the record straight about our *heated discussion*, and before you all speculate we're breaking up, and the rumors morph into more insane gossip, earlier on that evening I'd had dinner with Amie, our manager. She'd dropped a bombshell about the changes our record company wanted to make. I wasn't happy . . . not at all." I paused for dramatic effect. "Because they asked me to go solo."

The crowd gasped. Several people cried out. "Noooo."

"They *what*?" Jimmy's eyes widened. He slapped his hand hard against his chest.

For the first time since walking on set, my breathing eased. The news of going solo had the desired effect. The crowd's interest was no longer focused on Kyle and me.

"I said no. I'm not leaving these guys. Not ever." I slapped their thighs. "On the pier, Kyle kept badgering me, asking if going solo was something I wanted to do. It's a big no. That's it. End of story."

"I'm in shock." Jimmy gasped. "Solo? Can they do that?"

"They can ask all they want." I shrugged. "But it's not going to happen. We're not breaking up. We're stronger than ever and aim to be around for a very long time. Just like the Rolling Stones."

"You're stuck with us." Hunter leaned in and gave me a noogie.

Kyle play-punched me in the arm. "That's right. We're not going anywhere."

"Oh, thank God." Jimmy loosened his tie, relief washing over his face, all over-emphasized to please the audience.

"So now the slate is clean . . . well, until we cause another Internet meltdown." Hunter smiled and placed his arm on the sofa behind me. "The good news is we're about to hit the studio to record our fifth album. The first single will be released in a couple months, and the album will be out before Christmas."

"That's brilliant. We need more incredible music from you guys. We want more hits like 'Rise Up,' don't we?" Jimmy circled his hands in the air, hyping up the crowd. They cheered and clapped and whistled. "Who wants to hear Everhide sing?" The roar grew louder from the stands. Jimmy waved toward the band area. "Why don't the three of you head on over to the stage and sing for us?"

"We'd love to." I led Kyle and Hunter over to the mics.

We grabbed our guitars, put on our in-ear monitors, and exchanged we-nailed-it winks. Somehow, we'd survived another interview. We'd pulled it off without too much drama. But I could tell the lies were getting to Kyle. He'd gone along with the coverup without question, but every time we'd avoided the truth, the spark in his eyes faded.

If we could get through the next few days, the gossip would die down. Then we could put all the hurt and fear behind us. Stay low and get our relationship back on track.

The three of us would hit the studio next week. Recording was always fun. We could put the turbulent past few months behind us and look forward to the future.

All I had to do was make it through a few more interviews.

And survive Sunday brunch with my mother.

Chapter 33

GEMMA

On Sunday morning, I hopped out of the black SUV, stepped in behind Chester, and entered the lobby of the London Hotel on 54th. Trust my mother to pick one of the busiest restaurants in New York for brunch. There were people everywhere. With my chin down, dark sunglasses on and my baseball cap drawn low over my eyes, I prayed I wouldn't be recognized.

As I waited for the maître-d to serve the patrons in front of me, I pulled my cell phone out of my Gucci tote and quickly scanned my emails, searching for another update from Amie. She'd scheduled a meeting for me and the guys at SureHaven, but had failed to provide an agenda. I'd replied, asking for one, but she hadn't sent it through. We always had an agenda. The lack of one made me nervous. *Damn it. Still nothing.* I slipped my phone away and greeted the now-free host.

"Hi. Is Janine Lonsdale here?" My mother never used her current married name, not since I'd become famous. Mine got her into more places and more celebrity treatment. She abused my name to the nth degree. No surprise there.

"Yes. It's a pleasure to have you join us today, Miss Lonsdale." She grabbed two menus off the pile beside the check-in tablet. "I'm Petunia. If you need anything, I'll be happy to help. Please.

Follow me. I'll take you to your booth."

"Thanks." I straightened my tote on my shoulder and followed Petunia through the restaurant, past guests sitting in front of plates full of omelets and pastries, fry-ups, coffees, and Prosecco. But just as I reached halfway across the room, my mother's shrill voice filled the air.

"Gemma. Gemma." Janine slid out of the booth on the far side of the restaurant. She scuttled toward me in her ridiculously high, bright-green stiletto platforms and flung her arms around me. My face disappeared into her puffed-up, peroxide-blonde hair, reeking of sickly hairspray. She eased back and kissed me hard on the cheek. "Oh, my darling baby girl. It's soooo good to see you."

Ugh! I couldn't muster any form of excitement about being here. I rubbed my face, hoping no bright pink lipstick was left on my skin. "Hey, Mom."

Whispers from nearby diners reached my ears. *That's Gemma Lonsdale—from Everhide.*

So much for trying to be inconspicuous.

Sympathetic understanding flickered through Chester's eyes. He'd witnessed, overheard, and endured my mother's crap over the years. He knew what she was like. He waved toward the circular bar in the center of the restaurant. "I'll wait over here."

"Thanks." I slapped him on the shoulder. The lucky bastard didn't have to put up with my mother. "Make sure you eat something, okay?"

"Will do." He nodded and headed over to the bar.

I slid into the booth opposite my mother, dodging the ice bucket holding her Prosecco. Petunia handed us the menus, excused herself, and disappeared. But a roomful of guests watched my every move.

I smiled and gave them a little wave. The gentleman at the nearby table dipped his chin, then continued to read his paper and sip his cup of tea.

"So . . . Mom." I pulled off my baseball cap and placed it on the seat beside me. "What's it been? Nearly two years?"

"Oh, has it been that long?" Janine dug into her purse, grabbed her hand mirror, and retouched her lipstick. "I've been traveling. You've been busy. Time just disappears, doesn't it?" She snapped the case shut and put her makeup away.

"Yep." I scanned the restaurant, making sure there were no overzealous fans seeking photos or autographs. Normally I wouldn't mind, but my mother would relish the attention. Luckily, most of the diners were adults. Hopefully, I could eat breakfast without being interrupted. I checked where the exits were—a habit to always know the quickest route out of a place if I got inundated with fans. I nodded at Chester to let him know I was okay . . . for now. "So, Mom? Did you work things out with Victor, or are you still getting divorced?"

My mother ignored me and waved to the waiter. Once she had his attention, she pointed to her bottle of Prosecco.

The waiter glided over, bowed, and poured my mother another drink. He turned to me. "Good morning, Ms. Lonsdale. Would you like a glass?"

"No, thank you." I shook my head and flicked my finger at the bottle of Evian on the table. "Water's fine."

"Oh, come on, baby girl. You can have one glass of bubbly with your mother, can't you?" Janine tilted her glass toward me.

"No-pe." I shrugged. "Champagne or anything bubbly messes with my vocal cords. We're hitting the studio next week, and I can't risk any damage."

"Your loss. More for me." My mother downed the Prosecco like it was fruit juice. "Let's order food, and then we'll talk."

"Great idea." I grabbed the menu. The sooner I ate, the sooner I could get out of there. Talking to my mother was not my favorite pastime. We gave our order to the waiter. He bowed and hurried off toward the kitchen.

My mother happily helped herself to more Prosecco, pouring another glass.

"You didn't answer my question." I straightened my cutlery. "What's happening with Victor?"

Janine tapped her fingernails against the stem of her champagne flute. "Well . . . we've signed the divorce papers."

I puffed air through my nose. "Why am I not surprised?" I didn't feel sorry for my mother; I felt sorry for Victor. He was nice . . . gullible . . . old . . . sweet. "What happened?"

"We had very different needs. Especially in the bedroom. If you know what I mean." Janine fluttered her eyelashes as her loud voice carried. No doubt the three tables next to us heard every word. The man at the next table looked up. Janine winked at him, but he quickly returned to reading his newspaper.

I rolled my eyes at my mother. "I don't want to know what your needs are, Mom. So now what?"

"We're going to settle out of court. He's promised to look after me financially." Janine had a triumphant glint in her eye. It made me sick to the stomach. "You don't have to worry about me, baby girl."

"I wasn't," I mumbled, low and sharp.

"I'm only here until tomorrow night." She fanned her hand across her chest and shimmied her shoulders. "Then I'm heading to Florida to meet up with Antonio. Oh, you're going to love Antonio. I met him in Cyprus. He's *Italian*. I can't understand what he says half the time, but he's a great lover." My mother's eyes shone as if she'd won the jackpot on a casino slot machine. "I told him all about you. He can't wait to meet you."

"Is he going to be husband number five?"

Janine let out a high-pitched laugh and threw her head back. "Oh, you know how to make a joke."

But I wasn't laughing and wasn't even remotely close to doing so. "How rich is this guy, Mom? Is he better off than Victor? I bet my life he is."

Janine's smug smile was the confirmation I needed. "What can I say? I fall in and out of love easily."

"You're not with anyone long enough to fall in love. Do you even know what love is?" My hand went to my throat and touched Kyle's necklace. Had my mother ever felt for any of her men what I felt for Kyle? Would she go to any lengths to fight and protect a treasured relationship? I highly doubted it.

"And you do?" Janine arched her penciled eyebrow.

"You . . . who hasn't had a serious boyfriend since Ben? Or so you tell me. Are you jealous I've found a new lover who is fantastic in the bedroom?"

"Ew. Gross. No, I'm not jealous." I took a long drink of water to ease the nausea pooling in my gut. Something stronger would be good, but not around my mother.

"We're both adults. Sex is nothing to be ashamed of."

"I'm not ashamed." I shook my head. "I just don't want to talk about it with you in the middle of a restaurant."

The waiter delivered our food and took off. The smell of bacon and maple syrup wafted from my mother's plate. I pushed the granola around in my bowl, unsure if I'd be able to stomach it.

"We're not changing the subject." Janine's voice turned all sweet and innocent as she nibbled on a piece of crisp bacon. "So . . . while we're talking about sex, what's happening between you and Kyle?"

"I've already told you. There's nothing going on." I scooped a spoonful of granola into my mouth and swallowed hard. But in the past week, so much had gone down. Hunter had been unrelentingly supportive of Kyle and me. We'd had a dozen interviews. During each one, the three of us sat beside each other, played it cool, kept our story on point. It had gotten easier each time. Through it all, it confirmed how strong, committed, and protective we were of each other. We knew the truth. That's all that mattered.

It made me fall in love with Kyle a little more each day.

But my mother was not within my trusted circle of friends. I wouldn't tell her anything about our relationship. And I never would. I'd sooner rot in hell.

Janine finished her mouthful of bacon and leaned forward. Her huge breasts squished against the table, deepening the abyss of her cleavage. "Something happened on that pier, and I want the details. I've suspected something has been going on between you two since Hawaii. Did you break up? Is that what the fight was about? Then you had make-up sex in Hunter's car?"

The niggle in the back of my neck grew stronger. Why was my mother searching for details? There was something in her tone—a hunger, a desperate need, an obsession—that made my skin prickle.

"Why do you care?" I loaded my spoon with granola. "Is it so you can compare your failed relationships with mine? Score points? Will that make you feel better about yourself?"

Janine straightened and glared at me. She flicked her hand toward me, her fuchsia talons catching the light. "You think you're so perfect, living in your perfect little world, with perfect, hot guys dripping off you, traveling the world in first class, and playing your stupid guitar every day." She stabbed her finger on the table. Her wrist, full of gold bangles and chains, tinkled together. "You wouldn't be here if it wasn't for me."

I choked on my mouthful of food. "Oh, my God. My life is far from perfect. You, of all people, should know that. I've worked my ass off to get where I am today. Your view of the world is so fucking skewed. You wouldn't be here if it wasn't for *me*."

"I won't deny dropping your name helps in certain social circles." Janine pushed her empty plate aside, folded her hands, and placed them on the table. "Now, tell me what happened on that pier. If you won't, maybe Kyle will. He might be more forthcoming with information, like Ben was. He played the game well."

My heart faltered. The hair on my arms stood on end. "Kyle would say exactly the same thing as I have. But what do you mean? What information from Ben? What game?"

"Oh, it was so long ago." Janine swiped her hand through the air and laughed like it was no big deal.

"Tell me." My voice sliced through my teeth.

"My sweet, sweet Gemma. I can't believe how naïve you are sometimes." Janine sighed and shook her head. "Ben was the one who told me the name of the private villa you stayed in for your vacation. I made one quick call, cut a deal, and the photographers were there. It was all planned perfectly. Ben made a few bucks . . . and so did I. A lot, actually."

My lungs collapsed. My head spun. "You did what?" I dropped my spoon. I wanted to pick up my granola and throw it in my mother's face. Launch across the table and strangle her. "*You* sold me out for money?" My voice shook. My body shook. My blood boiled. "I was so humiliated and hurt after those photos went viral. How could you do that to me?"

Janine blinked and shrugged. There was no flicker of remorse in her eyes. No tears. No regret. No nothing.

The gentleman at the neighboring table glanced over, concern drawn on his face. *"Are you okay?"* he mouthed.

I forced my head to nod, but I was far from alright.

I closed my eyes. Nothing blocked my mother's voice from ringing in my ears. All this time, I'd thought it was just Ben who'd betrayed me. I'd never imagined my mother had been involved. My own goddamn shitty mother. She had no fucking soul.

Kyle was right. I was *nothing* like my mother. Never had been. Never would be. I loved Kyle. I loved Hunter. I loved my friends. I'd never sell them out or betray them. I'd protect them for as long as I lived.

Hate stung my eyes. "What have I ever done to hurt you?"

"Everything. Everything *you* do turns to gold. Your record deals, your hit-singles, your industry awards. You live the high life in your designer labels, your fancy cars, your product endorsements." The bitterness in my mother's tone punched me in the gut. "I'm entitled to a little piece of it. After all, I gave birth to you."

"Is that it? You're after money? Haven't you got enough out of your ex-husbands?"

"I certainly have. But I deserve more. And I get more by making a little cash on the side here and there." She pouted, and an evil smile curled one side of her lips. "That's why I'm here doing an interview."

"You're doing an interview for money? Who's the interview with, Mom?" Reality hit me like a blow to the back of the head. "Holy shit . . . you're going to the tabloids?"

"Yes." Janine tugged on her chandelier earring, playing an innocent act, but she was more twisted, evil, and heartless than the devil himself.

Ice shot through my veins and froze my heart, numbing the

pain from being betrayed by someone who was supposed to love me. I had always been cautious around my mother and her lust for gossip. Now I knew why. "You sold me out? Again?"

"You know I love you, baby girl." Janine waved at the waiter and pointed to the Prosecco bottle in the ice bucket for another one to be brought over.

"Love me? Bullshit." I pushed my bowl away, unable to eat any more than a couple mouthfuls. "If you loved me, you would respect me and protect what little privacy I have. Now . . . knowing you were behind the story with Ben, everything is clear. I haven't been in a relationship since Ben because I've been terrified. Terrified of being humiliated again. Terrified I'd end up like you, going from one relationship to the next. But for the first time in my life, I realize I'm nothing like you."

"I wouldn't be so sure about that. I think you and I are very alike." Janine took a gulp of her Prosecco, then threw me a thin grin. "We're both ambitious and have always been after something better."

Doubt crept through my veins. I'd always been hungry for success, but I'd achieved it through hard work. But shit . . . The guys and I had sold our souls to SureHaven for a record deal, for the opportunity to make something of our lives, to follow our music dreams. Was I the same as my mother?

No. No. No! I wasn't. Signing with SureHaven wasn't the same. The guys and I had entered into our contract fully aware of the costs. We'd understood the amount of blood, sweat, and tears we had to give and push through every day to be a success. We could've failed, not had a hit, never toured, been a waste of investment. Luckily, that didn't happen. Throughout our career, we'd never hurt anyone, never undermined anyone, and had never taken advantage of someone's vulnerability. We'd worked hard, were talented, and didn't have to sleep our way to the top.

Yep, I was nothing like my mother.

"There's nothing wrong with being ambitious, Mom." My shoulders slumped, overwhelmed by what I'd learned. "But how you pursue that ambition and treat those around you makes a difference. That's where you and I will always be opposites. I will always respect myself and will always respect Kyle and Hunter."

"Respect." Janine's mocking tone struck me like a cymbal. "You fucked Kyle in a supercar."

The blood drained from my face. Half of the restaurant turned their heads in our direction. The waiter clearing the table two rows down, dropped a coffee cup and spilled its remaining contents all over the cloth.

I shook my head, unable to tolerate my mother any longer. I'd had enough. I had to get out of there before I caused more of a scene. "We're done." I signaled to Chester at the bar to call for the car. "I'm not talking about this anymore."

Janine folded her napkin and placed it on the table. "You're so much like your father. So pathetic."

"Well, good. As long as I'm not like you. Go tell the gossip magazines about how ungrateful I am, or what a shitty daughter I am. Or go make up a wild tale about my love life. I've tried so hard and for so long to have you in my life, but I can't do it anymore. It's exhausting. So, from now on, don't call me. Stay away from me. Go back to Cyprus, or Nice or Florida or wherever the hell it is you crawled out from and leave me the fuck alone." I grabbed my baseball cap and jammed it onto my head, then picked up my tote bag. "Don't even bother sending me an invitation to your next wedding because I won't come. Not even if my life depends on it."

The moment I stood. Chester jumped to his feet. The gentleman who'd overheard most of the conversation gave me a sympathetic smile. At least now he might get to read his paper without being disturbed.

Chester led me out of the restaurant and into a throng of waiting cameras. *Shit.* I held my head down and hung on to my cap. There were flashes and snaps, and people calling out. Chester braced his arm around me, guiding me through the sea of paparazzi and into the waiting car. Unflustered, he slammed the door shut.

On the back seat, I drew my knees up to my chest and shuddered. All the anger and pain and hurt my mother had caused burned down my face in a flood of tears.

"Another delightful get-together with your mother, I see." Chester reached into his pocket and handed me his handkerchief.

"Thank you." I took it and dabbed my eyes. "She's a real piece of work. Fucking unbelievable." I was done. So done. She didn't deserve my tears. I owed her nothing. I sucked in a deep breath, sniffled, and set a new grit into my bones. "But that's it. I won't let her get to me anymore. Never again."

"Good for you." Chester dipped his chin. Dylan drove me home . . . to Kyle's.

The streets and avenues flickered past the window of the SUV. I wiped the last tears from my eyes. Brunch had been one of the worst encounters I'd ever had with my mother, but I was glad it had happened. I now knew the depths of my mother's shallowness, hatred, and disregard for me. How cruel and heartless she was. My intuition not to trust her had been right. She didn't deserve my time or effort ever again. I closed my eyes. With one deep breath . . . I blocked my mother out of my heart.

No regrets. No second chances.

I was nothing like my mother. That wake-up call was mostly thanks to Kyle.

A smile crept across my face. He was everything. So was Hunter. They were my life. They were the only ones I could trust. I loved them both. I always would.

Hunter was like a big goofball of a brother.

And Kyle . . . Warmth and light flooded my chest. Love thundered through my heart. All the covering up and the diverting from the truth about our relationship over the past week had reinforced one thing in my mind.

I loved him.

And he loved me.

Dylan and Chester dropped me off outside Hunter and Kyle's place. I let myself in with my access token and rushed upstairs. Guitar and piano music filled the hallway. I ran toward the music room and charged through the door. Hunter jumped in his seat at the piano.

"Fuck." Hunter's hand shot to his chest. "You scared the living shit out of me."

Kyle's eyes lit up when I walked toward him. I snaked my hands around his neck and kissed him. "I love you. I really fucking love you. And I want to show you how much. Your room. Now."

Kyle ripped the guitar off his neck and placed it on the stand.

"You've been crying." He brushed his thumb across my cheek. "What's your mom said or done now?"

"I'll tell you about it later. But right now, can we just fuck?"

"I'm already hard." Kyle slid his hands around my hips. I jumped up and curled my legs around his waist. As I threaded my fingers through his hair, I kissed his hot lips. He smelled so good, all sweet and spicy.

"Hello?" Hunter groaned and struck the piano keys. "Someone else is in the room."

"Back soon." Grinning, Kyle carried me out the doorway.

As we reached the middle of the hallway, Hunter called out, "Don't be long . . . We have to practice . . . I'll be here . . . by myself . . . waiting . . . Are you two done yet?"

In Kyle's old room, I kicked off my shoes, ripped his shirt over his head, and straddled him on the bed. Frantic hands discarded our clothes. Urgent kisses connected our minds, bodies, and souls. I was loved, cherished, and adored. I had Kyle. And music. And now, with my mother out of my life, surely nothing else could go wrong.

Chapter 34

KYLE

I followed Gemma and Hunter into Jeremy's lavish office at SureHaven Records on Madison Avenue and shut the cedar door behind us. Ambling past the wall of mirrored shelves lined with music awards and platinum album picture frames, I paused at the cluster of our statues and plaques. Seeing our achievements glitter under the display lights always brought a smile to my face. *Yeah, we're fucking good.* But being here had me on edge. All three of us were.

"Did you guys get an update about this meeting?" I scanned my email again. Still nothing. "I've emailed our team three times, and no one's replied with information."

"No. Something's not right." Gemma dropped her tote bag by the desk and sat on the corner. "Amie's been avoiding us. Kate and Bec haven't heard anything. I'm worried."

"It can't be good when all Amie said was, 'Bring your lawyer,'" Hunter headed for one of the two extra-long black leather sofas in the middle of the room, laid down, and propped a leopard-print cushion underneath his head. "I hope it's just about the Grant Entertainment Group takeover being finalized."

Here's hoping. We'd found out about the final acquisition via the news, not from SureHaven, Amie, or Grant. *Not cool.*

"Maybe it's good news." Gemma slid off the desk, stuffed her hands into the back pockets of her jeans and ambled toward the sofas. "Maybe the execs have decided to give us full creative control for this next album. That would be awesome." The smallest of sparks flickered through her eyes as she rounded her shoulders, but her tone came out flat.

"I love your optimism, Gem," Hunter sighed. "But don't get your hopes up."

I shook my head and eased over to her. "Gem, that would be nice, but I can't see that happening since they've been so anal about us sticking to the contract."

"True." Her shoulders slumped. She placed her hands flat against her stomach and winced. "It's shit . . . the vibe about this meeting is all wrong. I'm really worried."

"Don't be." I threaded my fingers beneath her hair and massaged her neck. "I'm sure this is just some bullshit business meeting."

After Gemma came home upset following brunch with her mother three days ago, I'd hated how distressed she'd been. Like always, I was there for her in whatever capacity she'd needed— even the hot, mind-blowing sex. Her kisses had stolen my breath more than usual. Our connection, extra intense. The light in Gemma's eyes had burned brighter after cutting the toxic ties with Janine.

Finding out her mother had been behind the whole Ben ordeal made me sick to the stomach. Janine was a horrible person. It was hard to comprehend that someone could be so narcissistic. I was glad she was gone . . . for good.

"I hope you're right, guys." Gemma snaked her arms around my waist and buried her face against my chest. I rested my cheek against the top of her head and inhaled the scent of her cherry blossom shampoo. *Perfect.*

Hunter sat upright and hugged the cushion against his side. "Since we have a few minutes, we need to talk about Amie."

Gemma tensed and turned her head toward Hunter. "Please tell me you're not back together."

"Fuck no. Definitely not." Hunter grimaced and shook his head. "I just needed time to think things through. Dumping her was a no-brainer after the shit she's pulled, but hard because I fucking liked her. I don't ever want to go through that shit again. But I had to make sure I made the right decision for our music. She's been a great manager . . . until recently. Over the past few weeks, she's been a bitch to work with and doesn't care about us as a band anymore. She cares only about money. I still can't believe she wanted to break us up. That's a huge no-fucking-way for me. There's no coming back from that. So, I'm with you. She's out. It's time to find a new manager. I don't want to spend the rest of our contract dealing with her."

"Neither do we." Gemma rushed over to Hunter and hugged him. "Thank you. If I had my way, we would've fired her after you first kissed her."

"Yeah, we should've." Hunter ruffled Gemma's hair as she sank onto the seat beside him.

"Hunt?" I rested my hands on the back of the sofa. "I'm sorry she screwed you over . . . and us. But this will be for the best. Trust me." I hated seeing him hurt. It had been a hard decision. Amie and Hunter had gotten along well. They loved making money, casual hookups, and materialistic things. They'd connected on that front. When he'd found out he was nothing more than a pawn in her corporate game of chess, it had cut him deep. Amie had tried and failed to tear us apart. Nobody could fuck with that. Our friendship . . . the three of us . . . our music . . . was everything.

Hunter kicked his leather boot against the leg of the glass coffee table. "Yep. She's gotta go. When Richard gets here, we'll get him to deal with firing her. I want her gone." He slapped his thighs, shot forward, and rose to his feet. As he drew his shoulders back, he painted on a cool smile and thumbed toward the door. "So before I end up an emotional train wreck like you two, I'm going for coffee. Want one?" He could wear a mask if needed, but I could see through it. Heartbreak sucked. *Damn* . . . Hunter's first.

Gemma pointed to the desk phone. "Sure, but just call Marcie at reception to bring them in."

"Nah. The guest lounge down the hall has coffee. I'll be back soon." Hunter strode across the room and headed out the door.

"Wow. He's more cut up over Amie than I thought." Gemma stared after Hunter.

"Yep." I quirked my mouth to one side. "But this *is* Hunt. He'll go out, get drunk, get laid, and he'll be back to his usual charming self."

Gemma pursed her lips, then giggled. Her eyes sparkled. "True. I can't wait to have the old Hunt back."

"Me too. I just want to put the past few crazy months behind us, record and focus on us and music again."

"Same." Gemma rose and came over to me. She wove her hands around my neck and drew me in for a kiss. "I can't thank you enough for what you've done for me, for always being there for me, for putting up with me. For getting through a rough week of interviews and the issues with my mother."

"I'd do anything for you, Gem." I wrapped my arms around her waist. "It will be good to let things calm down. Let's just enjoy being together. We're in the studio for the next month or two, so the paparazzi shouldn't hound us too much. I know we can't hide for all time, but a little while longer would be nice. Then I won't care who knows about us. Because you're mine. Forever. So you'd better get used to the idea."

"Forever?" She caught her lower lip between her teeth and rocked on her feet. "That's a long time."

"It's how I see things." Sporting a smile, I leaned in to kiss her.

"Wait. Just so we're clear . . ." She placed a finger over my lips and took a step back. "Don't get any stupid ideas about forever commitments like marriage. That's not on the cards."

I tugged on the bottom of her shirt. I'd known the moment I'd kissed her on the deck at my beach house she was my forever girl. "With your mom's track record, I know you have issues with marriage. But I don't. So, here's the thing. One day, I *will* marry you, Gem. But I won't ever ask you. When the time's right . . . you'll ask me."

"Then you'll be waiting a long fucking time." She pulled her shirt out of my hand.

Shit. Had I scared her? "Gem, I'm sorry. I didn't mean—"

"Kyle, I don't believe in marriage." She walked over to the sofa and sat down. She rubbed her hands up and down her thighs. "Isn't just being together enough?"

"Yes." I strode over and sank onto the seat beside her. I hooked my arm around her shoulders and kissed her on the forehead. Getting married one day would be nice, but if we didn't, it wasn't a deal breaker. "I don't need a ring, or a piece of paper, just you."

She brushed her fingertips down my jaw, smiled, and touched her lips to mine. "You're the best. Love you."

The door flung open, and Hunter returned with a tower of takeaway coffee cups. He handed us each a cup and plonked onto the sofa beside Gemma.

Before I took my first sip, Amie charged into the office with Richard, Jeremy, and three men I'd never seen before. I looked at Gemma and Hunter, but their faces were as blank as mine.

Jeremy came to the front of the group and tugged on his tie. "Gemma, Hunter, Kyle, this is Luke Wade, CEO of the Grant Entertainment Group, Patrick Mercure, their VP, and Neil Arnold, their lawyer."

We stood and shook everyone's hands. The new executives and Amie took a seat on the four-seat sofa opposite us. Richard sat in the armchair at the end of the coffee table and stretched out his legs. Jeremy turned a desk chair around and sat.

Jeremy folded his arms, the chair squeaking under his bulky frame. "Thank you, everybody, for coming. Let's get started. As you know, SureHaven has been acquired by Grant. These gentlemen are here to talk about the changes that will occur."

I glanced at the three men, all overweight, middle-aged, with salt and pepper hair, and dressed in expensive suits. My skin prickled at the sudden chill in the air and stone-cold eyes peering at us.

"It's nice to meet the three of you." Luke's toad-like throat wobbled. "I'm very excited about acquiring the pool of talent SureHaven has developed. We asked you to bring your lawyer because there are changes we need to discuss."

"Like what?" I jumped in before Gemma or Hunter got the chance. Gemma tensed beside me. Hunter's foot stopped wiggling on his knee.

"Several things," Luke said. "Moving forward, we'd like you to continue with the Grant Group under new contracts. As of this moment, your existing deal with SureHaven will end in ninety days. So, you won't be hitting the studio tomorrow—"

"What?" Gemma's high pitch pierced my ear.

"Our studio time is booked." Hunter's foot fell to the floor as he straightened. "We're ready."

My head spun. This wasn't good. "We've already had one delay. How long is this one for?"

"That depends on the three of you." Neil, the lawyer with greasy, thinning hair, pulled a pen from his jacket and opened his notepad. "On whether you will accept the terms and conditions of a new agreement."

Gemma's eyes lit up. "That depends on what they are. Let's negotiate a new contract right now. It's no secret we want full creative control—to sing, write, and record our own material."

I rubbed my forehead; Gemma was never subtle. But by the look in Luke's eyes, something bigger than we'd first thought was about to go down.

"See, Miss Lonsdale." Luke tugged on the lapels of his jacket. "That's where we have a difference of opinion. We run a refined formula, much like SureHaven, and we will continue to follow our format. That means you are presented with new and exciting opportunities. Amie has had preliminary discussions with you, Gemma. We want to know what else we can offer you to make your solo career happen."

"Nothing . . . You're not splitting us up. We're a band. The three of us are a package deal." Gemma clenched her hands so hard her knuckles turned white.

"That's a shame." Patrick drawled each word in a thick Texan accent. "This business is about marketing a product, and you fit our solo artist's profile perfectly. We want the guys to continue as a duo because we know they'll prove to be even more successful with the young female demographic."

"Just stop, right now," I squashed my empty paper coffee cup in my hands. "You're not listening. We stay together. End of story."

"Okay." Richard held his hand toward me. He cleared his throat and turned to the suits. "My clients have made it clear. They're not splitting. So, before they lose their cool, let's lay the options on the table. One, you honor the terms and conditions in the SureHaven contract so they can hit the studio under their current agreement. Two, we renegotiate a new contract today, one that everyone is happy with. Or three, you terminate their contract, and we walk out the door. But as Everhide are one of your biggest and most profitable artists, consider your options carefully."

All eyes turned to Luke. He clasped his hands together and tapped his index fingers in front of his mouth.

"I'm sure we can negotiate something agreeable." New nerves twisted in my gut. *Could we? Shit.*

"If it doesn't involve the three of us staying together and giving us full creative control of our music, then . . . there's no new deal." Gemma folded her arms and slumped back against the sofa.

"Gemma, we are offering you that if you go solo. We see the potential in your marketability." Patrick's gaze hardened. "But for the guys, the creative control stays with Grant."

I looked Amie square in the eyes. She'd been too quiet for my liking. Amie was supposed to represent us and fight for the deal we wanted, not bow to this new company's every whim. I jutted my chin in her direction. "Why are you sitting there listening to all this bullshit? What's in this for you?"

She crossed her ankles and folded her hands in her lap. "I'll head up the artist management division for Grant. I'll be managing an entire pool of artists, not just you."

"That's the best fucking news we've heard all day," Hunter cut in. "We were going to fire you anyway."

My blood boiled at the *I-couldn't-care-less* look on Amie's face. *Bitch.*

Richard raised his palm again. "Hang on. We'll deal with Amie later. One thing at a time." He turned to the men from Grant. "What reasonable offer are you willing to put on the table?"

Luke stroked his narrow goatee and stretched his thick neck. "If Gemma won't go solo, we can offer Everhide a one-album deal with one-option, similar to the SureHaven agreement. Our marketing and production costs are higher than SureHaven's, and we put more effort into artist support. You'll have a much bigger team behind you for promotional and touring opportunities. Therefore, any advance and ongoings will be slightly less. But in the long run, you'll get a significant financial reward."

"Are you joking?" A thud pounded at the back of my head. "You want us, one of the biggest artists on your books, to bend over and do this for less money?"

"No fucking way. We're not taking a pay cut." Hunter's jaw tensed and ticked. "You should at least match what we got with SureHaven. No, wait. You should pay us a fuckload more to stay."

"If you're confident in your skills, you'll have nothing to worry about. Otherwise, there are plenty of artists willing to take your place, Mr. Collins." Patrick strummed his fingers on the top of his leg.

"Hunter? Kyle? Gemma? Please, let me handle this." Richard straightened his tie. "There's no way we're agreeing to a reduction in fees. These guys are highly successful, and if you don't take advantage of that and negotiate a new and acceptable agreement in favor of my clients, then . . . in my view . . . there is only one option."

One option.

Holy shit!

My palms sweated. My pulse swooshed in my ears like a severe case of tinnitus. This meeting had taken a turn I hadn't seen coming. None of us had.

"Yes, they're a successful group," Neil sniffled. "And we aim to make them bigger. But it will be under our business model, Richard. We've been in this game for a long time and know what works for us. We'd like Everhide to be part of our future growth. That's the offer."

"Okay then." Richard dipped his chin, then tilted his head toward us. "Kyle, Hunter, Gemma? It's your call here."

My leg jiggled as I stared at the executives. We weren't some new kids on the block. We weren't nobody. This was ridiculous.

"Can we talk in private, Richard?" I waved toward the far end of the huge office.

He nodded.

Hunter, Gemma, and Richard followed me. We huddled together by the window.

Turning his back to the Grant executives, Richard lowered his voice. "Do you want to continue renegotiations with Grant . . . or walk away?"

I rubbed at the tension tightening my brow. "What are the penalties if we walk?"

"Technically, if SureHaven no longer exists as an entity, neither does your contract." Richard slid his hands into his suit pockets and kept his tone casual, like this was no big deal . . . But it fucking was. "As part of the acquisition, Grant should honor any existing agreements, but clearly they don't want to do that and have given you a timeframe to re-sign. That provides you with several legal options. They aren't offering you the same deal as SureHaven, so if you don't agree to their terms and conditions, you have the right to terminate at the end of the agreed period. They'll offer compensation, and there will be no penalty on your part. You could fight them to honor the SureHaven contract. Battle it out to get a more favorable new contract. And if they don't play nice, we'll take them to court. But I'm sure they won't want that option. They'll want to keep the news of any upset artists and failed renegotiations out of the media." Richard glanced at us. "So, what would you like to do?"

I held my breath, studying Hunter's and Gemma's faces to gauge their reactions. Hunter would want to ensure we kept on performing, but would his love of money weigh in on his decision? Gemma . . . well . . . I knew what she wanted, even though worry flickered across her eyes.

"I'm not signing a new contract for anything less than full

creative control," she said without hesitation. I smiled, knowing I was right.

"I'm not signing for less money." Hunter closed his eyes and shook his head. "They can go fuck themselves."

My heart hammered against my ribs. Nausea churned in my gut. What did I want to do? After everything SureHaven had done for us, it had come down to this. I'd always known the deal we'd signed was a steppingstone in our career. But taking the next step had come sooner than expected. I closed my eyes. Searched my mind. Only one logical path crystallized in my mind. Gemma was right. It was time to move forward and make our own music. "I agree with Hunt and Gem. I'm not signing if they don't have our interests at heart. The deal has to be better, not the same . . . and definitely not for less."

"Well then . . . let's see what we can do." Richard clapped his hands together. A fire flared in his eyes, as if he were ready to go to war.

We returned to our seats. The suits met us with steely gazes.

"My clients have made their intentions clear." Richard directed his attention toward Luke. "What's it going to be? Are you going to honor their current contract, meet their new requests, or do we proceed with termination?"

Luke shifted in his seat, puffed out his chest. His beady eyes jumped from Hunter to Gemma to me. "Your loyalty to each other is impressive, but it's also your downfall. So . . . I'm sorry. We can't accommodate your request. You, as a group, do not fit our long-term business model. So rather than investing time and money into one album, I think it's best for all parties to end our relationship before it begins. I'll have Neil draw up the letter of termination."

Holy fuck!

My mouth fell open. My chest constricted. It felt like my ribs would crack under the pressure. I couldn't believe what had just happened.

"Wise choice." Richard nodded.

"I'm sorry we can't be more accommodating," Patrick sighed.

Luke jutted his chin at us. "You will still be required to honor all obligations, including appearances and performances, over the next couple months. Our team will work with you until the agreed termination date."

"Wow. So, in ninety days, we're done." I swallowed, my mouth dry.

"It seems that way." Luke dipped his head and steepled his fingers together.

"We're disappointed you aren't willing to renegotiate, but we understand." Richard stood and buttoned his jacket. "Thank you for your time."

Stunned, I rose to my feet beside Gemma and Hunter. After a quick handshake with everyone, the four of us left the office and jumped into our waiting car.

"Fuck." Hunter wiped his hand down his face, then rubbed the back of his neck. "Did not see that coming."

"I can't believe we just lost our contract." A tear slid down Gemma's cheek. "This was not part of the plan. Now what the hell are we going to do?"

I stared out the window, numb. For the first time in a long time, I had absolutely no fucking idea. Only one thing came to mind. "Let's get wasted."

Chapter 35

GEMMA

"I should've kept my big mouth shut," I slurred as I concentrated on pouring another round of whiskey shots without spilling any onto the table. "I shouldn't have kept going on and on about wanting creative control. Fuck, I can't believe we lost our contract." It was mid-afternoon at an exclusive whiskey bar on 26th Street. Jazz music drifted softly through the sound system, a few businessmen and women wined and dined, and Sam sat at the main bar on guard. The guys and I remained unnoticed, tucked away in a dark corner at a private table, drowning our disbelief and sorrows.

This morning, we'd been excited about hitting the studio. And now . . . nothing. No contract, no manager, no deal.

"I can't believe they let us go." Hunter downed another mouthful of Jack Daniel's Sinatra Select whiskey and slammed the glass down on the table. The dim lighting added to the solemn mood that hung like gray clouds around us.

"I'm in shock." Kyle slouched over the table and twisted his shot glass around in his fingertips. "I thought Grant would give us what we wanted."

"I did too." Tears stung the back of my eyes. I'd always pushed the boundaries, always wanted more, and now I'd gone too far. I'd never contemplated we'd be dropped in the Grant takeover. "One thing though, I'm not sorry I didn't go solo. No way. I'd thought we'd strike a new deal. But now we have nothing."

"We're Grant's loss." Kyle swallowed his shot. "In this fucked-up situation there are some positives. We got out of the record deal we weren't happy with, and we got rid of Amie."

I smiled a half-drunken smile. A small sense of satisfaction rippled through me. The bittersweet ending hadn't come fast enough.

"I'm glad she's gone. But damn . . . don't you wish we could go back to the time when we first signed to SureHaven?" I swayed in my seat. "When everything was new and exciting."

"Geez, you can talk some shit when you're drunk, Gem." Kyle's eyes shimmered in the soft lighting. "I never want to go back to the beginning and start from scratch. We've come too far."

"I agree with Kyle." Hunter poured another shot, draining the bottle. He waved to the bartender and ordered another. He picked up his glass and waved it toward me. "Gem, what happened today with Grant sucks. It really does. But it's not the end. It's just a new chapter."

My eyes blurred as I stared at my glass. "I don't know where to begin."

Kyle's foot appeared on the seat next to me. My hand fell to run along his calf muscle, always craving contact with his body.

"We'll find a way forward together." He nudged my hip with his boot. "Maybe not today since we're drunk off our asses and I can't tell which way is up right now. But we're one of the biggest bands in the world. We'll find a new manager and have heaps of labels wanting to work with us. They'll be begging us to sign."

"Let's hope so." Hunter slapped Kyle on the shoulder and gave him a gentle shake. "Because all I want to do is record albums and get back on stage. Tour. Perform. Entertain huge crowds."

"Hell yeah." I raised my glass and downed my shot. Dizziness swam through my head as I jabbed my finger on the table. "But this time, it has to be *our* music. No one else's."

"It's always about the music, Gem." Kyle leaned forward, reached under the table, and ran his hands up my legs. "We'll use

Richard and Bec and Kate to contact everyone we know in this business. Don't stress. We *will* find a new label."

"If not, I'll build a fucking studio and we'll make our own damn records." Hunter slapped his hand on the table.

We had so much equipment in the guys' home studio that we probably could do that. Kyle loved producing our demo tracks. But at this stage in our careers, we knew our strengths and what we wanted to achieve. We were musicians, not marketing, distributing, and production powerhouses. I wanted a label and an entertainment organization behind us. One that would take us to the next level.

"Whatever we do, it's going to take months of talks and negotiations." A wave of nausea washed over me and swayed through my stomach. *Oh . . . that wasn't good.* "It's not like we can walk in off the street and say, 'Hey, we're Everhide, let's make a fucking album.'" We had an advantage; we had a proven track record. But that could also be an issue. We weren't a startup. Being established meant we were a bigger investment. A bigger risk. We had to align with company budgets and marketing schedules and business directives. Grant didn't want us. Others might feel the same way.

Whoa!

Stars appeared before my eyes, and a cold sweat broke out on my brow.

"We'll be fine." Kyle rubbed my knee but then stopped. "Gem? Are you okay?"

The blood drained from my face. Whiskey rose and fell like a rough sea inside my gut. The room spun. "No. I think I need to go home. Now."

"Move!" Kyle shoved Hunter out of the booth. "Gem's going to be sick."

Kyle helped me to my feet, hooked his arm around my waist, and grabbed my purse. "You coming, Hunt?"

"Nah," he slurred, waving his finger toward the far end of the room. "Those ladies over there have my name on their to-do list. Especially the blonde."

Yep. Hunt is back.

"Have fun." I blew Hunter a kiss, clutched onto Kyle's arm, and we staggered out the door. I planned to have fun, too. With Kyle. At home. In my shower . . . Once the world stopped spinning.

Chapter 36

GEMMA

A vivid hue of early fall colors filled the park across the road as late afternoon sunshine filtered through my picture windows. Curled up on my sofa, I plucked at the strings on my acoustic guitar. Song lists and ideas and notes lay scattered across my coffee table.

For the past two and a half months, the guys and I, along with Richard and Sophie, our new manager, had gone to meeting after meeting, held phone call after phone call, and had sat in on discussion after discussion with multiple record labels and entertainment companies. We'd flown to LA and London, had visited numerous music companies here in New York, and had spent way too much time sitting at desks with executives trying to cut a new record deal.

But nothing had come to fruition.

No contract had been signed.

It hadn't been easy. Just as I'd predicted. Kyle had thought we'd walk into any music company and get what we wanted based on our success, but many organizations were like SureHaven and Grant—they wanted to control every aspect of their artists' careers—the music, the money, and the marketing. That wasn't us anymore.

The tension and worry about finding a new deal grew with each day that passed. Fear and depression had taken their toll. We smiled for the cameras when we went to designated events. But behind closed doors, Hunter drank too much. He went out partying all the time and was back to his wild ways of sleeping around. Kyle worked constantly on his laptop. He spent too many nights away from me and left me wondering why. I couldn't believe that losing our contract had caused this widening gap between us.

I'd had enough of vacant talks with record companies. Every one of our meetings had left me frustrated, angry, disappointed and in the worst grumpy mood, like I had a severe case of PMS. So, in my spare time, to feel like I was working toward and achieving something, I'd sifted through all the songs we'd written over the years. I'd wanted to come up with a selection for our new album. For when it happened . . . not if.

My intercom buzzed. I glanced at the security monitor. Hunter and Kyle strode through the foyer and into the elevator. A few moments later, the security-code pad on my door blipped four times, and in they walked. Hunter carried a bottle of JD. Kyle, a stuffed backpack.

Oh shit. What has happened now?

"Why did your suit fittings take so long? I was about to send out a search party." I wriggled my eyebrows as I played "The Twilight Zone" on my guitar.

Hunter placed the bottle of JD on the coffee table and stepped over my legs. He flopped down into the armchair and put his boots up on the table. "Sorry. I couldn't decide on an outfit. You should've been there to help. I've gotta look good at the AMAs in a couple weeks. Kara kept mixing shirts and suits around. Every fucking thing was awesome. I couldn't make up my mind. So I just took everything, and I'll pick something on the day."

I giggled and slapped his shin. "Kara will love that. She's good, isn't she?" My bestie didn't work for one of the top fashion houses in New York for no reason. She understood her clients well, knew what they liked . . . even flamboyant ones like Hunter.

"More like annoying, so don't push it." Hunter narrowed his

eyes and shook his head. But then he grinned, so it couldn't have been too bad.

Kyle grabbed some glasses from the kitchen, ambled over, and sat beside me. "We also stopped by Richard's office."

"Is that what the JD's for? More bad news?" I put down my guitar and curled my hand around his leg.

Kyle poured everyone a drink. I swallowed hard. Queasiness swam through my gut. I hadn't touched whiskey since we lost our contract a couple of months ago. That had been a big afternoon. Too big. I'd spent the evening on my knees in front of my toilet, not with Kyle in the shower. But that was weeks ago. I loved whiskey. It was time to get reacquainted with my beloved JD . . . for whatever reason.

Kyle handed us each a glass. He sat forward, rolling his drink between his hands. Hunter's legs jiggled. My gaze darted between the two of them. Neither one could look at me. "Okay. What's going on? What's happened?"

Worry furrowed Kyle's brow. "I know I've been distant and distracted lately. I made Hunt promise not to say anything until the timing was right."

My grip tightened around my glass. "Tell me what?"

Oh shit. Dread crept across my skin and tightened around my throat. Had Grant got to them? Did the guys want to go out on their own? Without me? I'd never considered that option. *Fuck.*

Hunter dropped his head back and groaned. "Kyle, hurry up and tell her, or I will."

Kyle wiped his palm on his jeans. The glass shook in his other hand. "When I found out, I didn't believe it at first. But Gem, I don't want you to be pissed at me like Hunt was."

Oh God. Was he sick?

My mind exploded. Kyle had lost weight recently. We'd all been stressed. But had he been hiding something serious? I studied his face, looking for signs of illness, a discoloration in his skin, a dullness to the light in his gorgeous eyes.

"Kyle?" My voice caught in my throat. "Please tell me what's going on?"

With shaky hands, Kyle dug into his backpack and withdrew three thick documents. He put them on the coffee table side by side. "We've done it, Gem. We've done it. Not one, but three companies offered us contracts."

"ARRRRGH" I screamed. I screamed so loud my ears hurt.

I flung my arms around Kyle and hugged him tight. My heart pounded like it had been jumpstarted. "Oh, my God. The way you were so edgy, I thought you were sick or something. Don't scare me like that. But this . . . contracts . . . is fucking brilliant."

I high-fived Hunter and sat bouncing on the edge of my seat. My head reeled, wanting to know every detail.

"I told you Gem would think the worst." Hunter jabbed his finger toward Kyle. "Don't ever make me keep shit from her again."

"Agreed. But her reaction was priceless." Kyle's face broke into the hugest grin. I just wanted to kiss him.

"True." Hunter shrugged, raised his drink, and swallowed his JD.

I turned to the documents on the coffee table. The names on the contracts came into focus—Warner Music Group, Sony Music Entertainment, and Universal Music Group. I shook my head, trying to make sense of everything. "How did this happen? When we met with them, they weren't interested in giving us what we wanted. What changed?"

"I told Sophie and Richard to keep hounding them." Kyle smiled over the rim of his JD, then took a sip. "We needed someone big to take us onboard. I knew what we wanted, so all I've done was work with Richard to make sure those details were in the contracts."

"Why did you keep this from me?" A mix of hurt and sheer excitement ripped through my chest as I flicked through the pages of one of the documents. "I've been so worried about you. We don't make decisions without each other. We discuss everything."

"I didn't tell you because you were frustrated and upset by all the dead ends. You were disappointed. Depressed. You struggled after every meeting, setback, and rejection. I didn't want you to stress anymore." Kyle took my hand in his and kissed it. I had taken a blow, but I would've never given up. Not ever. "Once Hunt found out what I was up to, he wanted to tell you. But I wanted to do this for you, Gem. This is your dream. *Our* dream. When we started out, you never stopped. You booked all our gigs, entered us into every competition we could afford, pushed us to send demo after demo out into the world. If it wasn't for you, we would've never entered the SureHaven contest, won, and signed with them. I wanted to thank you for the incredible life we've had. For all we've achieved. Now, let's make it even better."

Shit. He'd done this for me. For us. Tears prickled my eyes. How could I be angry when he'd worked so hard to make this happen? *Contracts! We had fucking contracts!* "Thank you." I hooked my arm around his back and kissed him on the cheek. "This is incredible. It really is. But you should've told me."

"I wanted to surprise you. I'm not sorry about making our dream a reality." He pointed toward the documents. "Here it is. Ready for the taking. All we have to do is choose which one we sign. And, like always, the three of us will do that . . . together."

I splayed my hand over my racing heart. My buzz returned, skipping through my veins. Staring at the documents, I took a deep breath. *Wow.* Seeing our future in black and white made me fall in love with him even more. My hands trembled as I opened the pages of the quarter-inch thick Sony offer. "So, what are the deals?"

"We have full creative control over our music, production, and artwork. There are variations in management, marketing, exclusivity, terms, rights, and royalties. I ran some figures based on our past sales, and fuck, every contract is much better than anything we ever had with SureHaven. All these offers are for one album with an option. That's a good thing. We're not tied by the balls for multiple albums like we were with SureHaven."

It certainly is.

I downed my JD and held out my glass to Hunter for a refill. "Have you read through these?"

"No." He topped up my glass. "Not yet. I stayed out of it. You and I both know Kyle is much better with all this legal shit than we are. He made it all happen."

"How long do we have to decide?" I asked.

"Thirty days." Kyle finished his drink and slid the glass toward Hunter for more whiskey.

Unable to wipe the smile off my face, I gazed at the contracts. "Well, let's get started. Kyle, which one do you think is best?"

Grinning, he scratched his cheek. "I have one in mind, but I want to see if you and Hunt pick the same one."

A few hours and a bottle of JD later, we still hadn't reached a decision. Technical jargon messed with my head.

"Regardless of who we sign with, I have one condition to add." Hunter waved his glass at us. "We go into this deal clean. No more covering up your relationship. No one will give a shit about you two being together."

My heart lurched. It had been hard on everyone—us and our entourage—covering up our relationship. No one liked deflecting the truth or having to lie.

Since Ben, I'd fallen into a dark hole, afraid of what everyone thought. Embarrassed by what had happened. I'd grown paranoid, protective, and had avoided going out in public. I'd wanted to give the media wolves nothing to feed on. But I couldn't escape them. Never would. Not with the life I'd chosen and wanted. The past couple of months of lying low with Kyle had given me a new strength. I'd never felt this confident and comfortable in a relationship. He had my back. Went to extremes to protect me. Loved me for me. I was ridiculously in love. And insanely happy.

Hunter leaned forward. His eyes bore into mine. "Gem, I know you. I really care about you. Always have. Always will. Now, stop being stupid. You and Kyle love each other in a way that I can't comprehend. It defies everything, even the universe. You belong together. It's time to stop hiding, both of you. The media will go crazy for a few days when they find out you're together. Then they won't give a shit. Trust me."

Hunter was right. I'd learned that from him—to not let the gossip get to me, to brush it off with a laugh, and to always be honest. Like he'd done during interviews, admitting to being with Amie. I'd been in this game for long enough and through enough bad publicity, I should've known better. I'd been burned, but I'd survived. I was stronger thanks to the love and support of these two guys . . . especially Kyle.

I no longer had to worry about my mother harassing me for gossip, being ashamed of my actions, or being afraid of what people thought.

I was with Kyle. I loved him. That was all that mattered.

I nudged Kyle in the side. "I'm cool with that. Are you?"

"Fuck yeah. Absolutely." He kissed me on the lips, then smiled. "Love you."

"Love you, too. But right now, can we work out who we're going to sign with?"

"Hmmm." Kyle murmured against my lips. "Maybe we need a break."

"Yep. I agree." Hunter tossed the Warner contract onto the coffee table. "I've had enough for today. My head's hurting." He stood, kissed me on the forehead, and ruffled my hair. "I'm gonna leave you two alone so you can fuck each other senseless and celebrate our contracts."

"No. Wait. Where are you going?" I giggled as Kyle nuzzled into the small of my neck, sending goosebumps skipping down my arm.

"Maybe that whiskey bar again." Hunter shrugged, then threw me a mischievous grin. "So when I'm walking down the laneway, I want to hear you screaming Kyle's name."

"You're a sick fucker. You know that?" Chuckling, Kyle shook his head. But he grabbed me around the waist, half picked me up and laid me on the sofa. He stretched out, nestling between my legs. Hovering over me, he wriggled his eyebrows. "But I'm up for a challenge."

"Have fun. Catch you tomorrow." Hunter waved over his shoulder and left.

The second the door clicked shut, silence came over the living room like a heavy blanket settling on a bed. Warm, comfortable, content. Kyle braced his arms on either side of my head and touched his lips to mine.

I ran my fingers through his thick hair. "I can't believe we've got three contracts."

"It's very cool. I'm sorry I made you worry. But I did all of this for you."

I cupped his cheek. "Not just me. It's for us."

He nodded, just a fraction. "I hated not spending every night next to you. I struggle to breathe when you're not around."

My heart beat in sync with his. Being with him felt so right. "Then you better not stay away from me ever again."

He wriggled his hips and pressed his hard-on against my crotch. "Lucky for me, I only live around the corner."

"About that . . ." My pulse quickened as I ran my hands over his shoulders and linked my fingers behind his neck. "I've missed you like crazy when we haven't spent the night together. *I* want to be the one who finds out about stuff before Hunt. *I* want to be the one you confide in. I'm yours and plan on being so for a very long time . . . so what would you say to moving in with me?"

Kyle froze. His heavy breathing and the pounding of my heart were all I could hear. "Move in with you?"

Shit. Was it too soon?

"Yeah," I whispered, holding my breath.

"That *is* a serious step." He moved to the side, slid his hand down my arm and across my hip. He popped open the button at the top of my shorts. "Let me think about it . . . How does *yes* sound?"

"You will?" My heart cartwheeled up to my throat.

"Yes. I would love to move in with you."

I took his face between my hands and crushed my lips against his.

"Now we have even more to celebrate." A handsome, devilish smile inched across his mouth as he unzipped my shorts. "So, would you like to go fast or slow?"

"I don't like slow." I grabbed the bottom of his T-shirt and yanked it over his head.

"Good answer." He tugged my shorts off. "Neither do I."

***

Lying on my sofa in the aftermath of lovemaking, I wrapped my arms around Kyle and held him close. His head rested against my chest as I ran my fingers through his hair. With our legs entwined, our bodies side by side, he drew the throw-blanket over our waists. This wasn't just good. It was perfect. Finally, after tumultuous months, everything had fallen into place. We had a contract to sign. Kyle would move in. Our lives were about to change yet again.

I was ready. I wanted this.

It was time to go public. Time to tell the world I loved Kyle.

But first . . . We had to tell Hunter the news.

Chapter 37

KYLE

After having my fill of pancakes with maple syrup for breakfast . . . and Gemma, I walked beside her down the laneway back to my place. My palm sweated in hers. Excitement and nerves flipped through my stomach. The conversation that lay ahead would be difficult, but amazing. We had to tell Hunter our news.

As we reached the corner, Hunter stepped out of a taxi.

Chuckling, I stepped onto the curbside and slapped Hunter on the shoulder. "Looks like you had a good night." *I sure did.*

He shrugged and shaded his eyes against the bright sunshine. "The night was fine. The girl, okay. Served her purpose." But curiosity narrowed his eyes as his gaze jumped between us. He threw us a lopsided grin, turned and headed into our building. "Other than sex, what's got you two so fucking chirpy this morning?"

"Let's have a coffee." I drew Gemma closer, and we followed Hunter upstairs.

I sat on the sofa, rubbing my thighs and jiggling my legs. Hunter sank into the adjacent armchair. Worry darkened his eyes. Gemma placed three lattes on the coffee table and eased onto the seat beside me. I hooked my arm around her shoulders, and she curled into me, resting her hand on my thigh.

Shit. I stilled my leg.

"What's going on?" Hunter picked up a cup, blew on the hot latte, then took a sip.

I closed my eyes, cleared my throat, and took a deep breath. I'd known Hunter since the first day of elementary school. We'd been through so much together. There was no easy way around this, so I'd just better come out and say it. "I'm . . . moving in with Gem."

Hunter spluttered, choking and coughing on a mouthful of his drink. "You're what?"

My heart lurched. This was the hardest breakup of my life. "I spend half my time there anyway."

Hunter blinked, winced, and scratched his stubble. "Gem, why don't you move in here? This place is big enough for the three of us."

She shook her head and rounded her shoulders. "Hunt, if Kyle and I are going to do this couple thing, we need to do it in our own space."

"But . . ." Hunter closed his eyes and slumped deeper into the armchair. "Shit."

My stomach knotted like the ribbon in an old tape cassette. Why did this have to be so hard? But Hunter and I couldn't live together forever. We'd grown up. Life was changing. I had to do what was right for me and Gemma.

"Hunt, we're just around the corner." I softened my tone. "We'll be here all the time."

"It won't be the same," Hunter mumbled.

"No, it won't be, but it will be good." Gemma gave me a sexy wink as she nudged my side. Then she turned back to Hunter and shrugged her shoulder. "Maybe you could get a roommate."

"No. Never." Hunter shook his head as he waved toward the hallway. "Those bedrooms are yours. And always will be. Kyle, you own half this joint."

"That's fine for now. We can sort that out later, down the track, or in years to come." I ran my hand down Gemma's back and played with the long strands of her hair. Warmth flooded my chest. "It's time for Gem and me to be together."

Hunter stared vacantly out the window toward downtown and dragged his hand down his face. He sucked in a deep breath and let it out slowly. "Fuck. I guess it was inevitable." His voice was as dreary as the winter rain. "I was just hoping Gem would move in here."

"Sorry, Hunt." Gemma's eyes glinted as she softened her tone and wrinkled her nose. "I feel terrible about breaking up your beautiful bromance." *No, she didn't.* "It's my turn to live with Kyle. You've had him for long enough." She rested her head against my shoulder and curled her arm around mine.

"Yeah, it is." I kissed her forehead. Having her close eased the ache inside my chest. Hunter would always be my best friend, but my future was with Gemma. There'd be no looking back.

"When?" Hunter closed his eyes and pinched his eyebrows together.

I inhaled deeply and swallowed the dry lump in my throat. "From now."

"Shit. . . Really?" Hunter sank even lower into the chair. He rubbed his glassy eyes, then slapped the armrest. "Well, there's only one way you fuckers can make me feel better. Let's play some hard music, then go through the contracts and work out who the fuck we're going to sign with."

Chapter 38

GEMMA

Sitting between Kyle and Hunter in the back of the limousine on the way to the Microsoft Theater for the American Music Awards, I drew the split in my long dress closed over my knees . . . . for the twentieth time. I fidgeted with my dangling earrings, my straightened hair, and the strapless top of my dress, checking it hadn't slipped down over my boobs. Our security team sitting opposite us kept their eyes up and their faces void of all emotion. *Kudos to them for being professional.* The dress Kara had designed for me was exquisite. It just didn't cooperate when the car jolted over a bump.

"Stop fidgeting. You look stunning." Kyle slid his hand along my thigh in a comforting stroke. Dressed in a black Armani suit and shirt, his eyes glistened. His gaze ran along the length of my legs. A slow, sexy smile curled the corner of his lips. "You'll be the best dressed on the red carpet again. Trust me."

"Why are you nervous, Gem?" Hunter peered around Kyle. "We've done this a million times. A few photos, say hi to the fans, do a couple interviews, and we'll be inside."

I placed my hands on my stomach to settle the butterflies and took a calming breath. Tonight was our last obligation for

SureHaven. As of tomorrow, we had a new home with the Sony Music Group and would record under their Columbia label. I couldn't fucking wait.

But that wasn't what had me on edge. Yes, this was our first appearance since we'd announced we'd signed with Sony, but this was our first public outing since Kyle had been photographed moving into my place.

So much had happened in the past few days. I prayed tonight didn't turn into another shitshow. No . . . I wouldn't let it. Life was good, and I was excited about our future.

The car eased to a halt at the beginning of the red carpet. Fans and cameras and reporters lined the way up to the theater's entrance, a couple of hundred yards away.

"You ready?" Kyle kissed the back of my hand.

Yes, I was. "Let's do this."

An usher opened the limousine door and bowed. The air-splitting screams from the fans flooded in. Sam, Chester, and Mick climbed out onto the curb. The production crew guided guests along.

A short lady jostled over to our limo, waved and bellowed orders. "Good evening. We're five minutes behind schedule. I need Everhide to make their way to the media section pronto. Two minutes with fans. That's it."

"Sure." Sam nodded and flapped his hand at us to move.

"Time to party." Hunter pinned his dazzling smile into place, stepped out of the car, and buttoned up his bright red jacket. He blew kisses toward the fans, hollering behind the barricades.

Kyle was next. He eased out, turned and helped me exit the car. But the minute I was on my feet, he let go of my hand.

Like he normally did.

But something didn't feel right about that anymore.

I checked my dress, smiled and followed the guys over to the fans. Cameras flashed all around us as other guests made their way toward the theater. Sophie and Kate wove their way through the crowd, joined us, and hurried us along.

The guys and I posed for hundreds of photos, together

and individually. I usually hated the ones by myself where the photographers yelled to twirl around, show off some leg, look this way, glance over my shoulder, and give a 'sexy' smile. I was always glad when they were done. But tonight, I felt good. Every time I turned, I stole a glance at Kyle. My heart fluttered. I was sexy, confident . . . *his*.

We made our way along the line of reporters, playing it up for the photographers and answering reporters' stupid questions. *"Gemma, who designed your dress?" "Hunter, who dressed you this evening?" "Kyle, what hair products do you use?"* His response of "$1.99 hair gel from Walmart" always made me laugh . . . but that was true.

Kate herded us toward our next interview. But my footsteps faltered when I saw who it was.

"Great." I rolled my eyes. "It's that dickhead Gerard from *Entertainment On-Show* again."

I wedged myself between Hunter and Kyle, our arms hooked around each other's backs. Gerard checked his hair and his teeth in a handheld mirror before cueing his cameraman.

"Good evening. It's been a while since I saw you in Hawaii. Congratulations on being nominated for three awards tonight—Best Album, Best Single and Best Group. How are you feeling?" Gerard shoved the microphone toward Hunter.

"Amazing." Hunter's azure eyes sparkled underneath the bright lights. "It's an honor to be nominated. We have such amazing fans and thank them for supporting us."

"SureHaven must be sorry to see you go?" Gerard directed his question at Hunter again.

"I'm sure Grant, the new owners, are." His smile never faltered. *Damn, we were good at hiding the truth.* "SureHaven played an incredible part in our career, but for us, it was time to move on."

"It must be exciting, signing with Sony. When can we expect a new album?" Gerard thrust the microphone in my face.

"We're hitting the studio in the next couple weeks. We'll be recording right up to Christmas and aim to have the album out early in the New Year." I pulled back from the furry mic hovering too close to my chest. Kyle rubbed his thumb against my back in slow, sensual circles. His warm, reassuring touch grounded me and kept me calm.

"I'm sure your fans will be excited to hear that." Gerard's bald head glowed underneath the blazing lights. "So many exciting things have happened. A new record label. A new album to look forward to. And Kyle, a new home?"

Kyle's hand stilled on my back. I clutched the guys' jackets to stop myself from ripping the mic out of Gerard's hands and shoving it where the sun doesn't shine. I should've known this asshole would have asked us this question. But Kyle smiled, stayed cool, and nodded. "Yes, I did."

Yeah . . . he did. I glanced up at him. Heat touched my cheeks . . . but it was a good heat. I wasn't nervous or anxious or panicked. This was right. He was honest. And I loved him.

Gerard licked his lips and leaned forward, as if eager for a scoop. "Is it true you moved in with Gemma?"

Kyle smiled at me, took a breath, and nodded. "Yes. Yes, I did."

My blood pressure didn't skyrocket. Nausea didn't flood my stomach. Dizziness didn't spiral through my head. I loved Kyle so much. I couldn't deny it even if I tried. He'd stood by me through everything—my relationship with Hunter, and the issues with my mother—and he'd even lied to the world for me when we'd gotten caught together. There was nothing he wouldn't do for me. Or me for him.

"Gemma, is he your new roommate or are you . . . together?" Gerard raised an inquisitive eyebrow.

Unable to take my eyes off Kyle, my chest swelled. "Oh . . . we're definitely together."

"And how's that working out for you?" Gerard asked, prying for more information.

"Hmm. Let me show you." I let go of Hunter and turned to Kyle. With my heart hammering against my ribs, I grabbed the lapels high on his jacket and pulled his lips to mine. I didn't give him any time to think. He moaned, low and sexy, against my mouth, and caught me around my waist. He kissed me back, snaked his hands around me, and held me close. All I wanted to do was kiss him. Kiss him hard. Kiss him long. Kiss him hot.

Cheers and whistles erupted from the crowd. Flashes went off in a frenzy.

Kyle pulled back an inch and chuckled. His hot breath swept across my lips. "What are you doing?"

I cupped his cheek. "No more lying. No more hiding. I love you."

His smoldering eyes made my heart thunder even more. "I love you, too. Some warning you were going to do this would have been nice, though."

"Oh, shit." My throat seized. "I should've asked if it was okay."

His smile grew wider. "Gem, I've wanted to do this for months."

He tightened his hold on me, dipped me backwards, and kissed me again. My leg kicked up for balance. My split skirt fell open, exposing my bare thigh, like I was a tango dancer. Wrapped in his arms, I felt like I was soaring through the clouds, zooming through the stars.

The crowd went wild. The cameras went crazy. The progression of people halted and cheered.

Hunter ha-hummed and tapped my shoulder. "Okay, guys. You can stop now. You're taking the spotlight off me."

Kyle and I straightened. Laughing, he took my hand and kissed my palm. "You're crazy, Gem. You don't do things by halves, do you?"

"No-pe. Not when it comes to you." I kissed him on the lips again.

Gerard's greedy eyes widened, big and white. "So, I guess *all* those rumors were true?"

"No. Not all of them." I shrugged, not caring what this weasel thought. I refused to give him any more fodder.

"When did this happen?" Gerard waggled his finger back and forth between us. "How long have you been together?"

"A couple months." Vague was good. He didn't need the exact details. "All you need to know is we're together. We're happy. Nothing more to it. But tonight isn't about us. We're here to celebrate music and everyone's achievements, and to have fun. Oh . . . and we look forward to releasing new music very soon. Thank you. Nice to see you again." *Not.* "Have a good evening."

Gerard stood speechless as I entwined my fingers with Kyle's, spun on my stilettos, and the three of us moved down the carpet.

Kyle slapped Hunter on the shoulder. "Spotlight's all yours, Hunt."

"I've got no fucking chance after that." Hunter pointed at the TV monitors. "You're on every damn screen."

Reporters' arms waved in a frenzy, and microphones were thrust toward us. Camera flashes blinded us. The surrounding commotion and shouting became nothing but white noise.

I'd done it.

I'd told the world I was with Kyle.

It felt . . . incredible.

The three of us linked arms again and continued along the way. But Kyle held me just a little tighter and a little closer than Hunter. Just the way it was meant to be. And when Kyle leaned in and kissed me on the cheek, the cameras blinded us.

The world could see those pictures. See that we were in love.

Hunter goofed around, standing in front of us, holding his jacket open to block the photographers from taking pictures. "Nothing to see here, folks. Move along."

I loved him to death, but I loved Kyle more.

Friend versus soulmate—nothing could compare.

"You've gotta love his form." Kyle chuckled and drew me close.

I placed my hands on his chest. His heart raced as fast as mine. "I do, but I love you more."

"Good. Because now the world knows you're mine, better get used to me being around for a very long time."

"I'd like that. We're going to write and record our own music. Make a kickass album. Tour the world. Together. You've made all my dreams come true. Even my hot ones. Actually, you've exceeded them. Keep it up, and I think it's safe to say I want to spend the rest of my life with you. Forever sounds damn fucking good."

EPILOGUE

GEMMA

In front of the sold-out crowd at the Gillette Stadium in Boston, I placed my guitar on the rack at the back of the stage. We were only three-quarters of the way through our show, and no matter how hard I tried, my stomach wouldn't stop somersaulting. I sucked air into the depths of my lungs, returned to my mic, and unclipped it from the stand. I held it to my lips, pointed to the crowd, and hollered, "Is everybody having a good time?"

The crowd screamed and shouted. *"Yes!" "Woohoo!" "We love you, Gemma!"*

Laughing, I wiped the perspiration off my brow. "You guys are fucking awesome."

Over the past eleven months, Sony management had taken the guys and me to new levels of stardom, exceeding our wildest expectations. It had been incredible to record an entire album of our own music, release three singles, and, after months of rehearsals, we'd kicked off another world tour. Now . . . there was only one thing that could make life better.

The arena lights came up, and the audience roared. I took a few steps toward Kyle on the left-hand side of the stage, but Hunter dashed over and caught my arm.

"Are you sure about this?" Nervous excitement and concern

glistened in his eyes.

I held my mic out to the side so it couldn't pick up my voice. "Yes." I nodded, ignoring the butterflies in my stomach. "You got my back?"

"Always." Hunter ruffled the top of my head.

Kyle turned toward us, held out his hands, and mouthed, *"What's going on?"*

"Just go with the flow." I stepped over to him and waved at his bass. "Take off your guitar. Come with me."

Looking confused but intrigued, he did so.

Taking his hand, I led him down the runway to the front of the stage. With a huge grin beaming on my face, I spoke into my mic. "Boston . . . can anyone here tell me what's special about today? Something other than it being an exceptionally hot September evening?"

A cacophony of distorted voices hovered across the stadium.

Chuckling, Kyle shook his head. His cheeks flushed red. "Gem, I'm going to kill you."

I held my hand up to my ear and leaned toward the crowd. "What was that?"

Finally, their responses synced. *"It's Kyle's birthday."*

"That's right." I nodded and patted Kyle on the shoulder. "So, Kyle, if you could be so kind, please take a seat."

On cue, a chair rose onto the center of the stage via one of the hydraulic platforms.

He ran his hand through his hair and rubbed the back of his neck. I gave him a gentle nudge on the shoulder, and he sat.

I pointed my finger and waved it across the crowd. "Would you all please join me . . . and Hunter, who's hanging back with our band . . . and sing 'Happy Birthday' to Kyle, who turns twenty-five today."

The band erupted with music, and the crowd sang along to "Happy Birthday".

Happy birthday to you
Happy birthday to you

Happy birthday dear Kyle
Happy birthday to you

At the end of the tune, Kyle clapped, tapped his hand over his heart, and mouthed his thanks to the crowd. But just as he went to stand, I placed my hand on his shoulder. "Oh, you're not going anywhere just yet."

My stomach flipped. I grabbed the neckline of my damp shirt and shook it to cool my body down. The brush of air against my sweaty skin helped to clear my mind. This was it. I was ready. But first, a bit of fun.

I raised my mic. "As you all know, Kyle and I have been dating for nearly a year now . . . but I struggled with what to buy him for his birthday. You wanna know what I gave him?"

Girls and guys created megaphones with their hands in front of their mouths and yelled, "Yes!"

I glanced down at Kyle. Laughing, he shook his head and raised his hands. "Fine, tell them."

With my hand resting on his shoulder, I spoke to the crowd. "So I bought him a pair of Star Wars boxer briefs . . . " I lowered my voice and injected a touch of sexiness into it. "Which he's wearing . . . and dare I say, he looks damn hot in them." Giggling, I returned to my normal tone. " . . . and a new coffee cup. Do you think that's okay? Was that enough?"

"No!" they all called out.

"Damn." I jammed one hand on my hip, my mic poised in my other. "Well, I'd better come up with something else. If it's okay with you, do you mind if I sing him a song?"

The stadium erupted and cheered, sending a storm of thunder crashing against my chest. My heart barreled up to my throat, and I closed my eyes for a second.

I-can-do-this. I-can-do-this. I-can-do-this.

"Alright." My pulse thudded through my veins. "Let's do this. I'd like everyone to take out their cell phones, turn on the flashlight, and wave them in the air." I took a deep breath to calm my nerves and winked toward our crew in the control panel. All systems were go.

Kyle's smile broadened as he rubbed his hands up and down his thighs. "You wrote me a song?"

"Yeah," I whispered. "That okay?"

"Sure is."

The stadium lights dimmed, only to be replaced by thousands of tiny lights, transforming the place into a sea of stars. A lone spotlight shone down on me and Kyle. It was like we were the only two people in existence. That was what I had to focus on. I had to block everything else—the cameras, the phones, the photos, and the thousands of people watching us.

Hunter ambled toward us, strumming his acoustic guitar softly. Adrenaline charged through my veins at NASCAR speed. He stopped short of the stream of light. *Here we go.* I nodded to him. He plucked the strings and played a dreamy melody.

Kyle threw Hunter a *what's-going-on* look, but Hunter ignored him.

I wiped my sweaty palm on my jeans, took Kyle by the hand, and he stood. I led him a few steps forward, away from the chair. I met his warm gaze and smiled.

Fuck, I loved him.

I could do this.

It was just a little song.

I wet my lips, swallowed, and sang.

Do you remember when we met at school?
I was nothing but a bumbling fool
Little did I know, the universe had a plan
Took us to heights I couldn't imagine
For so long, I did not see
What was right in front of me

The crowd swayed their arms in time with the music. All the lights shining around us were magical. They shimmered across Kyle's eyes, filling them with golden shards. A sexy smile curled across his lips. If he kept looking at me like that, there was no way

I'd get to the end of my song. But the strum of Hunter's guitar in my in-ear monitor provided the gentle coax I needed. *Kyle* was all I needed.

> *You captured my heart with the touch of your hand*
> *You changed my life and made me who I am*
> *You took my broken heart, pieced me back together*
> *You healed my soul, now everything's better*

Kyle squeezed my hand, and tears filled my eyes. I nearly lost it, struggling to maintain even breaths. This was harder than I'd thought.

> *When I'm with you, I see forever*
> *I hope you feel the same, because I love ya*
> *I wouldn't be here if it wasn't for you*
> *So guess now there's only one thing to do*

My heart beat like a million bass drums against my ribs. I couldn't tell who was shaking more, Kyle or me. His eyes shimmered as he kissed the back of my hand. His warm lips sent shivers up my arm and down my spine. I entwined our fingers and gripped my mic tighter. Out flowed my shaky lyrics.

> *I'll be yours, if you'll be mine*
> *You have my heart, 'til the end of time*
> *So right now, on bended knee*

I dropped onto one knee and looked up at him.

> *Kyle McIntyre, will you marry me?*

The crowd erupted and roared, but the sound of my pulse thundering in my ears drowned it all out. Kyle fell to his knees in front of me, cupped my cheeks, and kissed me so hard I could barely breathe. He wrapped his arms around me and crushed me against his chest.

He tugged out my in-ear monitor and murmured in my ear. "Yes. Yes, I'll marry you, you crazy woman. I love you so much." He swept my sweaty hair off my face and kissed me again. And again, and again.

With fire burning in my cheeks, I sat back on my heels and mouthed. "*I love you.*"

Unable to stop smiling, I found some composure and held my mic to my lips. "In case you didn't hear, he said yes."

The audience stamped their feet, clapped, and hollered. The lights came up, and Kyle helped me stand. He hugged and kissed me again. Hunter rushed forward and wrapped his arms around us.

"Congratulations . . . That was fucking awesome. I'm crying. And I don't cry," he said, wiping his eyes. "Now . . . Get your shit together. We have a show to finish."

***

Somehow, we made it through our final set and encore. We rushed offstage into a sea of celebrations. Champagne bottles popped. Our backup band, entourage, and road crew cheered and hugged Kyle and me. Before my legs buckled beneath me, Kyle caught me in his arms, lifted me up, and spun me around.

"How the hell did you pull this off without me knowing?" He placed me back on the ground. It took a moment for my head to stop spinning.

"Weeks of planning and a lot of late nights." Excitement skipped through my voice. *I'd done it. I'd proposed. Holy shit . . . I'd done it.* "Everyone was in on it—Hunt, the crew, absolutely everyone."

Hunter handed us flutes of champagne. We clinked them together and took a sip.

I was still riding the high. Not sure I'd ever come down from this. "I couldn't have done this without your help, Hunt. So, thank you."

"You owe me one." He nudged his arm against my shoulder. "I can't believe you went through with it. You proposed . . . in front of all those fucking people."

"But I did." I latched my arm around Kyle's waist and drew him close. "I've learned my lesson. When I don't hide anything, no one gives a shit. There's no gossip, no speculation, and my mother never calls. It's fucking brilliant."

Kyle kissed the side of my head. "This is the best birthday present ever. I honestly never thought you'd ask me to marry you."

My cheeks ached from smiling so much. "I'm only ever going to get married once, so we better do it right."

"Deal." He hugged me tight.

"When can we have your engagement party?" Hunter grabbed a champagne bottle off the nearby table and refilled our glasses.

"I honestly have no fucking idea." Kyle shook his head and placed his hand on Hunter's shoulder. "I'm still in shock."

I hooked my arm around Kyle's waist and drew his hip against mine. "I've actually thought of that, too. In a month, we have a week off before we continue the tour. Why don't we do it then?"

Kyle's eyes widened. "In four weeks?"

"Sure. Why not? It's just a party." I shrugged. "Bec can organize it." I knocked back my champagne and savored the sweet taste sliding down my throat. "But . . . as for getting married . . . that can wait." I winced and had another drink. The "M" word still caused me to break out in a cold sweat. The thought of weddings, white dresses, and the world's interest in the two of us walking down the aisle made me nauseous. But I couldn't wait to spend the rest of my life with Kyle. "I just proposed in front of thousands of people. Let me deal with one phobia at a time."

"You take all the time you need. I'm not going anywhere." I didn't think the grin on Kyle's face could get any wider. "We're engaged. That's more than I ever dreamed of happening. It's fucking awesome."

"Congratulations. I'm so happy for the both of you." Sophie hugged us. "But we have to continue the celebration back at the hotel. Sorry, but it's time to move." She swirled her finger in the air. "Let's get this mob out of here so the road crew can get to work. The car's waiting for the three of you outside. Security is in place.

Let's move."

Hand in hand, Kyle and I followed Hunter down the corridor. We waved to the fans lurking outside the venue's rear entrance fence-line and jumped into our waiting SUV. I rested my head against the seat and turned to Kyle. He leaned over and kissed me on the lips. So gentle. So soft. So warm. I entwined my fingers with his and got lost in his hypnotic gaze. His eyes were so dark and beautiful. They owned every part of my soul. I'd do anything for him.

He was my soulmate, my best friend, my music.

Our future was together.

But right now . . . it was time to party.

***

The first few weeks of the tour disappeared. The guys and I headed home to New York for a week off before we continued touring for the next eight months—the United States, United Kingdom, Europe, Asia, Australia, New Zealand, and South America were all on the agenda. After a long day of travel, it was good to be home. I showered, threw on my pajamas, and walked into my bedroom.

Kyle lazed on the bed, reading. His chest was bare. He wore the Star Wars boxer-briefs I'd given him for his birthday. His skin glowed golden in the soft light.

"Hey." He put his tablet down and held out his hand.

I crawled onto his lap and pressed my lips against his. "Whatcha reading?"

He slid his hands around my hips. "Aren't I allowed to have any secrets?"

"Never."

His eyes twinkled. "If you must know, I was looking at ideas for our wedding."

I froze. But my mind spun. He was already looking? We hadn't even talked about it, let alone set a date.

"You still want to marry me, don't you?" He slipped his hand underneath my shirt and rubbed my lower back, sending warm pulses across my skin.

"Yes. But I thought we agreed not to worry about anything until after the tour."

"I'd marry you tomorrow if you let me." His eyes did that *I'm-so-in-love-with-you* shimmer that set my soul ablaze.

"We can't get married before our engagement party. It's only a few days away."

"We could." He shrugged. "We could sneak down to the city clerk's office."

My fingers trembled as I trailed feather-light strokes across his collarbone. "You just want to go sign the papers?" The idea had some merit. We could get it over and done with. But this wasn't just about me. "Is that what you want to do?"

He curled a strand of my hair around his finger and tugged it gently. "No."

"Okay." Panic skipped through my veins. "What kind of wedding do you want?" Visions of cathedrals and chandeliers and Kyle, dressed in a tuxedo, complete with a cravat, flooded my gut with nausea. I flicked the stupid notion aside. He wouldn't want a church wedding. That wasn't his style.

His warm smile touched my heart. "I'd actually like something small. Lowkey. Private."

We had a million friends, but not a lot of family. Was a tiny wedding possible? I stared at the tablet on the nightstand, my head faint over the whole wedding fiasco. I wanted to marry Kyle more than anything, but I could easily skip having a ceremony. "How small is small?"

"Do you want to see what I had in mind?"

I nodded and slid off his lap to sit beside him. He grabbed the tablet and turned it on. A picture of a quaint, secluded island with a gorgeous white beach, clear waters, and a stunning reef filled the screen. A beautiful house, surrounded by gardens and palm trees, was set back from the jetty.

"This is a private island in Belize." He scrolled through the stunning pictures. "The only way to get there is by boat or helicopter. The media and paparazzi wouldn't be able to follow us. We could fly an officiant in for the day. We'd invite Hunt, Kara, Lexi, and Hayden to stay for a couple nights. Then we'd send them home and we could have the place to ourselves for as long as we wanted."

That was it? That's all the people he wanted to invite? Tears welled in my eyes. The place was so remote, so beautiful . . . so right. "That would be perfect." I draped my arm across his waist and kissed the tip of his shoulder. "I'd love that."

"There's one more thing." He hesitated before putting his tablet down. "I have something for you."

Darting off the bed, he dashed into the walk-in closet and dug around in his drawers. He returned to the side of the bed and dropped to his knees. He let out a steady breath and placed a small red jewelry box on the mattress.

My heart slammed against my ribs. Dizziness swam through my head. "Kyle? What did you do? You bought me a ring?"

He twisted the box in his fingers. "I didn't *buy* you a ring. But I will if you want me to."

"Then what's in the box?"

He opened it. A dainty carat-sized pear-shaped diamond ring glistened on a black satin cushion.

"This . . . was my mom's ring." His voice, raw and raspy, caught in his throat. "If you don't like it . . . I'll get you something else."

My hand shot over my mouth. Tears stung my eyes. "Oh, Kyle."

"I know you loved my mom as much as I did. She played a huge part in getting us together."

I placed my hand over my pounding heart. Kyle was right. I'd loved Claire. She'd taught me to sing and play and saw the magic the three of us shared before anyone else.

A tear slid onto my cheek. "It's in the shape of a guitar pick."

"Yeah. But . . . " His brow furrowed as his gaze darted across my face. "If you want a bigger rock or something different, I'll buy you whatever you want? You don't have to—"

"Kyle . . ." I placed my hand on his. "It's perfect. It really is."

His eyes glistened as he nodded. "Well, then." He took a deep breath, grabbed the ring out of the box, and took my trembling hand in his. My pulse thudded in my ears. His gaze locked onto mine. "Gemma Lonsdale . . . With this ring, I promise to love and protect you for all time." He slid the diamond onto my finger and kissed my hand. His lips warm against my skin. "You're my life, my love, my music. I can't wait to marry you, to be your husband, to be together forever."

"I love you." I bobbed my head and entwined our fingers. "It hasn't been an easy ride to get here, but like we wrote in our song 'Horizon' all those years ago, we've traveled far and reached the stars. Now we're here on a new road, and I'm yours. I hope we keep writing incredible songs together forever, because I can't imagine life without music or you."

"So, can I book this island for our wedding? How about for twelve months from now?"

I glanced at the image on the tablet. *A wedding. On a private island. With just a few friends. Perfect.* I turned back to Kyle. "Yeah. I'd like that."

I brushed his long fringe off his brow. He crawled onto the bed, edged between my legs, and lay on top of me. My temperature soared as our lips connected. His kisses, hot and delicious, sent fire rushing through my veins. Every part of me craved more of him.

I wound my arms around his shoulders and held him tight. Our hearts beat as one.

This was love. True love.

Like I'd sung in my song when I proposed, the universe had a plan for us right from the start. It had tried and tested our loyalty and friendship, nearly ripped us apart and pushed us to be true to ourselves. We learned so much—how strong we were.

Every setback, every success, every broken heart—every experience we'd shared side by side. Every song we'd ever written . . . had been worth it.

We'd ended up here . . . Together.

Every line and every lyric had led me to love—to Kyle. My forever.

Thank you for reading **RIPPED – The Price of Loyalty**.

Gemma and Kyle found each other. These two best friends were destined to be together. They have more challenges to face in **RAPT – the Price of Love**, Book#3, but for now . . .

What about Hunter?

Hunter hides behind his ego, but why? What, or who, will it take to tame his wild heart . . . or break it? What happens when a one-night stand with an uptown girl sets him on a path he never saw coming?

If you are ready for a powerful, heartbreaking story that may cause a few tears, you'll love this enemies-to-lovers rockstar romance. Continue the series with Book 2 : **RUINED – The Price of Play**

AVAILABLE ON AMAZON and KINDLE UNLIMITED

PS. If you loved **RIPPED – The Price of Loyalty,** would you kindly take a moment and leave a quick product review on Amazon. They are music for an author's soul.

Thank you.
Tania Joyce

BEFORE YOU GO.

Would you like a BONUS EBOOK for FREE?

Find out how my world of rockstars began with the Everhide Rockstar Romance series.

ROCKED – The Price of Dreams is the origin story to my bestselling Everhide Series. Find out how the band met in high school, experience their heartbreak and hardships, and follow their journey to stardom. It is the pre-romance to the adult relationships that develop, evolve, and change throughout the six books. (Three standalones, three follow-ons—all happily ever afters, no cliffhangers).

This series will have you falling in love, shedding tears, and laughing out loud.

Read the prequel, **ROCKED – The Price of DREAMS,** for **FREE** when you subscribe to my newsletter. I only send emails about once a month, so your inbox won't be inundated with my news. Please subscribe here: https://taniajoyce.com/subscribe.

OTHER BOOKS BY TANIA JOYCE

Rockstars, bad boys and billionaires . . . something for everyone.
For eBooks visit Amazon. Paperbacks are available at all
good online book retailers. Author Signed Copies and Bookplates
are available from my website.

The Flintlocks Series

The Everhide Series

Billionaires and College Romance

NEWSLETTER

For information about my new releases, events, and special
offers, please subscribe to my monthly newsletter.
Join at: https://taniajoyce.com/subscribe
REMEMBER: You get a BONUS BOOK if you join.

***

FOLLOW TANIA JOYCE

You can follow and find Tania Joyce on the following social media
platforms.

Amazon: https://amazon.com/author/taniajoyce
BookBub: https://www.bookbub.com/authors/tania-joyce
Facebook: https://www.facebook.com/taniajoycebooks
Goodreads: https://www.goodreads.com/taniajoyce
Instagram: https://www.instagram.com/taniajoycebooks/
Pinterest: https://www.pinterest.com/taniajoycebooks
TikTok: https://www.tiktok.com/@taniajoyce
Web: http://taniajoyce.com

ABOUT TANIA JOYCE

Tania Joyce is an author of rockstar, contemporary and new adult romance novels. Her stories thread romance, drama and passion into beautiful locations ranging from the dazzling lights and glitter of New York to the rural countryside of the Hunter Valley.

She's widely traveled, has a diverse background in the corporate world and has a love for sparkles, shoes and shiraz.

Tania draws on her real-life experiences and combines them with her very vivid imagination to form the foundation of her novels. She likes to write about strong-minded, career-oriented heroes and heroines that go through drama-filled hell, have steamy encounters and risk everything as they endeavor to find their happy-ever-after.

Tania shuffles the hours in her day between part-time work, family life and writing. One day she hopes to find balance!

She loves to hear from her readers.

Visit: www.taniajoyce.com
or email her at: tania@taniajoyce.com

***

MORE BY TANIA JOYCE

Visit Tania Joyce on Amazon.Com